Gypsy

Lesley Pearse was told as a child that she had too much imagination for her own good. When she grew up she worked her way through a number of jobs, including nanny, Bunny Girl, dressmaker and full-time mother before, at the age of forty-nine, settling upon a career that would allow her gifts to blossom: she became a published writer. Lesley now lives just outside Bristol. She has three daughters and one grandson.

Find out more about Lesley and keep up to date with what she's been doing by signing up to Amongst Friends – the Lesley Pearse Newsletter. Simply go to www.penguin.co.uk, type your email address in the Free Penguin Newsletter panel and tick the box marked Lesley Pearse. And you'll soon be getting emails direct from your favourite author!

Gypsy

LESLEY PEARSE

MICHAEL JOSEPH
an imprint of
PENGUIN BOOKS

MICHAEL JOSEPH

Published by the Penguin Group

Penguin Books Ltd, 80 Strand, London WC2R 0RL, England

Penguin Group (USA) Inc., 375 Hudson Street, New York, New York 10014, USA

Penguin Group (Canada), 90 Eglinton Avenue East, Suite 700, Toronto, Ontario, Canada M4P 2Y3

(a division of Pearson Penguin Canada Inc.)

Penguin Ireland, 25 St Stephen's Green, Dublin 2, Ireland

(a division of Penguin Books Ltd)

Penguin Group (Australia), 250 Camberwell Road, Camberwell, Victoria 3124, Australia

(a division of Pearson Australia Group Pty Ltd)

Penguin Books India Pvt Ltd, 11 Community Centre, Panchsheel Park, New Delhi – 110 017, India

Penguin Group (NZ), 67 Apollo Drive, Rosedale, North Shore 0632, New Zealand

(a division of Pearson New Zealand Ltd)

Penguin Books (South Africa) (Pty) Ltd, 24 Sturdee Avenue, Rosebank, Johannesburg 2196, South Africa

Penguin Books Ltd, Registered Offices: 80 Strand, London WC2R 0RL, England

www.penguin.com

First published 2008

1

Set in 13.5/16 pt Monotype Garamond
Typeset by Rowland Phototypesetting Ltd, Bury St Edmunds, Suffolk
Printed in Great Britain by Clays Ltd, St Ives plc

A CIP catalogue record for this book is available from the British Library

ISBN: 978-0-718-15284-0

www.greenpenguin.co.uk

To my grandson Brandon.
My greatest treasure and delight.

Chapter One
1893, Liverpool

'Stop playing that Devil's music and come and help me,' Alice Bolton yelled angrily from the kitchen.

Fifteen-year-old Beth smirked at her mother's description of her fiddle playing and was tempted to continue louder and wilder. But Alice had been very irritable recently and was likely to come in and snatch the fiddle, so Beth put it back into its battered case and left the parlour to do as she was asked.

She had only just reached the kitchen when a thud, quickly followed by the sound of heavy objects falling, came from the shop below their flat.

'What on earth was that?' Alice exclaimed, turning round from the stove with the teapot in her hand.

'I expect Papa knocked something over,' Beth replied.

'Well, don't just stand there, go and see,' her mother snapped.

Beth paused on the landing, looking down over the banisters on to the staircase which led to the shop. She could hear something rolling around down there, but there was no sound of the cursing that usually accompanied any accidents.

'Are you all right, Papa?' she called out.

It was dusk, and although they hadn't yet lit the gas lights upstairs, Beth was surprised to see no glow at the bottom of the stairs from the lights in the shop. Her father was a shoemaker, and as he needed good light for close work he always lit the lamps well before daylight began to fade.

'What's the clumsy oaf done now?' her mother bellowed.

'Tell him to leave his work for tonight. Supper's nearly ready anyway.'

Church Street, one of Liverpool's main shopping streets, had few carts or carriages upon it at seven in the evening, so her father should have heard his wife's insulting remark clearly. When he didn't respond to it, Beth thought he must be out in the privy in the backyard, and maybe a stray cat had got into the shop and knocked something over. The last time this had happened the contents of a glue pot ran all over the floor and it had taken hours to clean up the mess, so she ran down quickly to check.

Her father wasn't in the privy as the door out to the yard was bolted on the inside, and when she went into the shop she found it in semi-darkness as the blinds had been pulled down.

'Where are you, Papa?' she called out. 'What was all the noise about?'

There was no sign of a cat, or indeed anything out of place. The street door was locked and bolted; furthermore, he'd swept the floor, tidied his work bench and hung his leather apron up on the peg just as he did every evening.

Puzzled, Beth turned and looked towards the storeroom where her father kept his supplies of leather, patterns and other equipment. He had to be in there, but she couldn't imagine how he could see anything with the door shut for even in bright daylight it was gloomy.

A strange sense of foreboding made her skin prickle and she wished her brother Sam was home. But he had gone out to deliver some boots for a customer a few miles away, so he wouldn't be back for some time. She didn't dare call her mother for fear of getting a clout for being 'fanciful', the expression Alice always used when she considered Beth was overreacting. But then her mother felt that a fifteen-year-old should have nothing more on her mind than improving her sewing, cooking and other domestic skills.

'Papa!' Beth called out as she turned the storeroom door knob. 'Are you in there?' The door only opened a crack, as if something was behind it, so she put her shoulder to it and pushed. She could hear a scrape on the flagstone floor, maybe a chair or box in the way, so she pushed harder until it opened enough to see round it. It was far too dark to make anything out, but she knew her father was inside, for she could smell his familiar odour, a mixture of glue, leather and pipe tobacco.

'Papa! Whatever are you doing? It's pitch dark,' she exclaimed, but even as she spoke it struck her that he might have been knocked out by something falling on him. In panic she rushed back across the shop to light the gas. Even before the flame rose enough to illuminate the glass mantle and bathe the shop in golden light, she was back at the storeroom.

For a second or two she thought she was seeing a large sack of leather in front of the storeroom window, but as the shop light grew brighter, she saw it was no sack, but her father.

He was suspended from one of the hooks on the ceiling, with a rope around his neck.

She screamed involuntarily and backed away in horror. His head was lolling to one side, eyes bulging, and his mouth was wide open in a silent scream. He looked like a hideous giant puppet.

It was all too clear now what the sound they'd heard earlier had been. As he'd kicked away the chair he'd been standing on, it had knocked a box of oddments, tins of shoe polish and bottles of leather dye, on to the floor.

It was early May, and just a few hours ago Beth had been grumbling to herself as she walked to the library because

3

her father wouldn't allow her to get a job. She had finished with school the previous year, but he insisted daughters of 'gentlefolk' stayed at home helping their mothers until they married.

Sam, her brother and senior by one year, was also disgruntled because he was apprenticed to their father. What Sam wanted was to be a sailor, a stevedore, a welder, or to do almost any job where he could be outside in the fresh air and have the company of other lads.

But Papa would point out the sign above the door saying 'Bolton and Son, Boot and Shoemaker', and he expected Sam to be just as proud now to be that 'Son' as he himself had been when his father had the sign made.

Yet however frustrating it was to have their lives planned out for them, both Beth and Sam understood their father's reasons. His parents had fled from Ireland to Liverpool in 1847 to escape slow starvation during the potato famine. For years they lived in a dank cellar in Maiden's Green, one of the many notorious, squalid slum 'courts' that abounded in the city. Frank, Sam and Beth's father, had been born there a year later, and his earliest recollections were of his father going from door to door in the better parts of Liverpool with his little cart to find shoes and boots to mend, and his mother going out each day to work as a washerwoman.

By the time Frank was seven he was helping both his parents by collecting and delivering boots for his father or turning the handle of the mangle for his mother. It was impressed on him, even when he was hungry, cold and tired, that the only way out of poverty was to work hard until they had saved enough money to get a little cobbler's shop of their own.

Alice, Sam and Beth's mother, had an equally tough childhood, for she had been abandoned as a baby and brought up in the Foundling Home. At twelve she was sent out to be a scullery maid, and the stories she told of the exhausting work and the cruelty of the cook and housekeeper were the stuff of nightmares to Beth.

Frank was twenty-three when he met sixteen-year-old Alice, by which time he and his parents had achieved their goal and had a tiny shop with two small rooms above. Alice had often said with a smile that her wedding day was the happiest day of her life because Frank took her to live with his parents. She still had to work just as hard, but she didn't mind that, for the purpose was to get even better premises where her father-in-law and husband could make shoes instead of just repairing old ones.

The hard work finally paid off and brought them here to Church Street, with two floors above the shop, where both Sam and Beth were born. Beth couldn't remember her grandmother, as she'd been only a baby when she died, but she had adored her grandfather and it was he who taught her to play the fiddle.

Since Grandfather's death five years ago, Papa's shoe-making skills had become well known and now he made shoes and boots for some of the wealthiest people in Liverpool. He still worked extremely hard, from first light until dusk, and most nights he fell asleep the moment he had eaten his supper, but until tonight Beth had always thought he was a very happy man.

'What on earth is going on down there? I heard you scream,' her mother called peevishly from the top of the stairs. 'Is it a rat again?'

Beth was brought up with a start. Appalled and terrified as she was, her instinct was to protect her mother.

'Don't come down,' she called back. 'I'll get Mr Craven.'

'You can't disturb neighbours when they're having their supper. Surely your father can deal with it?'

Beth didn't know how to answer that, so she went to the stairs and looked up at her mother, hoping something would come to her.

Alice Bolton was thirty-eight but looked far younger for she was tiny, with blonde hair, wide, pale blue eyes and the kind of delicate features and complexion that suggested frailty.

Sam had inherited her blonde hair and blue eyes, but he was nearly six feet tall, with his father's vigour and strong features. It was said that Beth was a double of her Irish grandmother, with her curly black hair, dark blue eyes and an impertinent manner that would get her into trouble one day.

'For goodness' sake don't stand there looking so gormless,' Alice snapped. 'Just tell your father to come now or the supper'll be ruined.'

Beth gulped, all too aware that lies and attempted smoke screens wouldn't help in something like this. 'He can't come, Mama,' she blurted out. 'He's dead.'

Her mother never grasped anything quickly. This time was no exception; she just stared at Beth blankly.

'He's hanged himself, Mama,' Beth said, fighting back tears and mounting hysteria. 'That's why I wanted to get Mr Craven. You go back up into the kitchen.'

'He can't possibly be dead. He was fine when he came up for his tea.'

Beth was controlling the desire to scream the place down, and her mother's disbelief almost made her lose that control. Yet it was true what her mother said, her father *had* appeared perfectly normal at teatime. He'd remarked on how good the seed cake was, and he'd told them that he'd finished the boots he was making for Mr Greville.

It didn't seem possible that he'd gone back downstairs, finished his work for the day, tidied his bench and then calmly taken his own life knowing his wife and daughter were just upstairs.

'He *is* dead, Mama. He's hanged himself in the storeroom,' Beth said bluntly.

Her mother shook her head and started down the stairs. 'You're a wicked girl to say such a thing,' she said indignantly, brushing Beth aside as she got to the bottom. 'I'll deal with you later.'

Beth caught hold of her arms and tried to prevent her from going into the shop. 'You mustn't go in there, Mama,' she begged. 'It's horrible.'

But her mother wouldn't be deterred; she thrust Beth aside, rushed over to the storeroom and wrenched the door open. Her scream when she saw her husband reverberated through the whole building. But the scream was shut off abruptly as she slumped to the floor in a faint.

An hour later Sam arrived home to find the shop was not in darkness as he'd expected. Through the window he saw rotund Dr Gillespie and burly Mr Craven, their neighbour, but even before they opened the door to him, he knew something was seriously wrong.

It was the doctor who explained that Beth had run to Mr Craven when her mother collapsed. Mr Craven sent his son to fetch the doctor, and came back with Beth to cut Papa's body down. When Gillespie arrived he had told Beth to take her mother upstairs, give her some brandy and put her to bed.

Sam was a tall, lanky boy of sixteen. He swayed on his feet at the news, the colour draining from his face and the shock of it almost making him collapse too. His father's body was on the floor, covered in a blanket, all except for one hand which was stained brown with leather dye. If it hadn't been for that hand Sam might have refused to believe what the men told him, but Frank's hand was as familiar to him as his own.

He asked why his father had done such a thing, but they couldn't tell him. Mr Craven scratched his head and said it was a mystery to him as only that morning he'd dropped into the shop for a chat, and Frank had been in good spirits. Dr Gillespie was equally baffled and spoke of how well respected in the community Frank was. It was clear both men were as horrified and shocked as Sam.

The doctor caught hold of both Sam's arms, looking right into his eyes. 'The mortuary cart will be here soon,' he said gently. 'There has to be an inquest in situations like this. You must be the man of the house now, Sam, and take care of your mother and sister.'

Sam felt as if a trapdoor had opened beneath his feet and he had fallen into a place he didn't recognize. For as far back as he could remember, there had always been order and absolute certainty in his life. He had often baulked at the dullness of the daily routine, with his father working in the shop from seven in the morning till late in the evening, and his mother cooking and cleaning upstairs. Yet he had always felt safe in the knowledge that if he did fall flat on his face while seeking out a more adventurous life for himself, everything would remain the same here and he could come back to it.

But at a stroke all that precious certainty was gone.

How could such a mild-mannered, thoughtful and kind-hearted man have such demons lurking inside him? And why didn't those closest to him ever catch a glimpse of them? Just that morning Sam had watched his father go to the foot of the stairs and listen while Beth was playing her fiddle. He made no comment, but his face had been alight with pride in her talent. Later, when Sam had finished repairing a pair of boots, Frank had clapped him on the shoulder and praised his work.

Time and again both he and Beth had witnessed the loving way their father looked at their mother, seen him holding her and kissing her. If they all meant that much to him, why did he want to leave them?

And what would happen to the family now, without the man who had been their provider, their rock and comforter?

Chapter Two

The grandfather clock on the landing struck midnight but Sam and Beth were still in the kitchen, too stunned and upset to even think of going to bed. Their father's body had been taken away hours ago, and Sam held Beth's hands tightly as once again she went over how she'd found their father. From time to time he would wipe the tears away from her cheeks with his handkerchief, and smooth her hair comfortingly. Likewise, when Sam became overwrought and his voice rose in anger, Beth would reach out to caress his cheek.

Dr Gillespie had given their mother a draught to make her sleep because she'd been hysterical, pulling at her hair and screaming that someone else must have strung Frank up, for he would never have chosen to leave her. While both children knew it was impossible for anyone else to have had a hand in tonight's work, they shared her sentiments. Their parents had been loving and happy.

'The doctor asked me if the business was in difficulties,' Sam said, his voice strained with bewilderment. 'But it wasn't. I can't even think of anything unusual happening in the past weeks that might account for it.'

'Could it have been a customer who upset him?' Beth asked.

There were difficult and unpleasant customers sometimes. They complained if Father couldn't make their shoes or boots as quickly as they wanted them, and often when they arrived to pick them up they tried to find fault with his workmanship so they could beat him down in price.

'He would have said. Anyway, you know he took all that in his stride.'

'You don't think it was us, do you?' Beth asked anxiously. 'Me complaining that I was bored at home, and you always slipping off to the docks?'

Sam shook his head. 'I don't think so. I heard him laughing about me once with a customer. He said I was a good lad, even if my head was in the clouds. And you certainly hadn't upset him; he was proud of you.'

'But how are we going to live now?' Beth asked. 'You aren't experienced enough to keep the shop going!'

It was often remarked on how different Beth and Sam were. Not just their looks, one tall and blond, the other small and dark – their natures were quite different too.

Sam's head was always in the clouds, living in a dream world of fantastic adventures, riches and exotic places. One day he could be wasting time down by the docks gazing wistfully at the ocean-going ships; another he could be peering through gates of big houses, marvelling at the way the wealthy lived. Although he had never admitted it to Beth, she knew the real reason he didn't want to be a cobbler or shoemaker was because no one became rich or had adventures that way.

Beth was far more practical and logical than her brother, thorough and diligent when she was given a task to do. She had sharper wits, and read books to gain knowledge rather than to escape reality. Yet she could understand why Sam lived in a fantasy world, because she had her fantasy too, of playing her fiddle to a huge audience and hearing rapturous applause.

It was of course an unattainable dream. Even if she had been taught to play classical violin, she'd never seen a female violinist in an orchestra. She played jigs and reels, tunes passed down from her grandfather, and most people considered that was gypsy music, suitable only for entertainment in rowdy ale houses.

Yet for all the differences between Beth and Sam, they were very close. With only a year between them, and having never been allowed to play in the street like other children in the neighbourhood, they'd always relied on each other for companionship.

Sam got up from his chair and knelt beside Beth, putting his arms around her. 'I'll take care of both of you, somehow,' he said with a break in his voice.

In the days that followed, Beth's emotions see-sawed between overwhelming grief and rage. She had never known one day without her father; he had been as constant as the grandfather clock chiming away the hours. A wiry man of forty-five with thinning grey hair, a carefully trimmed moustache and a rather prominent nose, he was always cheery and, she thought, transparent.

He might not have been overly demonstrative – a pat on the shoulder was his way of showing affection and approval – but he had never been a distant figure like so many fathers were. He liked her to come down to the shop and chat while he was working; he had always been interested in what she was reading, and her music.

But now she felt she hadn't really known him. How could he come up to the kitchen for his tea and sit with his wife and daughter while all the time he was intending to go back downstairs, finish his work and then hang himself?

He had talked about a pair of buttoned boots a lady had ordered just that morning, laughing about her because she wanted pale blue ones to match a new dress. He said they wouldn't stay looking good for long in Liverpool's dirty streets. Why would he say that if he knew he was never going to make them?

If he had died of a heart attack, or been run over by a carriage while crossing the street, it would have been terrible, and the pain they all felt now would have been just as agonizing, but at least none of them would have felt betrayed.

Their mother wouldn't stop crying. She just lay in her bed, refusing to eat or even to allow them to open the curtains, and Sam was like a bewildered lost soul, convinced it was his fault because he'd been less than enthusiastic about being a shoemaker.

Only a few neighbours had called to offer condolences, and Beth felt their real motive was not real sympathy but to gather more information to bandy around. Father Reilly had called, but although he'd been kindly, he'd been quick enough to say Frank Bolton couldn't be buried on hallowed ground as it was a grievous sin for a man to take his own life.

The result of the inquest would be in the newspapers, and all their friends and neighbours would read it and shun them afterwards. She thought it was cruel and cowardly for her father to have done this to them all. And she didn't think her mother would ever want to go out of the house again.

Five days after her father's death, Beth was in the parlour making black dresses for herself and her mother. Outside the sun was shining, but she had to keep the blinds closed as was the custom, and the light was so dim she was finding it hard even to thread the needle.

Beth had always enjoyed sewing, but as her mother wouldn't rouse herself to help, she'd had no choice but to dig out the patterns, cut the material on the parlour table and sew the dresses alone, for they would be disgraced further without proper mourning clothes.

She would give anything to be able to get out her fiddle and play as she knew she could lose herself in music and perhaps find some solace. But playing a musical instrument so soon after a bereavement wasn't seemly.

In irritation Beth threw down her sewing and went over to the window where she drew back the blind just an inch or two to peep out and watch the activity on Church Street.

As always, it was crowded with people. The omnibuses, cabs, carts and carriages created piles of horse droppings, and the smell was more pungent than usual today because of the warm sunshine. Ladies of quality in elegant frocks and pretty hats strolled arm-in-arm with gentlemen in high wing collars and top hats. There were matronly house-keepers in severe dark clothes carrying baskets of fruit and vegetables, and here and there young girls, perhaps maids on their afternoon off, dreamily looking in shop windows.

But there were plenty of poor people too. A one-legged man on crutches was begging outside Bunney's, the shop on the crossroads which was generally known as Holy Corner because Lord Street, Paradise, Chapel and Church Streets all met there. Worn-looking women held babies in their arms, smaller children tagging along behind; tousle-haired street urchins with dirty faces and bare feet loitered, perhaps on the lookout for anything they could steal.

There was a queue at the butcher's opposite, and because of the warm sunshine the women looked relaxed and un-hurried, chatting to one another as they waited to be served. But as Beth watched them, she saw two women turn and look straight up at the windows above the shop, and she realized they'd just been told that the shoemaker had hanged himself.

Tears welled up in her eyes, for she knew that the gossip would gain even more momentum after the funeral. People could be so cruel, always delighting in others' misfortunes. She could imagine them saying that the Boltons had always thought themselves a cut above everyone else, and no doubt Frank had killed himself because he was in debt. Beth almost wished that was the reason; at least it would be understandable.

Turning away from the window, she looked around the parlour. It was her mother's pride and joy; everything, from the patterned square of carpet and the china dogs sitting either side of the fireplace to the stiff, uncomfortable button-backed armchairs and the heavy tapestry curtains, were copies of things Alice had seen in the big house when she was a scullery maid.

Wanting a piano was part of it, and it had to be hauled up through the window by six men. Neither of her parents could play the instrument, but to her mother it was a sign of refinement, so Beth had to learn. She had no doubt her mother hoped it would wean her off the fiddle, an instrument she saw as 'common'.

Although Beth often felt hurt by her mother's attitude to her beloved fiddle, she was very glad when she found Miss Clarkson to give her lessons on the piano. She might have been a thirty-year-old spinster, with grey hair and a cast in one eye, but she was an inspiring woman. She not only taught Beth to read music and play the piano but she introduced her to a whole new world of books, music and ideas.

For five years Miss Clarkson was her ally, friend, confidante and teacher. She loved to hear Beth play her fiddle as well as the piano, she would bring books with her she thought Beth should read, she taught her about all kinds of music and sometimes took her to concerts too. Yet what

Beth liked best about her was that she didn't have the same narrow outlook as her mother. Miss Clarkson felt strongly that women should have equal rights to men, be that to vote, to have a good education or to work at anything they pleased.

Beth wished Miss Clarkson was still in Liverpool now because she was the one person who might have been able to help her and Sam understand why their father had done such a terrible thing. But she had emigrated to America because she said she felt stifled by the hypocrisy, class system and lack of opportunities for women in England.

'I shall miss you, Beth,' she told her with a resigned smile when they said their last goodbyes. 'Not just because you are my most accomplished pupil, but because you have a lively mind, a stout heart and boundless enthusiasm. Promise me you won't marry the first suitable man who asks you, just so you can have a home of your own. Marriage may be considered by most to be a holy state, but not if you pick the wrong man. And keep up your music, for it lifts the spirit and allows you the freedom of expression a girl like you needs.'

Beth had found Miss Clarkson was right about the music. It transported her to a place where her mother's repeated instructions on mundane domestic matters couldn't reach her, a world where fun, freedom and excitement weren't frowned upon.

Sadly, she knew Mama had never understood that. She had always liked to boast to the neighbours of her daughter's talent, but she didn't actually listen to her playing the piano and she resented the fiddle. Papa had listened and liked nothing better than to sit and hear her play the piano on a Sunday evening – Chopin was his favourite – yet he also enjoyed it when she played and sang popular music-hall songs. Even for him, though, the fiddle had been a slight bone of contention, perhaps because it was a reminder of his childhood and he feared the wild Irish jigs his father had taught Beth to play would draw her into bad company.

Hearing Sam coming up the stairs, Beth began sewing again. She heard him go in to see Mama in her room down beside the kitchen, and a few minutes later he came into the parlour.

He looked pale and drawn, his brow knitted in a frown. 'The Coroner is releasing Papa's body tomorrow,' he said wearily. 'He didn't find anything to explain why he did it, he wasn't sick. But at least we can bury him now.'

'Did you tell Mama?' Beth asked.

Sam nodded despondently. 'She was crying still. I don't think she's ever going to stop.'

'Maybe she will after the funeral,' Beth said with more optimism than she felt. 'I must fit this dress on her soon. I hope she won't make another scene.'

'I saw Mrs Craven outside. She said she'll come round later and try to talk to her; maybe it will be best if you try the dress then. However bad Mama feels, she won't want a neighbour knowing she's leaving everything to us.'

Beth heard the bitterness in his voice and got up to put her arms around him. He had been in the shop from first light till dusk most days, finishing up all the repairs, and she knew how frightened and worried he was. 'You said we'd manage the night it happened, and we will,' she said.

'I've got a feeling Mama knows why he did it,' Sam said in a low voice, leaning his chin on her head as she held him. 'I've gone through the accounts and although there isn't very much money, he wasn't in trouble. He never went out, so he wasn't drinking or gambling, and he certainly didn't have another woman. It can only be something to do with her.'

17

'Don't think that, Sam,' Beth begged him. 'It won't help putting the blame on Mama.'

Sam caught hold of her arms tightly and looked right into her eyes. 'Don't you realize everything is going to be different from now on?' he said fiercely. 'We are going to be poor. I wish I could promise you that I could keep the shop going, but all I can do is repairs. I'm not skilled enough to make boots and shoes, and that was what Papa made the money on. I'm going to have to get another job, but that won't pay enough to keep all three of us.'

'I can get one too,' Beth said eagerly. 'We will manage, Sam.'

He looked at her doubtfully. 'It may come that we have to find a cheaper place to live, or take in a lodger. We won't be able to live the way we've been used to.'

Anger flared up inside Beth again. All her life she'd heard Papa telling her that he wanted her and Sam to have all the advantages he'd never had. He'd made her believe that they were gentlefolk, a cut above most of their neighbours. But he'd shamed and ruined them without even an explanation as to why.

Chapter Three

As Beth laid the table for the evening meal she watched her mother stirring a pot of stew on the stove. As usual she was in her own private world, barely aware even that her daughter was in the room with her.

Three months had passed since she was widowed, but this was how she had remained. While she did the washing, cooking and cleaning in much the same way she always had, she only spoke when asked a direct question, and she took no interest in anyone or anything.

Mrs Craven, their kindly neighbour who had been so supportive at the time of their father's death, had said that Beth and Sam should be patient with her, for grief affected people in many different ways and their mother would come out of this silence when she was ready. But a month ago even Mrs Craven lost her patience when Mama told her to go away when she'd called round.

''Er face was as cold as a marble headstone! Fair gave me goose pimples, cos it was like she didn't know me,' she reported indignantly to Beth.

It seemed incredible to Beth that her mother could dismiss the one person who had been a true friend. But then she didn't show any appreciation for all Sam had done for her either.

He had tried so hard to keep the shop going, but the people who used to bring in their boots and shoes to be repaired stopped coming. Whether this was because of the suicide, or because they didn't think Sam could do the job, wasn't clear. So Sam rented the shop out to someone else. Mama merely shrugged when he told her.

For a dreamy and previously very lazy lad, Beth thought her brother had proved himself to be a real man by dealing so masterfully with all the family problems. With someone downstairs paying almost the entire rent for the building, they only had to find a small balance so they could continue to stay in the flat. Sam had got himself a position as a junior clerk with a shipping company and he brought home every penny he earned to keep them all. Mama should be praising him to the skies, not just ignoring him.

But then she hadn't praised Beth either when she found a position as an assistant in a hosiery shop. She never asked what the hours would be or how much she would be paid.

A while ago Sam had remarked that it was as if their mother had been replaced by a sullen servant. He said it jokingly, but that was exactly what it was like, for she made and served their meals without a word. She had never been a great conversationalist, a little gossip about the neighbours had been her limit, but she'd always been a good listener and was aware of any little changes in either of them, showing concern if they felt poorly or seemed sad. She didn't notice now whether they were tired or had a cold; she didn't even make a remark about the weather. If they asked her what she'd done during the day she would reply with one bald sentence: 'I did the washing' or 'I changed the beds'. Beth would seethe inwardly, wanting to scream out that she still had them and the home she loved, while her children's world had been turned upside down. Sam was tied to a desk for ten hours a day, at the beck and call of men who treated him like dirt on their boots. He couldn't wander off to the docks for an hour or two the way he used to; every penny he earned was needed.

Maybe Beth *had* wanted to work in a shop, but she soon found that working in Hooley's Hosiery wasn't anything like she had imagined. She and the other shop assistants had to line up each morning for a check that their nails were clean and their boots polished, and just a couple of strands of hair coming loose was a serious misdemeanour. Customers were often rude, but she had to smile sweetly as if they were royalty. She couldn't even go to the privy without asking permission, and just talking to another assistant was to risk being fired. She was spied on all the time, there were countless petty rules, and she found being on her feet all day exhausting. Their mother rarely went out, so she didn't see the sneers on people's faces or overhear their cruel remarks. Sam and Beth lived with that every day.

But all the feelings of anxiety, resentment and irritation that Beth had felt in the past couple of months were eclipsed today by something far more serious.

It was early closing day, and Beth got home soon after one. She intended to have something to eat, then try to persuade her mother to come out with her for a walk in the sunshine.

The people taking over the shop were going to sell shoes, and during the last week a carpenter had been building shelves and a counter. As Beth came in through the back door, a painter was working in the shop with the door wide open. He apologized for the paint fumes and said he hoped that wasn't what had upset her mother, for he'd heard her being sick in the privy.

Beth was naturally alarmed and ran upstairs to see Mama. But she denied there was anything wrong and said the painter was mistaken.

The paint fumes were very strong in their flat, but even so her mother refused to go out with Beth. So Beth had some bread and cheese and went out alone.

21

They only used the back door now, but as she came up Church Street the shop door was wide open, so she slipped in that way to save going round the back. It was about half past three, and she paused in the small lobby by the stairs up to their flat, because through the open back door she could see her mother in the yard taking the washing off the clothes-line.

She was stretching up to reach one of Sam's shirts, and Beth was shocked to see that her belly had grown very big.

Her mother was short and she'd always been very slender, in fact her waist had been so small that her father used to encircle it with his two hands. Three months ago, when Beth had fitted her mourning dress on her, it had still been the same. But it wasn't like that any more. She was wearing a linen apron over her black dress, but the waistband of the apron was well above where it should have been, and her swollen belly was clearly defined.

Beth was so shocked she almost cried out and alerted her mother that she was watching her. It wasn't an overall fatness for Alice's face had grown much thinner since she was widowed. Beth knew exactly what swollen bellies meant, even if properly brought up young ladies weren't supposed to be aware of such things.

That was yet another matter Miss Clarkson had explained to Beth. She said it was absurd to keep young girls in the dark about something so natural, and ignorance was dangerous too as men could take advantage of it. So Beth knew how babies were made.

While she had found it embarrassing to discover that her parents had continued to perform that act after she was born, Beth's real concern now was how she was going to broach such a delicate subject with her mother. But she knew she must, for if there was a baby on the way plans would need to be made.

A little later, once her mother was back indoors, folding up the dry washing, Beth studied her, hoping she was mistaken, for with the apron in its right place Alice's belly wasn't obvious; she just looked a bit thicker around the waist.

Beth had a cup of tea while she tried to pluck up some courage, for she anticipated hostility. But time was getting on, and once Sam got back her chance would be gone, for Beth knew she couldn't discuss pregnancy with a male present, not even her own brother.

She took a deep breath and plunged right in. 'You are going to have a baby, aren't you, Mama?'

Beth wasn't sure how she felt about having a baby brother or sister. But her mother's reaction to her question made it quite plain she considered it a catastrophe. Her face crumpled, she put her hands over her belly as if to hide it and let out a wail of anguish.

Beth had half expected to be told to mind her own business, but she certainly hadn't anticipated such a dramatic reaction. 'I know it must seem awful now Papa's gone, but Sam and I will help you,' she said quickly, going over to her mother. She didn't try to embrace her, for during the last three months when she'd attempted it, her mother had backed away as if she'd been scalded.

But surprisingly she flung herself at Beth, crying like a child against her shoulder. 'I didn't know how to tell you,' she sobbed. 'I've been so afraid of what was going to become of us.'

Beth just held her, so relieved that at last her mother was communicating with her that any other concerns seemed unimportant. 'There's nothing to worry about,' she said soothingly. 'We've managed all right so far, and we can manage a baby too. Maybe it's just what we need to make us all happy again. Do you know when it will be born?'

'December, I think,' Alice said, dabbing her eyes with her apron. 'But I'm too old to be having another baby. It's bad enough having the shame of your father going the way he did – now people will start talking about us all over again.'

'You aren't too old,' Beth said firmly. 'And what does it matter what other people say? It's none of their business.'

She made another pot of tea, and her mother blew her nose and admitted it was a relief to have it out in the open. 'I've behaved very badly to you two,' she admitted. 'But I was that worried and frightened I couldn't think of anything else. What's Sam going to think?'

'Just the same as me, that we're going to have a baby brother or sister,' Beth said calmly. She felt relieved that her mother's odd behaviour had finally been explained. 'I know everything looks a bit daunting now, Mama, but it will get better. And you'd better make friends with Mrs Craven again because you'll need her help when the baby comes.'

Mrs Craven, among her many talents, had something of a reputation of being an excellent midwife.

'That's why I told her to go away, I was that scared she'd guess,' Alice admitted. 'It was too much for me after Frank going the way he did.'

Later that evening after their mother had gone to bed, Beth and Sam sat in the kitchen talking. Sam had looked horrified when Beth took him to one side earlier and, with a great deal of embarrassment, told him the news. He whispered that this was the last thing they all needed, but he did have the diplomacy not to show his feelings to their mother.

Now they were alone and he'd had time to think about it, he had softened a little. 'I can't say I relish the thought of a squalling brat around the place,' he admitted. 'But at least it explains what was wrong with Mama. I thought she might end up in an asylum.'

'It must have been very frightening for her,' Beth said. 'Especially as her own mother must have had her without a husband, or she wouldn't have abandoned her. That place she grew up in was attached to a workhouse. I expect she was afraid that was where she'd end up.'

'I'd never let that happen,' Sam said stoutly. 'But it will tie us.'

'Whatever do you mean?' Beth asked.

He pursed his lips and frowned. 'Pa didn't leave much, and most of that was eaten up with the burial expenses and just living until I got work. Our joint wages are only just enough to scrape by on. But I'd hoped that in time Mama would marry again and we'd both be free.'

Beth had never imagined her mother remarrying, and she said so.

'Well, you'd better start hoping for it,' he said with a tinge of sarcasm. 'If you meet some chap who wants to marry you, he won't want to be saddled with your mother and her baby too. And I hadn't planned on staying put here for ever either. I want to see the world.'

Beth wanted to reproach him for being selfish, but she couldn't because she knew he wouldn't really run out on them. 'Let's not worry about the future for the time being,' she suggested. 'Something will turn up, you'll see.'

It was a long, hot summer, the milk turning sour by mid-morning, privies and drains stinking to high heaven, leaves on trees drooping listlessly with a coating of dust. The city didn't even become quiet once darkness fell because it was too hot for anyone to sleep. Babies cried, dogs barked, children played in the streets till all hours, and there were more drunken brawls outside the public houses than usual.

Beth found each day in Hooley's Hosiery a trial of endurance. By midday the shop windows got the full blast from the sun, and inside the temperature soared to over ninety degrees. Customers were tetchy and often very rude as they got her to open drawer after drawer of socks or stockings. Beth frequently had to bite her tongue to prevent herself answering back. In a high-necked black dress, with petticoats beneath, she was sweltering, her feet swelled and ached, and she often wondered why she'd once thought it would be marvellous to have a job.

Sam fared better at his work, for the clerks' office overlooked the sea, and with the windows wide open there was a cooling breeze. But with a stiff wing collar and a jacket, he too often admitted to nodding off in the heat or gazing longingly at the ships out at sea, wishing he was on one.

But their mother was suffering even more. She had no appetite, she felt faint in the heat, and her ankles and legs were so swollen by mid-afternoon that she couldn't walk. It alarmed Beth to see how thin and gaunt her face was becoming, yet her belly seemed to grow larger each day.

The hot weather finally broke at the end of September, when it rained almost constantly for two weeks. At long last they could sleep at nights again, the streets were washed clean, and their mother began to eat a little more.

Alice had apologized to Mrs Craven for her rudeness, and the neighbour was kind enough to pop in every day and help with a few of the heavier chores. Together the two women had dug out a stored box of baby clothes that had been both Sam's and Beth's, and another neighbour lent them a cradle.

Winter didn't set in until the end of November, but when it came it was with high winds and bitter cold. In the second week of December, when it was snowing, Beth arrived home on the Friday evening to find Mrs Craven in the kitchen, filling up a big pan with water to heat up on the stove.

'She started around midday,' the woman explained. 'It was lucky I called in on the way back from the market. I want you to go and get Dr Gillespie to come and take a look at her.'

Beth was immediately alarmed, but Mrs Craven gave her a reassuring hug. 'It's just a precaution,' she insisted.

It was the first time Beth had seen the doctor since the night her father hanged himself, and she felt acutely embarrassed about having to tell him why she needed him now.

'Having a baby!' he exclaimed, his round red face breaking into a wide smile. 'What a surprise! And how are you and your brother doing? It must have been hard on you these past months.'

'We're managing fine, doctor,' Beth said. His smile of pleasure made her feel a little less anxious, and his interest in her and Sam was comforting. 'Of course, the baby was a bit of a shock to all of us. But Mrs Craven said she wanted you to call round just as a precaution.'

But it wasn't just a precaution, Beth realized later, as she stood at the bedroom door listening to what the doctor was saying to Mrs Craven. 'She's a very small woman and the baby is big. Mrs Bolton isn't young either, nor is she very strong. I'll leave her in your capable hands for now, Mrs Craven, but don't hesitate to call me again later if you have any concerns.'

Beth's heart began to hammer with fright, and as the evening progressed and she heard Mama shrieking with pain, she grew terrified. It didn't help that Sam hadn't come home. There was just Mrs Craven, and she wouldn't allow Beth into the bedroom. 'I'll call you if I need help or to get the doctor again,' she said firmly. 'Babies can sometimes take an age to come, but don't worry yourself about the screaming – most women do that, it don't mean much.'

Sam arrived back soon after ten, just in time for Mrs Craven to send him out again for the doctor, and though she wouldn't be drawn on why she needed him, Beth could see anxiety etched into her big face.

Dr Gillespie came back with Sam, and once again disappeared into the bedroom for some time.

Around twelve Gillespie came back into the kitchen and asked for a bowl of hot water to wash his hands. He had already taken off his jacket and rolled up his shirtsleeves, and as he scrubbed at his hands and forearms he glanced over his shoulder at Sam and Beth.

'I've got to get the baby out quickly,' he said. 'Please get me more clean linen and towels. I can see you are both frightened, but try not to worry – your mother will be all right.'

Beth rushed to get the linen, and the doctor took it back into the bedroom with him, closing the door behind him. Mama's moaning stopped soon afterwards and Sam said the doctor must have given her ether.

It was very quiet now. Outside snow was still falling, deadening the sound of late-night carriages in the street. The only sound inside was the occasional cough or muffled instruction from the doctor to Mrs Craven, and the coal spluttering and shifting in the stove.

Sam and Beth didn't speak. They just sat on either side of the kitchen table, white-faced and anxious, both lost in their own fears.

Suddenly there was noise – rustling, feet moving and the doctor's low voice. 'My, she's a big girl,' they heard

Mrs Craven exclaim, and just moments later they heard the baby cry.

'Thank God for that,' Sam exclaimed, wiping his sweaty brow on his sleeve.

Shortly afterwards Mrs Craven came out of the bedroom with the baby wrapped in a blanket in her arms. She looked exhausted, but she was smiling. 'This is your baby sister. A real little porker,' she said with some pride.

For Beth, the sight of Mrs Craven's blood-drenched apron diluted any joy and wonder she might have felt at seeing her little sister. 'Mama – is she well?' she asked.

'She will be soon, the doctor's stitching her up now,' Mrs Craven replied. 'But you can do your bit by taking care of this little one,' she said, handing the bundle over to Beth. 'Put her in the cradle close to the stove to keep her warm. I've got to go back and help the doctor.'

While Sam got the cradle from where it had been left in the parlour, Beth stood looking down at the baby in her arms. She'd never seen a newborn baby before, and although Mrs Craven had said this one was big, to her it looked tiny, red and wrinkled. Its hair was dark, and although she couldn't see its eyes for they were all screwed up, she liked its little mouth which it kept opening and shutting like a fish.

Sam brought in the cradle. 'I think we'd better warm up the mattress and the covers first,' Beth suggested, for there hadn't been a fire on in the parlour since the weather got really cold. 'What do you think of her?'

Sam looked down at the baby and tentatively stroked its cheek with one finger. 'She's a bit ugly,' he said, wrinkling his nose with distaste.

'No she's not,' Beth said defensively. 'She's sweet, and it's just the same as looking at a newborn puppy or kitten.

They all look like little rats at first, but they soon get really pretty, and so will she.'

What with all the preparation of the baby's cradle and making yet more tea for Mrs Craven and the doctor, they temporarily forgot about their mother. It was only when their neighbour came back into the kitchen with a big bundle of bloodsoaked linen and asked Sam to get the tin bath from the yard to put it to soak that they were sharply reminded.

'She'll be poorly for some time,' Mrs Craven said gravely. 'We'll have to build her strength up again with some good beef tea, eggs and milk. When the doctor has finished with her, you can go in for a minute or two to see her. Don't expect much from her though, she's had a tough time.'

It seemed like hours before Dr Gillespie finally came out of the bedroom, though in fact it wasn't more than half an hour. He looked weary as he stripped off a bloodstained apron and went over to the sink to wash his hands. 'Have you any brandy in the house?' he asked.

'I think so, sir,' Sam said, going into the larder to get it.

'Good lad, give your mother some in hot milk.' He walked over to the cradle and looked down at the sleeping baby. 'She at least seems in very good health and Mrs Craven will explain what she needs. I'll come back in the morning to check on your mother.'

He took a small dark brown bottle from his bag and put it down on the table. 'If your mother is in pain during the night she can have three or four drops of this in hot water. Try and get her to drink some water too.'

'Go on! You can go and see her now,' Mrs Craven urged them once the doctor had gone. 'Then I must be away to my bed too.'

Sam and Beth crept into their mother's room on tiptoe, not knowing quite what to expect. Everything looked surprisingly orderly and normal considering what had gone on here, though it was very hot with the fire lit and there was a funny smell. But Alice seemed to have shrunk; she took up no more room in the big brass bed than a child, and her face had a strange mottled appearance in the gaslight.

'How are you feeling, Mama?' Sam asked.

'I hurt,' she croaked out. 'The baby?'

'She's fine, all wrapped up and in her cradle sleeping,' Beth said softly. 'You've got to drink this,' she added, going closer so she could lift her mother enough for her to drink the milk and brandy. 'I'll sleep in the kitchen with her tonight so she'll stay warm and I can keep an eye on her. It's snowing outside.'

When her mother had finished the drink and Beth laid her down again, she caught hold of her daughter's forearm. 'Please don't hate me for this,' she said pleadingly.

'Hate you for what?' Beth frowned, looking at Sam in puzzlement.

'For leaving you with such a burden,' she said as she closed her eyes.

Beth tucked the covers around her mother and turned the gas down till it was just a faint glow. Sam put a few more coals on the fire and they crept quietly out of the room.

'Does she think she's going to die?' Beth asked Sam once Mrs Craven had gone home.

'That will just be the effect of the medicine the doctor gave her,' he replied knowledgeably. 'Don't pay it any mind.'

'I won't be able to go to the shop tomorrow if I've got

to look after the baby,' Beth said. 'Mr Hooley won't be pleased when it's so close to Christmas. What if he won't hold my position until Mama is better again?'

'Don't worry your head about that,' Sam said wearily. 'You write a note for him and I'll put it through the door on my way to work. Now, I'd better put more coal in the stove to keep our little sister warm. I wonder what Mama will want to call her.'

'I think she looks like a Molly,' Beth said, peeping into the cradle again. 'I just hope she doesn't wake up until Mrs Craven comes in. I don't know a thing about babies.'

Beth slept fitfully in the old armchair by the stove, with her feet up on a stool and some blankets over her. She kept waking at the slightest noise, but each time it was nothing more than crackling from the stove, or a little murmur from the baby. But whenever she tried to go back to sleep, her mind kept mulling over that plea from her mother.

At six in the morning Beth was cuddling the baby and trying to get her to stop crying, when to her relief Mrs Craven came in through the back door, stamping her feet to get rid of the snow on her boots.

'Baby needs changing and feeding,' she said bossily, and throwing off her coat, she took the baby from Beth and proceeded to remove the soggy blanket, ordering Beth to go and get the box of baby clothes and napkins.

Beth watched in fascination as the older woman carefully washed the tiny baby and gave her instructions about changing the piece of lint around the stump of its umbilical cord and sprinkling a special powder on the cord until it fell off. She then folded a napkin into a triangle and fastened it around the baby's bottom.

'Later, when the shops are open, you must go and see if

you can buy a pair of india-rubber waterproof pants for her,' Mrs Craven said. 'They didn't have them when my babies were born, but I believe they are a godsend as they keep their clothes and bedding dry. You must change the napkin every two or three hours. If you leave her wet she'll get sore.'

As she dressed the baby in a little nightgown, she imparted a great deal more information about babycare, most of which went over Beth's head.

'Now, we'll take her to your mother for a feed,' she said, handing the baby back to Beth. 'She might protest as she's feeling poorly, but a mother always gets better quicker when she holds her baby.'

Alice did look marginally better, in as much as the awful blotching on her face had faded, and she opened her eyes and tried to smile. She winced with pain as Mrs Craven helped her to sit up a bit so she could put more pillows behind her, and she was terribly pale.

Beth knew now that Dr Gillespie had performed what was called a caesarean, and it should have been done in the hospital. But he had no choice: Mama couldn't be moved and the baby had to be removed quickly or they would both have died.

'We'll just let baby have a little feed,' Mrs Craven said, unbuttoning the front of Mama's nightgown. 'Then I'll get you a drink, something to eat and make you more comfortable.'

Beth blushed at seeing her mother's breast, but as Mrs Craven put the baby to it and she latched on quickly, sucking eagerly, embarrassment turned to delight at the sight of such greed and Beth had to smile.

'She's a little fighter, that one,' Mrs Craven said tenderly. 'Now, what are you going to call her?'

'I think she's a Molly,' Beth said, and sat down on the edge of the bed.

'Then Molly it shall be,' her mother said with the ghost of a smile.

Chapter Four

In the days following Molly's birth Beth didn't get a minute to herself, for it was a continuous round of changing and comforting Molly, seeing to her mother, including helping her on to a chamber pot because she couldn't get down to the privy, then doing all the washing and other household chores. The snow still lay thickly on the ground and most days there were more flurries. It was so dark inside the flat that Beth often had to light the gas during the day. When she rushed out to get groceries, she didn't linger, for however inviting Church Street looked, with the shop windows all decked out for Christmas, the hot-chestnut sellers and the organ grinders, it was too cold to stay outside.

She had become entranced by her baby sister. Looking after her was a pleasure, not a chore, and she didn't feel hard done by with everything else she had to do either. But within a week the joy was replaced by anxiety about her mother.

At first Alice had seemed to be getting progressively better. On the third day after the birth she asked Beth for an omelette, and she'd eaten every scrap of it, and some rice pudding. She was holding Molly for long periods after she'd fed her, and she was glad to talk to Beth, explaining little things about babies and cooking to her.

On the fourth day she was much the same until the evening, when she suddenly said she was very hot. By the following morning Beth had to run round and get Dr Gillespie because she was feverish.

The doctor said women often became that way on the fourth or fifth day after confinement, and recommended Beth make her drink lots of fluids and keep her warm. But Alice grew worse and worse, so feverish she hardly knew who she was. A nasty smell was coming from her, and she was racked by terrible pain in her stomach that even the medicine the doctor had given her didn't stop.

Mrs Craven called it childbed fever, but Dr Gillespie had a much more fancy name for it. He came in twice a day, irrigating Mama's womb with some kind of antiseptic solution and then packing it with gauze.

They carried on putting Molly to her breasts, even though Alice couldn't hold her, but this morning Mrs Craven had brought in a glass bottle with a rubber teat. She didn't have to explain why; it was evident that Alice's health was so poor that she couldn't produce enough milk.

Molly took to the bottle with gusto and Beth got a great deal of comfort too from sitting in the comfortable chair by the stove nursing her. She loved the way Molly's eyes opened very wide as she began to feed; they looked like two dark blue marbles, and she waved her tiny hands as if that helped her to get the milk down faster. But as she reached the end of the bottle, her eyes would droop and her hands would sink to her sides.

Often Beth would sit for an hour or more holding Molly up by her shoulder, rubbing her back the way Mrs Craven had advised to get her wind up. She loved the smell and the feel of her, the little sighs of contentment and everything about her. Even when she'd finally changed her napkin, swaddled her in a blanket so just her little head was visible and tucked her back into the cradle, she would stand and watch her sleeping, marvelling at the miracle of new life.

Yet the joy was marred by her mother's poor health. Neither Dr Gillespie nor Mrs Craven had even hinted that Alice wasn't going to recover, but however hard Beth tried to be optimistic, she could sense death approaching in the next room.

Their goodhearted, competent neighbour was popping in every two or three hours now, and Beth knew by the increase in bloodstained sheets, the foul smell, the way Mrs Craven kept piling more coal on the bedroom fire and the tightness of her expression that it was only a matter of time.

Beth didn't tell Sam of her fears, for she knew he was worried about money. Mr Hooley at the hosiery shop had taken a dim view of Beth wanting time off at his busiest period, and there was no question of him holding her job open until she could return. On top of that Sam was freezing in the shipping office and he said that it was hard to write neatly when his fingers were numb with cold. The thought of another two or three months of winter in such an icy workplace filled him with dread. Beth reasoned that if she told him that their mother was likely to die and he'd single-handedly have to support Beth and Molly, he might just be tempted to take to his heels and run off.

However, on Sunday evening, when Sam had been home all day observing the frantic activity, Beth could see by his anxious expression that he had finally realized how serious things were.

'Why didn't you tell me?' he asked Beth reproachfully as she sat cuddling Molly.

'You had enough to worry about,' she said truthfully. 'Besides, I hoped she might improve.'

The little bell Beth had put by their mother's bedside so she could call if she needed anything, tinkled. Beth got up and went into the bedroom with Molly still in her arms.

37

It was very hot and stuffy, and the unpleasant smell had become even stronger.

'A drink, Mama?' Beth asked with her eyes averted from her mother's face. It hurt to look at her, for the flesh on her face seemed to have sunk back into her bones and her eyes stood out like those of a fish on a fishmonger's slab.

'No. Get Sam, I must speak to you both,' she replied, her voice a mere croaky whisper.

Sam came in immediately, his nose wrinkling at the smell.

'Come closer,' their mother whispered. 'It hurts to speak now.'

Brother and sister edged closer to the bed, Beth holding Molly tightly against her chest. 'What is it, Mama?' Sam asked, his voice shaking.

'I have something bad to tell you,' Alice said. 'I know I am dying but I can't go with it on my conscience.'

Sam started to say she wasn't going to die and anyway, she was pure and good, but she waved her hand feebly to stop him. 'I'm not a good woman,' she said, her voice faltering and rasping. 'Your father killed himself because of what I did.'

Sam looked sideways at Beth questioningly. His sister shrugged, thinking their mother was just rambling with the fever.

'There was another man. Your father discovered it a few weeks before he took his life. He said he would forgive me if I made a pledge that I would never see the man again.' She broke off, coughing weakly. Neither Beth nor Sam moved to help her drink.

'I made that pledge,' she went on as the coughing abated. 'But I couldn't stick to it and continued to see the man when I could get away. The last time I saw him was the morning of the day Frank hanged himself.'

Beth was stunned. 'How could you?' she burst out.

'You, you . . .' Sam exclaimed, his face turning red with anger and disgust. 'You whore!'

'There is nothing you can say which will make me feel worse than I do,' Alice rasped out. 'I betrayed your father and I am responsible for his death. He was a good man, too good for me.'

'And Molly? Who is her father?' Beth shouted.

'The other man,' her mother said, closing her eyes as if she couldn't bear to see her children's angry faces. 'Look in the drawer where I keep my stockings,' she said. 'A note I found that night, Frank had tucked it under my pillow.'

Sam opened the small top drawer in the dressing table and rummaged for a moment or two, then pulled out a sheet of writing paper. He took it over to the gaslight to read it.

'What does it say?' Beth asked.

Dear Alice, Sam read.

I have known for some time that you are still seeing your lover. By the time you find this I will be gone and you will be free to go with this man you care for more than me. All I ask is that you wait a respectable time after my death before taking up with him, for our children's sake.

I loved you, I'm sorry that wasn't enough.

Frank.

Beth had begun to cry as Sam read the note. She could imagine her quiet, gentle father penning it down in the shop and coming up here at teatime to slip it under the pillow. Even with a broken heart he hadn't resorted to anger or spite, but had carried on being a loving husband and father till the end.

Sam moved over to Beth and put one arm around her,

looking down at Molly asleep in her arms. Tears were rolling down his cheeks.

'Why, Mama?' he cried out. 'Why did you have to do that?'

'I did love your father, but it was the sweet love of a friend,' she replied brokenly. 'Passion is quite another thing. Maybe one day you'll discover that for yourselves and understand.'

'But why didn't this other man come for you?' Sam shouted in anger. 'If it was true love, why isn't he with you now?'

'My biggest failing was to confuse passion with love,' she replied, her eyes burning as she looked at her son. 'He vanished into the night as soon as he heard Frank was dead. That was my real punishment, to know I had thrown in my lot with a philanderer who cared nothing for me, and Frank died thinking he'd found the way to make me happy.'

'Did this other man know you were carrying his child?' Beth sobbed.

'No, Beth. I didn't realize until after the last time I saw him.'

She began to cough and wheeze, and it was plain she was too weak to say anything more. 'Go to sleep now,' Beth said curtly. 'We'll talk again tomorrow.'

In the kitchen later, Sam walked up and down, white with anger. 'How could she?' he kept repeating. 'And if she doesn't recover, are we supposed to look after that brat?'

Beth was crying as she nursed Molly in her arms. 'Don't say that, Sam. She's just a baby, none of this is her fault, and she's our sister.'

'She's no sister of mine,' he raged. 'Our father might have been weak enough to accept his wife had a lover, but I'm not going to follow in his footsteps – she can go.'

'Go where?' Beth asked through her tears. 'Are we to take her to the Foundling Home? Leave her on someone's doorstep?'

'I can't and won't keep the child of a man who seduced my mother and caused my father to take his own life,' Sam said flatly, his mouth set in a determined straight line. 'Get rid of her!'

Beth stayed up for a long time after Sam had gone off to bed. She fed and changed Molly and put her down in the cradle, then sat in the chair trying to make sense of everything.

But nothing did make sense to her. Until tonight she hadn't thought it possible that a woman who had a good husband, children and a comfortable home could ever want anything else. She had of course heard whispers of loose women who went with men other than their husbands, but she had always had the idea that they were the kind of sluts who went into ale houses and painted their faces. Not ordinary women like her mother.

'Passion', in the way her mother had meant it, she had no understanding of. Miss Clarkson had been fond of the word, though she had mostly used it in connection with music. But once, when she was talking about how babies were made, she had said that 'passion' overtook some women and robbed them of their own will. Beth had to suppose that was what had happened to her mother.

Beth was still sitting in the chair crying when she heard a sound from her mother's bedroom. Something had fallen to the floor, perhaps the water glass. She didn't want to see Alice again tonight, but she knew she had to go in there and check on her.

Her mother was lying over to one side of the bed, trying

to reach for the family photograph which stood on the bedside table. It had been taken a year ago in a booth on New Brighton Beach when they had gone there for the August Bank Holiday. Reaching for it, she had knocked over a bottle of pills the doctor had given her.

'Is that what you want?' Beth said, picking it up and holding it out for her mother to look at.

Her mother lifted her arm with great difficulty and put one finger on the picture. 'Don't tell anyone about Molly,' she whispered. 'Let everyone think she was Frank's. Not for me, but for her, and give her this when she is grown up, so she'll know what we looked like.'

Her hand went from the picture to catch hold of Beth's wrist. It felt as dry as an autumn leaf, so small and bony, and she was gripping tight. 'I'm so very sorry,' she said. 'Tell me you forgive me.'

Instinct told Beth that this was the end or very close to it. Whatever her mother had done, whoever she had hurt, she couldn't let her die without a kind word. 'Yes, I forgive you, Mama,' she said.

'I can go then?' Alice asked in a whisper.

The grip on Beth's wrist loosened and her mother's hand fell to the blanket. Beth stood looking at her for some little time before she realized she had stopped breathing.

Chapter Five

'We *will* have the cheapest funeral,' Sam argued stubbornly. 'Because of her, Father couldn't be laid to rest in hallowed ground and no one came to the funeral to say what a good man he was. So why should she have anything better?'

'We can't let her have a pauper's funeral,' Beth said wearily, for they'd been over this several times already since he came in for his supper, and it was nearly eleven o'clock now. 'What would people think of us?'

'Why should we care about that!' he exploded. 'Apart from the Cravens, everyone's been whispering maliciously about us since Papa died. Let them carry on doing it.'

Beth began to cry because she didn't know this stony-hearted person who had taken the place of her brother. Their mother had been dead for less than twenty-four hours, her body was still lying in the bed, and yet Sam had gone off to work this morning as if nothing had happened. She understood of course that he was afraid he'd lose his job if he didn't, but he could have explained that to her, just a few gentle words to let her know he wasn't angry with her too.

'Don't cry, Beth,' he said, his eyes growing softer. 'I don't mean to be cruel, but things are desperate now. We can't spend money we haven't got on her funeral. And that baby has got to go!'

Beth moved protectively over to Molly's cradle. 'Don't say that, Sam. She's our sister and I will not abandon her. You can sell the piano or anything else to get some money, we'll take in a lodger or move somewhere cheaper, but Molly stays with us.'

'I can't bear to see her,' he said, and his eyes filled with tears. 'She's always going to be a reminder of what Mama drove Papa to do.'

'If Mama hadn't been so honest and brave admitting the truth, we'd have been none the wiser,' Beth argued. 'Besides, Papa would turn in his grave if we turned our backs on a helpless baby, even if it wasn't his. So you've got to find the humanity to accept that we have to do right by Molly.'

Sam just looked at her thoughtfully.

It was some little while before he spoke again. 'Put like that, I suppose I'll have to agree.' He sighed. 'But don't expect me to ever feel anything for her. And don't blame me when you find out what being poor is really like.'

It was enough for Beth that Sam had backed down. 'Then I'll compromise and arrange the cheapest funeral. But you mustn't blame me either if later you find it makes you feel bad about yourself.'

Christmas was bleak; they had neither the money nor the heart to attempt any kind of festivity. They left Molly with Mrs Craven just long enough to go to church on Christmas morning, but that gave them no comfort for it only served to remind them of joyful Christmases past. A few people approached them to offer condolences, but there was no ring of sincerity in them, only curiosity.

The funeral took place two days later, and Mrs Craven's eldest daughter minded Molly. Heavy rain had melted the snow, but an icy wind blew across the churchyard, almost cutting them in half as the cheap coffin was lowered into the grave. Apart from Sam and Beth, there were only three other mourners: the Cravens and Dr Gillespie. As Father

Reilly intoned the final words of the committal, Beth glanced over to where her father was buried in unhallowed ground. She thought how unjust it was that a man who had never sinned against anyone should be there, while his adulterous wife lay in the churchyard.

By the first week in February, when Sam became seventeen and Beth sixteen, they were forced to sell the piano. Beth didn't really care much about it, after all she still had her precious fiddle, but seeing the piano being lowered out through the window to the street below brought home to her how tragically ironic it was.

To her parents the piano was a symbol that they had succeeded in lifting their children up to the middle classes, and as such they would never suffer the hardships they themselves had endured. Yet by being protected from want and shielded from the hard facts of real life, both she and Sam lacked the resources to cope with poverty.

Beth could bake cakes, lay a table properly, starch and iron a shirt, and had acquired dozens of other refined accomplishments, but she'd never been taught to plan a week's meals on a tiny budget. Sam might be able to haul in coal for the stove, shovel snow out of the backyard and be on time every day for work, but he had no idea how to unblock a sink or fix a broken sash cord in the window.

All their childhood there had always been a fire in the parlour, the stove in the kitchen and even fires in the bedrooms when it was really cold. The gas was lit in all the rooms before it grew dark, there was always fruit in a bowl, cake in the tin and meat every day.

The coal ran out soon after Christmas and when they ordered more they were shocked at the price and could only keep the stove in the kitchen going. The gas ate up pennies so fast that they were afraid to light it. Fruit and cake disappeared from their diet.

Sam's wages were spent on food long before Friday came round, and once they'd eaten all the preserves and stores of sugar and flour their mother had so frugally tucked away in the pantry, they were down to bread alone until pay day.

Maybe Sam should have held out for a better price for their mother's prized round mahogany table and matching chairs, but they needed the money to pay for the coal and the bill from Dr Gillespie. There was no doubt they were swindled when the grandfather clock was sold. But neither of them had any idea of the real value of these items, or that second-hand furniture dealers could smell desperation.

Although Beth loved caring for Molly, she hadn't reckoned on the loneliness of being home all day alone with a baby. She never seemed to have a minute for herself to read, play her fiddle or take a bath. Sam wasn't interested in hearing about Molly when he came in from work, she had no one other than Mrs Craven she could talk to, and she was continually worried about money.

By the middle of March Sam could see no alternative other than to find lodgers to make ends meet.

One of the more senior clerks in his office suggested his cousin Thomas Wiley and his wife Jane, who had been staying with him and his family since Thomas moved from Manchester to take up work in the Liverpool post office. The couple were in their mid-thirties, and Beth took an immediate dislike to Jane. Everything about her was sharp – her eyes which darted around the room as she spoke, her nose and cheekbones, and even her voice had a sharp edge to it.

She showed no interest in Molly and she looked Beth up

and down as if pricing up the value of her clothes. When Beth tried to suggest they figured out a plan when each would cook their evening meal, Jane dismissed her by saying she wasn't one for cooking.

Her husband, Thomas, was easier to take to, a jovial, ruddy-faced man who appeared very grateful to be offered the parlour and Beth's old bedroom up on the top floor above the kitchen, for she and Molly were now in her parents' old room. Thomas said he had begun to despair of ever finding anywhere decent, or even clean, for he had been to view rooms that he wouldn't even keep a dog in.

Sadly it soon transpired that Thomas liked the drink more than he did his wife or home. Most evenings he didn't roll back till after ten.

Beth tried hard to get along with Jane, but it was clear from the start she thought a lodger should be waited on. She ordered Beth to fill the tin bath in the bedroom for her on her second day there. When Beth said she and Sam always had a bath in the kitchen as it was far warmer and more convenient, and anyway Jane must fill it and empty it herself, the woman flounced around indignantly, declaring 'she'd never heard the like'.

As it was, she spilled water all over the kitchen floor and made no attempt to clean it up. She complained that the sound of Molly crying in the night woke her and that the mattress on the bed was lumpy. Beth rushed to feed Molly if she woke in the night, and she spent a good hour shaking the feather mattress outside to make it fluffier, but Jane didn't reciprocate in any way. She could make a mess even making a cup of tea, and never cleared it up. She would fill the sink with washing and then disappear, which meant Beth had to do her washing for her or was unable to use the sink.

Day by day Beth saw the comfortable and orderly life

she'd been brought up with, and had struggled to maintain, eroding away. As she was bathing Molly in the sink, Jane would come in and start frying bacon, knocking the clean nightgown, vest and napkin from where they were airing by the stove to the floor. If Beth wanted to sit in the armchair to feed Molly, Jane was already sitting there. She helped herself to their food; she didn't wash up her plates or pots. Beth soon gave up hope of her ever offering to take a turn cleaning the kitchen, the stairs or the privy, yet Thomas would walk in at night with muddy boots and next morning Beth would see a trail all along the landing and up the stairs.

Beth felt unable to complain. Not only was she a little afraid of Jane, but she knew how desperately she and Sam needed the rent money. Yet it was so hard to see the home which had always been so clean and tidy degenerate into squalor, to listen to Thomas's drunken ramblings late at night, and never to have any real privacy. Playing the piano or her fiddle had always been her tried and tested way of escaping from her problems, but she no longer had the piano, and with Jane stalking around she didn't feel able to play her fiddle. She could feel herself becoming wound up like a watch spring, and she was afraid of what might happen when that spring finally snapped.

It happened one morning in July. Sam and Thomas had left for work about an hour earlier. Beth went into the kitchen with Molly in her arms, ready to feed her, and found Jane pouring some of the milk in the baby's bottle into her tea.

'What are you doing?' Beth exclaimed. 'That's Molly's!'

'There's no other milk left,' Jane said.

'Well, go out and get some,' Beth retorted angrily. 'What sort of person would take a baby's food?'

'Don't you speak to me like that.' Jane's eyes narrowed

48

and she stuck her thin face right up to Beth's menacingly. 'You feed her too much anyway, that's why she's so fat.'

At seven months old Molly was plump, but Beth took a pride in her being so healthy and strong. She had masses of dark hair, four teeth, and she could sit up unaided now. She was a happy, contented baby who smiled and gurgled all day long.

'She's beautiful, not fat, and you should be ashamed of yourself,' Beth snapped back. 'It's bad enough you stealing our food. Have I got to hide Molly's milk now too?'

'Are you calling me a thief?' Jane shrieked, and catching hold of a clump of Beth's hair pulled her head back sharply, making her cry out. 'That's right, snivel. You think you're so high and mighty, don't you? But what've you got to be high and mighty about? Yer pa topped hisself, and everyone knows why.'

She let go of Beth's hair and looked at her contemptuously. 'Don't yer know everyone talks about yer ma? Me and Tom heard about it afore we even moved in. Yer pa must've been soft in the head, topping hisself instead of throwing her out on the streets. No wonder yer brother don't want nothin' to do with the bairn.'

Beth backed away with Molly in her arms. She was horrified that the truth about her mother had got out, and she was afraid of Jane too, but she'd had enough, and she wasn't going to let the woman get the better of her.

'What you've just said is completely untrue,' she shouted back at her. 'I won't have anyone slandering my mother, so you can pack your bags and get out of my home now.'

'And how do you think you're going to make me?' Jane put her hands on her hips challengingly. 'Big brother going to throw me out, is he?' She cackled with laughter. 'He's as soft as shit.'

All at once Beth knew she had to be strong and fight for her rights. She turned, darted into the bedroom and laid Molly down safely in her cradle. She howled in protest, but Beth ignored her and returned to the kitchen to face Jane.

'I don't need my brother,' she said defiantly. 'I'm perfectly capable of dealing with the likes of you. Get out now and I'll pack your stuff and put it down in the yard for Thomas to collect later.'

Jane leapt towards her, one hand raised to slap her, but Beth was quicker, catching her by the wrist and twisting it, making the woman squeal in pain. 'Out!' she yelled at her, still twisting her wrist as she pushed her towards the stairs. 'And if you try to come back I'll make you sorry.'

Beth had never fought anyone before, apart from play-fighting with Sam when they were younger, but anger made her strong and determined.

Jane tried to fight back, clawing at her with her free hand, but Beth had youth and righteous indignation on her side, and she managed to haul the older woman down the stairs towards the back door. Once she'd got her out into the backyard she pushed her so hard that Jane fell over.

'I'll make you pay for this,' Jane shouted back as she lay sprawled on the ground, her grubby petticoats and drawers on display. 'You won't get away with it. I want my things.'

'You can have them,' Beth said. 'I'll throw them out the window to you.'

With that she turned away, went in through the back door, locking it behind her, and ran upstairs. It took only a couple of minutes to scoop up the woman's coat, hat, purse and a pair of boots from the bedroom, then she threw the kitchen window open and dropped them down into the yard below.

'Be grateful you've even got those,' she yelled. 'The rest

will be left in the outhouse for you to collect this evening.'

Mr Craven had come out into the alley beyond the back-yard and he was looking up curiously at Beth in the window. 'I'm just chucking her out for slandering my parents,' she shouted to him. 'Would you mind helping her on her way?'

She stayed just long enough at the window to see her neighbour escorting Jane out of the back gate, and to hear the woman's vitriolic stream of abuse.

Somehow Beth managed to give Molly her bottle, even though she was trembling like a leaf from shock. She heard Mrs Craven calling from the yard and went down to let her in.

'Oh, lovey!' she exclaimed when she saw how pale and agitated Beth was. 'We heard the yelling, and that's why my Alfie went looking to see what was going on.'

The sympathy in her voice made Beth cry, and Mrs Craven embraced her, then took Molly from her arms. 'I'll make you a nice cup of tea, and you can tell me all about it.'

'There isn't any milk. That's how it all started,' Beth began.

'Then I'll just go and get some,' Mrs Craven said. 'And you'd better change Molly's napkin while I'm gone. She stinks!'

Half an hour later, Beth had explained everything. The tea and her neighbour's concern had made her feel better.

'I knew she was a baggage the first time I clapped eyes on her. Common as muck and hard-faced too,' Mrs Craven said, bouncing Molly on her knee. 'As if you haven't had enough to cope with! But you mustn't pay any mind to what she said about your mother.'

'But is that what people are saying?'

Mrs Craven frowned. 'No one has said it to me. If they

had I'd have put them straight. But my Alfie did say there was talk in the Fiddlers.'

The Fiddlers Inn was around the corner in Lord Street. Papa hadn't been a drinker, but most of their male neighbours drank there, and Thomas Wiley did too.

It hadn't occurred to Beth before that anyone would suspect Molly wasn't her father's child, and she was horrified to learn they did, but she had no intention of admitting the rumours were true, not even to kind-hearted Mrs Craven.

'Why are people so cruel?' she asked in bewilderment.

'Sometimes it's from jealousy. Your family looked so perfect, your mother was a pretty woman, your father had a good business and two children to be proud of. No one could understand why he took his own life, so they make guesses at the reason.'

'What will become of us now?' Beth asked sadly. 'We needed lodgers to manage. Sam's going to be so cross with me.'

'I don't think so, Beth.' Mrs Craven reached out and took Beth's hand across the table. 'You showed a lot of spirit, he'll admire that. Now, let me help you pack up the Wileys' things. My Alfie will keep his ear open for when they come back for them, and help if they start any trouble.'

Chapter Six

'I wish we could emigrate to America,' Sam said dejectedly as he ate his supper. 'This place is full of bad memories. I hate it now.'

It was the day after Beth had thrown out Jane Wiley. Sam hadn't been angry about it, only demoralized. He had pointed out that there were hundreds of people needing somewhere to live, but it was impossible to know who might rob them or make their lives a misery.

Beth had been badly shaken by the whole thing. When she'd gone to clean out the Wileys' room, she'd found the chamber pot hadn't been emptied for days, and there were crusts of stale bread dropped on the floor and filthy under-wear strewn all over the place. Even the sheets on the bed were bloodstained and there was a big scratch right across the dressing table which looked as if it had been made by a knife.

Sam had gone downstairs when Thomas arrived to collect their things and Mr Craven had stood out in the alley too in case of trouble. But Thomas had seemed resigned rather than fighting mad. He'd just picked up the bags and left with them.

'But we'd need money to emigrate,' Beth said wistfully.

'We couldn't go with Molly anyway,' Sam retorted.

Beth felt a pang in her heart, for she knew that what he really meant was that he wouldn't want her with them. He hadn't softened towards her as she'd hoped; he never picked her up or played with her. Even when Molly laughed it didn't make him smile.

'If it wasn't for her we could sell everything to raise the fare,' he said bitterly. 'As it is, I'll have to take those two silver photograph frames tomorrow and sell them, just to keep us going.'

Beth went into the bedroom soon afterwards and opened the back of the photograph frames to take out the pictures. One was of her and Sam when they were around nine and ten, taken in a studio just down Church Street. She was wearing a white dress with a little straw bonnet, her hair in ringlets beneath it. Sam was standing beside her chair in a dark jacket and knee-length knickerbockers, looking very serious. Their mother had loved the picture, and Papa had bought the frame specially for it.

The other picture was the one she'd been asked to keep for Molly. Her parents were both smiling, and Beth remembered that seconds after the picture was taken they had all burst into helpless laughter because when the photographer bent down to put his head under the black cloth to take the picture he broke wind.

If only they could have all stayed as happy as they had been that day! Mama looked so pretty in her best dress and Papa distinguished in his striped blazer and boater. It had been very hot, and they'd all taken off their shoes and stockings and had a paddle in the sea together.

Beth could understand Sam's bitterness. There were times when she too felt like cursing her mother for bringing all this down on them. Why couldn't she have been satisfied with a good, kind husband who loved her?

The following morning Beth was feeling rather more positive and decided to write out an advertisement for two male lodgers. Later, with Molly in her arms, she took it down to the sweet shop further along Church Street. After handing it in to be displayed, she stopped to read the advertisements already on the board, and noticed one requiring a woman for a few hours a week to do laundry and sewing.

It was in Falkner Square, in one of Liverpool's best districts. Beth had often walked around its wide streets and leafy squares to deliver shoes and boots for her father.

Thinking such a position would be ideal for her, Beth rushed round to ask Mrs Craven if she would mind Molly while she went there.

'I'd be glad to, my dear.' Mrs Craven smiled, holding out her arms for the baby. 'And if it's only a few hours a week I'd be glad to mind her then too.'

Beth polished her boots, then put on her best dark blue dress with a lace collar and cuffs and a plain dark blue bonnet that had been Mama's. It was the first time she'd worn anything other than black since Papa died, and she felt slightly guilty at not wearing mourning, but both her black dresses were looking a little shabby now, and dark blue was hardly frivolous.

Beth's spirits lifted as she set off for it was a lovely warm day and it felt good to be going out without Molly for once, almost an adventure.

The gardens in the centre of Falkner Square looked pretty, with many flowering shrubs in full bloom. She stopped outside number forty-two, looking speculatively at the steps down to the basement area behind the black iron railings and the marble ones up to the front door beneath the pillared porch.

Beth had been told about life below stairs in big houses by her mother, and so she knew the basement door was the one she should knock on. But it had been made quite clear to her all through her childhood that she wouldn't ever be a servant to anyone, so she wasn't inclined to think of herself as one now.

Taking a deep breath, she marched up to the front door and rang the bell. It clanged loudly, echoing through the house, and suddenly she felt dry-mouthed and nervous.

The door was opened by an elderly woman in a grey dress with a white apron and frilly cap.

'I came in answer to the advertisement for someone to help with sewing and laundry,' Beth said, a little too loudly. 'My name is Miss Bolton.'

The woman looked her up and down. 'Where are you from?' she asked.

'Church Street,' Beth said.

'You'd better come in,' the woman said, and frowned as if puzzled. 'The mistress is out at the moment, but I'll take your particulars and tell her when she returns.'

The woman led her to the back of the house to a small, simply furnished room. Beth got the idea it was her room, for she'd caught a glimpse of the drawing room as she walked down the hall and that was very grand, with fancy carpets and lovely couches and armchairs.

'Sit down, please,' the woman said. 'I'm Mrs Bruce, Mrs Langworthy's housekeeper. How old are you?'

'Sixteen, mam,' Beth said.

'And do you have a character?'

Beth had no idea what she meant by that.

'A letter from your last employer?' Mrs Bruce said rather tersely.

'I had to leave the hosiery shop where I worked in a hurry,' Beth said, and breathlessly explained that her recently widowed mother had died in childbirth. 'I couldn't go back to my position at the shop as I had to stay home and take care of my little sister.'

*

Beth was peeling potatoes for the evening meal, with Molly, propped up against some cushions in a wooden box beside the sink, gnawing on a crust of bread, when Mr Filbert, the man who ran the shoe shop downstairs, called up to her.

'Miss Bolton, a young lad has just brought a letter for you!'

'I'll be right down,' she called back, rinsing her hands and drying them on her apron. She felt certain the letter could only be to turn her down, but at least Mrs Langworthy or her housekeeper had been polite enough to write.

'Not bad news, I hope?' Mr Filbert asked as Beth stood in the doorway through to his shop gasping at the contents of the letter she'd just opened.

'No,' Beth said, looking up at him with a broad smile. 'Quite the opposite.'

She could hardly wait for Sam to come home to tell him the good news. Mrs Langworthy wanted her to start in the morning. She suggested that Beth work two five-hour days, as she thought this would make it easier for her to arrange for someone to take care of the baby. And she was going to pay her ten whole shillings! Beth had only got seven shillings and sixpence for working all week at the hosiery shop.

'Our luck has finally changed, Sam,' she yelled exuberantly the minute her brother came in. His face broke into a wide smile and he hugged her.

'Mrs Bruce must have fallen for your charm,' he insisted when she told him how she thought she'd talked too much. 'I just hope Mrs Craven doesn't get fed up with minding Molly.'

'She said she'd be glad to have her,' Beth said. 'She isn't any trouble anyway, and I'll give her a shilling a day.'

*

All Beth knew of how gentry lived was from what her mother had told her of her experiences in service, but she was fairly certain right from the first day at the Langworthys' that it was a most unusual household.

She arrived at eight as arranged, and Mrs Bruce offered her a cup of tea and some toast in the basement kitchen. 'You can't work on an empty stomach,' she said, 'and I'm fairly certain you rushed here without a bite. Now, we'll wait until Mr Edward, that's the young Mr Langworthy, has left for the office and I'll take you up to meet the mistress.'

Twenty minutes later, Beth was in the dining room on the ground floor where Mrs Langworthy was having her breakfast. It was at the back of the house overlooking a yard, next to the housekeeper's sitting room where Mrs Bruce had taken her the previous day.

Beth was surprised by Mrs Langworthy. She had expected someone middle-aged and grey-headed, not a relatively young woman with flaming red hair, sparkling green eyes and such a warm smile.

'Welcome, Beth,' she said, getting up from the table and offering her hand. 'I'm sorry I wasn't here to meet you yesterday, but Mrs Bruce told me all about you and your circumstances. I am so sorry to hear of your recent loss, and I do hope your little sister won't mind me sharing you with her.'

Beth was so staggered at that unexpected warm greeting that for once she was tongue-tied. She shook her new mistress's hand and looked at Mrs Bruce for guidance.

'Molly is with a neighbour who she is well used to,' Mrs Bruce explained.

'Then I'm sure she'll be quite happy,' Mrs Langworthy said. 'I'll let Mrs Bruce show you around and tell you what's needed today. I have to see to my father-in-law now, but I shall see you later in the morning.'

A small, slender, dark-haired Irishwoman in her twenties was making the bed in Mrs Langworthy's bedroom, which overlooked the square. Mrs Bruce introduced her as Kathleen and explained once they left the room that Kathleen lived in and had a room up on the top floor. 'She is a general maid – she does all the cleaning and lights the fires. We have a cook who comes in daily, you'll meet her later, and then there's myself. Just a small staff, but the Langworthys don't entertain much, and of course Mrs Langworthy takes care of old Mr Langworthy.' Mrs Bruce indicated the other room at the front of the house and explained that was his room.

'This is Mr Edward's room,' she said, opening a door at the back. It was starkly masculine, with a vast, highly polished mahogany wardrobe, its own washbasin with brass taps and a large bed, already made and covered with a heavy dark blue quilt. 'The bathroom,' she said, opening the next door. 'One of the beauties of this house was that it was built with modern facilities.'

Beth had never seen an indoor water closet before, only pictures of them in magazines, and couldn't resist saying so.

'Neither had I until I came to work for the Langworthys.' Mrs Bruce smiled. 'There is another water closet on the ground floor too, along with the one in the backyard.'

The final room was a guest room. Mrs Bruce said her own bedroom was up next to Kathleen's.

Mrs Langworthy's clothes, which it would be part of Beth's duties to take care of, were in a dressing room off her bedroom, but the housekeeper said that for today she wanted Beth to do only laundry.

It wasn't until they got back to the basement, having viewed the large drawing room which took up half the house from front to back, and Mr Edward's study, a small room also looking out on to the square, that Beth realized she wasn't going to be paid so well for doing nothing.

The laundry room had its own door out to the yard, with two big white sinks, another low one which was called a sluice, a mangle and a large gas boiler, which had to be lit from underneath.

There was a big basket of sheets smelling strongly of urine, which had to be boiled, and then Mrs Bruce lifted the lid on an enamel pail to reveal soiled napkins.

'Try and think of this as no worse than your Molly's,' she said, even though she had her nose turned away to avoid the horrible stench. 'Rinse them off thoroughly in the sluice, then they must be boiled with the sheets. There will be other washing, though there is none today, but I want you to remember that old Mr Langworthy's linen goes in the boiler alone, after everything else has been done.'

'How long do I boil it for?' Beth asked, trying not to gag at the very thought of what was in the pail.

'Twenty minutes to half an hour,' the housekeeper said. 'While it's boiling you can wash any delicate items by hand in the sink.'

'Mrs Langworthy has to change him?' Beth just had to ask. She couldn't imagine anyone as lovely and well bred as her doing such a thing.

'Yes, she does, Beth. He always was a difficult man, even before he had his stroke. But since then he's become very much worse because one side of him is paralysed and his speech and sight are impaired. We've had dozens of nurses here over the years, but he frightens them away. Mrs Langworthy is the only person he allows to touch him, and she has the patience of a saint. She should have children, friends visiting and a life of her own.' Mrs Bruce stopped abruptly and blushed. 'I shouldn't have said that.' She sighed. 'It's just . . .'

'That you get angry for her?' Beth ventured.

'Yes, Beth.' Mrs Bruce nodded. 'But I spoke out of turn.'

'I won't repeat what you said,' Beth said as she turned on the tap above the boiler to fill it. 'She was good enough to give me work when I needed it. For that you both get my loyalty.'

'So what's it like?' Mrs Craven asked eagerly when Beth returned in the early afternoon.

Beth picked Molly up from the rug she was sitting on and tickled her till she laughed. 'Mostly wonderful,' she said. 'It's a beautiful house, they've even got a water closet inside. But I wish old Mr Langworthy could use it.'

There weren't words to describe how disgusting she found sluicing out those napkins. She gagged and retched, hardly daring to breathe, they smelled so bad. She wondered how nurses managed to cope with such things day after day, and if she could ever get used to it and not mind any more.

But she'd told herself as she walked home that the horrible part only lasted some twenty minutes at most, which left four hours, forty minutes of pleasant duties. She didn't mind rinsing and putting the clean linen through the mangle. Hanging it up to dry out in the yard was lovely. And she'd spent the last hour darning Mr Edward's socks while she sat in the kitchen chatting to Mrs Cray, the cook, and Kathleen, the soft-spoken Irish maid. What's more, she'd had a huge slice of delicious meat pie for her dinner, and Mrs Cray had given her a couple of pasties to bring home.

'You can get used to anything in time,' Mrs Craven said philosophically. 'And I loved having Molly, so it's good for both of us.'

*

Mrs Craven was right. Beth found she did get used to washing those napkins. Or maybe it was just that the good parts of the job heavily outweighed the bad. It was nice to get out twice a week, to have other people to talk to, and to know she was helping Sam keep things going.

She didn't see much of Mr Edward. He had usually left for his office around the time she arrived, but on the odd occasion she ran into him she found him pleasant enough. He was tall and slender, with thinning sandy hair and a military-style moustache, at least ten years older than his wife. He struck Beth as a studious, quiet man who took life very seriously.

Mrs Langworthy was quite the opposite. She was so kind and merry, and always found time to come and find Beth for a little chat. She loved to hear about Molly, and it was clear she wished she had a child. She had a wonderful ability to hold her position as the mistress of the house yet empathize with those who worked for her. Beth understood why Mrs Bruce was so devoted to her, and she resolved that if ever she found herself in a position to have servants, she would model herself on this admirable woman.

It seemed as if Sam's and Beth's fortunes had finally turned, for just a week later they found two new lodgers, Ernest and Peter, both respectable young men who worked for an insurance company and were friends.

Sam thought it better for Beth that the lodgers should have the two rooms upstairs and so he moved down to the parlour. Right from their first night the young men proved to be ideal lodgers, polite, tidy and sensitive towards Beth and Molly.

They were both keen cyclists, and every Sunday they went out with a cycling club for jaunts into the countryside. They ate whatever Beth put in front of them, they were grateful she did their washing, and neither of them drank. Sam enjoyed their company, and often in the evenings the four of them played cards together. Sometimes they begged Beth to play her fiddle and clapped their hands and tapped their feet to accompany her. Those were the best nights of all because for a couple of hours all her cares fell away with the music and she felt as free and untroubled as a bird.

It seemed to Beth, too, that Sam was actually growing fond of Molly at last. Sometimes, if he came in from work and she was sitting on the floor, he'd bend down and pat her head, as Ernest and Peter often did. Beth didn't say anything – she was sure that if she did remark on it he would never do it again – but she'd watch him out of the corner of her eye and note that he was playing peekaboo with Molly, or tickling her to make her laugh.

One evening in August after Beth had put Molly to bed, she'd gone across to see Mrs Craven for a few minutes and came back to find Sam holding the little girl in his arms.

'She woke up crying,' he said defensively. 'I thought she might have a tummy ache.'

The following day when she had to go to Falkner Square Beth felt like skipping the whole way, she was so happy. Later that morning she was in the little room off the kitchen where they kept the sewing machine, singing as she turned some worn sheets sides to middle and sewed them up again, when Mrs Langworthy came in.

'And what has turned you into a little songbird?' she said with a wide smile.

'I'm just feeling happy because my brother seems to be getting fond of Molly at last,' Beth admitted. 'We had so many problems after our mother died, you see. It was difficult for him to accept Molly.'

'I don't think men have that instant love for babies that

women feel,' Mrs Langworthy said thoughtfully. 'Many of my friends have told me their husbands showed no interest at first. It must have been harder still for your brother, you both being so young.'

Beth chatted on about their two lodgers, and how Sam seemed much happier lately. 'He hasn't even mentioned emigrating to America for ages,' she said.

'Would you have liked to do that?' her mistress asked.

'Well, yes,' Beth replied. 'What an adventure it would be! But it wouldn't be possible with Molly, would it? I'd have to work too if we wanted to make a real go of it. Without any friends or family there we'd have no one to mind her.'

'It seems a shame to me that you and your brother have to sacrifice your dreams or ambitions,' Mrs Langworthy remarked, and patted Beth on the shoulder in sympathy.

One hot, sunny Saturday right at the end of August Sam came home from work and suggested they should catch the ferry to New Brighton the following day. Ernest and Peter were planning to go out early on their bicycles, and as they had already said they wouldn't want any supper as they were eating out, it meant Sam and Beth wouldn't have to rush back.

Beth was thrilled at Sam's suggestion, not only because she had so many good memories of going to New Brighton for the day with their parents, but because he was including Molly.

'Put on something pretty,' he suggested. 'You've been in mourning for quite long enough. It's time we had some fun.'

Just a week or two before, Beth had gone through her mother's clothes to see what could be sold, or altered to fit her, and she'd found tucked away at the bottom of the cupboard the pale blue and white striped dress Mama had been wearing in the photograph. Beth had been longing to

64

wear it, for it was very pretty, with a lower neckline than she usually wore, leg-of-mutton sleeves and a pin-tucked bodice. She'd had to let the waist out a fraction and drop the hem an inch or two, but it fitted everywhere else perfectly.

'You look lovely,' Sam said appreciatively when she came into the kitchen on Sunday morning, ready to leave.

Beth was quite giddy with excitement, for with her hair left loose and a pert little straw boater perched on top at an angle, she felt quite the young lady of fashion. Molly seemed to pick up on her excitement for she began laughing and clapping her fat little hands as Beth carried her downstairs and put her into the perambulator.

As they turned into Lord Street to make their way down to the docks and the ferry, Sam was clearly equally excited, for he began playing games with Molly and making her laugh as he walked along beside the perambulator.

There were hundreds of people making their way in the same direction. New Brighton, with its sandy beach, carousels, donkey rides and promenade, was a popular day out for working people.

It was the best day ever. They ate ice cream, candy floss, shrimps and meat pies, and they laughed uproariously at Molly who wanted everything they ate. She was so greedy for the ice cream that she almost stood up to try to reach it, and it became daubed all over her face.

They took off their boots and paddled, rode the carousel with Sam holding Molly in front of him, and Beth won a jar of bull's-eyes on the hoopla stall. Sam tested his strength and only got the indicator to rise as far as puny, while other lads far smaller than him were making the bell ring. But he did win a coconut on the coconut shy. They had their photograph taken in a booth on the beach too. They had to queue for ages while the mothers in front of them turned to their grubby children and wiped their faces with a spit-dampened rag and pulled combs through unruly hair.

Beth found it hard not to laugh when she finally got into the booth and was told to sit on the chair with Molly on her lap. Sam stood behind, one hand on her shoulder. The background scenery was of a castle and a lake. She wondered if one day in years to come Molly would look at the photograph and ask where that castle was in Liverpool.

It was almost eight before they arrived home, and Sam's sunburnt face was the colour of a lobster. 'I'll make some tea while you put Molly to bed,' he said and bent to kiss the little girl as she lay sleepily in Beth's arms.

That was the crowning moment of the day for Beth. It might have taken eight months to come, but it was all the sweeter for knowing he hadn't done it out of duty, but real affection.

'You little charmer!' Beth whispered to Molly as she took off her clothes and napkin to wash her. 'You finally won him round.'

Beth stayed in the kitchen long after Sam, Ernest and Peter had gone to bed. She thought how good it had been to see Sam laughing again, to feel hope for the future in her own heart, and a certain pride that she'd done so well at being a stand-in mother for Molly. Molly's dark hair was curly now, her cheeks like little apples, and a great many people had stopped to admire her today. Soon she would be walking and talking too. Beth smiled as she remembered how frightened she'd been that night she was born and Mrs Craven said she must take care of her. But she'd done all right and so had Sam.

*

66

Beth woke up suddenly, and finding she was very hot, she sat up to push the blankets back to the foot of the bed. She didn't think she'd been asleep long for she could still faintly hear drunks in Church Street. But as she turned her pillow over and lay down again, she heard a sound out in the back alley.

She stiffened. She was well used to people walking up and down the alley – nearly everyone who lived above the shops used their back doors to go in and out. And people like the Cravens who lived in the houses in the street behind Church Street had access to it as well. But the sound she heard wasn't someone walking home purposefully, or even stumbling drunkenly, it was more like someone creeping, trying not to be heard.

Beth had double-checked that she'd locked the back door when she went out last thing to the privy, so she knew no one could get in. But remembering Ernest and Peter's bicycles were out in the yard, she thought it might be someone trying to steal them.

She got out of bed and went to the window, but although she could just about make out the back gate in the moon-light, she couldn't see the bicycles because the boys had probably leaned them against the side wall of the privy, and the roof of the lean-to was obscuring her vision.

As she couldn't hear anything more, she decided it was probably only a cat and got back into bed. But when she heard another small noise a few moments later, she jumped up and padded out of the bedroom into the kitchen to look out of the window where she had a view of most of the backyard.

She pulled back the lace curtain, and while there wasn't enough light to make out anything more than a dark shape against the privy wall, she could see a glint of chrome, so that satisfied her that the bicycles were still there. But as she dropped the curtain she heard another sound, and snatching it up again, this time she saw a silhouette as someone ran across the yard, pulled open the gate and disappeared through it.

The shape was in her line of vision for no more than a second, but she felt certain it was a woman. Yet while she knew thieves could be of either sex, she couldn't imagine a woman prowling around at this time of night. She stood there for a moment in puzzlement, considering whether she should go and wake Sam. Deciding that was pointless as the intruder had gone and Sam had to be at work early in the morning, she turned to go back to the bedroom.

But as she reached the door she smelled paraffin and heard a whooshing sound.

It could only be fire.

In horror she ran to the top of the stairs and looked down to see flames flickering. It hadn't been a thief, but someone intent on burning them all alive.

'Fire!' she screamed at the top of her voice. 'Sam! Ernest! Peter! Fire! Get up now!'

Chapter Seven

Scooping Molly out of her cradle, Beth snatched up a blanket and ran along the passage to the parlour where Sam was sleeping.

'Wake up, Sam!' she yelled, shaking him. 'There's a fire!'

He hadn't drawn the parlour curtains before going to bed and there was enough light from the street lamps outside for her to see him clearly. He opened his eyes and looked blankly at her for a second, but when she repeated the warning he leapt out of bed, snatched up his trousers and jumped into them.

'Get Ernest and Peter!' she shouted, and he was off down the passage like a shot. Smoke was billowing up the stairs now, and Beth knew she had to think of an alternative way to escape.

Shutting the parlour door and putting Molly down on Sam's bed, she flung up the sash window as wide as it would go and screamed out, hoping a policeman or anyone nearby would hear her. But the street below was deserted, with not so much as a cat prowling around.

The boys came thundering down the stairs and burst into the parlour. 'How did it start?' Peter asked, his voice shrill with fright.

'Never mind that now,' Ernest said as he leant out of the window. 'It's too high to jump from here. Maybe the back windows would be easier?'

'I'll go and look,' Sam said, taking command. 'You stay

here, use the sheets and anything else to make a rope. Beth, carry on screaming for all you're worth.'

He was gone in a flash, only to return seconds later coughing from the smoke and carrying a pile of bedding. 'The fire's got the whole staircase and it's too dangerous to try to get out of the bedroom window because the flames are right beneath it,' he gasped. 'We'll have to get out this way. Beth, stop up the gap under the door with the rug. Ernie, help me throw the mattress out to soften our landing, then we'll lower you. Beth and Molly can go after that.'

Beth did as he asked, ramming the rug against the door bottom as tightly as she could. Ernest and Peter had already got two sheets knotted together, and they tugged at it to make sure it was strong enough, yelling for help at the top of their voices as they did so. Beth snatched Molly up again as the boys manhandled the mattress out of the window, then Ernest got out on to the window sill and took the end of the sheet, and with Sam and Peter holding the other end, they gradually lowered him down.

As the boys were busy at the window Beth looked for something secure to put Molly into. Seeing the coal scuttle, she grabbed it and tipped out the coal into the fireplace. Molly was crying now, frightened by all the noise and panic around her, Beth sat her in the scuttle and wedged her in with a pillow.

'Good girl,' Sam said approvingly. Ernest was yelling fit to bust down on the street, Peter joining in at the window. Sam quickly tied the sheet rope around the coal-scuttle handle and tested it for strength.

Beth's heart was in her mouth as she watched Molly's descent to the street below. Sam and Peter were lowering her very carefully, but the coal scuttle was swaying precariously. If Molly struggled it would tip over to one side.

Fortunately she remained still and reached the safety of Ernest's arms.

'Now you, Beth,' Sam said as he pulled the sheet rope up again. 'You cling on to the sheet like grim death. I'll lower you.'

Beth was terrified as she crawled backwards on to the window sill. She had bare feet and was wearing only her nightgown with nothing beneath it. Even in such a desperate situation she couldn't bear the thought of anyone seeing her private parts.

'Wind it round your wrist and hold it tightly,' Sam ordered her. 'Use your feet to help you down the wall. We'll let it down gently, we won't drop you.'

Nothing in her life had been so frightening. She was terrified of plunging down and breaking her neck and all too aware that the breeze had got under her nightgown and that Ernest was looking right up at her. But she had to do it quickly because Sam and Peter needed to get down too.

'Good girl, only a few more feet and you can jump,' Ernest called out. 'The mattress is right below and I'm here to catch you.'

She got a bit hooked up on the signboard along the top of the shop window, but she managed to get beyond it and then Ernest told her to jump.

People were spilling out of their homes now to see what all the noise was about, and the sound reassured her a little. She let go of the sheet and dropped to her feet on the mattress.

Snatching Molly out of Ernest's arms, she glanced into the shop window and to her further horror saw flames licking all around the door at the back which led to their flat. Smoke was billowing overhead too and more and more people were coming out on to the street. She hoped the fire brigade would get here before the whole terrace of shops burned down.

'I've got a ladder!' yelled a male voice. 'Two minutes and I'll get it to you.'

Sam, meanwhile, was assisting Peter out of the window. 'How is Sam going to get down?' Beth asked Ernest. 'There isn't anything to tie the sheet to up there.'

'The ladder might be here by then,' Ernest said. 'Come on, Pete,' he shouted. 'Mind how you go when you reach the signboard of the shop.'

Peter jumped the last ten feet and turned to Ernest. 'The fire's at the door up there now,' he said. 'How's Sam going to get down?'

Beth could see the flames leaping across the shop floor. Before long the fire would be raging up the front of the building and trapping her brother.

'Sam!' Beth yelled. 'Drag the bed over to the window. The headboard is too big to go through it, so you can tie the sheet to that.'

She felt sick with fright and wished she could see if Sam was obeying her – it would be just like him to try to collect up a few valuables before he left. It was mayhem out in the street now, some people shouting that they should start a chain of buckets of water, others panicking that their homes might be at risk, barefooted children in their nightclothes crying because they couldn't see their parents. A few people were blowing whistles and more were banging on other doors in an attempt to get the occupants out.

But just as Beth was beginning to think Sam was lost to her, the sheet came spilling out of the window and he was outside on the sill, bare-chested, the street light shining on his blond hair, her fiddle case in his hand.

'Catch this,' he yelled, and tossed it down into Peter's

hands. Just as the flames behind the shop window began to crack the glass, Sam came down the sheet hand over hand.

Beth ran to hug him. 'What made you think of rescuing the fiddle?' she asked.

'Something told me I must.' He shrugged. 'I know how much it means to you.'

It was some fifteen minutes later that the first fire engine arrived, the firemen leaping off and fastening the hose to the water supply, but by then the front of the building was ablaze. The horses were taken out of the shafts and led further down the street away from the fierce heat, and Beth and the boys huddled together on the other side of the street, watching the scene in horror.

It was then that Beth realized they had lost everything. Their home, their clothes, their money. All gone.

They were destitute and homeless.

Their landlord and Mr Filbert, the tenant in the shop, would have insurance, but they had none. Sam hadn't even got a suit of clothing to put on to go to work in the morning. As for Molly, she had just a nightgown, a napkin and a blanket.

Beth shivered with fear, not the cold. Someone put a blanket around her shoulders and she heard them asking if they had someone they could go to. Tears came then, scald-ing hot tears that splashed down her cheeks on to Molly, who had fallen asleep in her arms.

Two more fire engines arrived, one going to the back of the building, but the fire was still raging and it looked as if the ironmonger's on one side and the haberdasher's on the other would go up too. Policemen were trying to get the huge crowd to move right back well out of the way.

'How did it start?' someone shouted.

'Someone set it purposely,' Beth called back. 'I saw them

running out the back gate. They put paraffin through the letterbox, they wanted to kill us all.'

One of the policemen came over to her and asked her to repeat what he'd just heard her say. 'Have you any idea who it could have been?' he asked.

'Try looking for Jane Wiley.' She spat out the name. 'She used to be our lodger.'

Mrs Craven suddenly appeared through the crowd with her husband beside her. 'I'm here, lovey,' she called. 'We won't see you and Sam homeless after all you've been through.' She pushed her way over to Beth and opened her big arms to encircle her and Molly. 'You come with us now.'

Barefoot, with only a cotton nightgown and her fiddle to her name, and Molly in her arms, Beth walked with the Cravens to their home, leaving Sam to follow once he'd found someone who could take in Ernest and Peter. The Cravens' two small rooms had been the haven Beth had run to many times in the past months when she had a problem, or just needed someone older and wiser to talk to. But she was very aware that it could only be the most temporary refuge now, for her neighbours were too old to have the disruption of unexpected guests, and too poor to have to feed them.

Beth couldn't sleep. It wasn't just the hiss of water jets playing on the fire, or firemen shouting to one another less than forty yards away across the back alley. It wasn't even the hard floor of Mrs Craven's living room, or the smoke-laden air that kept her awake. It was the knowledge that Jane Wiley had started the fire viciously and wantonly.

She didn't know how anyone could be that wicked, for even if she hadn't actually intended to kill them, she must have set out to destroy their home.

Everything gone – clothes, furniture and money – but even worse, to Beth, was the loss of all the little personal things and family photographs, mementos of her parents and grandparents which could never be replaced. She was touched that Sam had thought to rescue her fiddle, but it seemed such a frivolous item to save.

Practical as ever, Mrs Craven had found a couple of napkins and a baby gown for Molly and made an impromptu cradle for her out of a drawer. She'd said that the Salvation Army helped people in their position by giving clothes and boots, and she had no doubt the neighbours would make a collection for them too. But Beth was too demoralized to find any comfort in that.

'It's the best we can do for now,' Mr Craven said as he handed Sam a shirt, jacket and boots belonging to a neighbour the following morning.

Sam put them on gratefully, but their owner was clearly a great deal bigger than Sam and they made him look like a clown.

'At least I've got my own trousers still,' Sam remarked. 'I won't have to worry about them falling down round my ankles.'

'They'll understand at your work,' Beth said, sensing he was anxious about what the office manager was going to say about his appearance. She went over to him and straightened the shirt collar.

'Don't worry, Beth,' he said. 'On the way home tonight I'll go and see the Salvation Army and see if they've got some things I can have.'

Beth was still in her soot-blackened nightgown, but Mrs Craven had gone round to her daughter's to see if she had some clothes to lend. It had brought Beth up sharply to discover that most other people had just two sets of clothes, one for everyday and one for best. She'd been fortunate to have five or six dresses and it had never occurred to her that this was unusual.

The fire was completely out now. Mr Craven had been to inspect and said the entire staircase had caved in, the windows had exploded, and the frames and interior doors had all burnt out along with the furniture. The shop below was completely gutted too. Mr Filbert hadn't arrived yet, but when he did he was going to have a tremendous shock.

Mrs Craven arrived back from her daughter's soon after Sam left for work. 'This is really shabby,' she said, pulling a very worn and faded green dress out of her bag. 'It's the only thing my Cathy could spare, but it should fit you. There's these boots too.'

Beth looked down at the boots and saw the upper on the right one had partially come away from the sole; they were also two sizes too big for her. But at least she had something to put on.

'I was supposed to go to Falkner Square today,' she said. 'Should I still go?'

'Of course you should, you can't afford to lose that job now,' Mrs Craven said a little sharply, as if she'd already begun to regret taking Beth and Sam in. 'Now, take a bowl of water in the other room and have a good wash. You've still got soot smuts on your face.'

By the time Beth got to Falkner Square she had a blister on her foot from the overlarge boots.

'Beth!' Mrs Bruce exclaimed as she came limping into the kitchen. 'What on earth has happened to you?'

As Beth told the story she began to cry. Mrs Bruce made

her sit down and gave her a cup of tea and her undivided attention.

'So that's why I look the way I do,' Beth finished up, wiping her tears away with the back of her hand. 'I don't know where we're going to live or how we'll manage. We had such a lovely time yesterday at New Brighton, I really thought we'd turned a corner and everything was going to be better.'

Mrs Bruce gave her a pat on the shoulder. 'I am so sorry, my dear, it must have been a terrible shock to you. But for now I suggest you take those horrible boots off or the blister will just get worse. You get on with the laundry and I'll talk to you later.'

That sounded very much as if the housekeeper thought Beth had wallowed in self-pity for long enough, and however wretched Beth felt, she knew keeping this job was all-important. She took her boots off and got on with the laundry, almost glad to see a huge pile for it would take her mind off her problems.

It was after twelve when Mrs Langworthy came out into the backyard as Beth was hanging out the last of the washing. She looked very lovely in a pale green and white dress, her red hair fixed up on top of her head with a couple of tortoiseshell combs.

'Mrs Bruce has been telling me about the fire, Beth,' she said in a concerned tone. 'I am so very sorry.'

'I daresay I'll get over it,' Beth replied. She really didn't want to play for sympathy and it was enough for her that the mistress had come to speak to her.

'But where will you live?' Mrs Langworthy asked. 'It's very difficult when you have a baby to consider.'

'We're all right for the next couple of nights with our neighbour. We'll get somewhere at the end of the week when Sam gets paid.'

'I can imagine the kind of places on offer when you are desperate.' Mrs Langworthy pursed her lips in disapproval. 'I really can't bear the thought of it, so I want you to take the rooms above the stable. They've been empty since my father-in-law had his stroke and we dispensed with our coachman.'

Beth could only stare at her mistress in amazement.

'I didn't put you down as a girl with nothing to say for herself.' Mrs Langworthy laughed lightly.

'I'm sorry, mam,' Beth said quickly. 'I was just that surprised. I can't believe you'd be that kind.'

'Maybe you won't think it so kind when you see how dusty it is!'

Beth's face broke into a wide smile. 'I don't care if it's like the Black Hole of Calcutta. I'd work for you every day for nothing in return for a place to live.'

'That won't be necessary,' Mrs Langworthy said crisply. 'Just pop up there now and give it a clean before you go and get Molly and your brother. I'll ask Mrs Bruce to sort out some bedding and linen for you.'

Beth stood at the top of the wooden stairs inside the disused stable looking into the first of the two rooms, and her spirits rose. It was small and very dirty, but she could see that once she'd cleaned the windows it would be light and airy because it had windows both on the side which overlooked the Langworthys' backyard and on the mews side. It had a sink, a stove and a table and chairs. Excitedly, she rushed across to look in the other room and found there was an old iron bedstead and a truckle bed, which she could put in the kitchen for Sam.

She had no real idea what kind of accommodation she and Sam could have got for a rent they could afford. But she was absolutely certain it would not have been anything like this, and probably just one room in a slum.

Beth worked like a beaver cleaning the rooms for two hours. She propped the two mattresses up in the sun to air, scrubbed the floors and cleaned the windows. When she'd finished there wasn't a single cobweb anywhere, but she looked like a chimney sweep and her bare feet were black.

Mrs Bruce and Katherine came across the yard just as she finished, each laden down with a pile of blankets, pillows and clean linen. They helped Beth make up the two beds, and Mrs Bruce put a red and white checked cloth over the table.

'Isn't it wonderful?' Beth gasped. 'I can't believe any one could be as kind as Mrs Langworthy.'

'She's had more than her share of bad luck and hard times,' Mrs Bruce said knowingly. 'And she said you're to go upstairs and have a bath and wash your hair before you go to get Molly. She's found a few clothes for you too.'

As Beth lay back in the warm water, letting her hair drift on the surface, she was staggered by how she could have gone from sheer desperation to bliss in such a few hours.

She'd only ever been in a tin bath before, and not since she was five or six had she been able to lie down in one. She just hoped people had been as kind to Sam today as they'd been to her.

The clothes Mrs Langworthy had given her were folded on the bathroom stool. A dark blue skirt, a blue blouse with white spots, a chemise, drawers and a petticoat. She wondered if Mrs Langworthy knew she'd had nothing under that horrible green dress today. Mrs Bruce had given her a pair of her boots and some stockings as Mrs Langworthy's were too big.

Lovely as it was in the bath, Beth knew she must hurry now and get back to Mrs Craven and Molly.

'Well, blow me down!' Mrs Craven gasped as Beth turned into her backyard in new clothes and her hair shining like polished ebony. 'Someone's done you proud, and I know it weren't the Sally Army!'

Beth smiled, partly because she felt more like her old self again, all clean and neat, but also because it was pleasing to find Mrs Craven outside in the sunshine with Molly.

She picked her little sister up off the blanket she was sitting on, and hugged her. 'Beth's got a nice surprise for you,' she said.

'Well, you've fallen on your feet and no mistake,' Mrs Craven exclaimed after Beth had told her about the morning's events. 'Talk about lucky!'

Beth felt a little embarrassed then, for it sounded as if her neighbour was almost disappointed that her luck had turned so soon. 'It won't be the same without having you just across the alley,' she said quickly. 'You've been so very kind, Mrs Craven, right since Papa went. I don't know what Sam and I would've done without you.'

Her neighbour beamed at that. 'Just make certain you come round to see me now and then. I shall miss you all, but specially my little Molly.' She held out a finger to the baby who grasped it eagerly. 'Now, I've got some news for you too. The police have arrested Jane Wiley. That copper what talked to your Sam last night came round this morning after you left and told me. She's denying it of course, but they could smell paraffin on her clothes. The copper said someone round at her lodgings said they saw her go out later at night too, and it was after Thomas rolled back from the pub.'

'What will happen to her?'

'Prison, of course,' Mrs Craven said with relish. 'And a long stretch too, I expect. I hope she rots there.'

Beth nodded in agreement. 'Have you heard how Mr Filbert and the other two shopkeepers are?' she asked. 'It must be terrible for them to lose their businesses.'

'I heard they was savage about it. A few looters got in the ironmonger's before they got the window boarded up.'

Beth shook her head in disgust. 'Any news of Ernest and Peter?'

'They come and took their bicycles away this morning, and asked after you. Someone in Lord Street took them in last night and got them fixed up with some clothes, but they'll be all right, they've got families with a bit of brass to help them.'

At that, Beth remembered she had brought back the dress and boots she'd borrowed. She handed them over and then drew out of the bag a large meat pie Mrs Cray, the cook, had given her.

'I wish I had some money to buy you something to show how grateful I am for your kindness,' she said, 'but maybe we could all share this before we leave later, and when I come to visit you again I won't be empty-handed.'

'Bless you.' Mrs Craven's eyes lit up at the sight of the pie. 'You're a good girl, Beth, your mother would be proud of you.'

Sam turned up at half past six, carrying a brown paper parcel. He was still wearing the overlarge jacket and shirt, and said the other clerks had teased him all day. But the office manager had given him five pounds from the company relief fund intended to help employees in distressed circumstances.

81

'I bought some clothes for myself in the second-hand shop,' he said. 'I was going to say you could take some of it and get yourself some clothes tomorrow, but it looks like you are all fixed up. That will leave us with more for rent for a new place.'

Beth told him her news then, and Sam looked staggered. 'Why would she do that?' he asked.

'Because she's kind and generous, so we'd better make sure we don't make her regret it.' Beth smiled.

It transpired that the perambulator left in the back shed was unscathed by the fire, just covered in soot. After supper, Beth and Sam tucked Molly into it, along with a small bag of baby clothes people had brought round for her, and the fiddle, and said goodbye to the Cravens and made their way to Falkner Square.

'I can't really believe we've lost everything,' Sam sighed as they cut down a back alley which would bring them out on to Seel Street. 'You said you didn't like Jane Wiley the first time you met her. I wish I'd trusted your judgement.'

'I can take no satisfaction in that,' Beth replied grimly. 'Maybe if I hadn't been quite so hasty in throwing her out, she wouldn't have done it. But let's not dwell on that. No one died in the fire thankfully, and maybe a new start will be good for us.'

'But we've got to toughen up,' Sam said thoughtfully. 'We can't let things keep happening to us. We need to work out what we really want and strive towards that.'

'What do you want?' Beth asked. It was a beautiful warm evening, and though she was terribly tired, she actually felt she had everything she wanted right here: Molly asleep in the perambulator; Sam beside her, and a new home waiting for them.

'To go to America,' he said. 'I don't want to be subservient to others, sitting on a stool scratching away at ledgers and feeling I should be grateful for the pittance I get each week. Neither do I want you growing old before your time scrubbing other people's clothes. America is a vast, young country, full of opportunity. We could do well there.'

'I'm sure we could.' Beth was afraid to ask whether he was including Molly in this dream. 'But first we have to get back on our feet.'

Chapter Eight

Edna Bruce was checking the monthly account from the butcher's when she heard Beth sigh. Looking up, she noticed the girl looked unusually pensive as she sewed some buttons on to one of Mr Edward's shirts.

They were in what had once been the butler's parlour, the room at the bottom of the basement steps. In the absence of a butler it was used now as a sewing and ironing room, and as it was raining hard outside, Molly was there with them in her perambulator having her midday sleep.

It was six weeks since Beth and her little family had come to live in Falkner Square, and Mrs Bruce was delighted by how well it was working out.

She only ever saw Sam on Sundays because he left for work early in the morning, but she had found him to be a very pleasant young man.

Beth came in for three hours each weekday now, which suited everyone better as the laundry didn't mount up into unmanageable amounts. She brought Molly over with her, and in good weather she stayed in her perambulator outside in the yard.

Not that she was ever in it for long! Mrs Bruce, Cook and Kathleen were all guilty of getting her out to cuddle her, as was the mistress too. On the odd occasions Mr Edward was home during the morning and came down to the basement, he too fell for her charms and stopped to play with her.

In truth, Molly had become everyone's pet. Her curly

hair, treacle-brown eyes and ready smiles made fools of all of them. She was a remarkably happy baby, she hardly ever cried, and would go willingly to anyone.

But the most surprising consequence of Beth coming to live in Falkner Square was that old Mr Langworthy had taken to her. That had never happened with anyone before. It came about because Beth volunteered to sit with him one afternoon while the mistress popped out for an hour. When she got back she found her father-in-law engrossed in listening to Beth reading from a penny dreadful. Apparently she'd put it in her pocket to read, expecting him to be asleep, but on finding him wide awake, she thought she might as well see how he liked it.

As old Mr Langworthy had been something of an intellectual snob before his stroke and wouldn't have allowed such lowbrow reading matter in the house, both his son and daughter-in-law found this very amusing.

Now Beth often read to him, or just went in and chatted to him. She didn't seem in the least put off by his incapacity, or that he spoke in grunts and odd sounds; in fact she spoke to him as she would to anyone else, about things in the news, books she'd read in the past, and about her late parents.

Yet however well things were working out, both Mrs Bruce and Mrs Langworthy were a little concerned that such a vibrant young girl had such a narrow life. It wasn't a hard one by any means; most girls in service worked from six in the morning until their master and mistress went to bed. In fact, if Beth was married and Molly her own child, it could have been said to be a charmed life. But Sam was not her husband, and as he'd now got a second job as a barman at the Adelphi Hotel and was out every evening, Beth was always alone.

Mrs Langworthy herself had said it was no life for such a young girl to be stuck in a couple of rooms with a baby, and no family or friends to visit. Mrs Bruce thought perhaps this was what was ailing Beth now.

'Is there something troubling you, Beth?' she asked. 'You are awfully quiet today.'

'I was just thinking how hard Sam works,' Beth said with a little shrug of her shoulders. 'He wants to go to America, you see, that's why he took the barman's job. He thought some experience like that would stand him in good stead.'

This was the first Mrs Bruce had heard of this. 'Is he planning to go without you?' she asked.

'No, he wants me to go too. But I don't see how I can, there's Molly to think of.'

'People emigrate with children all the time,' Mrs Bruce said evenly. 'They manage. I've heard of some going with five or six children.'

'Yes, but it's different with Sam being my brother.' Beth sighed, her blue eyes suddenly very sad. 'I wouldn't want to spoil his chances, and having us two to support would be difficult for him.'

Mrs Bruce thought about that for a few moments. 'Yes, I suppose you are right, he wouldn't be free to travel and look for the best prospects, and later if he wanted to get married, that could be a problem. But it's hardly fair that you should be left behind with all the responsibility of Molly, either here or over there. She's his sister too.'

'That's the nub of the whole thing,' Beth replied, her voice flat and dispirited. 'He's far too conscientious to leave us, but I feel bad that I'm holding him back.'

'I see.' Mrs Bruce nodded. 'Tell me, if you didn't have Molly, would you like to go to America?' she asked.

'Oh yes,' Beth exclaimed, her eyes brightening. 'It sounds

such a wonderful place. I often daydream of playing the piano in a big hotel.'

'You play the piano?'

Beth smiled shyly at her surprise. 'Yes, though I'm probably rusty now because we had to sell ours when Mama died. I play the fiddle too. Sam managed to save it in the fire. I like that best, but Mama called it Devil's music because they play the fiddle in low ale houses.'

Mrs Bruce smiled. She had heard someone playing jigs on a fiddle on many an occasion but she'd never guessed it was coming from the coach house. She didn't think it was Devil's music either; it was gay and bright. 'Why didn't you ever tell me this before?' she asked. 'It's such a wonderful accomplishment.'

'I thought it might sound like I was boasting. Servants aren't supposed to do that.'

'I would never have thought it boastful, and I would love you to bring your fiddle over here sometime and play for me.'

The way Beth's eyes lit up made Mrs Bruce smile. 'And don't you stop dreaming or planning for your future,' she went on. 'I made the mistake of always putting duty before my own desires and ambitions, and because of that I missed out on marriage and children. I wouldn't want that to happen to you.'

'What wouldn't you want to happen to Beth?'

Both Mrs Bruce and Beth turned their heads in surprise on hearing Mrs Langworthy's question. They hadn't heard her come down the stairs to the basement. She looked stunning in her apple-green silk dress with leg-of-mutton sleeves and her hair arranged in sleek, fat curls on the top of her head.

'Beth was just telling me that Sam is dead set on going to

America, and I suspect she really wants to go with him,' Mrs Bruce said.

'I can understand that.' Mrs Langworthy nodded. 'It sounds such a wonderful, exciting place. But don't go rushing off just yet, Beth, I've just got used to having your help. And seeing this little one every day!' She stood by the perambulator looking down at Molly adoringly. 'She is just the most perfect baby. I wish she'd wake up so I could cuddle her.'

Mrs Bruce could feel her mistress's raw longing for a child as she leaned over Molly. When she first married Mr Edward she used to say she wanted at least six children, and she was so strong and healthy that Mrs Bruce had expected it would come about in the fullness of time. But it hadn't, and as each year passed it seemed less likely.

Molly woke and stretched. On seeing Mrs Langworthy, her face broke into a wide smile and she lifted her arms to be picked up.

'She'll be wet and spoil your dress,' Beth said in alarm.

'As if I care about that!' Mrs Langworthy laughed and eagerly scooped the baby up. 'So, little Molly, it must be nearly your dinnertime,' she said. 'What is it to be today?'

Molly was busy playing with Mrs Langworthy's necklace, and tentatively tried to chew it.

'Cook saved some of the lamb stew from last night for her,' Mrs Bruce said. 'She's such a joy to feed, I've never seen her refuse anything.'

'Could I feed her?' Mrs Langworthy asked.

Beth couldn't understand why her mistress would want to do such a thing, but she readily agreed. 'You'd better put an apron on, though, she's a bit messy,' she added.

Mrs Bruce busied herself with her duties, but made a point of going in and out of the kitchen as Mrs Langworthy fed

Molly. To her surprise the mistress looked entirely at ease with the baby on her lap, spooning the food into her greedy little mouth. Yet even more amusing to watch was Beth, for as she sat on the opposite side of the table to the mistress, her mouth kept opening and shutting in time with Molly, and every now and then her hand would move involuntarily as if unable to believe Mrs Langworthy could scoop uneaten food from around the child's mouth and pop that in too, the way she did.

Her mistress clearly picked up on Beth's tension. 'I have had some previous experience,' she said with a gay little laugh. 'I used to feed my younger brothers and sisters regularly. I just haven't had any encounters with babies or small children since I married.'

'You are really good at it,' Beth said admiringly. 'I was scared stiff of Molly at first. I'd never even held a newborn baby before, much less fed and changed one.'

'I must try changing her too,' Mrs Langworthy said, her face all aglow. 'Babies are much more agreeable to take care of than grumpy old men.'

Mrs Bruce turned away so that neither Beth nor her mistress would see the tears well up in her eyes. She sensed it could only end badly because Beth would move on before long and take Molly with her.

All through the autumn, at Christmas and into the New Year of 1895, Mrs Bruce watched Beth and Molly gradually working their way into everyone's hearts at Falkner Square. She knew it wasn't her imagination because she too was falling under their spell.

It was hard not to love someone who could sing even when she was sluicing filthy napkins. Her merry laugh enlivened the basement; her eagerness to help everyone with their chores created a happy atmosphere. She would gladly spend the afternoon cleaning silver, pressing Mr Edward's clothes or reading to old Mr Langworthy, even though she wasn't paid to do any of these extra duties. Perhaps it was because she preferred to work than be alone with Molly in her rooms, but whatever the reason, Mrs Bruce liked having her around.

They had celebrated Molly's first birthday before Christmas in the kitchen. Cook made a special iced cake and a trifle, Kathleen the maid had blown up balloons, and even Sam and Mr Edward came home earlier to be there. Beth had made Molly a new pink dress, which she immediately daubed with trifle. She had been able to walk a few steps holding on to someone's hands for some little time, but that afternoon she took four or five steps unaided to reach Mrs Langworthy.

It was undoubtedly because there was a child in the house that Mr Edward brought home a Christmas tree, for they'd never had one before. Sam fixed it securely in a large tub and placed it by the drawing-room window, and Beth helped Mrs Langworthy trim it with candles and glass baubles.

As always in the past, various relatives came for Christmas dinner and Sam was on hand to carry old Mr Langworthy down to the dining room. But although the festivities upstairs were much the same as in previous years, downstairs it was a far jollier affair.

Once the dinner was over upstairs, old Mr Langworthy had been taken back to his room and the master and mistress were entertaining their guests in the drawing room, the staff dinner took place in the kitchen.

Mrs Bruce asked Sam, as the only male, to sit at the head of the table and carve the goose. Mrs Bruce sat at the foot, with Cook on one side of her and Molly perched up on a box on a chair on the other. Kathleen and Beth, both wearing paper hats, sat either side of Sam. Whether it was the wine they drank, or just that there were three more people than usual around the table, the laughter started when Sam fooled around pretending to be a surgeon as he attacked the goose with the carving knife, and it didn't stop.

Cook didn't live in but had lodgings nearby. She'd been in service since she was a young girl, always in households with a big staff. She related hilarious stories about some of the blunders they made, and how the rest of the staff covered them up.

Sam told them tales too about people who came into the bar at the Adelphi Hotel. He could mimic their voices and mannerisms so well, it was almost as if these people were in the room.

Mrs Bruce studied Sam as he was talking and noted how much he'd come out of himself since he became a barman. He was more confident now, looking directly at whoever he was talking to, not dropping his eyes the way he used to. He was a handsome lad, with his blond hair, peachy skin and brilliant blue eyes, and his easy manner with women was very attractive. Mrs Bruce thought he'd be irresistible once he'd put a little muscle on to that lean frame.

But she also noticed how little attention he paid Molly. After the dinner, as she staggered around the room going from one person to another, Sam didn't watch her as every-one else did. He picked her up when she fell over by him and he offered her small pieces of an orange he was eating, but he didn't take her on his knee or make a fuss of her. Mrs Bruce decided that while he certainly wasn't unkind to her, he was actively avoiding any involvement.

She wondered why this was, and the only logical reason

she could find for it was that he intended to walk out on Beth and Molly. He probably felt he could do that more easily if he didn't allow his heart to become engaged with his baby sister.

Mrs Bruce found herself fretting about this a great deal as the New Year came in. She told herself that Beth could be fine, for with or without her brother, the Langworthys would continue to employ her. Yet whenever Beth played her fiddle over in her rooms, and she heard the joy and hope in her music, she couldn't help but feel dismayed that her life was never going to take her beyond Falkner Square. Mrs Bruce could already see the shackles binding her here. Right now it was just because of her duty to provide for Molly, but the longer she stayed, the bigger she'd feel her debt to the Langworthys was. By the time Molly was old enough to work, Mrs Bruce would be old, and Beth would slip into her shoes. She'd never get the chance to play in public, to see more of the world. Most likely she'd never marry either.

Chapter Nine

'Mam, mam,' Kathleen screeched out at six in the morning. It was early February, bitterly cold and still dark, the master and mistress asleep. Mrs Bruce had just gone down to the kitchen to put the kettle on the stove for tea.

She rushed back upstairs to find Kathleen in the doorway of old Mr Langworthy's room. Kathleen's first job each morning as maid was to stir up the fire in his room, and on seeing the girl's horrified expression Mrs Bruce guessed that the old man was dead.

'He had his mouth and eyes open,' Kathleen sobbed. 'I asked him if he wanted a cup of tea. But I think he's dead.'

'Control yourself,' Mrs Bruce said sharply. She was just going to add that Kathleen should have come down and told her quietly without waking the master and mistress, but it was too late – both their bedroom doors opened simultaneously. Mr Edward was in his long nightshirt and the mistress was clutching a shawl around her shoulders.

'Is it my father?' Mr Edward asked.

Mrs Bruce nodded and went into the old man's room. Kathleen had put the oil lamp on the mantelpiece, so there was enough light to see exactly what she had seen. He was lying awkwardly, his head right at the edge of the mattress, as if he'd been struggling to get out of bed.

Mrs Bruce went over to him and found he was indeed dead. She lifted him back on to the pillow and closed his eyes and mouth. 'He has passed on then?' Mr Edward asked from the doorway, his wife standing beside him as if they were both afraid to come in.

'I'm afraid so,' Mrs Bruce said, straightening up the bed-clothes. 'I am so sorry. But you two must go back to bed or you'll catch your death of cold. I'll get Kathleen to take a note round for the doctor.'

When Beth came over to the house with Molly at nine that morning, she found Mrs Bruce, Cook and Kathleen sitting at the kitchen table looking very woebegone.

Mrs Bruce explained what had happened, and said that the doctor was up with the Langworthys now signing the old man's death certificate. 'It is for the best really,' she sighed. 'He had no real life any more, and the mistress will be spared all that hard work. But just the same, it's hard to see him go.'

'His eyes made me think of a fish, so they did,' Kathleen blurted out. 'And I touched his hand and it was cold as ice.'

'That's enough now, Kathleen,' Mrs Bruce said sternly. 'I know it was a shock to find him but we must all show respect for him and support the master and mistress.'

Beth's eyes filled with tears. She had been scared of the old man when she was first asked to sit with him. His face was distorted because he was paralysed all down one side and he was so thin that he looked almost skeletal. When he tried to speak his mouth was all over the place and the sounds that came out were unintelligible and frightening. But she had grown used to it and after she'd read to him a few times she began to understand what he was trying to say. He could convey pleasure with his eyes, irritation with a wave of his good hand, and sometimes she could make out real words in his grunts, and if she repeated them to him he would nod.

She sensed his delight when she came to see him, knew when he was enjoying a story, and the more time she spent with him, the more she felt for him. She thought it must be the worst thing in the world to have a keen mind trapped in a body you couldn't control, to suffer the humiliation of being fed and changed like a baby, and to have no real way of showing that you knew what was going on all around you.

'Don't cry, Beth,' Mrs Bruce said, picking up Molly who was looking anxiously up at her big sister. 'He's gone to a better place, his suffering is over and he can join his wife again.'

A pall of gloom descended on the house, which seemed to grow heavier daily as the master and mistress made the arrangements for the funeral.

For Beth the atmosphere was all too familiar, and on top of disturbing reminders of her parents' deaths and funerals, there was the niggling worry of what might become of her now. Without all the old man's laundry there wasn't going to be a lot for her to do. Mrs Bruce, Cook and Kathleen ran the house like clockwork between them. Would Mr Edward want to pay wages for someone he no longer needed?

Beth's seventeenth and Sam's eighteenth birthdays came and went that week without celebration. Beth was kept busy helping Cook prepare cakes and pastries for the funeral wake, and making minor alterations to the mourning clothes their mistress had worn when her mother-in-law died.

On the morning of the funeral, Beth woke when it was still dark, but there was enough light outside from the lamp at the end of the mews to show it had snowed during the night. She sat up in bed for a minute or two looking out of the window. Everything looked beautiful, grime, rubbish and ugliness hidden under a thick blanket of pristine, sparkling white. It brought to mind the snow just over a year ago when Molly had been born. Beth remembered standing at the kitchen window with the baby in her arms, marvelling that the back alley and the rooftops beyond had been miraculously transformed into something magical.

Just a few days later her mother was dead, and rain washed the snow away. She had looked out of that same window and seen that everything had become grey, bleak and ugly again. It had seemed significant at the time, a warning perhaps that happiness and beauty could only ever be fleeting.

So much had happened since then. Such despair, hurt and worry, then finally the loss of their home in the fire. Yet the fire had been fortuitous in as much as they came here to live and found a measure of security and happiness again.

Both she and Sam had been forced to grow up fast, but perhaps the most important thing Beth had learned was that she couldn't count on anything. Not on the Langworthys' kindness continuing, nor that this job and home would last for as long as she needed it. She couldn't even rely on Sam staying with her for ever.

The only thing she could be absolutely certain about was her own self. But that was a lonely, chilling thought.

Sam wasn't expected to attend the funeral because the only time he'd met the old man was at Christmas when he'd carried him down to the dining room. But he had to go to work, so Beth put a shawl around her shoulders and crept into the living room to light the oil lamp, stir up the fire in the stove and put the kettle on.

Sam looked so peaceful and untroubled, curled up in the narrow truckle bed. It hadn't occurred to him yet that old

Mr Langworthy's death might bring them more trouble, and she was reluctant to air her fears because he'd seemed so happy since he began working at the Adelphi.

'Time to get up, Sam,' she said softly, and shook his arm.

He opened his eyes and yawned. 'Already! It feels as if I've only been in here an hour or two.'

'It's six o'clock and it's been snowing,' Beth said, struck by how handsome he was becoming. His face had filled out, he'd grown a little moustache, and his long eyelashes drew attention to his lovely blue eyes. She felt a little pang in her heart that before long he would find a sweetheart and she'd have to take second place.

He smiled and leapt out of bed, rushing over to the window like a child. Wearing just his woolly combinations he looked slightly ridiculous. 'I love snow,' he said, turning to grin at her. 'In parts of America it comes in November and lasts right through till spring.'

'I can't think of anything worse,' Beth said archly, kneeling down to pull out the ash box under the stove. That wasn't true – she loved snow as much as he did and some of her best childhood memories were of going tobogganing with him – but she was tired of his constant references to America. 'The water in the kettle should be warm enough for you to wash and shave. Your clean shirt is hanging on the bedroom door.'

'You're becoming like an old maid,' he retorted.

Beth, Kathleen and Cook could only find room to stand at the back of St Bride's, for they had been last in the procession of mourners following the six carriages taking family members to the church, and now all the pews were full. With the thick snow as a backdrop for the black plumed horses and the coffin banked high with flowers, it had been an impressive sight. Beth had expected that the snow would deter a great many people, but it looked as if half of Liverpool's population was there.

Once the first hymn, 'Abide with Me', had been sung and the prayers had begun, Beth's thoughts wandered to Sam's remark earlier that morning. She supposed she *had* become like an old maid. Everything she did, or even thought about, these days was centred round Molly or the Langworthys. She didn't care anything for how she looked, her clothes were hand-me-downs, she didn't even go and look in shop windows any more, not just because she couldn't afford to buy anything, but because she had nowhere to go to wear such things.

Before her father died she spent a great deal of time indulging in romantic daydreams, but she never did now. There was no point: she was never going to go to balls and parties or drive around in a carriage and pair wearing a fur coat and diamonds. Even the more humble dreams that Miss Clarkson had prompted, training to be a teacher, a nurse or working in a shop, were ruled out now because she had to take care of Molly.

In truth the only time she ever escaped into fantasy was when she played the fiddle. Alone in the coach house she could imagine she was wearing a beautiful, brightly coloured silk dress, with glittery pins in her hair and pretty shoes on her feet. For an hour or so she could float with the music, all responsibilities falling away.

As Reverend Bloom began to speak about Mr Langworthy, Beth came out of her reverie.

'Theodore Arthur Langworthy wasn't born with a silver spoon in his mouth,' he said. 'His father was a poor Yorkshire farmer, and he expected his eldest son would follow in his footsteps. But young Theodore had other plans.'

Beth had known nothing about Mr Langworthy's background, not even that his name was Theodore, and it was difficult to imagine the bedridden old man as anything but sick and frail.

'Already fascinated by machinery, he ran off to Liverpool where he got himself an apprenticeship as an engineer,' Reverend Bloom went on. 'He was just twenty-two when he designed and made a water pump in a shed at the back of his lodgings. Ten years on he had fifty men working for him and exported his pumps all over the world. Later he diversified into making steam engines for ships, and Langworthy Engineering became one of Liverpool's biggest employers.'

Reverend Bloom's eyes scanned the congregation. 'Many of you here today owe your present prosperity to him for he took you on when you were young lads, showed a fatherly interest in you and trained you well. Others of you connected with charitable institutions will remember how he championed your causes and made generous donations to keep them going.'

Maybe it was because Mr Langworthy had followed his dream that Beth found herself drifting off again in thoughts of Sam. She had hoped that when he made new friends at the Adelphi he would lose interest in America. But he hadn't. He pored over maps, read books and articles in magazines and saved every spare penny to go.

Until now Beth had been inclined to view Sam's passion to emigrate as merely adventuring, but it suddenly occurred to her that it wasn't so different to Mr Langworthy wanting to be an engineer. If he hadn't been bold enough to defy his father and strike out for what he really wanted, many of the people here today wouldn't have had work, charities would have been poorer, and who would have made those water pumps and steam engines he sent all over the world?

Maybe Sam's desire to go to America wasn't going to benefit anyone else, but on the other hand if he didn't go, he might become bitter and end up blaming her. Beth was afraid of being left here alone with Molly, especially now when the future was so uncertain, but she thought she was more fearful of losing her brother's affection by holding him back.

At five that afternoon Beth was washing up in the kitchen while Cook put leftover food away in the pantry, when she heard Mrs Langworthy saying goodbye to the last of the guests at the front door. Even from some distance she could hear the weariness in her mistress's voice and feel the strain she had been under all day as she tried to hold her emotions in check.

The front door closed. Beth heard Mrs Langworthy asking Mrs Bruce and Kathleen to clear away the last of the glasses and food in the dining room, then a few minutes later she came down the stairs to the basement.

She looked pale and wan in her black dress, but she smiled at Beth and Cook. 'I just wanted to thank you for doing so much today,' she said.

Cook looked up from putting away some leftover cakes. 'We were glad to,' she said. 'But you look very tired, mam. Can I get you anything?'

The mistress sighed and put her hand to her forehead as if it hurt. 'No, thank you, Mrs Cray, you've done quite enough for one day, you go on home. If we want some supper later, we can find something ourselves.' She turned to look at Molly who was sitting on a blanket in the corner playing with a couple of wooden spoons.

'You've been a very good girl today,' she said, bending down to pick her up. 'I haven't heard a peep from you.'

'She's a little angel,' Cook said fondly. 'I think she knew we were all too busy to play with her.'

Holding Molly in her arms, Mrs Langworthy slumped down on a chair and cuddled her. She remained silent, bent forward with her face against the baby's hair.

Beth suddenly realized her mistress was crying, and in alarm she moved forward. 'What is it, mam?' she asked.

'Losing my father-in-law has made me realize how empty my life is,' Mrs Langworthy said, lifting her head a little and trying to wipe her tears away.

'You're bound to feel a bit adrift for a while,' Beth said soothingly. 'But you'll be able to do all the things you never had time for now. Shall I make you a nice cup of tea?'

'This is what I want,' Mrs Langworthy said, holding Molly against her chest. 'A baby to love. Without a child a woman has nothing.'

Mrs Cray made a warning face at Beth and a little sipping movement with her hand as if to explain the mistress had had one sherry too many.

Beth put her hand comfortingly on the older woman's shoulder. 'We can all share her,' she said.

'I don't want to share her, I want her all for myself,' Mrs Langworthy replied and she looked up at Beth with a pleading expression.

At that moment Mrs Bruce came down the stairs with some dirty glasses on a tray. 'This is the last of them,' she said cheerily, unaware she had walked in on something.

'They certainly all ate and drank their fill,' Cook said loudly, clearly trying to break the tense atmosphere. 'Isn't it time you took Molly home now, Beth?'

Mrs Langworthy got up abruptly and handed Molly back

to Beth. 'I'd better get back to my husband,' she said, her voice trembling. 'He's feeling a bit low too. I'm sure everything will be fine by tomorrow.'

The mistress didn't get up the following day. Kathleen took in her early morning tea as usual, and reported back in the kitchen that she was feeling poorly.

'Too much sherry,' Cook said with a wink at Beth, but she kept her voice down so Mrs Bruce wouldn't hear.

Mr Edward was out of sorts too. He snapped at Kathleen because his breakfast toast was cold, then went into his study and stayed there instead of going to his office.

'It wouldn't be fitting for him to go back to work today,' Mrs Bruce said, as if she was trying to justify his actions. 'He'll have to sort out his father's affairs and he must have dozens of letters to write. But I must say he's taking this harder than I expected.'

Beth understood why Mrs Bruce was a little perplexed, for Mr Edward had gone to his office even on the day his father died, and had seemed perfectly composed yesterday at the funeral. It was understandable that Mrs Langworthy had taken to her bed – she had after all been run ragged for over a week arranging everything. But putting together Mr Edward's uncharacteristic behaviour today, and his wife's emotional state yesterday, Beth felt sure they'd had a quarrel last night.

Had she blamed him because she didn't have a child of her own?

Three days after the funeral, Mrs Langworthy was still in her bed. Mrs Bruce had been taking up her meals on a tray, but she only picked at them.

'The doctor said he can't find anything wrong with her,'

Beth heard her saying to Cook. 'He thought it was just melancholy and that perhaps Mr Edward ought to take her away for a holiday. But who would want to do that in this weather?'

It hadn't snowed since the day of the funeral, but the temperature was so low that the snow was still lying and the wind was icy. It was so cold in the coach house that Beth stayed over in the house as long as possible, and she had been taking Molly into bed with her at night to keep her warm. Sam had been staying later at the hotel too, perhaps for the same reasons, so Beth hadn't even had an opportunity to speak to him about America.

'Beth, why don't you go up and see her?' Mrs Bruce suggested. 'Take Molly with you, I'm sure that will cheer her up.'

It was mid-afternoon, and as there was no more work Beth could find that would give her an excuse to remain in the house, and it was far too cold to go out anywhere, she was only too glad to agree.

Mrs Langworthy was lying back listlessly on the pillows, not even reading, but when she saw Beth and Molly her face lit up. 'What a nice surprise. I was just thinking about Molly. Let her come on the bed with me,' she said, patting the coverlet.

Beth lifted her on and pulled up a chair for herself by the bed. Molly bounced around, then made the mistress laugh by playing peekaboo with her with the blanket.

'What *is* wrong, mam?' Beth asked after chatting about Molly for a little while. 'Do you hurt anywhere? Have you been sick?'

'No, nothing like that,' Mrs Langworthy replied, and looked down fondly at Molly who was now snuggled up beside her as if intending to go to sleep. 'I just feel weary with the pointlessness of my life.'

'My mother said something like that to me once,' Beth said thoughtfully. 'I was a bit hurt at the time, but I suppose she meant just cooking and cleaning all day.'

'Women do get weary.' Mrs Langworthy sighed. 'I know I should be counting my blessings, I've got a lovely home and a kind husband, but you see, I always counted on having children, and now it doesn't seem as if I'm ever going to be blessed with any. I didn't let myself think about it too much when my father-in-law was alive, I had too much to do. But now I can't stop thinking about it. I feel so sad.'

Beth felt a little uncomfortable hearing this. To her Mrs Langworthy had a perfect life, and she thought she ought to go down to some of the squalid courts in the Scotland district of Liverpool and see how life was for the women there.

Perhaps her mistress picked up her thoughts because she reached out and put her hand over Beth's. 'I'm sorry, my dear, I was forgetting how much sadness you've had in your young life. Whatever must you think of me?'

'I think of you as the very nicest, kindest person in the world,' Beth replied truthfully. 'You took us in when we had no one else to turn to. I'll always be so grateful for that.'

'You've more than repaid me,' Mrs Langworthy said. 'But tell me, Beth, don't you ever feel aggrieved that you were burdened with Molly?'

Beth looked down at her sister and smiled because she'd fallen asleep with her thumb in her mouth. 'I haven't ever seen her as a burden,' she said. 'Maybe I'm tied, I have to think about what's right for her, instead of me, but I don't feel aggrieved about it.'

'That's a very selfless attitude,' Mrs Langworthy said. 'But tell me, have you and Sam had any more thoughts about going to America?'

Beth's heart sank, sure that this was Mrs Langworthy's way of getting around to telling her she was no longer needed. 'It's never out of Sam's thoughts,' she said carefully. 'But since Mr Langworthy died, I have been rather more troubled about our position here. With so much less laundry, you won't be needing me any more.'

'Not need you!' Her mistress looked shocked. 'Of course I'll still need you. You didn't surely think I would put you out?'

'You mean I can stay on with Molly?'

'Of course, my dear. It never even crossed my mind to dismiss you. You are invaluable – I know you have always done jobs that weren't really yours.'

'Thank you so much, mam, I was so scared of what might become of us,' Beth admitted. 'And it will make it so much easier for me to let Sam go to America on his own. You see, I'd come to the conclusion that was the right thing to do. Then maybe in a few years' time, when he's settled, Molly and I could join him there.'

'But you could go with him now if you left Molly with us.'

Beth looked hard at her mistress, a little puzzled by what she'd said.

'I couldn't do that,' she said. 'It's not as if I could be back in just a couple of weeks.'

'I didn't mean just minding her for a few weeks,' Mrs Langworthy said, looking intently at Beth. 'I meant permanently.'

Beth was so shocked her mouth fell open. 'Permanently?'

'Don't look so startled, Beth! Surely you can see this is the best possible solution for you and Sam? My husband and I would love her as our own, she'd live in this lovely house, go to the best schools and never want for anything.'

Beth was scandalized. 'But she's my flesh and blood!'

'But that's all the more reason to let us ensure she has a good life,' Mrs Langworthy said, two bright red spots of colour appearing on her cheeks as if she were feverish. 'When I was a girl I knew several big families that allowed one or two of their children to go and live with a wealthier relative. It was common practice.'

Beth also knew people who had done this. 'But you aren't a relative,' she pointed out. 'I couldn't let Molly grow up thinking I gave her away!'

'I wasn't for one moment suggesting that you sever all connection with her.' Mrs Langworthy looked affronted. 'You could write to her, come back and visit her. I would tell her I was her guardian, I would never claim to be her mother. She could call me Aunt Ruth.'

Beth felt as if someone had opened a trapdoor beneath her feet and she was falling into space. She knew the Langworthys could give her little sister everything a child could want or need, but for almost fourteen months Molly had, to all intents and purposes, become Beth's own baby, and her instinct was to fight tooth and nail for her.

She reached out and ran one finger down Molly's little face, suddenly afraid Mrs Langworthy had the power to take her even if she and Sam refused their permission.

'Think about it long and hard, Beth,' Mrs Langworthy said softly, reaching out and touching her arm. 'I know I've shocked you and perhaps you even feel that I'm insulting you by suggesting this. But you must believe me when I say that no one could have done a better job of rearing Molly so far, especially as you are so young.'

'I couldn't let you have her,' Beth said fiercely. 'I love her too much.'

'I know you love her, but don't dismiss my offer out of hand,' the older woman said. 'Think what it could mean to you. You'd be free as a bird to go with Sam. Your life could be your own again, you could do what you want to do. But you'll still be Molly's sister, nothing and no one could take that from you.'

Beth couldn't bear to hear any more. She gathered the sleeping child up into her arms and backed towards the door, apologizing as she went.

Sam arrived home at half past eight. Normally it was gone midnight before he got home, but it had been so quiet in the Adelphi Hotel that the bar manager had told him to go early. When he saw the windows glowing from the lamp, he was pleased because that meant he and Beth could have a chat. She was normally fast asleep when he got in.

But as soon as he opened the door and saw her sitting hunched up in front of the fire, a blanket around her shoulders, he knew something was wrong.

'What's happened?' he asked. His hands and feet were like blocks of ice and he went over to the stove to warm them. 'They haven't told you they don't need you any more?'

Beth had raised that anxiety just last Sunday, but Sam didn't believe they would dispense with her, for at Christmas he'd sensed how fond both Mr and Mrs Langworthy had become of her.

'Mrs Langworthy wants us to give Molly to her,' she blurted out, and promptly burst into tears.

Sam knelt on the floor in front of her and prompted her till she eventually told him exactly what had been said.

'Is that so bad?' he asked when she'd finished. 'She's right, it would be good for Molly.'

'You've never cared about her,' Beth accused him bitterly. 'If you'd had your way she'd have gone to the Foundling Home.'

'Maybe I wasn't too nice about her when she was born,' Sam agreed, blushing with shame. 'I'm sorry for that now. But she could have a much better life with them than she could with us. We could get a passage to America, have a high old time. Think how marvellous that would be!'

'I don't want a high old time, I want Molly.' Beth began to cry and covered her face with her hands. 'I'd made up my mind to tell you to go alone. I know it isn't fair of me to hold you back. So you go and I'll keep her.'

Sam said nothing for a while, just knelt at Beth's feet while she cried into her hands. He did often think about their mother's infidelity, and felt bitter that his father took his own life because of it, but he didn't feel any resentment towards Molly any longer.

How could he? She was the sweetest little thing; in fact he was sure that if he had been with her constantly as Beth had, he'd be just as indignant and horrified at this suggestion as his sister was.

As it was, he was able to view the situation more dispassionately. There was no doubt the Langworthys could give Molly the best of upbringings. They were wealthy, influential people, but they had kind hearts too. But for their generosity in giving him and Beth a home after the fire, they could well have been forced to live in a slum, and Molly wouldn't be the healthy, happy baby she was.

Maybe he was thinking of himself to some extent. It would be wonderful to sail for America with Beth, unfettered by a small child. They could go where they wanted to, be free to do as they pleased, and with both of them able to work they could accumulate far more money.

Above all else he wanted Beth to have a good life, a loving husband and children of her own. But she wasn't going to get that with Molly in tow, for people would always think she was Beth's illegitimate child. Beth could hope for nothing more than being a servant, and she deserved better than that.

But how could he convince his sister that he wasn't just thinking of himself?

'I could go to America, then send for you once I'm settled,' he said. 'But I don't want to go without you, Beth. And now this has come up with the Langworthys, how are they going to be with us if we turn them down? What if they ask us to leave? What then?'

'They won't do that,' Beth said quickly, but she looked at Sam questioningly. 'Will they?'

'I don't know,' he admitted. 'Mr Edward might feel that Molly's presence upsets his wife. People do turn nasty when they don't get what they want.'

Sam decided he would stop at that. Beth knew only too well that they would never find another place like this to live. Nor was she likely to find another job where Molly was welcome. She was intelligent enough to take that into account when she made her decision.

That night Sam couldn't sleep, for he knew Beth was lying awake in the next room worrying. They had talked round and round the subject, and he sensed that Beth knew in her heart that for Molly, giving her to the Langworthys was the kindest thing they could do. The events and struggles of the last year had taught them both how precarious life could be. They didn't have to stray far from Falkner Square to see how easy it was to fall into the abyss of poverty.

But Sam was also aware that Beth couldn't be entirely rational because she loved Molly so much. She wasn't able to think as he could, of herself, to get excited by the prospect of freedom and adventure. Or even to believe that maybe once Molly was grown up she could come out and join them in America.

And despite all he'd said tonight, and in the past, Sam had looked in on Molly asleep in the room next door before he went to bed, and his heart had swelled with affection for her. He couldn't imagine a day without seeing those big brown eyes, hearing her merry chuckles and watching her toddling around the room. He had done his best not to let his heart become engaged, but he had failed, and it wouldn't be only Beth who felt the pain of parting.

Beth woke him the following morning as she always did. Her eyes were red and she was very pale. She handed him a cup of tea and sat down on the end of his bed.

'Will you come home this afternoon?' she asked.

It was Saturday, and Sam finished work at the shipping office at noon. Usually he visited friends in the afternoon and went straight to the Adelphi in the early evening.

'If you want me to,' he said.

'I do. I want you to come over to the house and talk to Mr Langworthy about Molly,' she said, her voice cracking with emotion. 'If he really wants this as much as his wife does, then I think it's best we agree to it.'

A lump came up in Sam's throat, for he knew how much pain she was in. He couldn't bring himself to offer any platitudes. 'I'll come straight home,' he said. 'You are so brave, Beth.'

'It's not brave. Brave would be taking her to America with us or walking out of here with my nose in the air. But I got to thinking what Papa would have made of this. I believe he would have said we should give Molly what is best for her.'

Sam privately thought that as his father hadn't considered his own children when he killed himself, he would have had no views on this situation, but he kept that to himself. 'Yes,

I think he would too.' He nodded. 'But before we agree, we must get them to promise they tell Molly about us and make sure she writes to us when she's old enough.'

Beth's eyes filled up with fresh tears. 'I think we should say it has to be done quickly too. I couldn't bear to have to wait weeks with this hanging over us.'

'I've got enough for our passages now,' Sam replied. 'But only just.'

'We'll manage,' Beth said fiercely.

Beth was hoping against hope that when they spoke to Mr Edward he would tell them that his wife wasn't in her right mind because she was poorly. But at three o'clock, the time she'd asked Mrs Bruce to fix for her and Sam to talk to him, he opened the drawing-room door as they came up the stairs from the basement and there was a kind of glow in his eyes.

He didn't have the warmth his wife had; he was starchy and cool with everyone. Beth knew that was due mostly to his upbringing and his business responsibilities, but she had seen him unbend when talking to Molly.

'You want to discuss the proposition my wife put to you?' he asked.

'Yes, sir,' Beth said, her legs turning to jelly.

'Come on in and sit down,' he said.

The fire was roaring up the chimney and the lamp had been lit as it was such a dark grey day. Mrs Langworthy was there too, wearing the same black dress she'd worn for the funeral, but she looked much better than she had the previous day. She was seated by the fire, and Mr Edward indicated for Beth and Sam to sit down on the couch in front of it. He remained standing, his elbow on the mantelpiece.

'My wife fears you may think she made her suggestion rashly, without consulting me. But in fact she raised it with me back at Christmas,' he began.

'And your views at that time?' Sam said archly.

'That Molly was a delightful baby, one I could certainly care for as my own. But we weren't in a position to discuss the possibility of it with you, not while my father required so much care.'

'But just a few days after his death you felt it was appropriate to tackle Beth on the subject?' Sam said sarcastically.

Mr Edward blushed. 'I was very alarmed when my wife informed me she'd spoken out so bluntly. It should have been handled with tact and at a far more appropriate time.'

'Please forgive me for that.' Mrs Langworthy spoke up, wringing her hands anxiously. 'I'm afraid my affection for both Molly and Beth made me too impulsive and if I did offend or even frighten her, then I am so terribly sorry.'

'We do understand that Mrs Langworthy wishes the very best for Molly,' Sam agreed, looking straight at Mr Edward. 'But what we need to establish today is whether you are both of the same mind.'

Beth was surprised Sam could be so bold and forthright. She had been a little afraid he would just allow himself to be railroaded into agreeing with everything the Langworthys said.

'Indeed we are,' Mr Edward said firmly. 'I can assure you both I share my wife's wish to cherish her, protect her and give her everything we would have given our own child had we been blessed with one. I have very little previous experience with small children, I admit, but I find Molly utterly delightful.'

Beth could only stare at Mr Edward, for she hadn't expected him to show that degree of warmth or commitment.

'Beth!' Sam looked sharply at his sister. 'Have you anything to add?'

'If we let her stay with you, will you promise that you will write and let us know how she is, until she's old enough to write herself?' she asked, her voice shaking with emotion.

'You have our word on that,' Mr Edward said gravely. 'If you should come back, you will be welcome to come and see her too. All that I ask is that you allow us to become her legal guardians, to take our name. We need that security.'

Beth and Sam exchanged glances, realizing that in the eyes of the law this would mean they were relinquishing their rights to their sister.

'No child could be more wanted,' Mrs Langworthy pleaded. 'She will have us, Mrs Bruce, Kathleen, and Cook too. It will be a stable, happy home full of love. We know what a wrench this will be for you both, but by putting her in our care you will be safeguarding her future.'

Sam looked to Beth and she nodded. 'When she's older you must tell her that we didn't do this easily, only because we believed it to be the best for her,' Sam said tremulously.

'We certainly will, my dears.' Mrs Langworthy got up and took Beth's hands, drawing her up from her chair to embrace her. 'We won't let her forget you. And we promise we will never give you cause to regret today's decision.'

Mr Edward moved closer and cleared his throat before speaking. 'Can I just say how much we will miss you, Beth? You have brought light and colour into this house.' He paused for a moment, looking at Sam, then back at Beth. 'I believe you will both do well in America, but if it isn't to your liking, return and come back to us. We will always have room in our hearts and home for you.'

Beth heard the sincerity in his voice and she felt deeply touched.

'Thank you, sir,' she whispered, tears springing into her eyes. 'I think it best that we leave as soon as possible. It will be easier for everyone that way.'

Chapter Ten

A stiff north-easterly wind forced the passengers on the decks of the *Majestic* to clutch at their hats as they waved goodbye to their friends and relatives. The choppy sea and the sky were a sullen dark grey, but the red-jacketed bandsmen playing spiritedly on the quay and the streamers being hurled at the ship created a carnival atmosphere despite the bleak March day.

Mrs Bruce, Kathleen and Mr Edward had moved back from the pressing crowd to the shelter of a shed but they were still waving frantically, the green feather in Kathleen's hat bobbing in the wind.

'They should go now. They'll catch their death of cold,' Beth shouted to Sam. What with the wind, the band and people shouting all around her, she could barely hear herself think.

What she really meant was that she couldn't bear to look at them for another moment, for they represented all she was unwilling to give up. She was of course forcing a gay smile, but now she was chilled to the bone she was finding it increasingly hard to pretend joy and excitement. She wanted to be back in the warm kitchen of Falkner Square with Molly on her lap. She didn't want to leave Liverpool.

But she couldn't say any of that to Sam for he was genuinely excited enough for both of them. His cheeks and nose had turned red with the cold, but his wide smile said that his long-awaited dream had at last begun.

'There's Sally!' he exclaimed jubilantly, pointing down

into the waving crowd. 'She's there by the crane! The one in a red cloak. I didn't think she cared enough to come and see me off.'

Seeing the girl her brother had mentioned so many times in the last couple of weeks was a distraction from Beth's misery. Sam had been introduced to the burlesque dancer by one of his friends at the Adelphi. Even from a distance of some two hundred feet, Beth could see she was everything she'd expected – a raven-haired, curvy floozy with paint on her face.

Since he'd met her, Sam had been coming home at three in the morning stinking of her cheap scent and his lips swollen from kissing. Beth had sometimes secretly hoped he'd find Sally's attractions greater than those of America and give up his plans.

'Do you love her?' Beth asked, forced to shout again.

He turned to her and smiled wickedly. 'I did while I was with her, but there'll be scores of girls like her in New York.'

Beth realized by the sparkle in his eyes he'd done far more than just kiss the girl, and she hoped he hadn't left her carrying his child. She thought she ought to reprove him, but as she was a little envious that he'd experienced that mysterious thing their mother had called passion, she didn't know what to say.

Clanging bells and a booming order that anyone not sailing was to leave the ship immediately prevented any comment, but as Beth watched her brother waving and blowing kisses she noted that a couple of elegantly dressed young ladies further along the ship's rail were also studying him. It occurred to her that her handsome brother was very likely to become the object of attention for many women on this voyage.

The whole ship was draped in paper streamers now and

the excitement was mounting palpably as the crew began to haul in the gangways and prepare to cast off. There were just as many people crying on deck as there were on the quay. In the past Beth had watched this scene dozens of times, but she'd only ever been aware of the sorrow among those left behind. It had never occurred to her that anyone on the ships could be anything but happy to go. She knew better now, for her heart felt as if it was being torn out at leaving Molly behind, and she realized that many of her fellow passengers must be leaving whole families, not just one little girl, and perhaps, like her, they feared they'd never see them again.

She had got up extra early this morning and crept into the house to watch Molly sleeping. Mrs Langworthy had had her father-in-law's bedroom stripped and redecorated just as soon as Beth had agreed Molly could stay with her. The room was finished a week ago and it was fit for a princess, with pink roses on the wallpaper, a proper cot and a new apple-green rug with white fringes. Mrs Langworthy had suggested Molly slept in it as soon as it was ready, thinking it would be less of a shock to her after Beth had left. But Molly hadn't seemed the slightest bit daunted by her new surroundings, and slept like a top from the first night.

Since then Mr Edward had been out and bought her many toys, including building bricks, a furry dog on wheels to push around and a rocking horse. Beth knew she ought to be glad he was showing his delight at becoming her sister's guardian, yet somehow each new acquisition made her feel more dejected and inadequate.

That morning Beth had sat in the room with just the palest of early-morning light to see her sister by. She had silently worshipped her, drinking in her long eyelashes on her plump, rosy cheeks, her dark curls, and the way her first finger curled around her nose as she sucked her thumb. Her head told her she was doing the right thing for Molly, that her future would be immeasurably better with her Uncle Edward and Aunt Ruth, but she still felt like a condemned woman waiting for her life to expire.

Even worse was the final leave-taking. Mrs Langworthy held Molly in her arms at the front door as they got into the carriage with Mr Edward, Mrs Bruce and Kathleen. As the carriage rumbled away down the street, Beth had to steel herself from jumping out to snatch Molly back.

Down on the quay a woman was wailing loudly. She was old, perhaps a grandmother, too old to go with her family. She held her arms outstretched, tears streaming down her wrinkled face, as if begging them not to leave her, and Beth had to turn her face away as the sight was too tragic to bear.

The gangways were stowed away, sailors cast off, then coiled the ropes away, and suddenly the gap between ship and shore widened. The band struck up a jolly sea shanty, the last of the paper streamers were thrown, and in a last-ditch attempt to show Mr Edward she was happy to be going, Beth took off her new straw hat and waved it, even though tears were rolling down her cheeks.

'You'll feel better soon,' Sam said, putting his arm around her waist. 'Molly will be happy with the Langworthys. You've still got me, and so much adventure to come. It's time too that you had some fun.'

Beth's only reply was to lean her head against his shoulder. It helped to know he hadn't been fooled by her pretended delight, and understood her pain. But it was so long since she'd had any fun, she wasn't sure she'd even recognize it when it came again.

Just this morning Mrs Bruce had said that she believed true happiness came to those who actively sought to bring it to others through kindness and thoughtfulness. She said Beth must look upon everyone on the ship as potential friends, not strangers, and to remember that they were all as apprehensive about what lay in wait for them in America as she and Sam were.

The ship was gaining speed, the faces of those on the dockside a pale blur. There was no turning back now, so she had to be brave and think of how lucky they were to be getting this chance to shake off all the sadness of the past and build a new future. As Sam had so rightly said, there was so much adventure to come.

'Let's go below decks and meet the people we're going to be sailing with,' she suggested more brightly than she felt. 'And don't you go off with another Sally, leaving me on my own!'

Sam chuckled and gave her a hug. 'That's better, sis,' he said. 'And don't you worry, I'm not going to leave you. There's too many men casting sly looks at you. I won't let you out of my sight.'

The steerage passengers were housed right down in the bowels of the ship, and as if that didn't make their humble position clear enough, there were metal grids preventing them from slipping into the first- and second-class areas.

As Beth and Sam made their way down the companion-ways, they caught glimpses of the rarefied world beyond the grids. Soft carpets and polished wood cabin doors with brass fittings; white-jacketed stewards carrying trays of drinks to the fortunate occupants, and well-scrubbed and beautifully attired children trying to escape from the clutches of their nursemaids.

As they reached the lower levels, the doors and floors became metal, the paintwork scuffed and grimy. Here there were people elbowing their way through the narrow corridors, their anxious and sometimes angry faces relaying the message that no steward was going to arrive down here with a cup of tea, a blanket for a child or even words of reassurance. The noise of the engines almost drowned out the sounds of babies crying and frantic mothers trying to round up their children, and Beth's heart sank even further.

The single men were housed forward, single women in the stern, with families in the middle section. Sam had been making jokes for days about what steerage actually meant. Some said it was so called because it was where the steering mechanism was housed, but Sam was of the opinion it referred to steers, or cattle, for that was how they'd travel. But Beth, who had seen illustrations of how steerage passengers fared in the days of sailing ships, with four or five people to one bunk and the only sanitation a bucket, was relieved to see that the bunks were canvas, designed to be stowed away during the day to make more room, and that there were lavatories and washrooms in each section.

It was claustrophobic though, and very gloomy, and looking around her at her fellow passengers' pinched faces and shabby attire, she was glad she'd acted on Mrs Bruce's advice and sewn their money into their clothes, for instinct told her it wouldn't be wise to trust anyone.

Yesterday Mr Edward had given them thirty pounds; he said they were to look on it as an emergency fund for use if they couldn't get work immediately. This was on top of all the other things he and his wife had given them – luggage, two warm quilts, towels and items of clothing – and they thanked him with moist eyes.

As Sam put Beth's valise down in the women's section a

stern-faced older woman in a grey dress advanced on them. 'Out of here, young man,' she said sharply.

'I was just getting my sister settled in,' he retorted.

'She'll be fine in my care,' the woman replied. 'I am Miss Giles, the matron. I do not allow single women to fraternize with the opposite sex. If you wish to see your sister during the voyage you must arrange to meet on deck.'

Sam looked incredulous and a couple of pretty young Irish girls began giggling.

'I'll meet you again in an hour,' Beth said, anxious not to get on the wrong side of Miss Giles. 'Don't worry, I'll be fine.'

The realization that almost everyone was as apprehensive and scared as she was made Beth feel a little better. There were around twenty-six other girls in her section and the vast majority were under twenty, like her. Most were travelling with their parents and younger siblings and hated being separated from them, though there were four like Beth with older brothers. The remainder were either with a sister or a friend, and only one woman, one of the oldest, was entirely alone; she said she was joining her fiancé in New York.

One of the many gifts Mrs Langworthy had given Beth was a new brown coat with a fur collar. She had almost new shiny buttoned boots and a brown wool travelling dress, and in comparison to the other women she looked rich. They clutched worn-looking shawls around thin shoulders, they had holes in their boots and patched dresses. Most were Irish, pale and poorly nourished, yet for all that they had a look of eager expectancy in their eyes, and spoke of their destination with such hope and fervour that Beth felt ashamed for being so reluctant.

Bridie and Maria, the two Irish girls who had been so

amused by Sam, suggested she claimed the bed next to theirs. Their lilting voices full of warmth and friendliness reminded Beth of Kathleen and acted as a salve to her bruised heart.

'We can meet with the single men in the family quarters,' Maria said with a hint of mischief in her eyes. 'My uncle emigrated last year and he wrote home to say there was dancing and singing in the evenings. Miss Giles is only here to make sure no men come into this room, so she is, but she can't stop us having fun outside it.'

'Have you left your sweetheart behind?' Bridie asked. 'You have the red-eyed look of a girl who's been crying for days.'

All at once Beth found herself confiding in them about Molly, crying again as she described how hard it was to leave her. Maria put her arms around her and drew her head down on to her skinny shoulder. 'Sure, and don't we know how hard that is! When I said goodbye to Mammy and the little ones I thought my heart would break. But we're on our way to somewhere better, Beth. We'll do well there and before long we'll get them to join us. You can do the same for Molly.'

By the following morning they were out in the Atlantic and as the sea became rougher many people began to suffer from seasickness. Beth felt well, but knowing the sound of retching and the smell of vomit in the stuffy quarters were likely to make her ill too, she went up on deck.

It was very cold and windy, but after the constant noise of the ship's engines and people shouting to one another over it below decks, it was good to have quiet and solitude. Beyond the railings which separated the steerage passengers' small part of the deck from the remainder, a couple of stewards were exercising dogs, and one lone man in a heavy overcoat and a fur hat with ear-flaps was walking briskly up and down the deck.

Beth stood at the ship's rail staring out at the huge expanse of empty grey sea before her stretching to infinity and smiled at the memory of the previous evening.

She had gone with Bridie and Maria into the family area to be introduced to some of the people they had come over from Ireland with. At first she had been repulsed because almost everyone was very shabby and rather dirty, and they all seemed to have so many children. They made her think of the Irish back in Liverpool who lived in such terrible squalor in the slum courts. Her parents had brought her up to think that the men were good-for-nothings, always drunk and fighting, and that their women bred like rabbits and neglected their offspring.

But she was soon to see that however poor these people were, and whatever conditions they'd lived in back in Ireland and Liverpool, they loved their children and wanted a better life for them. She found it impossible to remain aloof when she was greeted with such warmth and interest, and when all about her were such gaiety and optimism. One man with a beautiful tenor voice began to sing, and before long everyone was joining in. An old man got out his fiddle and two little girls were encouraged to show off their Irish dancing talents.

It turned into a real party when Sam and some of the other single men came in to join them. Drink was being passed around, but most were just drunk on sheer delight to be on their way to America. The fiddler broke into a jig and to Beth's surprise Sam began the dancing by catching hold of Maria's hands and urging her up on to her feet. Beth would have been content to sit and watch, but as others began to get up and dance, the jig became faster and soon her feet were tapping. When a young man with red hair and an even redder face held out his hand to her, she was only too happy to be his partner.

It was not the kind of sedate dancing she'd learned at school but an outpouring of excess energy and exuberance. As one tune ended, another man would claim her. It felt good to be twirled about with so much energy. Her partners had rough, callused hands, their hobnailed boots beat a tattoo on the wooden floor and sweat poured down their faces, but even if they were not the sort of men she'd always imagined would lead her at her first dance, she felt happy.

Later, back in the single women's cabin, Beth lay in her canvas bed listening to the other girls whispering excitedly about the young men they'd met tonight, and she felt proud that her brother appeared to be the one they all admired most. She could still hear the sound of the old man's fiddle ringing in her ears, such joyful, wild music, as if he was pouring every experience of his life into it. She had never heard the instrument played quite that way before, and she felt inspired to emulate him.

She put out her arm and groped around under her bed until her fingers met the worn black case with its peeling leather. Just touching it was enough. Her talisman for good fortune.

'Huge, ain't it?'

Beth was startled by the male voice behind her on the deck, and turned to see it was one of the lads she'd danced with fleetingly last night; she recognized him by the scar on his right cheek. It was the scar, which looked as if it had been made with a knife, that had made her wary of him. He was tall and whip-thin, the mop of black hair she remembered thinking needed a wash and a cut now hidden beneath a cap. Although he was probably a couple of years older than her, his shabby, too large jacket and moleskin trousers gave him the look of a young street urchin.

'So huge you could get scared by it,' she replied. 'It makes me feel very small.'

'They say it's that cold if you fell in you'd die of shock in two minutes,' he said.

'That's a cheerful thought!' she said with some sarcasm. 'Why don't you try it? I'll check if they're right.'

He laughed. 'You've got an acid tongue. Just like me ma.'

'Is that why you're going to America, to get away from her?'

'In a way, s'pose I am,' he said with a grin. 'Not to mention Pa, with his drinkin' an' all. Why are you going?'

'Same as most of us,' she shrugged. 'To seek my fortune; for the adventure.'

'You're Sam Bolton's sister, ain't yer?' he said.

Beth nodded. 'I'm Beth Bolton. And you?'

'Jack Child,' he said, and gingerly held out his hand. 'Pleased to meet you.'

She shook his hand briefly. 'Where are you from? That's not an Irish or a Liverpool accent.'

'Down south, from the East End of London. I came to Liverpool a year ago to get on a ship for America, but I had my money stolen and so I had to find work until I had enough to get another ticket.'

'That was bad luck,' she said, warming to him a little because he had soft brown eyes and an engaging, lopsided grin.

'It's made me more cagey,' he said thoughtfully, leaning on the rail beside her. 'But that's a good thing. They say New York is full of rogues and they prey on us immigrants.'

'Really?'

He nodded sagely. 'A pal of mine went six months ago. He wrote and said men lie in wait outside the immigration hall looking for suckers to fleece. They offer to get you work and a place to live, but once you've handed over some money they scarper.'

Sam had told Beth that men down in the docks in Liverpool sold forged tickets for passages on ships that didn't exist; they promised to take foreigners to hotels and then stole their luggage. She supposed such things went on everywhere in the world.

'We'll just have to be on our guard then.' She shrugged.

'You and Sam will make good,' Jack said. 'You've both got something about you.'

'And what's that?' Beth asked, amused by the way he was studying her. By no stretch of the imagination was he handsome – he had a raw complexion and his features looked too big for his face. His accent, a mixture of London and Liverpool, sounded peculiar, yet there was something very likable about him.

He looked a bit sheepish. 'Well, Sam, he's 'andsome and got that cock-o'-the-walk way about him. You're classy and beautiful.'

'Well, thank you, Jack.' She smiled. 'I just hope when I go looking for work they think so too.'

They stayed at the rail talking for some time. Jack told her that while he'd been in Liverpool he'd worked for a carter and had lodged with a family in Leeds Street. 'They was worse than me own,' he laughed. 'Rough as they come and always fighting and drinking. Glad to get out of there I was. But they took me in when I didn't have a penny to me name, not many would do that.'

Beth in turn told him about her parents dying and how

126

she'd left Molly behind. 'You did the right thing by her,' he said with a look of real understanding. 'I was lookin' at some of the folks down there last night with all their little 'uns and wonderin' 'ow on earth they thinks they can get a start in New York. It'll be hard to get a place to live, and if the men can't get work straight off, how they gonna feed 'em?'

This same thought had been in Beth's mind too. It was comforting rather than painful to imagine Molly toddling around the house at Falkner Square, adored by everyone. Her life would remain constant and secure and she would always have a warm, clean bed, good food and plenty of love. Beth thought that if she reminded herself of that each day, in time she might be able to be truly glad she gave her to the Langworthys.

The sea became even rougher in the late afternoon and as the ship bucked and rolled, more and more people became sick and took to their beds. For most of the day Beth had felt dutybound to help those affected, washing their faces, getting them drinks of water and emptying the vomit bowls, but as the evening progressed and the smell below decks began to make her feel queasy too, she put on her coat and went up on deck again for some fresh air.

It was freezing cold up there, and deserted, but she could hear an orchestra playing in the first-class saloon even above the noise of the wind and sea.

To hear the music better she walked right down the deck to the railing which kept the steerage passengers contained in their section, and seeing a lifejacket locker, she tucked herself into the side of it to get out of the wind and listen to the waltz music. In her imagination she was in a pale blue dress with a satin sash, being twirled around the floor by one of the ship's officers.

She became so immersed in this happy little fantasy that she came out of her little shelter to dance alone. But a sudden burst of louder music and a pool of golden light spilling out on to the deck alerted her that someone had come out of the first-class saloon. She slunk back into her shelter when she saw a man in formal evening dress lighting a cigarette, but she couldn't resist peeping out to look at him.

He was tall, slim and dark-haired, and although he was some forty yards from her, and the light poor, she thought he seemed jumpy, looking around him in a nervous manner.

A few minutes later the door opened again and a lady came out.

She was like a beacon in the dark because of the white fur stole around her shoulders, her blonde hair and light-coloured, shiny dress. As she raised her hand to greet the man, her bracelet twinkled brightly, suggesting it was diamonds.

The couple embraced, and Beth wondered why they would come out on to a freezing cold deck when they could have been dancing together in the warm saloon.

The reason became obvious when they began kissing frantically, for clearly they couldn't do that in front of people. Beth thought it rather romantic and wondered if they were engaged and had given their chaperone the slip.

But the man was clearly concerned at them being caught, for even as he kissed the woman he was manoeuvring her down the deck towards Beth and the shelter of the lifeboat suspended there.

'I daren't stay more than a minute or two,' the woman burst out breathlessly, her words carrying clearly on the wind. 'He's watching me like a hawk.'

'You've got to leave him,' the man said fiercely. 'I want to kill him each time he paws you.'

Beth suddenly felt very uncomfortable at being a witness to this clandestine tryst. She wanted to move away, or at least cough so they knew they weren't entirely alone, but it was too late, for the couple were only feet from her now, just the other side of the railing, so close she could smell the woman's perfume.

Silence made her peep out again. They were kissing so passionately it made Beth blush. The woman's back was to her, and the fur stole had slipped down from her shoulders, revealing the flesh on her shoulders and neck which was very white and smooth.

Their breathing was heavy, there was a rustling of clothes, and though Beth couldn't be sure, she thought the man was touching the woman in an indecent manner.

'I need more than this fumbling, Clarissa,' he sighed. 'I want to make love to you on a bed, to see you naked beneath me. Come to my cabin tonight.'

Beth was burning up with embarrassment now, but if she moved they would hear her and it would look as if she'd been purposely spying on them.

'I'll try,' the woman replied. 'I'll slip Aggie one of my powders.'

There was more frantic kissing and fumbling, then Beth heard Clarissa say she really must go, and a second or two later she heard her heels tapping back along the deck.

The man remained where he was and Beth saw him light up another cigarette. As she was now frozen to the marrow she began to sidle away towards the door of the companion-way. But in the darkness she didn't see there was a small ledge in front of her and she tripped over it, falling down on to the deck.

'Who's there?' the man barked out.

Beth knew without turning her head that he was just four or five feet behind her, looking straight at her as she lay sprawled on the deck, and that only the railing was preventing him coming over to her.

'Get up and speak to me,' he ordered her.

She was so used to doing what she was told that she didn't even consider running away, and obeyed him.

'How long have you been there?' he asked.

'A while. I came up because it's so stuffy below.'

She couldn't help but stare at him for he was so handsome, impeccably dressed and had such a cultured voice. She guessed he was in his mid-twenties.

Until that moment Sam had been the yardstick she measured men's looks by, and she'd seen few as handsome as her brother. But Sam looked almost girlish in comparison to this man, for his hair was coal black and he had deep-set eyes, a proud nose and high cheekbones.

'Are you in the habit of spying on other people?' he said with a sneer.

'Are you in the habit of being rude to people?' she retorted with some indignation. 'I was here first. You should have checked to make certain you were alone if you were intending to do something secret.'

'You're a cheeky minx,' he replied, looking her up and down. 'Will a florin buy your silence?'

Beth didn't understand that question and just stared at him.

'Five shillings?' he said.

All at once she realized what he meant. Witnessing an adulterous meeting was shocking enough to her, but to be offered a bribe not to speak of it was insulting. 'How dare you assume my silence can only be bought?' she said indignantly. 'I have no interest in you or your lady friend. It would have been quite sufficient just to ask that I didn't tell anyone what I saw.'

He looked slightly chastened. 'I apologize,' he said. 'It's just that –' He broke off lamely.

Beth felt bolder now. All day she'd been aware that the ship's company cared little for the comfort or well-being of their poorer passengers, and having something over someone from first class made her feel she was evening up the score. She moved closer to him, right up to the railing. 'That she's another man's wife?'

He could easily have snapped at her, but he just looked saddened. 'You are too young to understand,' he said with a sigh.

'You'd be surprised what I understand,' she retorted, thinking of her mother's dying confession. 'I know passion makes people behave recklessly.'

He gave a humourless laugh. 'And what, oh Wise One, should I do if I love a woman who is married to a man who makes her utterly miserable?'

Beth was surprised and a little touched by his honesty. 'So why did she marry him?' she asked.

'She was pushed into it by her family,' he replied.

Beth thought about that for a moment. 'Then why doesn't she just leave him?'

'You surprise me,' he said with a touch of sarcasm. 'I always thought girls of your class believed in the sanctity of marriage.'

Beth bristled at the mention of her class, and his assumption that a girl like her couldn't have an open mind. 'As I see it, there is no sanctity in a marriage of convenience.'

'You sound bitter,' he said, looking at her intently. 'If you weren't so young I'd think you were speaking from experience. But what you suggest is impossible anyway; her husband has her watched.'

'By a servant?' Beth asked. She remembered the woman had mentioned someone called Aggie.

He nodded.

For reasons she didn't understand, Beth felt drawn into his problems and wanted to help him. 'She'll be easily distracted once we get to New York. Maybe your lady should make plans for then?'

'And what kind of plan would a devious little minx like you devise?' he said, a faint smile tweaking his lips.

Beth could well understand why the woman Clarissa was taking such risks for him. It wasn't just his face that was attractive, he had an easy manner too. 'I think she would need help from another woman,' she said thoughtfully. 'Her servant wouldn't think to watch her so closely if she was with a friend.'

'I'll bear that idea in mind,' he said, this time giving her a beaming smile. 'Shame you aren't in first class too, it could be you!'

Beth laughed lightly. 'I wish I was in first class. I don't suppose so many people are seasick there. That was why I came up here, to get away from it. But I must go now, I'm frozen.'

'And can I rely on you not to speak of this to anyone?' he asked, raising one eyebrow questioningly.

'Discretion is my middle name,' she giggled.

'Then, Miss Discretion, I hope we run into one another again,' he said with a little bow. 'And you must run along now before you freeze to death.'

The rest of the voyage passed slowly and uneventfully, without Beth catching sight of the lovers again. As sickness had descended on so many of the steerage passengers there were no more nights of dancing, music and revelry, and Beth filled her days nursing, cleaning and minding the children of those too ill to take care of their own.

There were many she'd helped who claimed she was an angel, but to Beth there was nothing extraordinary in taking care of others; she was used to it. Besides, the light was too bad to read, it was too cold to go up on deck for more than ten minutes at a time, and the people she liked most, Maria and Bridie in particular, were too poorly for fun or conversation.

Sam would call for her to go up on deck with him several times during the day, and Jack Child invariably turned up too. Beth assumed it was because he had become friends with Sam, but her brother was quick to point out that she was the attraction.

Beth didn't really believe this because she'd become aware that everyone, male and female, admired Sam. He was funny, kind-hearted, daring and often outspoken.

Yet whatever Jack's reason for wanting to spend time with them, Beth was always pleased to see him. He was entertaining, quick-witted and worldly. He made her feel slightly giddy, and he always understood her little jokes and came back with sharp retorts that made her giggle. She often wished that it wasn't so cold on deck so they could stay up there longer; as it was, she often prolonged their meetings until she was almost a block of ice. On the way back down the companionway they lingered chatting until one of the crew or stewards told them off for blocking the way.

Sam's activities were not curtailed by mere rules. He managed to flout them all by sheer charm, his smart appearance and his good manners. He'd somehow managed to get to know a young lady called Annabel in second class, and spent part of each day with her and her family in various places around the ship, even to the extent of eating with them and avoiding the disgusting daily meal of stew given to the steerage passengers.

Beth might have been jealous if he hadn't smuggled her back cake and fruit. Jack was awestruck by Sam's cool-headed nerve and by his bearing which enabled him to get away with it.

'If I walked through one of those grids they'd know straight off where I came from,' he said with a wry grin. 'I'd do better to nick a steward's jacket and carry a tray to get in there. But the minute I opened me mouth the game would be up.'

'They say there's no class distinction in America,' Beth pointed out. 'All you need to better yourself is the ability to work hard.'

Beth hadn't really been aware of class distinction until her mother died. Before that, almost everyone she came into contact with had been the middling sort, respectable and industrious, just like her family. She was of course aware of the very poor; she saw them daily begging in the streets. But the gentry were so far removed from her, with their big houses, servants and fancy carriages, that they never touched her life.

Going to work and later to live in Falkner Square had changed all that. Then she was a servant, observing the gentry from close quarters, and she became aware of the huge, unbridgeable gulf between her and them. The Langworthys had never made her feel inferior, but she had been made to feel so on this voyage just because they couldn't afford a higher fare.

At night as she lay in her bed, trying to blank out the groans of the sick around her and the ever-present smell of vomit, she would think about the promised classless society in America. Clearly there had to be some kind of hierarchy there too, but if it was based on wealth rather than birth or education, maybe if she and Sam worked hard they could end up with the kind of status the Langworthys held.

Chapter Eleven

'Land's been sighted!

At the excited yell from one of her fellow steerage passengers, Beth rushed to get her coat and joined the throng of other people pushing and shoving to get up on deck. It was early afternoon, eight days since they left Liverpool, and it seemed odd that even those who had spent the entire voyage prostrate with seasickness had suddenly found the strength to get up.

Rain was coming down heavily, the visibility very poor, and all Beth could see ahead was a slightly darker grey line on the horizon, yet that didn't send anyone back to the warmth below decks. All around her she could hear people asking one another how long it would be until they landed, and then discussing what they'd do first once they'd been through immigration.

After having the entire deck to herself for most of the voyage, it felt strange to be jostled by so many people. Sam wasn't there – she assumed he was with Annabel – and she couldn't see Jack either. To try to avoid the crush, and to find a spot from where she might get her first glimpse of land, she elbowed her way through the throng of people, right up to the railings that separated them from first class.

There, to her surprise, just the other side of the railing, was Clarissa, huddled under an umbrella with a gentleman.

Beth might have only had a brief glimpse of her in the dark, but she knew without any doubt it was Clarissa, even before she heard her speak. She was wearing a long, light brown fur coat and matching hat, a few tendrils of blonde hair fluttering in the breeze around her face.

Beth kept looking straight ahead, but her eyes were swivelling sideways to study the woman. She was what most people would call a classical beauty: an oval face, porcelain-like complexion, a perfect straight nose and high cheekbones. Beth couldn't see her eyes straight on, but she assumed they'd be blue. Yet her looks were not as interesting as the way she was with her companion. He held the umbrella above them with one hand, but she was holding his other arm almost possessively and looking right up into his eyes each time he spoke.

Beth assumed he must be yet another admirer, because he didn't fit the image of an old, stout man she had created in her mind for this woman's husband. He was around forty and tall, with a little goatee beard and neat moustache, as straight-backed and slender as a guardsman in a stylish dark blue coat with an astrakhan collar. Unusually, he wasn't wearing a hat, and he had a good head of wavy brown hair. While not rakishly handsome like the other man Beth had seen, he had a pleasant, good-natured face, and he was laughing at something Clarissa was saying to him.

'I'm afraid I may lose the brolly soon,' Beth heard him say as a gust of wind almost turned it inside out and he had to struggle to bring it under control.

'I did say, my darling, that it was a mistake to bring it out here,' Clarissa replied, smiling fondly at him. 'Umbrellas don't belong on ships, only in cities.'

'And let my lovely wife get wet?' he exclaimed jovially.

Beth was so surprised to discover this was the cuckolded husband that she almost jerked her head round towards the couple, but she controlled herself just in time and kept her eyes fixed firmly on the horizon.

137

'I did suggest it would be wiser to watch for land from the saloon,' she heard Clarissa retort.

'Maybe wiser, but there's a more exciting atmosphere out here,' her husband replied, waving one hand at the steerage passengers. 'Look at them all, clamouring for their first sight of America.'

Beth knew she ought to feel disgusted that this woman thought so little of marital fidelity. Clearly her husband wasn't an ogre, and she'd been playing fast and loose with the handsome younger man's feelings. Yet what she felt was more like disappointment, and sadness that the other man was going to be badly hurt.

A few minutes later, the mist and rain lifted just enough for land to be dimly sighted, and this took Beth's mind off Clarissa and her lover.

The passengers learned to their frustration that they wouldn't set foot in New York that evening, for the ship had to lie at anchor in the Hudson River until an immigration official came aboard. It was said that he had to check there was no disease on board, and then, providing all was well, they would be allocated a berth in the New York docks the following morning.

The calmer waters and the delight at being so close to their destination cured seasickness instantly and everyone wanted their last night to be one to remember. Even Miss Giles, who had watched the women in her care like a hawk, relaxed her vigilance.

When the customary cauldron of stew was brought down for the evening meal, there was a near riot in the rush to be served. Some of the passengers had eaten nothing but a few spoonfuls of thin gruel and dry bread since Liverpool, and now they were ravenously hungry.

Beth could hardly believe her eyes as they fell on the greyish-brown, greasy liquid with a few pieces of vegetables and more lumps of gristle than meat floating in it. She had forced herself to eat some of the nauseating concoction each night, because there was nothing else on offer, but they all looked as if they were positively enjoying it.

Once the meal was over, out came the fiddle, the spoons and the mouth organs and the singing, dancing and drinking began in earnest. Jack had a bottle of whisky and offered it to Beth. She took a swig and winced as it burned her throat, but, determined to be daring, she took another and found it went down more easily.

Maybe it was only the whisky, but that evening Beth felt like a butterfly coming out of a cocoon. The sheer number of young men clamouring to dance with her proved that she was attractive; she felt excited and optimistic about the adventure awaiting her in the morning. While she knew she was going to miss Molly dreadfully in the weeks ahead, she suddenly realized she wasn't sorry she'd left England.

'Get your fiddle and play, Beth,' Sam urged her.

She tried to refuse because she'd never played in public before, and she was afraid she wasn't as good as the old man. But Sam wouldn't leave it, and soon all the other people around them were clamouring for her to play too.

Beth had always played the fiddle by ear, even though she read music for the piano, and when she came back with her instrument she listened to a few bars of the tune the old man was playing, and once she thought she'd got it, she joined in with him.

It was far faster than she was used to, yet it felt right, the way the fiddle was intended to be played. Her fingers moved like quicksilver on the strings and her bow was making them sing. She moved her whole body in rhythm, closing her eyes and completely immersing herself in the music.

She sensed rather than saw her audience's appreciation: the foot-tapping grew louder, and whoops of joy came from those dancing. All at once she knew this was what she was made for, to play soaring, happy music that lifted her and all those around her to a better place. She forgot she was on a ship surrounded by grubby, pale-faced people and felt as if she were dancing barefoot across a buttercup-strewn meadow in bright sunshine.

When the tune ended and she opened her eyes again, she saw she had taken everyone to that place too. Their eyes were shining, they were smiling broadly, and sweat poured from their faces.

'Ah, you're a little gypsy!' a man in the crowd shouted out. 'Sure and wasn't that the best fiddling outside of Dublin!'

Beth played a few more times before putting her fiddle down and joining in the dancing. It was even more frantic than on their first night, the music louder, and as she was swirled around in a frantic polka, she laughed with sheer joy.

Sam passed her by again and again, each time with a different girl in his arms, and his wide, approving grin at the sight of her enjoying herself made her feel even more elated. It occurred to her that he'd probably harboured doubts that she could ever break out of her prissy ways, and maybe he'd even feared she would be a liability.

She vowed to herself then that she would show him she could be as good as any man in taking the rough with the smooth, and she would throw herself into the big adventure wholeheartedly.

A couple of hours later, the pipe and cigarette smoke and the sheer number of hot sweaty bodies in a confined space with little fresh air coming in, made Beth head for the deck.

As she went up the stairs she realized to her consternation that she was a little tipsy because she found it hard to coordinate her movements. Just as she was about to topple backwards, she felt two hands clutch her round the waist from behind to steady her.

It was Jack.

'Steady on, girl,' he said. 'If you're sure the deck is where you want to be, I'll come with you.'

As they finally got up to the top, the cold fresh air felt wonderful. The rain had stopped, the sky was clear and studded with stars and the sea was flecked with silver lights.

'This is better,' she sighed, taking deep breaths. 'How beautiful it all looks.'

'That it does,' Jack agreed. 'The sea looks like black satin, and see that moon!'

It was just a crescent, but it appeared far closer and brighter than Beth had ever noticed back in Liverpool. They found a locker to sit on and stayed there in companionable silence for some time. The band was playing along in the first-class saloon, and now that they were going up the Hudson River it was far warmer than out at sea, so much so that several other couples had come up and were standing further along the deck.

'You're a dark horse,' Jack said, grinning at her. 'You never said you could play like that. I thought when I saw your violin case you only played that screechy chamber stuff.'

'It's an Irish fiddle,' Beth said with a smile. 'I don't think it knows anything but jigs. My mother never approved of it; she always said it was ale-house music.'

'You'll never be short of work playing that way,' Jack said. 'But where are you going tomorrow? Have you got plans?'

'I think Sam has,' she said. 'What about you?'

'I'm going to my friend's place,' he replied. 'I don't think it's much, a kind of lodging house, but it will do until I get work.'

'And what will that be?'

'Anything that pays well,' he replied. 'I just wish I had a talent like yours. You'll surely have people falling over themselves to hire you.'

'Hire me?' she exclaimed. 'To play my fiddle?'

'Isn't that what you were gonna do?' he asked, looking puzzled.

'I thought I'd have to do domestic work or be an assistant in a shop, like back home,' she said.

Jack snorted with laughter. 'Well, you'd be crazy if you did when you've got a talent like that up your sleeve.'

'But they won't take a girl on, will they?'

'That would be an even bigger attraction,' Jack said. 'Especially someone as pretty as you.'

'Well, thank you, Jack,' she said, blushing a little.

'I'd be glad to come and listen, but I don't suppose you'll want to know me once you start moving in fancy circles!'

'Of course I will,' Beth said indignantly.

'Nah!' He shook his head. 'I'm too rough for someone like you. Your friends will look at my scarred face and think I'm a wrong 'un.'

'How did you get it?' she asked, and reached out to touch the scar gently.

'My pa done it. He was hitting Ma, I tried to stop him, and he picked up the knife and slashed me. That's why I left London. Couldn't take no more.'

'If you got it defending your mother, there's no reason to be ashamed of it,' Beth said, and kissed the scar.

Suddenly his arms were round her and he was kissing her.

Beth was startled, but not unpleasantly so. Jack's lips were soft and warm; she liked the way one of his hands was caressing her face and the tingle she felt down her spine. Without even being aware of what she was doing, she nestled into his arms and put hers around him.

As his tongue insinuated itself between her lips she thought he was taking liberties, but it felt good and she didn't want to break away. He was breathing heavily, holding her tighter and tighter, and it was only then that she realized she ought to call a halt.

'We should go back now,' she said as she broke away and stood up. 'We've got an early start tomorrow and so much ahead of us.'

'I don't ever want to let you go,' he whispered. 'You're so lovely.'

Beth smiled at him and patted his face. 'That's sweet, but you'll see me tomorrow.'

'I'd do anything for you,' he said, catching her fiercely by her shoulders. 'Anything!'

By the time Beth got back below decks, the party had broken up. A few drunken men were still staggering around, but the women and children were all in bed. In the single women's dormitory Maria and Bridie were waiting for Beth; it seemed someone had reported back that she had been seen with Jack.

'Is he your sweetheart?' Bridie whispered, her freckled face alight with eagerness.

'No, at least I don't think so,' Beth said, hurriedly pulling off her dress and boots and clambering into her bed. She had no idea whether a few kisses amounted to being someone's sweetheart. She liked Jack, but then he'd been the only man on the ship that she'd got to know. And for all she knew, she might meet someone far more suitable when they landed.

'Did he kiss you?' Maria whispered.

'Yes.'

'What was it like?' Maria asked.

'Nice,' Beth whispered back. 'But I don't know how it compares as it was the first time.'

'You've never been kissed before?' Bridie said incredulously.

Miss Giles came in then to check everyone was in bed, so Beth was spared having to say anything more.

She pretended she'd fallen asleep before Miss Giles left, shutting the door behind her. With her eyes closed she could relive Jack's kisses, and savour the delicious sensation all over again.

'What's happening now?' Beth asked Sam. It was ten in the morning and a clear, sunny day. They had been woken at first light by the ship's engines starting up again, and someone yelled out that it was time to disembark.

Suddenly it was utter chaos down in steerage with everyone rushing to pack up the remainder of their belongings. Even the crew shouting out that it would be several hours before they left the ship made no difference to the mass panic.

Beth was swept up in it too, and rushed up on deck to see for herself.

There was New York spread before her, looking exactly the way it had in a picture she'd seen in a magazine. She could even see the spire of Trinity Church which she knew was an aid to shipping as it was the highest building.

She was spellbound. The church spire might be the tallest building, but all the others appeared remarkably tall too. It was the sheer volume of ships that really astounded her.

Countless piers jutted out into what a sailor told her was the East River. Apparently the Hudson, which they'd sailed up the previous evening, was on the other side of the island, and a ship was moored at each and every pier. Despite the early hour the quay was crowded with every kind of cart, wagon and carriage imaginable, and hundreds of men were unloading and loading cargos.

As they came in closer, the noise of barrels being rolled over the cobbles, horses' hooves, wagon wheels, ships' engines and human voices was tremendous, and when Beth looked away from the quayside she saw thousands of craft of every kind, from tugboats to old sailing ships, out on the river. Looking back in the direction the ship had come from, she caught sight of the Statue of Liberty, which she'd seen so often in pictures at home. But nothing had prepared her for the sheer mammoth size of it, towering over the harbour, or the emotion it awakened in her.

She remembered her teacher reciting a poem. Beth couldn't recall if it was actually something to do with the statue, or just America in general, but the part of it which had remained in her head seemed to fit both of them: 'Give me your tired, your poor huddled masses yearning to breathe freely. The wretched refuse of your teeming shore.'

Beth didn't see herself, Sam or anyone on this ship as 'wretched refuse', but she supposed the woman who wrote it had watched many thousands of people from all over Europe hobbling through the immigration halls. With their worn suitcases, drawn faces, and shabby clothes they probably did look like so much refuse, though she thought the poet could have used a kinder word.

The Brooklyn Bridge was far bigger and longer than she expected too. She couldn't imagine how anyone could conceive of erecting something so huge over a river.

Her final thought before going back below decks to await instructions about when they would disembark was to wonder, if the port of New York held all these marvels, what more incredible sights there would be in the rest of the city.

'It seems the first and second classes are too grand to pass through immigration,' Sam said gloomily later as he and Beth watched gangways being lowered and the upper classes happily tripping down them, most with porters carrying their luggage. 'We get taken on a ferry to Ellis Island to be checked out. If they don't like the look of us we get sent back to England.'

'They aren't likely to send us back,' Beth pointed out. 'We're strong and healthy.'

'I wasn't afraid we'd be sent back. It's how long it will take to be cleared. Look how many ships there are here, all full of immigrants. It will be hard to find somewhere to stay tonight once it's dark.'

By four in the afternoon Beth was growing very anxious as the queues to be interviewed by immigration officers didn't appear to be moving at all. It was nearly twelve o'clock before the ferry had brought them to the island and the huge, pine-built building in which they were to be 'processed'. She had heard from a sailor on the ferry that this building had only been opened in 1892, but it was filled with thousands of people with unwashed bodies, and what with the poor ventilation, her stomach rumbling with hunger and her legs aching with standing for so long, it felt like an ancient torture room.

So much noise too – thousands of voices all talking at once, and many of them speaking foreign languages. There was a palpable undercurrent of fear as well, which perhaps was why so many small children were crying. Word passed back down the queues that they were to be questioned along with a medical examination, and although this didn't bother Beth or Sam, it was clear that it was creating anxiety for many.

'Public charge' was a phrase Beth kept hearing people use. She gathered that the officials were refusing entry to anyone they thought might become one. She saw a wizened old couple who looked barely able to stand and hoped that they could prove they had family to take care of them. There were whole families who seemed so dreadfully poor that they were bound to be treated with suspicion, and what of those who looked thin, pale and coughed a great deal? Were they harbouring tuberculosis?

By the time Beth was called forward to the doctor, she felt faint with hunger and thirst, but the doctor only looked her up and down and waved her on. The questions were simple enough: how much money she had, what sort of work she would be doing, and a few others which were obviously intended to discover if she was mentally competent.

After waiting for so long for the interview, it seemed absurdly brief, almost a disappointment. She was waved on, Sam right behind her, and suddenly they realized it was all over. They'd been accepted and they could get aboard the ferry bound for the city.

The hours on Ellis Island had been horrible, frustrating and tiring, and they had expected that once they were over that, everything would be fine. But as they walked down the gangway from the ferry on to the quay in New York, Beth was terrified.

It was now after eight in the evening, dark and cold, and it felt like being thrown headlong into a maelstrom:

thousands of bewildered, luggage-laden people, and preying on them the jackals who were determined to relieve them of some of their money.

Intimidating burly men in checked suits and homburg hats elbowed their way through the crowds, offering to change their money into dollars and get them a hotel room or a bus or train ticket. There were ragged, barefooted urchins tugging at their clothes begging for money or offering to carry their bags, and a huge negress with a turban on her head urged them to come to her restaurant for something to eat. One stout man wearing a frock coat and top hat blocked their way, insisting that he could take them to a 'swanky apartment' for a small consideration.

Beth might have been tempted to put her trust in someone, for she was hungry and cold, wanting a cup of tea and a sit-down more than anything in the world, but Sam, carrying their luggage, swept her on, brushing aside all these pedlars and warning her to keep a tight hold on her fiddle.

'Annabel's father told me of a hotel to make for,' he said. 'We'll just get away from here and find something to eat, then we'll take a cab to the hotel.'

'What about Jack?' she asked, for she'd turned and seen him trying to catch up with them.

'Jack can look out for himself,' he said sharply.

Chapter Twelve

'I never thought it would be so hard to find somewhere to live,' Sam sighed despairingly. 'Nor that there would be so many people out to cheat us. I really don't know where to turn next.'

Beth was unpicking the lining of her jacket by the light of a candle to get at the last of the money they'd brought from England. As Sam spoke, she looked across to where he sat hunched by the meagre fire, a picture of misery.

They had been in New York for a whole month, but they had not bargained with being the target for quite so many crooks. It was almost as if they were wearing placards saying 'Greenhorn'.

There was the booth down by the docks which invited immigrants to register for work. The form they had to fill in looked official; the man who advised them was smartly dressed and seemed concerned for them. The twenty-dollar fee didn't seem that much, not if it meant they would be sent out to good, well-paid work. But after three days, when no message arrived at their hotel as he'd promised, they called back to the booth, only to find it had gone, and their twenty dollars with it.

Another time they answered an advertisement for accommodation in the newspaper. They met the landlord at the boarding house and were shown two pleasant rooms which they were told the present tenant would be vacating at the end of the week. They paid him twenty-five dollars' advance rent and were given a key. But when they turned up, ready to move in, the key didn't open the front door of the building, and when they managed to rouse one of the other tenants they discovered the man they'd met wasn't the landlord at all. There were no vacant rooms there.

It didn't make them feel any better to discover that dozens of other people had fallen for these tricks too. They had lost what seemed like a fortune to them, and they felt embittered that such trickery was commonplace, yet no one had warned them about it.

There were many other unhappy incidents too, offers of work which turned out to be a hoax, accommodation they rushed to see, only to find it consisted of sharing one room with half a dozen other people. They'd been spun very believable hard luck stories and been talked into 'Sure Thing' gambling games which would make them rich. Mostly they were realistic about the latter, and only risked a dollar at most, but they had fallen for some of the hard luck stories, and realized after they'd parted with money that they'd been suckered.

This hotel was the fourth they'd stayed in, each time moving to somewhere cheaper until they got to this flea-pit in Division Street. But although the room was tiny, grubby, cheerless and cold, they knew it was a palace compared with most of the accommodation on offer to immigrants with little money.

Unless they found work soon, though, they wouldn't be able to afford to stay even here. Sam might not know where to turn to next, but Beth did, and she knew her brother wasn't going to like it.

'We could turn to Jack,' she said quietly, bracing herself for his anger. 'I saw him earlier today.'

'What!' Sam exclaimed, his face darkening.

Beth shrugged. 'I know you don't approve because he's

sweet on me, but he can help us. He's already got a job, he knows people here, and with him on our side we won't be fleeced any more.'

'We don't need help from someone like him,' Sam said woodenly.

'You're holding out for someone from Fifth Avenue to rescue us, I suppose?' Beth said sarcastically. 'Or waiting for the Waldorf to send someone round to beg you to be their new barman?'

'Don't be ridiculous,' he snapped. 'You know how many jobs I've been after.'

'Yes, but they've all been well out of your league,' she retorted bluntly.

Sam had such grand ideas that he'd gone after jobs far beyond his limited experience. He was only eighteen and he'd only ever mended shoes, kept ledgers and served drinks. But he'd got it into his head that he could leap into a top position here just because he was English.

'Don't be a snob about Jack,' she said reprovingly. 'He might be a bit rough and ready but he's a good sort, and he's sharp too. We aren't; we get taken for suckers because we don't know what's what. The only way we are going to make our way in this country is by getting down there with common folk, learn the ropes and then find a way to climb them.'

'We weren't brought up to live in a slum,' he said sullenly. 'Surely you haven't forgotten that place?'

Beth hadn't. She still shuddered at the thought of the area they'd stumbled upon by accident on their first night in the city.

Sam had been given directions to Broadway and a reasonably priced hotel, but they must have taken a wrong turning in the dim light and ended up in the hideous slum area they now knew was the infamous Five Points, named because five streets, including Park and Worth, converged there.

It was a thousand times worse than any slum in Liverpool, a poorly lit, veritable rabbit warren of narrow alleys lined with decaying old houses. Filthy, ragged and barefoot children huddled in doorways, bent old men were hugging open fires on waste ground, and slatternly-looking women yelled abuse as they walked by. The five-storey tenements, which loomed over the older houses like grim fortresses, appeared to house thousands, judging by the cacophony of noise coming from them.

By then it was almost ten in the evening, the stench was like walking through an open sewer and everyone appeared to be drunk or demented. They were approached threateningly several times, harassed for money, and savage-looking dogs snarled at them. They actually feared for their lives.

The following day, in the temporary safety of a neat, clean hotel, they were informed that twenty years earlier, Five Points was said to be the worst slum in the whole world. Even now, in its improved state, it was the last refuge of the desperate, both the poor and criminals. As many as sixteen people could be sharing just one room, gangs of children lived rough on the streets, and hardly a night passed without someone being murdered.

Since then they had explored New York, and while there were many other areas where immigrants lived in substandard and often hideously overcrowded tenements, the terrible sights they'd seen in Five Points were not encountered again.

There were the mansions on Fifth Avenue, beautiful quiet squares with elegant houses, and shops crammed with goods they'd never seen before. Central Park was vast and magnificent, and there were buildings so big and grand they could only stand and stare at them. They marvelled at the elevated railtrack on which the train chugged along over their heads, and at the new, amazingly tall buildings which people called skyscrapers.

The sheer volume of traffic – carts, cabs, carriages and omnibuses – was staggering, as was the number of restaurants, oyster bars and coffee shops. It was such an exciting, noisy, vibrant city, and the huge mixture of different nationalities, all with their own languages, customs, music and cuisines, created an alluring and mesmerizing circus of delights.

Beth felt that if they could just get work and a decent place to live she was sure they could be very happy here.

'I wasn't suggesting we live in Five Points,' she said indignantly, for she was growing tired of her brother seeing the worst in everything. 'You've got to stop comparing everything to back home, Sam. We were really lucky that the Langworthys gave us a home after the fire. But that kind of luck is rare. I sometimes think we might have been served better back then if we'd been forced to live the way most people do; that way we'd be more worldly now. And if you hadn't escaped out of steerage every day on the ship, you might have learned a thing or two about ordinary people.'

He shuddered, and Beth sighed inwardly. It was only in the past few weeks that she had discovered her brother had failings, and she wasn't sure he could overcome them.

It wasn't so much that he was a snob – he didn't actually look down on people. He just believed he was due the better things of life and refused even to consider doing any kind of manual work. He was mesmerized by wealth and in the thrall of anyone who had it, and because he'd charmed himself into second class on the ship so easily, and been favoured by the wealthy customers back at the Adelphi, he couldn't see why his charm wasn't working here.

But Beth could see why. New Yorkers were by and large loud and often aggressive. Sam's appeal was his good looks, soft voice, the twinkle in his blue eyes and his very Englishness. He would do very well with just that if he were already rich and living on Fifth Avenue, but for a man looking for work he needed to project himself as strong and capable.

Jack was working in a slaughterhouse on the East Side. He said it was the hardest work he'd ever done, a stinking, horrible job, but the pay was good and he'd made many friends there. He'd offered to get Sam in too, but Beth knew her brother would sooner die of starvation than work there.

It had been so good to see Jack today. They had made a pact on arrival in New York that they would meet one month to the day on Castle Green, which was close to where they disembarked, at half past five.

Beth hadn't really expected Jack to turn up – a whole month in a new city was enough to make anyone forget hasty promises. But there he was, looking very smart in a checked jacket, well-pressed trousers and polished boots. He told her he'd managed to get off a couple of hours earlier by telling his boss a relative of his was arriving from England.

He was honest enough to say he was living in a tenement, sharing a room with six other people, but he pointed out that he'd lived in similar places back in Liverpool. He laughingly admitted he'd got his jacket and trousers from a second-hand shop and sweet-talked a girl in a laundry to press them for him. But however awful his job sounded, it was clear he'd really thrown himself into his new life. He looked healthier and more muscular than he had on the ship, and much more confident.

Beth had left him feeling a great deal more hopeful, not just because they planned to meet again in a few days, but because he'd made some suggestions as to how she and Sam could get on their feet.

'Look, Sam,' Beth said in a firm tone. 'Why don't you get a barman's job on the Bowery? There's plenty of work going there.'

His eyes opened wide in alarm. 'I couldn't work in one of those rough houses.'

'Almost all the bars in New York are a bit rough,' she said patiently. She hadn't been in any herself but Jack had told her this. 'You need experience before anyone will give you work in a top hotel or private members' club. And I've got a plan. If you were working as a barman, I could come in and play my fiddle there.'

Sam looked at her in horror. 'On the Bowery! With all those –'

'Yes, rough men.' Beth cut him short. 'I couldn't do it without someone to look out for me, but I know those men will really like my playing. Besides, some of the men who drink down there own saloons uptown. We'd get ourselves noticed. Not many saloon owners could have a handsome gent like you behind their bar with a sister who gets everyone's toes tapping. We'd be a real money-spinner for them.'

These were words right out of Jack's mouth. But she wasn't going to tell Sam that because she knew he'd dismiss the idea out of hand.

'You'd really want to play in one of those dives?' Sam said incredulously.

'Why not? It's as good a training ground as anywhere, better than a snooty place where some clever devil would notice if I hit a wrong note,' she said defiantly. 'You know I've been to almost all the respectable hotels to ask if they need a pianist. They take one look at me and show me the door without even inviting me to show what I can do. I've been to shops, restaurants, oyster bars and no one will even give me a job washing dishes. Besides, I'd rather play the fiddle. If I got a name for myself on the Bowery it might change everything.'

'They'll think you're a whore down there,' Sam said disapprovingly. 'I couldn't watch over you if I was behind the bar.'

'It would be enough that men knew you were my brother,' she insisted, for this was what Jack believed. He also said he'd be around, and all his chums too. 'I'll be fine – a man would find it hard to do anything improper to me while I'm playing a fiddle.'

Sam said nothing, but she sensed he was weakening, if only because he thought her fiddle-playing might enhance his own image.

'Let's give it a try,' she wheedled. 'I was told Heaney's is one of the best bars, and they need a barman. What have we got to lose? We do one night, see how it goes, and if you hate it, we don't go back.'

Jack had said that Sam would be a magnet for all the dancing girls in that area and he thought he'd soon come round once he was the centre of attention. Beth wasn't too happy about girls like that going after her brother, but then she'd be around to watch over him too.

'All right,' he said sourly. 'But it will be your fault if something terrible happens.'

'What could be more terrible than to be starving and homeless?' she said sharply. 'And that's what we'll be once our money runs out.'

At eight o'clock the following night, for all her brave talk, Beth was terrified.

*

She and Sam had gone into Heaney's at midday and asked Pat 'Scarface' Heaney, the owner, for work. He was a short but extremely muscular man in his forties, and what little hair he had left was ginger. He wore a bright green waistcoat which, though startling, didn't detract from the formidable razor scar running from his right eye right down to his chin. Jack had told Beth that he received this in his youth when incarcerated in the Tombs, the huge prison built to solve the problems of Five Points, where Heaney had been a gang leader.

The Bowery was a street of entertainment, lined with bars, music and dance halls, theatres, German beer halls and restaurants. At night the sidewalks were crammed with stalls, selling anything from hot dogs to fruit and candy. There were also what were called 'museums', though in fact they were freak shows, where for a few cents you could see the Bearded Woman, dwarfs, trained monkeys and other curiosities. Prostitutes mingled with the crowds, and inevitably there were pickpockets too. But in the main it was the playground of ordinary working folk.

Jack had said that Heaney's clientele was comparable to those who drank in the big, noisy, ale houses near Lime Street Station in Liverpool – cab drivers, carpenters and engineers. He'd also pointed out that Heaney's was one of the smartest saloons on the Bowery, with its shiny mahogany bar, huge mirrors behind it and a great deal of well-polished brass and clean sawdust on the floor.

Sam looked quite relieved when he saw it, for the men drinking at the bar were ordinary, not the bruisers or degenerates he'd expected.

Pat Heaney clearly liked the look of Sam right off, and after only a few questions, he told him to get behind the bar and serve the customers while he talked to Beth.

'I'll be straight with you,' Heaney said, swigging down a large tumbler of whisky and keeping one eye on Sam. 'Girls, specially pretty ones, are trouble in a bar. But I like the idea of a girl fiddler, and you've got spunk coming in here and asking to play when yer just off the boat.'

Beth lied and said she'd played publicly in Liverpool but he waved his hand in a gesture that said he didn't care what she'd done before, he was only interested in what she could achieve in his saloon.

'I'll give you one chance,' he said. 'Tonight at eight. If they like you, you're on; if not, then finis. Out you go. I can't say fairer than that. I'll get one of the boys to hand round the hat for you, and I'll take half of it.'

It struck Beth that the odds were all in his favour. He wasn't going to lose even if she played badly.

He was an intimidating man, not just because of his scar, or the muscles that showed under his thin shirt, but through his blunt manner and the way he looked at her. There was no light in his pale brown eyes, just cold calculation. He asked why they'd come to America, and when she said both their parents had died and they wanted a new start he made no comment, not even to say he was sorry for their loss.

Instinct told her he had no soft side, and that she and Sam would have to tread very carefully with him. Jack had recommended they tried this bar first because Heaney considered himself 'the man' on the Bowery: he liked to be first with anything different, and a girl fiddler was certainly that. But Jack had also warned her he had a reputation as a dangerous man to cross.

'How long will you want me to play for?' Beth asked cautiously.

He took his eyes off Sam for a minute or two to give her another cold stare. 'That depends on if they like you,' he said. 'If I wave my hands after the first three numbers, you go. If not, you play for an hour. At the end of that I'll tell you what next. Right?'

Beth nodded nervously.

'Got something more colourful to wear than that?' he asked sharply, looking at her brown coat with disdain. 'They won't like you if you look like a school marm.'

Beth gulped. She had very few clothes and all of them were dark in colour. 'I'll try and find something,' she said.

He got to his feet and looked down at her. 'Off you go then. Be back at eight sharp. Your brother can stay on.'

She hesitated at the door, looking back at Sam. He was polishing a glass as Heaney spoke to him. He glanced around at her as the man walked away and made a cheerful thumbs-up sign. But she saw a flicker of anxiety in his face which she guessed was because he wouldn't be able to escort her here tonight.

'I'll be fine,' she mouthed, and gave him the thumbs-up sign back.

That afternoon she practised her fiddle for a couple of hours and made a list of all the numbers she knew best so she wouldn't run out of ideas that evening. She was very nervous, for there was a world of difference between playing when she chose to, and in front of a room full of strangers.

Later she washed her hair and went through her clothes as it was drying. She guessed Heaney expected her to wear something flashy, but she had nothing like that. The brightest dress was one Mrs Langworthy had passed on to her just before they left; she'd said at the time it might be useful if Beth got invited to a party or a dance. It was slightly shiny with green and white stripes, a rather low neckline, leg-of-mutton sleeves and a small bustle. Beth had been dying to put it on as it was very pretty, although she wasn't entirely happy about wearing it to a saloon full of men. But she thought that if she sewed a little lace across the low neckline, at least she wouldn't show any cleavage.

At half past seven she was ready, stays pulled in extra tight, her hair left loose on her shoulders, a couple of green ribbons in her hair and her boots polished. She hadn't been able to button up her dress at the back, and had to go and ask the woman in the room below to do it for her. But she was pleased with the end result: she didn't look like a loose woman, but neither did she look like a schoolmistress. The combination of nerves and excitement had given her a rosy glow, and her hair was very shiny.

Picking up her fiddle case, she locked the room and left.

Pat Heaney leaned back on the door that led to a room he kept for private gambling and watched the girl performing, a smile twitching at the corner of his lips.

He hadn't expected much. Her soft English voice, the clarity of her skin and the innocence in her eyes had all made him think she would play like one of those stiff-backed spinsters in a drawing room. How wrong he was!

The first surprise, when she arrived bang on time, was how she looked with her hair down. A real stunner, with shiny black curls tumbling on to her shoulders, nothing like the prim look she'd had this morning with her little governess's hat and her hair scraped up under it. He liked her dress too, a classy little number, though he'd rather rip off the lace across her chest and see what lay beneath it.

She was so scared when she got here that he thought she'd make a run for it. And her brother didn't help by keeping looking round at her all the time while she was waiting to go on. Was he really her brother? They weren't alike, except for their English accents.

But then he had announced her, and instead of faltering as he expected she almost leapt up on to the stage. She paused with that bow up in the air just long enough for every man in the place to turn and look at her. Then down it came and she was off and running, notes so sweet and fast he could hardly believe what he was hearing.

Maybe he had heard better fiddle players, but they'd never been pretty like her. She didn't just play with her arms and hands, but her whole body, undulating with the music, better than any of those hoochy-coochy girls he'd seen at the Burlesque.

She was on her third number now, and she had everyone's attention. Talking forgotten, drinks not quite getting to their open mouths, feet tapping, heads nodding, every man jack of them was in a trance.

She almost danced as she played, bending, swaying, those hips moving in a way that was sending messages down to his cock. He liked the way she tossed her hair back from her face, the way little strands stuck to the sweat on her cheeks. It was enough to make a man want to jump up beside her and stroke it back.

Liking something this much was something Pat wasn't used to. Knowing he had a winning hand at poker, sitting down to a big juicy steak, the first whisky of the day – they were about the only things he could really claim to like. He couldn't remember when he'd last listened to music, really listened; he guessed it was back when he was about her age.

Eighteen. He'd had fire in his belly then, always wanting to prove himself, and every nerve end twitching with life. When he wasn't fighting he was fucking; he never knew which he liked best. And there was plenty of both around Five Points.

He could still get a woman whenever he wanted one, and he could have a fight too at any time. But he was getting too old for fighting, and the women were all whores. Yet listening to this girl made him feel juicy again, like he could take on any one of those Young Turks who strutted up and down the street. Like he could take a woman to bed and keep hard all night.

He was going to be cock-o'-the-walk tonight. Every man in here would want to pat him on the back and buy him a drink for getting her in. They were spellbound; she'd wrapped them up like a spider binding a fly in her web. And they'd be back for more night after night.

Pat glanced at her brother. He was quite a find too, good-looking in that fragile, English aristocrat way. He had a nice manner about him, verging on the side of snooty, but with a disarming smile, and he served drinks fast and with style. Pat knew deep down in his bones the lad was honest too, and that was rarer than a horse that didn't shit.

But it wouldn't take long before someone tried to poach the pair of them away. He could see Fingers Malone up the end of the bar; his devious little mind was probably already whirling with plans to get them into his brother's fancy place on Broadway.

So Pat knew he would have to think of some way to keep their loyalty to him.

Chapter Thirteen

'That much?' Beth gasped as Heaney handed over her half of what had been put in the hat for her. It was all in nickels and dimes but it was such a large heap.

'Eight dollars and forty-five cents,' Heaney said. 'Do you want me to change it up for you?'

Beth nodded, too astounded to speak. She had played three hour-long sets, with a break between them. It was nearly one in the morning now and she was exhausted.

'Don't expect to get that much every night,' Heaney said dryly. 'You were a novelty tonight and it's Saturday. Come Monday it might be just nickels, but I like you, so I'll promise you'll never leave here without two dollars.'

'You want me back on Monday?'

'Yup. Monday, Friday and Saturday. Might get some other players in at the weekend too.'

'How will the money be divided up then?' Beth asked, fearing she would get a far smaller percentage.

He gave her a calculating look, perhaps surprised she'd dared to ask. 'You leave that to me,' he replied. 'But as I said, I'll see you right. You can go now, and your brother too. I wouldn't want a pretty little thing like you walking home alone.'

'He's a strange man,' Sam said reflectively as they walked home arm in arm. The Bowery was still every bit as busy as it had been early in the evening; drunks wove their staggering way through the more sober on the pavements, narrowly missing the food stalls. Music and guffaws of laughter wafted out from bars, the pounding sound of dancing feet from somewhere unseen, and shouted greetings from one group of people to another across the street. The air was heavy with odours, fried onions on the hot-dog stands vying with beer, tobacco, cheap scent and sweat, along with horse droppings from the cabs. 'He hardly spoke to me all day. I didn't know if he was pleased with how I was shaping up or not. Then he stuck a five-dollar bill in my hand and said I was to come back on Monday. Does that mean I get the job for as long as I want it? And how much will I be paid each week?'

'I think he's slippery, so we'll have to speak up and ask such things,' Beth said thoughtfully. 'I know the audience liked me, but he didn't say anything.'

'That'll be because he wants to keep the upper hand. Of course he liked you – I watched his face when you were playing. Just hope he doesn't have any ideas about you being his woman.'

'Surely not? He's far too old,' Beth exclaimed.

Sam chuckled. 'Most of the men watching you had thoughts like that. I could see it in their faces. I can see I've got to watch out for my little sister.'

'Who would have thought it?' Beth said dreamily as they turned into a side street to cut down to Division Street. 'A year ago we were frantic with worry about money, and now here we are in America.'

'Still worried about money.' Sam chuckled again. 'And we're working in a saloon! Papa would turn in his grave.'

'I think he'd be proud that we've been brave,' Beth said indignantly. 'Besides, the saloon is just a first step. We'll find a way to make our fortune.'

*

Fortunes, Beth found, weren't made so easily. By October, six months after they'd arrived in New York, she was still playing three nights a week in Heaney's and by day she worked in a second-hand clothes shop on the Bowery. In a good week she earned as much as thirty dollars, but the good weeks were rare; mostly it was only around eighteen dollars. Yet this, she had discovered, was far above what most women could hope to earn. Most single women worked as cleaners, shop assistants and waitresses, and all were badly paid and worked very long hours.

For married women with children, there was no choice but to work at home for people who exploited their desperation to earn some money. Some did piecework for garment manufacturers, working a fourteen-hour day at least in crowded, badly lit rooms. Others made matchboxes and got everyone in the family to help. Women like this were lucky to earn a dollar a day, and most got half that.

Beth didn't take her second job because of the money, but because she was lonely at home all day with nothing to do. She had gone into the second-hand shop close to Heaney's one day to see if she could find a new dress. Ira Roebling, the old Jewish woman who owned it, was very friendly and chatty, and by the time Beth left the shop, with a red satin dress in a parcel, she'd given Ira a potted version of her life story, heard some of Ira's, and had been offered the job.

Ira had come over from Germany back in the 1850s with her husband and his parents. They had owned a very successful pastry shop for years, but a year after both her in-laws had passed on from old age, her husband died in an influenza epidemic, and without him Irma couldn't manage the baking of the pastries. She turned to selling second-hand clothes because she loved clothes and had many contacts prepared to sell her their old finery. With each ship bringing in new immigrants, there were always people wanting cheap clothes, and just as many who wanted to sell theirs.

Ira was a shrewd, some said mean, old girl. She gave the very lowest price for clothes and sold them for the highest. Beth guessed her to be in her sixties, though it was hard to tell as she was slender, strong and very energetic. She always wore black, including a felt cloche hat which she never took off even when it was hot. But however eccentric she was, she was funny and quick-witted. Beth had seen her cast her black shoe-button eyes over a row of figures and add them up in a trice, and she never forgot anything, not the name of a customer, nor an item of clothing in her shop. The number of people who came in and out during the day just for a chat was testimony to the esteem in which she was held in the neighbourhood.

Ira did most of the selling, and Beth sorted the clothes into sizes, did the odd repair and generally kept the shop in order. This was no mean feat as it was crammed from floor to ceiling with stuff. There were huge boxes of shoes, all jumbled in together, and one of the first things Beth did was tie them up in pairs and sort them by colour and size. She often tried clothes on too, something Irma actively encouraged, for as she pointed out, they couldn't sell things unless they knew what they looked like on.

Ira lived above her shop, and her three rooms were just as chaotic. During the summer when it was unbearably hot, Beth wondered how she didn't pass out from lack of air, for she never opened her windows for fear of someone climbing in and robbing her. But although Ira was mean in many ways, never throwing anything out and haggling with customers over prices till the pips squeaked, she always gave

Beth something to eat at midday. Sometimes it was delicious chicken soup she'd made herself, but more often it was hot salt beef sandwiches from a Jewish delicatessen along the street, and some fresh fruit. She said she didn't think Beth ate enough and no man would want her for his wife until she'd put some meat on her bones.

Beth had laughed at that, for she saw Jack at least twice a week, and she knew he thought she was perfect the way she was. She liked him too, his sense of humour, reliability and the way he looked after her, and she supposed that if a girl spent that much time with a boy back in England, it would be considered almost an engagement.

But Beth was reluctant to encourage Jack beyond friendship.

Ira thought this wise, not because she didn't approve of Jack, in fact she liked him, but she felt Beth was too young to be serious about anyone.

'There are so many hundreds of nice young men out there,' she would say with a roguish twinkle in her eye. 'Enjoy your youth, it doesn't last very long.'

But Ira wasn't happy about Beth playing at Heaney's. 'He's rotten to the core,' she'd say emphatically. 'You must never be alone with him, and make sure your brother never lets him do any favours for him, otherwise when he calls them in, Sam will be in deep trouble.'

Beth *was* always careful to keep her distance from Heaney, for he made her flesh crawl. He looked at her as if he was mentally stripping her clothes away, and she felt his eyes on her all the time she was playing. But though she wished she could leave his bar and go to work for someone she liked and felt comfortable with, she knew he would make her regret it.

By all accounts Pat Heaney took slights very seriously. It

was rumoured that he had killed several men, and crippled many more, just for talking about him behind his back or refusing to obey his orders.

He had no real friends, only lackeys who supported him because they were afraid to do otherwise. According to Jack, he controlled dozens of prostitutes, taking at least half of what they earned. He owned two of the most dilapidated tenements in the Canal Street area and he charged such exorbitant rents that his tenants had to sublet again and again to be able to pay him. He had a hand in the thriving opium dens, dog-fighting and bare-knuckle fights. Even if only half the stories about his revenge attacks on people who had fallen foul of him were true, he was an exceptionally dangerous man. Beth was certain that if she left to work somewhere else in New York some 'accident' would befall her. He would never let her be a success anywhere but in his saloon.

Sam thought she was allowing her imagination to get the better of her. He not only didn't believe the man was dangerous, he felt he was Heaney's right-hand man because he let him run the bar without interference.

But Beth could see why this was. Despicable as Heaney was, he wasn't a fool. He knew Sam was honest and capable, and just as big an attraction to the chorus girls from the local theatres as Beth was to the male customers. She would often peep through the door during her rest period before the last set, and there were always three or four of these girls flirting with Sam. And of course Sam loved the attention.

But then Beth knew she was guilty too of loving the attention she got. There was no bigger thrill than to have an audience in her thrall, to know she was desired by most of the men who cheered her rapturously. It was good to put on a pretty dress, to know she could afford to buy another any time she wanted to. She was doing something most women could only dream of.

Soon after starting at Heaney's, she and Sam had found a room on the top floor in a tenement on Houston Street, sharing the kitchen with an Italian couple who had the other room in the apartment. To almost everyone they knew, a room for just two was luxury, and although Beth often complained because there was never any peace and quiet in the building with its five floors, each with four apartments and an average of eight to ten people in each, she thanked her lucky stars that it was only noise she had to put up with, not a room full of people.

The room wasn't much, with its stained old wallpaper, and it was like an oven during the heat of summer, but Beth had made it homely. She begged some theatre posters to cover up the stained walls, found a few sticks of furniture among the many second-hand shops in the neighbourhood, and Ira had let her run up some curtains on her sewing machine and given her an old bedspread to string up between their two beds to give them a little privacy.

Houston Street was a poor area, with lines of washing hanging from every window, scrawny, grubby children play- ing in the street, a grog shop on the corner, and she often saw women trudging up the street with huge bundles of clothing on their backs that they'd sewn at home. But it was a lively, cheerful neighbourhood. On hot evenings people sat out on the front steps and chatted, the women shared child-care duties with one another, and helped the Italians and Germans with their English. Everyone she spoke to was glad they'd come to America and believed that by working hard they would achieve all their goals.

The worst thing about the tenement was that there were

only two privies out the back for them all, stinking, horrible places that made Beth shudder and cover her nose when she entered. But Sam always emptied the slops pail each morning before he went to work, and their room overlooked the street, so the smell from the privies didn't come through their windows. The apartment was also so high up that they weren't troubled by rats, as many of those on the first and second floors were.

On days when she felt irritated by the noise and smells of cooking in the tenement, or daydreamed of the luxury of having a real bathroom with hot and cold running water like the one in Falkner Square, she reminded herself that these things weren't really important, and how much better her life had become since she'd been in America.

It would've been unthinkable for her to play her fiddle in a saloon back home, where there was none of the freedom for young women like there was here. She could meet Jack alone for a couple of hours in the evening or on his day off without anyone raising an eyebrow. She had more money than she could ever have dreamed of back in England, and no one knew about how her father died either. Then there was the huge variety of food available here. She rarely cooked anything herself for it was just as cheap to buy something out. She loved the hot dogs, baked potatoes, doughnuts, pancakes and waffles. A Chinese man had a stall selling noodles which she adored, and she liked the big bowls of spaghetti with a tomato and meat sauce at the café owned by Italians. Hardly a day went by without Ira introducing her to something new: pretzels, pastrami, salt beef, fish balls or some kind of German sausage.

The only thing from England she really missed was Molly, and that was like a dull ache inside her all the time. She couldn't walk past a mother with a plump, dark-haired little girl without stopping to speak, and in those brief moments she felt acute envy.

'I could give you a baby of your own,' Jack said once when they had been together and he'd watched her talk to a child. It was said light-heartedly, for every time they kissed he said he dreamed of making love to her.

Beth had laughed, for only a couple of days earlier she'd been talking to Amy and Kate, the two young women who lived in the apartment beneath her. They were a few years older than her, and appeared to have a great deal more experience with men than she did, but they were both funny and lively and Beth was very glad she had made two new friends.

The conversation that day had been about lines men used to get their way with girls. Amy recalled that her first sweetheart had said, 'I won't get you in the family way,' and Kate said hers had tried to blackmail her with 'You would if you really loved me.'

Beth thought Amy would find it very funny that Jack had turned the old line around.

But then Jack was a real treasure. He never complained about anything, not about his work, his living conditions, or her holding him at arm's length. Always an optimist, he could see the funny side of everything. He made Beth laugh, she could tell him anything, and she trusted him implicitly. During the summer they had often taken a walk on hot evenings down to the East River to try to get some cooler air. Neither of them had been prepared for how hot New York could be; in Liverpool there had always been a breeze from the sea, even on the hottest days.

They'd watch gangs of young boys diving into the murky water, probably the only bath they ever had, for these boys lived on the streets – they were known as street Arabs – sleeping in doorways and foraging for food.

With an ice cream each from a stall, they would talk about how cold it had been on deck on the ship coming over from England.

'In the winter we'll talk about how hot it was this summer just to warm ourselves up,' Jack would say.

It was an easy, uncomplicated relationship, for they were the very best of friends, but Beth always felt a little nervous when Jack began kissing her. She liked the tingly feeling she got in her belly, the way she seemed to melt into his arms and want to stay there for ever, but she was afraid where it might lead.

Amy had asked her once if she loved him, and Beth hadn't known how to reply. She looked forward to seeing him and was always glad when he came to Heaney's on Saturday night to watch her play. But she wasn't sure that was what people called love. He didn't make her heart beat any faster, nor had she gone off her food, the way it was in romantic books.

Jack was in the bar when Beth came out of the back room to play her final set on Saturday night. It was raining outside and he must have only just come in, for even across the big room she could see how wet his hair was. She waved before she jumped up on the stage to join the pianist.

She always enjoyed the last set on Saturday night. The crowd were mellow with drink, they hadn't got to work the next day, and they showed their appreciation with loud clapping and stamping. She'd also come to love having Amos playing with her. He was a negro from Louisiana, and he could play the piano like no one else she'd ever heard. Once they got going they fed off each other and took the tunes to new realms.

That night was even better than usual. The audience

172

cheered, clapped and hollered at every number, and Beth felt she had them eating out of her hand. She had difficulty ending it, for they kept calling for an encore. She did one, then another, before they finally let her go.

As she elbowed her way through the crowd towards the door to the back room where she'd left her coat, someone caught hold of her elbow.

To her astonishment it was the handsome man from the ship who had been with the married woman.

'Miss Discretion didn't tell me she was a fiddle player,' he said.

In the first week or so after arriving in New York, Beth had wondered what happened between him and Clarissa, but she certainly hadn't expected ever to see him again. But there he was, his English voice a reminder of home, and his appearance even more striking than it had been on their first meeting. He was wearing a sharply tailored dark green jacket and beneath it a fancy embroidered waistcoat.

'What on earth's brought you here?' she asked.

'I'm on business,' he said, but the way he glanced towards the back room, where she knew Heaney held card games, suggested what his business was. 'How did you come to be working for Heaney?'

'My brother and I just came in here and asked for work,' she replied, and pointed out Sam behind the bar. 'We've been here for six months now.'

All at once Jack was pushing his way through the crowd. 'Sam asked me to take you home tonight,' he said with a wide smile. 'He's got to work late.'

'Fine.' Beth acknowledged him with a nod, but looked back at the man from the boat. 'What happened with Clarissa?'

He shrugged. 'It sort of fizzled out once we landed.'

Beth could see Jack was growing edgy and she really didn't know why she wanted to hold this man's attention a little longer anyway. 'I've got to go,' she said. 'Mr Heaney doesn't like me talking to his customers.'

'It was good to see you again,' he said holding out his hand. 'Especially to find you were so talented.'

She put her hand in his and the touch of his skin on hers sent a shiver down her spine. 'And to see you. Good luck at the game tonight.'

'Who was that man?' Jack asked as they walked to Houston Street. The heavy rain had emptied the streets of people and their footsteps sounded very loud.

'Just a man who was on the ship.'

'I never saw him.'

'He was in first class. We spoke once when I was on deck,' she replied.

'So what would a toff be going in Heaney's for?'

Beth stopped short and pulled on Jack's arm till he was facing her. 'Gambling?' she suggested sarcastically. 'But he was as surprised to see me again as I was to see him. I don't know anything about him, not even his name, so don't get jealous.'

'I wasn't,' he retorted indignantly. 'It just looked as if there was something between you.'

'Nothing more than surprise,' she said shortly.

'Can I come in for a little while?' Jack asked as they got to her house.

'No, it's too late,' Beth said, taking her fiddle case from him.

'I'd be really quiet,' he said.

He had that boyish, eager look which usually made her smile, but for some reason it made her cross this time.

'It isn't that I'm afraid of you making a noise,' she said impatiently. 'It's how it looks after one in the morning. And Sam not being around.'

Sam still didn't entirely approve of her friendship with Jack, but it suited him to tolerate it, for Jack walking Beth home at night meant he didn't have to worry about her. He wouldn't even know if Jack came up for a while because he often stayed out all night himself.

'I only wanted to cuddle and kiss you,' Jack said dejectedly. 'It's too cold and wet to do that out here. You must know I'd never try to make you do anything you weren't happy about.'

Beth moved closer to him and kissed him on the lips. The gas street light made his face seem even more angular, his scar more livid, and gave his skin a sinister yellow tinge. She felt no desire for him at all and that made her feel bad about herself. 'I know that, I'm just tired and a bit grumpy, and you're very wet, so go on home.'

'I love you, Beth,' he said, catching hold of her face between his two hands. 'I think I fell for you the moment I first saw you. Don't you feel the same?'

He couldn't have picked a worse moment to tell her he loved her, and instead of being touched, she felt irritated. If she said no he'd be deeply hurt, but if she said yes she might be starting something she was likely to regret.

'This isn't the time, Jack,' she said wearily.

He took a step back. Rain was shining on his face and hair and his mouth was set in a hurt, straight line. 'There isn't going to be a time for us, is there?'

He turned and walked away then, not even glancing back to see if she was watching him.

Chapter Fourteen

When Beth woke up on Sunday morning to find it was still raining just as heavily as it had been the previous evening, her first thought was of Jack. Since she and Sam moved into Houston Street, he'd always come round here on Sundays to take her out somewhere.

She pulled back the dividing curtain, only to find Sam's bed hadn't been slept in again. All at once she realized how dependent she'd become on Jack's company and how lonely it would be without him. Knowing he'd be too bruised to come calling today, or any day, unless she apologized and told him she loved him, she pulled the covers up tightly to her neck and tried to go back to sleep.

Sam didn't arrive back until two and was very surprised to find her still in bed.

'Are you ill?' he asked, sitting down beside her.

Beth told him about Jack. 'There just didn't seem to be anything to get up for,' she finished.

'If you do really care for him then you'd better get round to his place and make it up with him,' Sam said, rubbing his stubbly chin. 'But it's always been my view you could do very much better than him.'

Beth sat up and glowered at her brother. 'Just tell me how I'll meet someone suitable. Heaney never lets me talk to anyone. You never introduce me to any of your friends. And it wouldn't be right to go round to Jack's and give him false hope just because I don't want to be on my own.'

Sam looked thoughtful. 'Practically every man that comes into Heaney's would like a chance to meet you. But none of them are good enough for you either.'

'Why should you decide that?' she snapped. 'I bet whoever you were with last night isn't right for you either, but that doesn't seem to bother you.'

'It's different for men.'

'Well, I don't see why it should be,' she said indignantly. 'If I can perform in one of the busiest saloons in New York, I don't see why I can't mix with anyone I choose to.'

Sam just looked at her for a moment. 'Get up and get dressed, we'll go out,' he said at length. 'I don't like to see you looking sad.'

On Monday evening when Beth went to Heaney's, she found Jack had been in earlier and left a note for her.

She had never seen his writing before, and the childlike print and terrible spelling were confirmation of the gulf between their upbringings. Yet however uneducated Jack was, his deep feelings for her shone through. He said he would still like to be her friend and he wouldn't expect anything else of her.

Beth was sorry she'd hurt him, and her instinct was to write back immediately and say there would always be room in her life for him. But she knew if she did they'd just slip back into the old routine, and before long it would erupt again. Perhaps it would be best to do nothing for a while.

On Tuesday at Ira's they had a big clear-out of summer clothes. Items that were too shabby or unfashionable would be collected by a man with a stall in Mulberry Bend, down in Five Points. The good things were packed away in boxes to be stored until next spring.

It was nice to be busy, and Beth realized at five o'clock,

when she put on her coat and hat to leave, that she hadn't thought about Jack once all day.

She had only just stepped out of the shop and closed the door behind her when she saw the man from the ship leaning nonchalantly against the lamp-post and grinning at her. 'Hello, Miss Discretion!' he said.

Beth was dumbfounded to see him. But she instinctively knew it wasn't by chance.

'How about coming and having a cup of coffee with me?' he said. 'Unless of course you've got something better to do?'

'But I don't even know your name,' she said.

'Well, that's easy enough to fix.' He grinned. 'It's Theodore Cadogan. Known to my friends as Theo.'

'Well, Mr Cadogan,' she said, suppressing the desire to laugh that he'd had the cheek to ask around to find out where she was. 'What makes you think I'm in the habit of going off with men I barely know?'

'Then how can you get to know anyone? I did only suggest coffee, not selling you to the white slave trade.'

'Who told you where I was?'

'Your brother, and I promised him as a gentleman that my intentions were strictly honourable.'

Beth doubted his honourable intentions, but Sam must have liked and approved of him or he wouldn't have told him where to find her. Besides, he was so handsome and he made her feel bubbly inside. 'Just a cup of coffee then,' she agreed.

An hour later they were still in the coffee shop. Beth was calling him Theo and he was calling her Beth. She had told him of the events which led up to her coming to America, and he had told her that his father was a wealthy landowner in Yorkshire, but as the younger son he wouldn't inherit the estate.

'Father wanted me to study law, but that bored me,' he said with a theatrical yawn. 'Mother thought I should go into the Church, but I certainly had no calling for that. I toyed with the idea of the army too.'

'So what made you come here?' Beth asked.

He rolled his eyes in a manner that said he didn't want to admit to the real reason.

'It was Clarissa, wasn't it?' she laughed.

He sighed. 'Not entirely. But let's just say I was duped into believing her marriage was an unhappy one. I booked to come on the same ship as them, imagining foolishly that it would all work out and he'd just let her go when we got to New York. But she was only toying with me, she never had any intention of leaving him.'

'Oh dear, Theo,' Beth tutted, 'you must have been destroyed.'

'Only dented, my dear,' he said with a grin. 'And once here in the land of opportunity, I realized I'd found the perfect outlet for my talents, and I certainly don't regret coming.'

'What are your talents?' she asked teasingly. 'That is, apart from being something of a charmer and ladies' man?'

'I play cards rather well,' he said.

Beth laughed. 'Will that make you a fortune?'

'I hope so.' He smiled roguishly. 'It has stood me in good stead so far.'

'If you play with men like Heaney you'll get fleeced,' she said.

'You underestimate me, my dear,' he said. 'I intend to own gambling places, not lose my shirt to them.'

He laughed at her look of surprise. 'And you, my pretty little gypsy, can play your fiddle in my very first one if you wish. I feel it was fate that we met up again, and that our fortunes will be inextricably linked.'

Beth felt fluttery inside as his hand reached out across the table and took hers. She thought he was going to kiss it, but instead he turned it and studied her palm, tracing the lines on it with his forefinger.

'There is great passion in your hand,' he said in a low voice. 'I see strength and courage too. Money will come to you, but love, both of men and your music, will always be more important.'

Beth giggled. 'You sound like a gypsy now! Can you see a husband and children?'

'Is that what you want?'

'Don't all women?'

'You are all told that is what you want from an early age,' he said thoughtfully. 'Our society encourages that idea too and creates no alternatives. But I think it would be such a waste for you to marry young and spend your life bringing up a brood of children when you have so much talent.'

He was still holding her hand, and slowly he bent his head down and put his lips to it. Beth felt a sharp pull inside her, a hot flush washed all over her and her skin tingled. She had to resist the urge to reach out and run her fingers through his hair. Instantly she recognized her feelings were the start of passion.

Three days later, Beth was with Ira in the back room of the shop where they repaired and laundered clothes, when Ira asked the name of the man Beth was seeing.

'I know you are seeing someone,' she said, looking sharply at Beth. 'You've been lost in a daydream since Wednesday.'

Beth lifted the flat iron from the top of the stove and spat on it to see if it was hot enough to iron the white cotton petticoat. She didn't want to answer Ira's question; she felt if she voiced anything about Theo, especially her feelings towards him, it might jinx everything.

He had asked her to supper when they eventually came out of the coffee shop, and much later he had walked her home to Houston Street. It was a cold evening and the street was deserted, just a handful of young men standing around the grog shop on the corner.

'I suppose you live somewhere smart?' she said as they came to a stop outside her place.

'Not really,' he said, and reached out to caress her cheek. 'Don't be embarrassed by being poor, Beth. The will to succeed is always strongest when you have the least.'

His hand on her cheek made that strange pulling feeling in her belly return. She wanted him to kiss her so badly that she felt faint with it. She didn't even care who saw her.

'Will I see you again?' she asked weakly, knowing that was too forward but unable to stop herself.

He kissed her then, as though it was his answer to her question. His lips touched hers, so gently at first, awakening every nerve ending in her body. Then, just as she was aching for something stronger, his arms went around her tightly, the tip of his tongue insinuated its way into her mouth, and she seemed to erupt inside.

She couldn't help but press herself closer to him; his kiss was so thrilling that her body was acting on its own volition. She could feel her nipples hardening and a kind of throbbing in her private parts, and she shamelessly slid her tongue into his mouth too.

It was he who extricated himself first. 'You kiss as beautifully as you play the fiddle,' he said softly. 'You'd make any man lose his head.'

Then he said he had to go and she remained there on the doorstep dizzy with desire, watching him walk back down the street. He moved with the grace of a panther, straight-backed, chin up. As he got to the street light on the corner he turned and waved and she felt her heart might burst.

Sleep eluded her that night, for she relived that kiss over and over again until her body was on fire. She was reminded of a neighbour's cat back in Liverpool that lay writhing on its back out in the backyard, making an odd, crying sound. Her mother had said it was in season and she threw a bucket of water over it to make it go away, for two tom cats were sitting on the wall watching the display. Mama said she didn't want any of that nastiness in her backyard. Beth hadn't understood the significance of how the female cat was behaving then, but she did now.

Since she was old enough to be curious about love, marriage and having children, she'd been led to believe that it was men who got the pleasure and women tolerated the act for their sake. Even pragmatic Miss Clarkson hadn't suggested otherwise. Her mother's dying confession was the first inkling Beth had that perhaps women could want or need sex, but she had been too horrified by the consequences of that illicit affair to have any sympathy.

'Not answering my question won't deter me,' Ira said, coming closer and putting one hand on Beth's shoulder. 'It's quite normal for a girl of your age to fall in love, but I know it isn't Jack you are mooning over. So who is this new man, and where did you meet him?'

'He's called Theodore Cadogan and I met him coming over on the ship,' Beth said somewhat reluctantly. 'I only spoke to him once then because he was in first class.

But I ran into him again last week in Heaney's and when I came out of here on Tuesday evening he was waiting for me.'

'So he's a gentleman?'

Beth nodded glumly.

'What was he doing in Heaney's then?'

Beth sighed; she had seen that question coming. 'He had gone there for a card game.'

Ira sucked in her cheeks. 'A gambler, eh! Well, they are usually very entertaining, I'll give you that. But you keep your head, girl, I wouldn't want to see you led astray.'

'I really like him,' Beth said weakly.

Ira looked hard at her until Beth blushed. 'I see,' she said at length. 'He's stirred up feelings you don't understand. Is that it?'

Beth just looked at her feet.

Ira laughed. 'You've been told good girls don't have those kind of feelings, I suppose? Well, that's plain daft, there'd be precious few babies come into this world if that was the case! I'll tell how I see it, there aren't women who like it and another bunch who don't, there are just women who've got good lovers and ones who haven't.'

'He isn't my lover,' Beth exclaimed, alarmed that Ira would even think such a thing. 'I've only spent one evening with him.'

Ira chuckled. 'If he can make you feel that way in one chaste evening I'd say you'd better not chance being alone with him, unless of course you want to find out what a good lover can do for a woman.'

Beth squirmed with embarrassment, making Ira laugh louder. 'I know there's plenty who will tell you that you must have a ring on your finger before you try the goods. But I was always glad I tried out my Gunter before marriage.'

'I may never see him again anyway,' Beth said in an attempt to wrap up this conversation which she was finding excruciatingly embarrassing.

'I'm sure you will,' Ira said. 'Not just for your looks or your curvy body, but your gaiety, brains, manner and your fiddle-playing. You are quite a prize, my dear. But you've got to protect yourself. Don't believe everything he tells you, don't loan him any money, don't expect him to marry you, and get some advice about how to stop yourself having a baby. That's been the ruin of many a good woman.'

'I wouldn't do that,' Beth said in horror. 'Risk having a baby, I mean.'

'Don't be so sure.' Ira patted her cheek affectionately. 'In my experience when a woman is physically attracted to a man, she loses her common sense.'

Beth had to play that evening, and Heaney got a cab to take her home as Sam was working late. She woke on Saturday morning from a dream about Theo, and that made her start worrying about what Ira had said on the subject.

She pulled back the curtain slightly between her and Sam's beds. To her disappointment it was empty once again, and the day loomed ahead of her devoid of any company.

When she heard Amy's voice out on the stairs a couple of hours later, Beth called down to ask if she'd like to come up for some tea.

Amy was second-generation American, of Dutch descent, but she'd left the family farm in Connecticut because her father was angry with her for walking out with someone he disapproved of. She had told Beth ruefully that the man in question wouldn't run away with her, and she'd arrived in New York alone. But she appeared to have done all right for herself: she and her friend Kate were always going out, they had nice clothes and they were happy and friendly. Beth often felt a little envious of them as they seemed to have far more fun than she did.

'Tea! Just what I could do with, it's like a crazy house down there,' Amy said as she came into Beth's room. She looked like a farm girl, tall, with broad shoulders and a wide, flat-featured face and flaxen hair. 'They've got even more of their family in now! I ask you, how can six people share one small room? As for getting into the kitchen . . . !'

Amy was referring to the Irish family who had a room in her apartment. There had been two adults and two children from the start, but with another two moving in it had become impossibly crowded. As Amy already shared her small room with Kate, and there were five people in the third room in the apartment, Beth could guess how difficult it was to get into the shared kitchen.

Amy flopped down on Sam's bed and while Beth poured their tea, she ranted for a while about her neighbours. She suspected one of the Irish family was pouring slops down the sink. She said they took her food, and there was always a child crying. 'I've got to find somewhere else to live,' she finished up. 'It's unbearable.'

Beth felt a great deal of sympathy for Amy and Kate, and she was very aware how lucky she and Sam were to have to share only with the Rossinis, who were middle-aged, quiet, clean and good-natured.

But Amy was never one to dwell on her own problems for more than a minute or two. By the time she'd drunk her tea she was making Beth laugh with a story about the grocer round the corner who had been caught with another woman by his wife.

'Where's Sam?' she asked a little later. 'I hardly ever see him these days. Has he got a lady friend?'

'I expect so,' Beth said. 'But he hasn't told me anything about her.'

'She's a lucky lady, whoever she is,' Amy said with a sparkle in her eye. 'He's real handsome.'

'If he's not careful he'll find himself having to get married,' Beth retorted.

'I'm sure he knows how to prevent that.'

'Can you prevent it?' Beth asked innocently.

'Of course, you silly goose.' Amy laughed.

'How?'

'Some men, the more thoughtful ones, withdraw in time,' Amy said airily. 'But I wouldn't trust any of them to do that. They can use a sheath too, but they can split and men don't like them. But most women I know use a douche afterwards. Or there's a little sponge that you pop in before you get going.'

Beth had got to like Amy in the first place because she was so direct and open, but she blushed with embarrassment at these intimate revelations. 'How do you know all this?' she asked.

When Amy's expression tightened, and she didn't come back with one of her usual quips, Beth felt she had to apologize. 'I didn't mean to be nosy, I won't ask you anything more.'

Amy looked back at her and sighed. 'I wish I'd had someone when I was your age to ask such things. But I didn't, so I got pregnant.'

'What did you do?' Beth asked in a scandalized whisper.

'An old woman in the know got rid of it for me,' Amy admitted. 'It was soon after I got to New York. It was terrible. I thought I was going to die.'

'That surely must have put you off men?'

The older girl chuckled. 'Sure, for a while, but then I met

another charmer. Only before I let him get anywhere near me, I got some advice from one of the girls at Rosie's.'

Beth's eyes widened with shock because she'd overheard some men in Heaney's talking about Rosie's, and it was a brothel.

'Don't look like that,' Amy reproved her. 'Not many of us have got a talent like your fiddle-playing to keep us. For some of us it's the only way we can keep a roof over our head. I soon wised up to that and went to work at Rosie's.'

Beth could hardly believe what Amy had just admitted. She had never asked her friend what she did for a living; she just assumed she worked in a store for her clothes were smart.

'Don't tell me you didn't know?' Amy threw back her head and laughed at Beth's shocked expression. 'I thought someone must've told you by now!'

'I don't really talk to anyone but you,' Beth said feebly. 'I would never have guessed. I mean, you're so nice.'

'Whores can be as nice as anyone else,' Amy said with a touch of acid in her voice. 'We don't advertise what we do by walking around half naked with our faces painted either.'

'I didn't mean it like that,' Beth said quickly. 'I meant I thought you worked in a store or a restaurant.'

Amy rolled her eyes skywards. 'Honey, I thought working at Heaney's would've opened your eyes! Few of us girls set out to be whores, but when you're hungry and you ain't got no place to call home, it ain't so bad to take a few dollars for givin' a man a bit of lovin'. Why would I be a maid, or work in a store for five or six dollars a week when I can make that much with one trick?'

Beth was floored. It did of course make sense of why Amy seemed to know so much about men, and indeed why she was often home during the day. She was trying to find something to say that wouldn't sound patronizing or disapproving when Sam arrived home, and Amy immediately got to her feet and said she had to go.

Not wishing to let Amy think she was too prim and proper to deal with such a revelation, Beth went to the door with her. 'I'm sorry,' she said. 'You just took me aback.'

Amy put her hand on Beth's shoulder. 'I guess you're still a greenhorn. You see, I thought you knew and I was so glad that you liked me despite it, but I guess that's the end of us being pals?'

'Not at all,' Beth said, and meant it. 'I like you even more for being honest with me. I just feel a bit foolish that I hadn't guessed before. But you've given me an awful lot to think about.'

'Quit thinking and have a lot more fun,' Amy said with a wide grin. 'Your brother's got the right idea.'

She was gone before Beth could ask her exactly what she meant by that.

Some little time later Beth was making tea and a sandwich for Sam before he left for work when she heard a strange swishing noise coming from their room. She hadn't questioned where he'd been all night, because he'd been washing and shaving, and anyway her mind had been on the things Amy had told her.

But as their room door was partly open she put her head round it to see what the noise was. To her surprise he was sitting at the little table by the window, playing with a deck of cards. As she watched, he shuffled them, then did what looked like elaborate tricks with them, swishing them into a row upon the table, each one partially overlapping the next.

'What's that?' she asked.

'Just practising,' he said without turning his head, and

188

flicking the row of cards so that they all turned over together.

'Is it a trick?'

'No. Just stuff a dealer does. I'm not fast or slick enough yet. But I'm nearly there.'

'Why would you want to do that?' she said, coming right into the room.

He put the cards down and looked up at her. 'Because I want to be a dealer. I want to learn everything about gambling, poker, roulette, faro and all the rest.'

Beth felt her little world had just turned upside down. First she found her only girlfriend was a whore, and now Sam was talking about becoming a gambler.

She could accept that Theo gambled – for gentlemen it was part of their way of life. But Sam had been brought up warned about the evils of it. Their father wouldn't even put a shilling on a horse, for he always said it was a slippery slope.

'I want to work in gambling houses, not to throw my money away in them,' he said, giving her a sharp look as if daring her to disapprove. 'There's good money to be made in them; the house never loses.'

'Has Heaney got anything to do with this?' she asked.

'No more than seeing how much he makes from the games at his place,' Sam retorted. 'That's why I have to stay late – he gets me to serve drinks to the players. I've been watching them closely.'

Beth slumped down on to his bed. She felt panicked for suddenly everything seemed threatening.

'What's wrong?' he asked. 'Oh, for God's sake don't go all holy on me, Beth! Gambling is big over here, people don't think badly about it, so why should we?'

'Don't you ever get afraid about losing the values we used to have?' she asked.

189

'That we had to remember our place? To kowtow to the gentry? To be poor but honest? You tell me, Beth, why shouldn't we be rich? Is it written in the stars that because our father was a shoemaker, we shouldn't aspire to more than that?'

'I suppose I'm scared we're getting corrupted,' she said weakly. 'You know very well, even if you won't admit it, that we're bound to Heaney, and he isn't a good man.'

'I know he's using us, but we can use him too, Beth. You're gaining experience and practice while you play for him, and I'm learning all about gambling. When the time is right we take all that experience and move on, out of New York and on to Philadelphia, Chicago or even San Francisco. We came here for adventure and to make our fortune, and that's just what we're going to do.'

'You won't just go off one day without me, will you?' she asked fearfully.

Sam moved over to sit beside her on the bed and hugged her tightly. 'Beth, you are the only person in this whole world I really care about. You're not just my sister, you're my dearest friend. I will never go anywhere without you.'

Sam had never been one for flowery speeches, and knowing he meant what he said made Beth burst into tears.

'Don't cry, sis,' he whispered, stroking her hair. 'We've done just fine so far, and we can do better still.'

Chapter Fifteen

After Sam had told her of his aspirations to run a gambling house, Beth sat by the window looking at the view of the rooftops and the grey sky above them, thinking of all the people she knew back in Liverpool. She wondered what they would make of how she and Sam were living.

She had written to the Langworthys every two weeks since they arrived here, and she knew that she was guilty of adding a kind of glossy veneer to everything. She used the word 'hotel' rather than 'rooming house', she described Central Park and Fifth Avenue rather than the Lower East Side. While she hadn't exactly told lies, she had created an image of Heaney's as a select establishment and implied that Ira's shop just sold clothes, not second-hand ones. She'd jubilantly announced their move into the apartment, but failed to add they had only one shared room.

Her justification for her omissions had been that everyone back home would be distressed if she described the poverty she lived amidst, and be worried for her safety if she was a little more frank about Heaney's. But now she was seeing all those people she cared about in her mind's eye, she felt they would be even more alarmed by the changes in her and Sam than by how they lived.

They certainly wouldn't approve of her flaunting herself in scarlet satin, or that she had a few tots of rum most nights she played at Heaney's. They'd be appalled that she'd made friends with a whore, and that the man she wanted was a womanizer.

As for Sam, they'd be shocked that he stayed out all night, and planned to have his own gambling house. Mrs Bruce would be opening her bottle of smelling salts!

It made Beth sad to think she was leading the kind of life her old friends would never approve of, yet she had no intention of returning to being an overworked but virtuous laundry maid. Every time she got up on that stage she felt like a bird being set free from a cage, and she loved being admired and applauded.

The only part of her old life she really missed was Molly. That was a dull ache inside her which never went away. Yet at the same time she was very glad her little sister was safe in England for this was no place for a small child.

Beth turned away from the window and looked objectively at the room. It struck her that the decorative touches she'd added to it represented how things really were. The blue counterpane which acted as a curtain between hers and Sam's beds was tied back for now with a red velvet ribbon to give it a semblance of elegance; the theatre posters hid the stained walls; the brightly coloured dresses she wore in Heaney's were a decoration too, and every week she bought a bunch of flowers to make the room seem more homely.

But these were like the veneer in her letters home. They only masked the fact that the place was grim.

It struck her that Sam, with his sensitive nature, had probably been aware of this from the day they moved in. Maybe that was why he was so dead set on becoming rich, so that they wouldn't have to pretend any more or be ashamed of anything.

Beth didn't hanker after very much more than she had now, just a quieter place, a room of her own and a real bath. But then, she did want to go home one day to see Molly, and she certainly didn't want to go back like a poor relation.

So maybe she ought to start thinking ahead and planning, like Sam was doing.

That night she played better than she'd ever played before. Her whole body seemed to be overtaken by the music, and she danced around the stage, whipping up the crowd to a near frenzy. The applause was deafening, no one wanted her to stop, and Pat Heaney had to get up on the stage to bring it to an end.

'Ain't our little gypsy swell?' he shouted out to the crowd. 'She'll be back on Monday night for you again, so make sure you don't miss her.'

He came out into the back room to bring her money as she was mopping the sweat from her face and neck. 'You were great tonight,' he said with far more warmth than he usually displayed. 'You've come on a treat since you started here.'

He held out her money and she saw that it was around seven dollars. But she had seen dozens of dollar bills fluttering into the hat.

'I think then that's it's time you began paying me better,' she said impulsively. 'Or at least give me the hat to count up the money myself.'

His smile vanished and Beth felt a pang of fear.

'Why, you ungrateful little bitch!' he exclaimed. 'Are you saying I'm cheating you? I took you on when no one else would.'

Beth knew this was a decisive moment. She must either back down or fight back. She was very afraid; his cold eyes and that fearsome scar told her that he was too dangerous to take chances with. But she had played her heart out and something deep inside her told her she must stick up for herself or go under his heel.

'You were the first person I approached to play,' she said

defiantly. 'And right from the first night here there were plenty of others who'd take me on. As for cheating me, well, I know you've done that from the start. You never give me half of what's in the hat.'

'I did you a favour,' he roared at her.

'No you didn't, you did yourself one,' she said, sticking her chin out. 'More people come in when I'm playing, and they stay and get drunk. It doesn't cost you a dime to have me here, and the customers put that money in the hat for me because they have enjoyed my music. So you're cheating them too by keeping it.'

'Do you know what happens to people who cross me?' he said, pushing his face right up to hers, so close she could smell his whisky breath.

'I haven't crossed you,' she said. 'But if you call leaving here and going to work in another saloon crossing you, then I shall do that unless I get what I'm due.'

She could see he was tempted to strike her, his hand holding her money was tightening into a fist, but she stood her ground even though she was afraid.

He let out a foul stream of expletives, but Beth reached for her coat and put it on. 'You've got just one minute to make that up to fifteen dollars,' she said, looking at the money still in his hand. 'Or I walk out and never come back.'

'I won't keep your brother on if you do that,' he said, his eyes narrowing like a snake's.

'Then you're a bigger fool than I took you for,' she said tartly. 'Where are you going to get another honest barman like him?'

His fist came up, but Beth was growing so angry now that she slapped it away. 'You hit me and I'll go and work in the saloon right next door just to spite you,' she hissed at him. 'Sam would never work for you again either. Your minute is up now. Either give me the fifteen dollars or step out of my way.'

She knew she had won when he reached into his pocket, brought out a roll of bills and peeled some off for her. In a strange way she was disappointed, for he had just proved how valuable she was to him, and now she couldn't walk out and work for someone else she would like and trust.

'I want to count the hat money myself from now on,' she warned him. 'I'll give you half because that's what I agreed, but try to cheat me again and I'm off.'

She flounced past him into the bar and made her way over to Sam. 'Be careful what you say to him tonight,' she whispered. 'I've just had a spat with him.'

Sam looked worried and glanced over towards the back room. 'He wants me to stay late for cards. Is he going to get you a cab?'

'I'll see she gets home,' a familiar voice spoke up just behind her. 'That is, of course, if Beth's agreeable!'

Beth spun round. 'Theo!' she exclaimed, unable to hide her joy.

As the cab jogged home to Houston Street, Beth told Theo the bare bones of what had been said.

'Of course you were right to stand up for yourself,' he said. 'And very brave. But Heaney is a vindictive man, Beth, I've heard many stories about him.'

'He won't hurt Sam, will he?' she asked fearfully.

'I don't think so, he needs him. I doubt he'd dare try to do anything to you either, there are too many customers who would string him up if he did. But both of you must be on your guard with him. It would be as well to try to butter him up a bit when you work next.'

'I'm not doing that,' she said indignantly.

'My dear,' Theo sighed, 'take a tip from me. Always disarm your enemies with charm, it works far better than fists, guns or knives.'

As the cab drew up to Beth's house, Theo took her hand. 'I'm going back there now, but may I take you out somewhere tomorrow?'

Beth beamed, her altercation with Heaney all but wiped out by Theo's request.

'I'd love that,' she said.

'Then I'll be round for you at one,' he said. 'Now, how about one of those lovely kisses?'

It was pitch dark on the stairs as always. The only gas light was by the front door, and that had been turned off long ago. Beth felt as though she'd been bewitched as she groped her way up the four flights. She was on fire from Theo's kiss, her heart racing, and out of breath from the climb. She stumbled several times when she missed her footing, but the excitement she felt because she would be seeing Theo the following day banished any thought of the scene earlier with Heaney.

Once in her room and the oil lamp lit, she slumped down on her bed, still panting. Theo wanted her, and that was all that mattered.

'You look very lovely, Beth,' Theo said as he jumped out of his cab to greet her the following day. 'I hope you haven't been waiting out here in the cold for long?'

'Oh no, I only came downstairs just now,' she lied. She had in fact been waiting on the doorstep for over twenty minutes, too afraid to stay upstairs in case he walked into the house through the ever open front door and saw, heard and smelled how grubby, noisy and smelly the place was.

She wished she'd had more notice that he was going to take her out, because then she could have got something new to wear from Ira's shop. As it was, she had to wear the same old brown coat, but she had borrowed a fox fur collar and hat from Amy to give it a lift. The dress beneath it was a dark violet-coloured crêpe with a wide cream lace collar and cuffs, but it wasn't very fashionable for it had been a hand-me-down from Mrs Langworthy.

'I thought I'd take you up to Central Park,' Theo said as he helped her into the cab. 'The trees should be beautiful in their autumn colours, and later we'll go to a restaurant I know near there.'

Beth hadn't been to Central Park since August, when the grass was brown from lack of rain. That day even the leaves of the trees had hung limply with a coating of dust. But it looked beautiful again now, the grass a lush green and the trees a blaze of yellow, russet, gold and brown in the sunshine.

Arm in arm, they walked around the lake, and Theo told her he'd had a big win the previous night at Heaney's. 'I won't be going back there for a while,' he said. 'Heaney's a nasty piece of work and I wouldn't put it past him to pay someone to attack and rob me as I leave his place. He knows I took you home last night too, so if he asks you anything about me, just say you hardly know me, that we only met once on the ship coming here.'

'That is all I could say,' she said impishly. 'I don't know anything much about you.'

He laughed. 'And I intend to rectify that today. Now, what would you like to know?'

They sat on a bench by the lake and he told her about his parents, older brother, two younger sisters and their home.

Beth had a picture in her mind of a mansion surrounded by farmland with a tree-lined avenue leading up to it. He'd been educated first at home with a governess, later at boarding school. His father ran the farm himself and Theo described him as a bluff, opinionated and selfish man who had no time for anyone who wasn't as strong, or didn't ride or shoot as well, as he did.

'It was fortunate I could ride and shoot as well, if not better, than him,' Theo said with a grin. 'But that didn't make up for my lack of interest in farming, and my reputation as a ladies' man. He blamed Mother for both, but then he blamed her for almost everything.'

He said his mother was a loving but rather fragile woman who was unable to stand up to her overbearing husband. His older brother was like his father and Theo felt he had nothing in common with either of them. He did have a great deal of affection for his younger sisters, but said despairingly that they were like their mother, indecisive, weak and without any opinions of their own, so he thought they were destined to marry men just like his father.

'I'm the odd one out,' he said with a shrug. 'I always wanted more than was offered – excitement, colour and new experiences. The thought of living the kind of sedate life my father approved of, which inevitably would mean marrying someone appropriate, filled me with horror. I want adventure, and when I marry it will be an adventure too, to someone with a mind of her own, passionate, with a sense of fun. I never want my children to suffer the kind of chilly formality I grew up in.'

Beth secretly thought that woman sounded like her,

but she kept that opinion to herself and told him instead how she had been destined to be the dutiful stay-at-home daughter, until her parents' deaths pushed her into a different kind of servitude.

She said her father had a heart attack and that her mother died in childbirth with Molly, but passed on quickly to how she went to work for the Langworthys, lightening the story by making it clear how good her mistress was to her.

'My heart wasn't really in leaving England,' she admitted. 'But it was for the best, and Mrs Langworthy writes every few weeks to tell me how Molly is getting on.'

'You're a very courageous girl,' Theo said thoughtfully. 'Not many could cope with so much while so young. I'm sure your parents would have been very proud of you.'

Beth laughed. 'I'm not so sure they'd have approved of me playing my fiddle in a saloon.'

'You are using a God-given talent, and you are making a great many people happy by doing so. To me that is commendable.'

'I used to dream of playing the piano in a smart hotel lounge,' she admitted. 'I certainly didn't think I'd end up living in a stinking tenement, or working for a thug.'

Theo shook his head in amusement. 'You'll be moving on upwards soon. Sam told me last night of his plans to work in gambling houses. I believe he can do it too – he's sharp, he's got charm and he's got you beside him. I'd bet on you two making a fortune.'

'You need money to begin.' Beth sighed.

'Not always.' Theo smiled and tickled her under the chin. 'Charm and a good idea will always get backers. I have a disreputable uncle who it is said I take after. He told me once, never put your own money into a business venture. He has lived by that and amassed a fortune.'

'What are your plans?' she asked.

'For now, to see how much money I can win in New York, while I keep my ears open for a whisper about the next boom town.'

'Boom town?' Beth exclaimed. 'What do you mean?'

Theo sucked in his cheeks. 'Like San Francisco in '49, for instance. It was a small fishing village until gold was found nearby. Then tens of thousands stampeded to get there, and fortunes were made.'

'Not many of them found gold,' Beth said, remembering that from a history lesson.

'The smart people don't go for whatever has created the stampede, be that gold, diamonds or silver,' he said with a chuckle. 'It's always very hard work, and only a few strike it rich. The really clever people, the ones like you and me, go there to offer services, shops, saloons, hotels, restaurants, dance and music halls.'

Beth giggled. 'And I play the fiddle in one of these places and they toss gold nuggets at me?'

'Exactly.' He smiled. 'It certainly wouldn't be any fun for them being rich unless they can spend it wildly.'

'But surely all the gold, diamonds and silver have been found now?' Beth said.

'Not necessarily. Parts of America are still virtual wilderness, and who knows what's under the ground? But boom towns can spring up for other reasons too. The railway, for instance – wherever that goes people will want houses, shops and the rest.'

'And gambling houses?' she asked, raising one eyebrow quizzically.

He smiled, a hint of mischief in his dark eyes. 'And gambling houses.'

'Well, if you get word of one of these boom towns,

you make sure you tell Sam and me. We'd be glad to tag along.'

Theo had been sitting with his arm along the back of the seat, and he suddenly moved it to her shoulders. 'I can't think of two people better suited to join me,' he said. 'Sam promises to be a force to reckon with because he's so determined. As for you, with your fiddle, you'd be an asset anywhere.'

Beth thought he was going to kiss her, but he must've remembered it wasn't done to embrace a young woman in public, for Theo suddenly said it was getting cold and it was time they found a coffee shop and got warmed up.

As they walked out of the park, Beth thought how perfect he was — handsome, a gentleman and so entertaining too.

Jack had been fun to be with, but in comparison to Theo he was just a boy, with no finesse or education. When he took her hand it was awkwardly, he lunged at her for a kiss, and he certainly didn't have the ability to say or do things which would make a girl tremble and shiver.

When Theo took her hand his thumb would caress hers; if he put his hand on her waist he gave it a little squeeze. They found a little coffee shop just across the road from the park and once they had sat down he took her hand and lifted her fingers to his mouth, not just to kiss them, but to give each one a delicate lick with the tip of his tongue.

'I want to kiss your mouth but this will have to do for now,' he whispered.

It was the unexpectedness of his little touches and compliments which made them so thrilling.

He was talking about the plight of some immigrants who hadn't been able to find anywhere to live and had been caught a few days earlier trying to camp out under the bushes in Central Park, but he suddenly broke off to smooth away a strand of hair escaping from beneath her hat. 'Your eyes are like deep forest pools,' he said, then carried on with what he'd been talking about before.

He slid one finger up under the sleeve of her coat, as if to feel her pulse, and the intimacy of it made her blush. 'Your skin is as soft and smooth as a baby's,' he whispered. When she dropped her teaspoon to the floor because he made her flustered, he reached down to get it and he put his hand on her leg, just above her ankle boot.

But it wasn't only his touch that set her on fire, it was the way he spoke too. His voice was deep, but soft and cultured, and almost everything he told her, whether it was about his life back in England or the people he'd met since he'd been in America, he made so vivid that she could see it clearly.

'Miss Marchment, my landlady, is living in greatly reduced circumstances,' he told her. 'She has the air of a duchess even though she's old and frail and has nothing coming in other than the rent for the rooms she lets out. She sits all day in a purple velvet chair worn thin with age, a lacy shawl around her shoulders, and gives her orders to her maid as if she were still in control of a staff of twenty. The house is crumbling with neglect, the rugs threadbare, a thick layer of dust on her pictures, mirrors and ornaments, but she invites me in for tea and orders her maid to make it in the battered silver teapot. Such a gracious old lady!'

'Does the maid clean your room for you?' Beth asked, not liking the idea of him living in squalor.

'Yes, she does, I guess she knows that if the tenants leave she'll get no more wages. But the poor soul has so much to do that she just doesn't have time to clean her mistress's rooms thoroughly.'

'Is she old too?' Beth asked.

'About fifty. She's worked for Mrs Marchment all her life.

But you don't want to hear sad stories about old ladies. Tell me about the people in your house.'

Perhaps it was because he described people so vividly that Beth found herself doing so too. She told him about the crazy Irishman on the first floor who shouted out every time someone passed his door, and the strange little Polish man who scuttled down the street clutching a brown leather satchel to his chest, his eyes swivelling from side to side as if he was carrying state secrets and believed someone was going to snatch them. Theo roared with laughter, making several other people in the coffee shop look round at him.

'I think it's time we got some dinner,' he said, chuckling as he took her hand again to kiss it. 'It's so good to be with someone beautiful who also makes me laugh. Most beautiful women, I find, have no sense of humour.'

By Thanksgiving Day in November, Beth was so deeply in love with Theo that she could think of nothing else from the moment she opened her eyes in the morning till she fell asleep at night.

She felt he loved her too, even if he had never said so, for he always made an effort to see her once a week, even when he had to go out of New York on business. Nor had he dropped her because she wouldn't let him have his way with her.

He had asked if he could come up to her room the second time they went out but she refused because she knew she was likely to get swept away by his kisses and caresses once they were alone.

On their third meeting he suggested taking her away to a hotel for a night. She pretended to be affronted at the suggestion, but in fact she was tempted, for at least her neighbours wouldn't know what she was getting up to. But sweet reason prevailed: she only had to think of what happened to her mother, and she knew she couldn't take the risk, not just of having a child, but maybe of Theo throwing her aside once he'd got what he wanted.

Since then Theo was always saying how much he wanted her, but although he tried plenty of gentle persuasion, he was never forceful. And when he talked of the future, it was as if his plans included her.

Sad as Theo's long absences made Beth, she was quite relieved that he was still away as Thanksgiving Day approached. Amy and Kate had decided that Beth and Sam's first Thanksgiving in America should be marked properly and they planned to cook them a traditional turkey dinner.

As there was so little room in their own apartment, they had asked Beth if they could cook it in hers, and suggested the Rossinis should be invited too. Beth asked Sam to invite his lady friend, but his look of horror suggested he had no intention of bringing his sweetheart to a dinner party with two whores and an elderly Italian couple who only spoke a smattering of English.

Yet as the day grew closer, Amy's enthusiasm for this special meal began to win both Beth and Sam over. Sam brought home an old door and fixed it over a couple of trestles to make a table big enough for them all; they borrowed chairs from different people in the house; Ira lent them an embroidered tablecloth, and Mrs Rossini dug out her old family recipes to cook a special dessert.

Amy and Kate surpassed themselves in cooking the meal. By six o'clock everything was ready, the turkey a deep golden brown and vegetables perfectly cooked. They were all just about to take their places around the table when Jack turned up.

Beth had seen him a few times since they split up, mostly in Heaney's when she'd only been able to wave from a distance, but he had come into Ira's shop a couple of times to say hello. The first time he came she was afraid he was pursuing her, but when he made it clear he was only being friendly, even mentioning a girl he'd taken dancing, she was glad they could be friends again.

'I wouldn't have come if I'd known you had company,' he said, looked a little embarrassed. 'I brought you some meat and some fruit.'

'It's lovely to see you and you're more than welcome to join us,' Beth said, taking the bag from his hands. It contained a quantity of lamb chops, some sausages, and apples and oranges. 'Thank you so much. It's very kind of you.'

'The boss gave us all a bag of stuff for Thanksgiving,' he said a little sheepishly. 'Too much for me to eat on my own.'

Jack's unexpected arrival turned out to be a blessing for he turned what might have been a dull party into a noisy, jolly one.

He made Amy and Kate laugh a great deal, stopped Sam from feeling awkward about having to entertain all the women, and as he had learned quite a bit of Italian from some of his workmates, he could include the Rossinis in the conversation.

Beth observed that the callow youth with few social graces she'd met on the ship had become a self-possessed and very amusing man. Hard physical work had given him muscle, his angular face had filled out, and the scar gave his face extra character. He was also far more articulate than she remembered. He told them stories about the men he worked alongside with humour, yet they were tempered with a great deal of understanding of the problems many of these foreign immigrants were facing.

Beth watched him flirting with Amy and Kate and guessed that he'd gained all this poise through women. He laughed when she asked him if he had a sweetheart, and charmingly said that his heart was still in her keeping. But that remark in itself proved someone was responsible for polishing him up. He would never have said such a thing when they were walking out together.

Everyone had drunk rather too much wine by the end of the evening. The Rossinis kissed them all on both cheeks and thanked them profusely before they went off to bed. Amy and Kate left too, and it was only when Jack remained, sitting on Sam's bed, that Beth felt a pang of anxiety that he was going to be difficult.

But she was wrong.

'I hope you don't think I come round tonight lookin' fer a free feed,' he said, looking from Beth to Sam. 'It weren't that, I came cos I heard sommat the other day what bothered me.'

'About Beth?' Sam asked.

'No, not about either of you, just about Pat Heaney. There's trouble brewing, he's fallen out with a geezer name of Fingers Malone. Both Fingers and Heaney have each got a gang behind them, blokes they've bin in with since they was young.'

Sam nodded. 'I've heard that much. I've met Fingers too – he used to come in the bar most nights when I first started there.'

'Yeah, well, the word is that there's going to be some kind of showdown soon. It won't be just a scrap between Heaney and Fingers, it could be all-out gang war. I thought I ought to warn you so that at the first sign of trouble you both get out of there.'

'We'll take your advice,' Sam said a little starchily, as if he resented Jack hearing this before he did.

'That's not all.' Jack looked sharply at Sam. 'I'm worried about Beth's safety. She's valuable to Heaney, and Fingers knows it. He may even think she's Heaney's woman.'

'How could anyone think that?' Beth exclaimed.

'Maybe cos Heaney's let folk think that,' Jack replied.

Jack left soon afterwards and the door was barely shut behind him before Sam claimed he was talking nonsense. 'What does he know? This will be a half-baked rumour that he's picked up on and he's using it to make himself look important.'

'That's a horrible thing to say,' Beth said indignantly. 'You're just cross because Jack heard it before you. But no one would dare tell you; you're too close to Heaney, and they'd be afraid you'd warn him.'

'Me close to Heaney!' Sam snorted indignantly. 'I can't stand him.'

'That's not the way it looks to other people. They all know he trusts you.'

'Jack just wants to worm his way back in with us,' Sam said scornfully. 'What better way to do it than by making out you are in danger? Before you know it he'll be offering to escort you home each night; he's jealous because he's heard you're walking out with Theo.'

Beth was less concerned about gang rivalry than she was about Theo, who was still away. Every night she played she searched the faces in the audience, hoping he'd be there.

Sam did take the precaution of always escorting her home in a cab after she played, even though it meant he often had to return to the saloon afterwards to serve drinks at private card games. But he made a point of saying it was the right thing for a brother to do, and that it had nothing to do with what Jack had said.

Snow fell during the night on Molly's second birthday in mid-December, and Beth woke to find the city under a white blanket, bringing back poignant memories of both her sister's birth and her mother's death. She had always tried hard not to dwell on her mother. Even when she posted a present and a card for Molly's birthday a couple of weeks earlier, she kept her thoughts to what her baby sister would be like now, not how she came to be born. But with Theo still away and no word from him, she couldn't help feeling she'd been cast aside, just as her mother had been.

More snow came and the New York shops looked beautiful, all decked out for Christmas. Many of the very smartest ones had the new electric light installed, and as darkness fell in the streets their fantastically dressed windows were ablaze with light and colour. Even the very smallest shops and stalls on the streets sported decorations and extra oil lamps, there were huge Christmas trees in many of the squares, and the air was rich with the smell of chestnuts roasting in charcoal burners.

Beth bought presents – a royal blue woollen muffler for Sam, scented soap for Amy and Kate, a bottle of lavender cologne for Ira – and hoped that the lovely red dress and the rag doll she'd sent home to Molly would arrive in time for Christmas. She wanted to buy a present for Theo too, but she decided to wait a little longer, to see if he would turn up again.

Two days before Christmas Eve, still with no word from him, Beth was feeling very glum. The shop had been very busy all day, and the constant cry of 'Merry Christmas' as people left the shop made it worse for her, knowing she had no one special to spend the day with.

Ira must have noticed that she wasn't quite herself. 'Honey, you should get Jack to take you out dancing,' she suggested out of the blue. 'You don't want to hang around waiting for a man who can't even send you a letter when he's away to tell you he's thinking of you.'

Beth didn't appreciate Ira making such remarks. She sulked for a while, but by mid-afternoon she came out of it and tried on a pretty, deep pink dress that Ira had remarked was perfect for her.

Ira was right, and when Beth asked if she could buy it, the old lady said she'd like to give it to her as a Christmas present.

'You're a good girl – I don't know how I managed before you came,' Ira said with slightly moist eyes. 'Giving you a dress that was made for you is the least I can do to thank you.'

'Then I won't hang around waiting for Theo,' Beth replied. 'I'll take up the Rossinis' invitation for Sam and me to have Christmas dinner with them. Maybe if Jack's in at Heaney's tonight, I'll even hint that he takes me dancing.'

It was bitterly cold when she left Ira's at five. She tucked the parcel containing her new dress under her arm, wrapped her muffler around her neck, and with her gloved hands in a fur muff Ira had also given her, set off for the market to buy some fruit, nuts and candy to share with the Rossinis.

There was a new cheeriness in people's faces as Beth walked down the Bowery. An organ-grinder had decked out his organ with glittery stars, and it was playing 'Silent Night', and she saw a group of children watching in awe as a man wound up some clockwork toys on a stall. She stopped to look at a bear clashing cymbals and a man rowing a boat.

She considered buying the bear and sending it home to Molly, but decided it was likely to end up broken in the post.

She turned the corner, and after the bright lights of the Bowery it was very dark. She was aware of someone close behind her, but there was nothing unusual about that for it was early in the evening.

When a hand clamped down on her shoulder, she dropped her parcel in fright.

'Don't make a sound,' a gruff male voice warned her. 'I've got a knife at your back.'

She froze, for she could feel something digging into her coat. Her first thought was that the man wanted to rob her, for that wasn't uncommon in this area.

'I've only got a couple of dollars,' she said. 'But you can have that.'

'You're worth more than a couple of dollars to me,' he said. 'Now walk, do as I say, and you'll be fine. Squeal, and I'll stick the knife in you.'

Chapter Sixteen

'Where's that sister of yours?' Pat Heaney asked Sam. He took his watch out of his vest pocket and looked at it. 'What's she playing at? It's nearly half past eight!'

The saloon was packed and Sam had been so busy for the last hour that he hadn't noticed the time. But at Heaney's words he checked the clock on the wall behind the bar. 'I don't know where she is,' he said, immediately feeling a cold chill run down his spine, for Beth was never late. 'She was working at Ira's today as usual. Pebbles went in there to buy something, he said he'd seen her.'

Pebbles was the pot man, so named because he wore thick glasses.

'If she lets me down tonight she'll be out of a job,' Heaney snarled.

'She wouldn't let you down,' Sam said defensively. 'Even if she was taken ill she'd get a message to you.'

'Maybe that old crow Roebling has been taken bad,' Heaney said. 'I'll send someone down there to ask.'

He walked away from the bar, and Sam saw him order Pebbles to go and check.

There were men clamouring to buy a drink, and as Sam poured their beer and took their money, he remembered Jack's warning.

He had been convinced Jack had made up all that stuff about Fingers Malone and Heaney as a ruse to get in with him and Beth again. The only reason Sam had been taking

Beth home at nights was to give the man no excuse to try to muscle in.

Yet now Jack's warning didn't seem so far-fetched, and Sam served drinks with one eye on the door. When Pebbles returned around ten minutes later and went over to Heaney, Sam could wait no longer.

Leaving the bar, he pushed his way through the drinkers towards Heaney. 'Any news?' he asked.

'She left the shop at five,' Heaney growled. 'She was going to the market before going home. You'd better get round and see if she's there.'

Sam ran the whole way, his legs going like pistons. He clattered up the stairs and into the apartment. Mrs Rossini was in the kitchen and looked round in surprise.

'Has Beth been home?' Sam asked.

She shook her head and added something in Italian. Sam felt she was trying to ask why he looked so worried. But he couldn't spare the time to try to find words she would understand, and went into their room. Beth's fiddle case was on the floor by the window, just where it had been when he left the room at midday to start work. He looked at the dresses she wore when she was playing and all three of them were still hanging on the wall.

He realized it was possible Theo had come back, met her at the shop and whisked her off somewhere. Under normal circumstances Beth wouldn't go anywhere if she was expected at the saloon, but as Sam knew, the heart took over from the head when romance was in the air, and she had been moping over Theo for weeks.

Yet even if she had done that, Sam knew she would've come back here first and left a note for him, if only to ask him to tell Heaney she was ill.

Amy and Kate were out and the Irish family they shared with hadn't seen Beth either.

Sam ran back to Heaney's. He was really scared now. Beth's safety was uppermost in his mind, but he didn't relish having to tell Heaney that he'd heard a rumour about Fingers and not divulged it.

In the room at the back of the saloon, Sam told Heaney he was afraid Fingers might have kidnapped Beth, and why, and predictably the man blew his top.

'You heard that Fingers was about to declare war on me and you didn't tell me?' he roared.

Sam apologized and explained that he hadn't believed it. 'I was told I should watch out for Beth, that's why I'm scared they've done that.'

He fully expected Heaney to scoff at this. But he didn't; instead he scratched his head and looked worried.

'Would they have taken her?' Sam asked.

'How would I know?' Heaney snarled. 'But one thing's certain, we'll soon know if the mother-fucker's got her because he'll make some demand.'

He had no sympathy for Sam. It was clear from his agitation that his main concern was not Beth's safety but his own loss of face.

'Get back behind the bar and keep this to yourself,' he ordered him.

Sam felt like punching the man for being so callous. He wanted him to get up on the stage, announce Beth was missing and ask if anyone knew anything. But reason prevailed, for although he knew the vast majority of men in the bar would be only too eager to help find her, New York was a big place. She could be held anywhere, and scores of men running around blindly with their blood up wouldn't achieve anything but further trouble.

It was the longest night Sam had ever known. He had to listen to Heaney's announcement that Beth couldn't make it to play that night, see the disappointment on the men's faces, and deal with many of them asking him if she was sick.

Heaney sent him home at midnight. 'They won't make a move until tomorrow,' he said, with a clap on Sam's shoulder which was as close as he could get to displaying a semblance of sympathy. 'I've been through this kinda thing before, lad. They'll make us sweat before they show their hand.'

It did make Sam sweat. Lying on his bed, looking at Beth's empty one, he cursed himself for dismissing what Jack had said. It was pure arrogance on his part; he just didn't want to acknowledge that a man he considered inferior might actually know more than he did. He'd never approved of Jack's friendship with Beth, yet he'd pretended he did because it let him off taking care of her, so he could spend more time with his women.

Until tonight, Sam had prided himself on his many conquests. It made him feel powerful that he could sweet-talk any girl into bed. Yet now, as he thought about Polly, Maggie, Nora and, more recently, Annie, he felt ashamed of himself. They were all either actresses or dancers, girls who had already been ruined by someone else, soft targets as they were vulnerable and desperate for love. In truth he knew that each one of them would probably become a whore before long. He didn't know now how he could have been so hypocritical about Jack, for even if he was a bit rough and ready, he had always treated Beth with the utmost respect and real affection.

Theo, on reflection, was a far more dangerous animal. He was not only handsome and well bred but also suave and calculating. Sam had watched him play poker several times and been in awe of his coolness and sophistication. At the last game he played at Heaney's he'd won over five hundred dollars, yet he'd acted as if it were nothing. Any brother worth his salt would have moved heaven and earth to stop his sister getting involved with such a man, yet Sam had openly admired him and given the relationship his blessing.

He felt nauseous as he considered that Beth could have gone the same way as their mother. He was reminded that he'd had no sympathy for her, and it shamed him now that he'd wanted to abandon her newborn baby. It had been Beth who held everything together. But for her resourcefulness and her personality they would never have been invited to live in Falkner Square and it was doubtful they'd ever have got to America.

He wished now that they'd never come here as his mind began to turn to where she might be and the conditions she was being held under. He knew it wouldn't be a comfortable or warm place; men like Fingers lived like animals. But even more terrifying was the possibility that he might never see Beth again. He couldn't imagine Heaney agreeing to pay a ransom for her. He'd see that as weakness. And Fingers would never let her go without payment; he'd sooner kill her than lose face.

At four in the morning when it was still pitch dark, Sam left the house to find Jack. He didn't know where he lived, but he did know he worked at the slaughterhouse by the East River and started there early in the morning.

It was freezing cold, with a thick layer of frost-covered snow from days earlier. He walked fast to warm himself up, but he felt sick with anxiety and lack of sleep.

Beth hadn't been able to sleep either. She was so cold it had crossed her mind that she could very well die from it.

For the first three or four hours after she was pushed unceremoniously into this dark cellar she had kept walking up and down and shouting, but eventually exhaustion had forced her to sit down on what felt like some old packing crates.

There was water on the floor, and it had seeped into her boots, and the air was foul. Whether this was a leakage of sewage, something dead or rotten in there with her, or just the sheer age of the building, she didn't know, but she wasn't inclined to grope around in the darkness to find out.

She did know that she was in one of the alleys off Mulberry Bend, the same area she and Sam had accidentally found themselves in on their first night in America. She'd taken note of where the man with the knife at her back was prodding her to because she hoped she'd be able to distract him at some point and run away from him. But she stood no chance of that, for his hand remained clamped down on her shoulder, and he moved the knife to her side and held it there.

Beth had never seen the man before. He was tall and powerfully built, with coarse, misshapen features that suggested he might be a prize fighter. His hands were huge, like hams, and what teeth he had left were blackened and broken. By the standards of Mulberry Bend he was well dressed, in a thick, dark wool coat with a velvet collar and a homburg hat, but he had the smell she'd come to recognize of a slum dweller – mildew, tobacco and wood smoke.

She knew he must have been ordered to capture her, for if robbery had been his aim he would have taken what she'd had and moved on. And he was definitely acting on Fingers' behalf because she had tried pleading with him, telling him she'd willingly play at his saloon as she had no loyalty to Heaney. He confirmed this by looking a little startled at

216

Fingers' name, and then told her to shut up. She didn't shut up, she continued to plead her cause, but then he struck her round the face.

Her fingers felt her swollen cheek tentatively. His blow had been like being hit with a sledgehammer. She was so dazed by it she could hardly see, and he grabbed her arm and almost dragged her the rest of the way here.

There had been dozens of people about. In the narrow, fetid alley they ended up in there had been a gang of men who had all looked at them curiously. Sadly Beth didn't think that would mean rescue was close at hand, for Fingers wouldn't have ordered her to be brought here openly if he hadn't been sure he could count on the locals' loyalty.

She had no idea what time it was now, but she felt it was still night, for there were no chinks of light coming in anywhere. The thought of rats made her flesh crawl and she hugged her arms tighter around her, trying hard not to think of that. Instead, she tried to work out how long it would be before Sam realized what had happened.

He would of course have known something was wrong when she didn't turn up to play. But how could he find her? It would be like looking for a particular pebble on an entire beach.

Chapter Seventeen

At six, when Jack arrived at the slaughterhouse to see Sam waiting there, the colour drained from his face even before Sam told him what had happened.

'Go on, say it,' Sam said miserably. 'I should've taken more notice of what you told me.'

Jack's eyes flashed dangerously, but he made an effort to control himself. 'I guess you couldn't have watched over her all the time.' He sighed. 'No one could, and who would've expected them to snatch her as she was leaving Ira's shop?'

'What can we do, Jack?' Sam asked miserably. 'I can't see Heaney sending his mob out to find her. He'll just order them to smash up Fingers' property and then the war will really start.'

Jack nodded in agreement. 'I wish I could skip work and stay with you, but I daren't. I finish at one today, though, so I'll keep my ear to the ground and meet you at Heaney's by two.'

Sam walked back home, but with every step his fear for Beth grew. He had been so complacent, believing he was better educated than most, attractive to the ladies and considered a gentleman by all. He lorded it behind the bar at Heaney's, never lapsing into American slang because he wanted to stand out as an Englishman.

But the truth was that he was a milksop. He had never been in a fight in his life, and he was afraid of violence, and if he was considered honest, that was because he was too scared to be otherwise.

His famous charm wasn't going to rescue Beth and he

had no money to pay a ransom for her either. What was he going to do?

Beth sat shivering on her box watching as faint chinks of light came through the boards of the cellar ceiling. But although this told her that it must be after seven on Saturday morning, there were no other chinks of light anywhere else. Somewhere up there was the trapdoor she'd come down through. There had been some sort of ladder, too, for the man had pushed her on to it, but she'd lost her footing and slithered the rest of the way down to the floor. He'd pulled the ladder up before shutting and locking the door.

She wished she could remember what the room above was like, but she'd been struggling and crying as he pushed her along a narrow dark passage from the alley, so even when he struck a match, she hadn't noticed anything more than the trapdoor he flung open.

But it struck her that even if she didn't see anything, she would've sensed if the room was lived in. There was no sound coming from there now, nor had there been all night, and if there had been anyone living there, surely her captor would've gagged her?

So perhaps it was a storeroom. Maybe there wasn't anyone else in the entire building?

That seemed very unlikely. Mulberry Bend and its surrounding rabbit warren of alleyways were by repute the most overcrowded part of the city. Anyone owning a building here would press it into service as a five-cents-a-night flop house.

She wanted to cry, from fear, cold and hunger, but she was determined not to. Fingers had snatched her because he considered her valuable. It didn't make any sense for him to leave her down here to die.

The light through the ceiling cracks was growing a little

brighter, which suggested there were windows in the room above. Most windows around here were broken, and if she made enough noise someone might hear. All she had to do was find something to make it with.

Sam was back at Heaney's at nine, to find the door locked, and when he peered through the window he saw Pebbles sweeping up the dirty sawdust on the floor.

He attracted the man's attention, and reluctantly he opened the door. 'Mr Heaney told me to keep the door locked and not let anyone in,' he said.

'He wouldn't have meant me,' Sam said, slipping in and locking the door behind him. 'Is there any news of Beth?'

'Dunno,' Pebbles replied, his expression saying that he cared less.

Pebbles was a bit simple, so Sam knew there was no point in questioning him further. He went through to the back and lay down on the old sofa in there, trying to think what he could do.

The next thing he knew, Heaney's voice was booming in the bar. Sam jumped up and ran in there, noticing it was now eleven o'clock and he'd been asleep for two hours.

'You look rough,' Heaney remarked, going behind the bar and pouring himself a whisky. 'I haven't heard anything, so get yourself home and cleaned up. It's business as usual until I tell you otherwise.'

His brusque tone made Sam angry. 'You don't give a damn about Beth, do you? Only that someone's pulled one over on you. What kind of man are you?'

'The kind that socks insolent young pups in the mouth,' Heaney retorted, finishing his drink in one long gulp. 'Now, get home and shave and put a clean shirt on.'

*

Jack was as good as his word; at two he came into the saloon. He'd changed his bloodstained working clothes for a very shabby seaman's navy blue pea jacket and an equally old cap. 'I was told Fingers owns property in Mulberry Bend,' he whispered to Sam across the bar. 'No address, and it's like a feckin' rabbit warren around there, but I'm going over now to look around.'

'I want to come with you,' Sam whispered back. 'But Heaney will throw a fit.'

'You'd stand out there like a dog's bollocks,' Jack said with a smirk. 'I'll go alone. Besides, it'll be better if you're here when Fingers does make a move. We need to know what his demands are. We can't trust Heaney to tell us the truth.'

'I don't think he'll pay anything to get Beth back,' Sam said fearfully.

'That's why we've got to find her, and if Fingers has hurt her then I swear I'll kill him.'

Jack lit up a cigarette outside a pawnshop in Mulberry Bend, leaned back against a wall and surveyed the teeming street impassively. Beth had told him how horrified and scared she was when she and Sam lost their way and found themselves here, but he hadn't had the heart to tell her that it wasn't so different to where he'd grown up in the East End of London, or for that matter the slums of Liverpool.

The main difference was that English people were a tiny minority here, and perhaps only half of the rest spoke little or any English.

They were Italians, Germans, Poles, Jews and Irish in the main, with a liberal sprinkling from other European countries, plus negroes who had moved up from the Southern states. The only thing they had in common with one another was the hopelessness of their situation, for this wasn't just a ghetto of poor people, this was the absolute bottom of the pit.

If you came to this hell-hole in desperation because you'd nowhere else to go, the sides of the pit were too steep and high to climb out again.

Jack knew that the rents charged here for one filthy, rat-and-bug-infested room were in fact higher than for a decent house or a complete apartment uptown. But then, these poverty-stricken immigrants would not be acceptable to the landlords of those places.

All over the Lower East Side people could only manage to pay high rents on low wages by sharing with others, usually friends or relatives. But here the only criterion for having some sort of roof over your head was the ability to pay a few cents per night, and for that you slept on a floor among dozens of others.

Living a hand-to-mouth existence, with no comfort, warmth or even facilities for keeping clean, people soon found themselves locked into a spiral which led ever further downwards. A man could hardly take on strenuous physical work when he had little sleep or a decent meal; a woman couldn't sew or even make matchboxes unless she had room and light to do it in. Who wouldn't turn to drink when it was the only thing which numbed the mind from complete despair?

In Jack's immediate view he could count five grog shops, three saloons, two second-hand clothes shops and two pawnshops. He thought that gave a fairly accurate picture of the needs of the community.

The one greengrocer's had a display of fruit and vegetables that even from a distance were clearly well past their best, and the dried goods store was only marginally better.

People were peddling things all along the kerbside. Two bent old crones were selling stale bread, and he watched as their dirty hands delved into even dirtier bags made from old mattress ticking to bring out another misshapen loaf. Another man was butchering a goat on a piece of wood balanced on one of the street's ash tins. But even worse were the two Italian men selling stale beer, the leftover dregs from a saloon, passing it out in old tin cans.

'The Bend', as it was generally known, because the road was shaped like a dog's leg, was at least swept from time to time by the council. But just a few steps away in the rabbit warren of narrow, dark alleys running from it, places where neither council brooms nor sunshine ever ventured, the rubbish lay rotting on the ground, mingling with the stink of human effluent. Thousands of people lived in the ramshackle houses, tenements, cellars and even sheds, a pile of rags passing for a bed, a beer crate for a stool.

Jack had no doubt that most of the ragged, half-starved children he could see hanging around today had no home, for living on the streets was often preferable to 'home'. At least that way they didn't have to hand over their meagre earnings from begging or thieving or risk being beaten by drunken parents.

Jack knew exactly how that was, for he had taken to the streets of Whitechapel at a very early age for just the same reasons. School was a place he only went to when the truancy man caught him; all his knowledge and skills, which were mainly those of survival, were learned on the streets.

Meeting Beth on the ship had been like a miracle. The only friends he'd ever had were those from the slime at the bottom of the barrel like him. He'd looked at girls like Beth from afar, wishing he could reach out and touch their silky hair, or just be close enough to smell their clean skin and clothes. He never dreamed he would ever have someone like that for a friend, much less hold her hand or kiss her.

But Beth talked to him as if he was the same as her. She laughed with him, she shared her sadness and her hopes with him. She made him think he could achieve anything he wanted. When she said goodbye on the ship, promising she would meet him in exactly one month's time on Castle Green, he didn't expect for one moment that she would be there. But the strength and belief in himself that she'd given him stayed with him.

He spent his first night here in the Bend, for it was the only place he'd been told about by acquaintances back in Liverpool. But for Beth's influence, he wouldn't even have noticed how appalling it was, he would've numbed his mind with drink and followed the lead of those he met that night. But she had changed his viewpoint, and by the following morning he knew he must get out immediately or find himself sucked in.

Working in the slaughterhouse was hideous. The terror of the cattle as he helped drive them from the ship towards their death, the casual attitude of the men who killed them and the stink of blood and guts made him feel sick to his stomach. But it was work, better paid than most jobs, and even though sleeping on the floor with five other men in one tiny room didn't seem as if he'd taken a step upwards, he knew he had.

He almost didn't go to Castle Green a month later. He'd caught Sam's parting glance at him, and it was cold enough to freeze a brass monkey. He also expected that Sam, with his looks and charm, would have found some fancy position, and that by now Beth would be walking out with someone her brother had picked for her.

It was sheer defiance that made Jack go. He had been

tempted so many times to backslide into his old ways of drinking and fighting, and he thought if she let him down he could justify it. But there she was, waiting for him on Castle Green, bright, eager and lovely.

He had been surprised that Sam wasn't in work, and when he sensed her anxiety about it, he tried to help, never imagining Sam would stoop to being a barman on the Bowery. Jack hadn't admitted how he was living, or how gruesome his job was – that would have been too much for Beth – but it spurred him on to improve his situation.

Getting moved into the butchery side of the slaughter-house wouldn't seem much of a step up to many, but it was. He was learning a trade which would stand him in good stead in the future, and he didn't have to see and hear the cattle's terror. Shortly afterwards he got a better room, sharing with three friends. It wasn't much, but it was clean, he had a real bed and a place to hang his clothes.

All through the summer he thought he had the sun, the moon and the stars because he had Beth. He worked extra hours to get more money so he could save a little; he even went to a night class to improve his reading and writing.

Then came the day he realized she didn't feel the same about him.

For a while he thought life wasn't worth living without her. It was like a knife through the heart hearing that his rival was a gentleman, for it brought back all his old feelings of worthlessness. So many nights he went down to Heaney's and stood outside just to listen to her playing, and he'd be choked up with tears.

It was on one of those nights that it came to him that even if she didn't return his love, maybe he could keep her in his life as a friend. He knew it wasn't going to be easy, for he'd have to pretend to like Theo the card sharp and put up with Sam looking down on him. But he thought he could do that, in the hopes that one day Beth might need him.

Well, she needed him now. He just hoped he could track down where she was being held and rescue her.

Jack was systematic in his search, up one alley, down the next, checking out each tiny dark court in between. He saw drunks lying insensible, near-naked children with hollow eyes sitting listlessly on stoops. Gangs of young lads eyed him up with suspicion, haggard whores offered themselves for a few cents.

Everywhere else in New York there were Christmas decorations, festooned trees and shop windows full of ideas for presents. But although tomorrow was Christmas Eve, there was no hint of any festivity here.

Jack spoke to many people. Mostly he pretended he was just off a ship and had been told that he'd got to look up someone called Fingers Malone. Mostly people shook their heads and said they didn't know anyone by that name. An old whore with a pockmarked face spat and said he was an evil bastard, but couldn't be drawn as to why, or where he could be found. A couple of lads of about thirteen bragged they'd done a few jobs for him. Jack was pretty certain they'd only heard his name and wouldn't even know the man if he stood in front of them.

In a dirty, smoky saloon on Mulberry, the barman said he owned a chunk of property in Bottle Alley, but a man drinking at the bar said it wasn't there, it was in Blind Man's Court.

By eight in the evening Jack's feet ached. He was so weary of repeating the same story to so many people that he doubted he was making much sense, and he'd scrutinized every inch of both Bottle Alley and Blind Man's Court. The

Bend was no place for a stranger to hang around at night, for the alleys were dark, full of drunks eager for a fight and young lads on the prowl looking for someone to rob. It was also bitterly cold, so he felt he had to go back to Heaney's to see if Sam had any news.

It was a relief to get back to the Bowery with its bright lights and gaiety. Music thumped out from the German Beer Gardens, and a marching band was playing Christmas carols. The pedlars were out in force, selling everything from cheap toys to men's suspenders. There were toffee apples, roast chestnuts and waffles, and the warmth from the stalls and the sweet smells reminded Jack that Beth might be cold and hungry.

Jack spotted a familiar face in the crowd ahead of him. He had only seen Theo once, but his striking good looks were memorable, and in the Bowery such a man would stand out, even without his full evening dress, complete with top hat and a cloak.

Jack stepped right into his path. 'Mr Cadogan!' he said.

'Do I know you?' Theo asked, looking Jack up and down as if astounded that a man so roughly dressed should know his name.

'No, sir,' Jack said. 'But I'm a friend of Beth's, and she's in great danger. I was just going down to Heaney's to see her brother, and I spotted you.'

Jack half expected the man to claim he had urgent business and couldn't stop now, but he didn't. 'In danger?' he exclaimed. 'Tell me what's happened!'

Jack explained and added that he felt she was being held somewhere in the Bend and how he'd just come from there. 'But sommat might have happened since I've been gone.'

'Poor dear Beth.' Theo sighed, looking genuinely distressed. 'I had intended to go and collect her later this evening, I've been away in Boston for some weeks. But I'll come with you now and perhaps with our combined force we can make that dreadful Heaney get her released.'

Heaney's was packed as usual on a Saturday night and a negro pianist was acting as a substitute for Beth.

Sam looked wild-eyed and frantic, his customary bonhomie with the customers gone. 'Thank God!' he exclaimed as Jack and Theo came up to the bar. 'I'd been thinking everyone had deserted me.'

Theo had a few words with him, but over the din of the drinkers Jack couldn't hear what he was saying. Then Theo turned back to Jack, caught hold of his arm and pointed to the back-room door. 'We're going in there,' he said.

Jack was somewhat bemused that the man he'd taken for an upper-class jackal who liked to scavenge in low places did appear to have some courage.

Theo didn't even knock on the door, just charged in. Heaney was sitting at a table writing in what looked like a ledger. His eyes grew wide at the unexpected intrusion.

'I hear you've had a demand from Fingers Malone for the return of Miss Bolton,' Theo bluffed, his voice cold as steel. 'You may have your reasons for not informing her brother what they are, but as her fiancé I insist on knowing.'

Jack was fairly certain Beth had not become Theo's fiancée because she would've said so at Thanksgiving. While he hated the idea that this might be on the cards, he was glad Theo had come up with a good excuse for his intervention.

'As the demand has been made of me,' Heaney said, getting out of his chair, 'it's my feckin' business.'

'Not when a young lady is in peril,' Theo snapped at him,

and took a threatening step towards the older man. 'Now, tell me what you know, and be quick about it.'

Heaney blustered and stalled.

'How much does he want?' Theo asked.

'It isn't the price so much as what could happen in the future,' Heaney said, a slight whine in his voice. 'He'll think he can take everything I've got, beat me down and stamp on me. I won't let him do that.'

'I take it that means you aren't intending to do anything,' Theo said contemptuously. 'You want to let her rot with Fingers, don't you? What sort of snake are you that a girl's life means nothing to you?'

'Fingers won't kill her,' Heaney said quickly. 'He wants her to play at his place.'

'She will do that if you don't lift a finger to help her.' Jack spoke out, tempted to wring the man's neck. 'You've got to rally some of your men and strike back. Why not snatch his missus?'

'That wouldn't bother Fingers, he'd be only too glad to see the back of her,' Heaney said with a shrug.

'Well, get one of his henchmen then!'

'I've checked out his place. He's got it tight as a drum, his men are everywhere.'

'You mean his saloon, I take it?' Theo said. 'What other properties does he own? D'you know where they are?'

'He's into everything from the stale beer dives to the five-cents-a-night doss houses,' Heaney replied disdainfully.

'Down on the Bend?' Jack asked.

'Where else?' Heaney snapped.

Jack looked at Theo and gestured to him that he wanted to talk to him outside.

'We'll be back,' Theo said to Heaney.

*

They had to go right outside on the street as the noise in the saloon was so loud.

'Heaney won't help.' Jack spoke in a low voice as he lit up a cigarette. 'So we've got to find her ourselves. Bottle Alley or Blind Man's Court, she's got to be in one of them. We pick five or six good men and storm 'em. Even if she's not there, we're bound to find someone we can put pressure on to tell us where she is. If we go in early in the morning everyone will be sleeping off the grog.'

'I've never been down there,' Theo said, his voice subdued as if this was all too much for him.

'I have, and I know my way around.' Jack grinned at him, for he liked the fact that he was in a position to command. 'I know which men to pick too. We don't want Heaney's blokes, nor Fingers'. This is just us, getting our girl back.'

Theo didn't speak for a moment. 'I'll have to go home and change,' he said eventually. 'Can I meet you later?'

'We'll meet up on the corner of Canal Street at six,' Jack said.

Theo nodded. 'What shall we say to Heaney?'

'Nothing, like he's told us nothing,' Jack said viciously. 'But there'll be trouble after this for all of us. Reckon we might have to leave town for a while.'

Chapter Eighteen

'Who's this other cove then, Jack?' Edgar asked as the men gathered at the end of Canal Street at six in the morning. It was well below freezing and their breath was like smoke as they huddled together under a lamp post.

'A flash geezer, name of Theo,' Jack replied tersely. He was wishing now he hadn't suggested Theo joined them, for he was likely to be a liability. 'Beth's been walking out with him.'

All five of the men worked at the slaughterhouse and none had any affiliation with either Heaney or Fingers. They were all big, muscular men, ranging from twenty to twenty-five, but Edgar was the only one born in America. The other four were immigrants like Jack: Karl, a Swede, Pasquale, an Italian, Thaddeus, a Pole, known to everyone as Tadpole, and Dieter, a German.

The bonds between these men had been formed while working alongside one another. Theirs was a hard, brutal trade and serious accidents could happen at any time, so they had to rely on one another. Jack had once knocked Karl out of the way of an enraged steer, and all the others had someone to thank for giving them a timely warning or helping them when they were hurt. There was a kind of code between all the men who worked in the slaughterhouse that if one of their number needed assistance, the others would give it.

Jack was one of the group who offered their muscle when Tadpole's younger sister was raped by three men as she walked home from a dancing class. One of the rapists would never walk again, let alone defile another woman, and the other two received a primitive form of castration.

Jack had known he could count on these men, for they not only knew that Beth was special to him but had all heard her play at Heaney's at some time. When he'd called at each of their lodgings, their only question had been, 'What time?' Each man had come prepared with a cudgel tucked beneath his coat.

Sam came around the corner to join them, looking as yellow as a Chinaman in the gaslight. Jack introduced him briefly to the other men, and patted his shoulder in sympathy because he knew Sam was no fighter and could see he was scared.

Finally Theo arrived. He was wearing working-men's clothes and Jack fleetingly wondered how he came by them as he doubted the man had ever done a day's real work in his life. He also wondered if Theo had considered running away from this. But he would have the man's full measure in an hour or two.

He introduced Theo, then urged everyone to gather round him so he didn't have to shout.

'The object of the raid is to frighten people into telling us where she's being held,' he began. 'Shout, push, but hold back on using your cudgels, they are only for those standing in our way, not the poor sods who live in the hovels.

'They'll be reluctant to tell us anything. They may be down and out but even they have a code of not squealing. They are out in the alleys at all hours, though, so some of them must have seen Beth brought there.

'Finally, watch out for the children. There'll be hundreds of them; it will be like stirring up an ants' nest. We don't want hurting one of them on our consciences.'

'Are we all to go in at once?' Karl, the big blond Swede, asked.

'No. I'll go in with Pasquale and Dieter, to make sure the Italians and Germans understand what we want. The rest of you block the door to stop any escaping. I've got some money to offer as a bribe, so keep your eyes and ears open for anyone who acts or looks like they know what we want.'

Jack handed Sam a spare cudgel, knowing he wouldn't have thought to bring any kind of weapon. He noted that Theo had a stout walking stick, which surprised him; he had expected the man to produce a knife.

Jack led the way, Sam beside him, and the others followed close on their heels.

It was odd seeing the alleys so empty and peaceful after the crowds and noise on the previous day. They passed many drunks lying insensible on the frosty ground. Jack wondered fleetingly how many of their number would never wake up, for he'd heard that the death rate in winter here included many who'd frozen to death.

But it wasn't entirely silent. They could hear snoring and babies crying, and there was the inevitable rustling of rats going about their business.

They began with Blind Man's Court, and Pasquale lit the lantern he'd brought with him. As Jack had expected, there was no lock on the front door, nor even any on the door of the first room they charged into. As Pasquale held the lantern up they saw there were at least fifteen people huddled in together on the floor like sardines in a tin.

'Where's the girl?' Jack yelled, prodding bodies with his cudgel. 'Come on, tell me where she is!'

One by one heads lifted, blinking in the light of the lantern. A woman screamed, a man swore at them, but Jack persisted. 'Someone brought a girl here by force yesterday,' he said. 'It was around six in the evening. Did you see her?'

Pasquale repeated the message in Italian when he heard some of his countrymen's voices. That brought forth a torrent of words and Jack looked questioningly at Pasquale, for though he'd learned a few Italian phrases, he couldn't understand them.

'They say to go away, they haven't seen anything. They are upset you woke them up.'

'D'you believe them?'

Pasquale nodded. 'We'd best try the next room.'

They went through the house systematically, and although they saw some two hundred people, ranging from babies to old folk, they learned nothing. Some of the younger men escaped from them and ran outside, where the others stopped them and questioned them. But they had run not out of guilt, just sheer force of habit. It seemed that a raid on that house usually meant some of their number being sent to the Tombs.

By the time they were ready to move on to the next house, the noise they had created had alerted most of the residents in the little court, and Jack's men had their work cut out to keep everyone contained within it. Fortunately, as it was still dark and bitterly cold, most were so frightened by the sight of the cudgels that they soon disappeared back inside.

'She wasn't brought here, Jack,' Theo said when they'd been in every house, searching from the cellars up to the attics. 'I've never seen such a pitiful bunch. You saw how hopeful they looked when it got around there was a reward for information! They are half starved – if they knew something they'd have been falling over themselves to tell us.'

'Let's hope we find something in Bottle Alley then,' Jack said wearily.

*

The situation in Bottle Alley was a repeat of what had gone on in Blind Man's Court, except it was harder to contain the people who came tumbling out to see what was going on, because it was an alley, with an exit at either end. By the time they were half-way down the alley, it was light, and their problems were exacerbated by people who lived elsewhere coming through it. Many stopped to ask what was going on, or just stood around watching.

Sam looked as if he was on the point of collapse. Dealing with so many people milling around him, all speaking different languages, when he hadn't slept for two nights, was indeed hard on him.

Jack was tired too. He felt he must have asked the same questions at least a thousand times, and there were moments when he was tempted to use his cudgel, just to provoke some real reaction rather than the blank stares. A few old crones clutching shawls around their bent shoulders held out filthy hands for money, many of the men hurled insults, and the children darted around them constantly, getting in the way.

To Jack's surprise, Theo was very good with the children. Most of them spoke English, or at least enough to communicate with him, and he worked his way diligently among them, questioning, cajoling and promising a reward for information.

'Come over here, Jack!' he suddenly called out, and as Jack pushed his way through the throng, he saw Theo was with a little girl of six or seven. She was typical of all the children, painfully thin and white faced, with matted hair, and her dark eyes seemed too large for such a small face. She wore only a thin, ragged dress, her feet were bare and dirty and a shawl was criss-crossed across her chest and tied in a knot at her back.

'She heard something,' Theo said as Jack reached him. 'But her English isn't good. She keeps going off into Italian.'

Jack got Pasquale, who knelt down in front of the child and spoke to her in his language. Pasquale was handsome, with curly black hair, olive skin and soft, dark eyes, and although the little girl was shy and peeped through her fingers at him, she gradually began to respond as he kept talking to her and smiling to reassure her. Theo held out a silver dollar, and her eyes fixed on it greedily. 'Tell her she may have it if she can tell us what she heard and where it was.'

The silver dollar seemed to work. All at once she was jabbering away.

'What's she saying?' Jack asked.

'She heard banging yesterday and someone calling out. She told her mother who said people are always banging and calling out here. But the girl said she'd never heard anyone calling like this lady was.'

Jack's heart seemed to leap into his mouth. 'Where was this?' he asked.

Pasquale asked the little girl and she took his hand as if to lead him there.

Jack followed with Theo, right along the far end of the alley they hadn't yet searched. The child stopped by a small piece of waste ground, clearly the site of a building which had burned or fallen down. It was full of rubbish and rubble and a crazy-looking tumbledown shack which could've once been a stable. She looked up at Pasquale and began speaking again.

Pasquale smiled. 'She hides in the shack when her pa is drunk. She slept in there and was woken up in the morning by the banging and calling. She said it came from over there.' He pointed to the house on the left.

Jack felt a surge of excitement. The houses on either side

of the waste ground were very old and shored up with big timbers, but squeezed behind them in what should've been a backyard, were newer buildings. These places, known as back lots, were a common sight all over the Lower East Side.

'Let's get in there,' he said.

Going round to the front of the house, Jack saw the door was padlocked and the windows boarded up. He asked the child if anyone lived there. She shrugged her shoulders and said something in Italian.

'She doesn't think so,' Pasquale said. 'But sometimes men come there.'

Before Jack could even express his opinion that they'd found the right place, Theo thrust the silver dollar into the little girl's hand, ran round the back again and shinned up the wall that joined the two parts of the house. It was about eight feet high, but he managed it with ease for it was rough stone with many hand- and foot-holds. He perched on the top for a second, then jumped down the other side.

Jack quickly followed him, calling back to Pasquale to get the others and bring the lantern. He dropped down into the tiny yard between the two buildings.

The space was only about four feet square, and ankle-deep in rubbish, fortunately frozen solid. The doors to both houses were padlocked, and all the windows boarded up save one by the door to the front house. The board there had been wrenched off, revealing glass which was partially broken.

Theo lifted his walking stick and smashed out the remainder of the glass.

'Wait for the others to get here,' Jack called out, but Theo took no notice and climbed in.

Jack was just about to follow him when he heard Karl yell that he was coming over with the lantern, so he waited until his friend was on the wall and had passed the lantern down to him.

Theo's heavy boots were making a racket on the bare boards inside the house, but as Jack climbed in through the window, he thought he heard something.

Asking Theo to stand still, he listened, and they both heard a faint cry.

'Beth?' Theo bellowed. 'Is that you? I've come to rescue you!'

The two men stood stock still, straining their ears to hear.

Then, just as Jack began to think they had imagined the cry, he heard Beth's voice.

'I'm below you,' she called, her voice tinny and weak. 'There's a trapdoor in the floor.'

'I'm just lighting a lantern to see,' Theo shouted back, indicating to Jack he was to do it. 'Hold on, I'll have you out in a trice.'

Once the lantern was alight they could see an old table and a few chairs to one side of the room, several large wooden crates and a quantity of empty bottles strewn around them. It looked as if men had been coming here for card games.

But they could see no trapdoor in the floor.

Karl came in, quickly followed by Pasquale, and all the men pushed at the packing cases to see what was beneath them.

As they moved the last one, which was heavier than the others, they finally saw the trapdoor. 'We've found it, Beth,' Theo shouted, and Jack pulled it open.

'There's a ladder here,' Pasquale called, dragging it along the passageway.

Jack moved to be the first one down the ladder, but Theo elbowed him out of the way and disappeared down into the darkness.

'I've got you now,' they heard him say above the sound of Beth crying.

Theo brought her out over his shoulder, and as he set her down at the top of the ladder, Jack thought he had never seen a sadder sight. Her face was black with dirt, her eyes red and swollen, and tears had made white tracks down her cheeks. Her skirt and boots were soaked and she was so stiff with cold she stumbled when she tried to walk.

'I thought I was going to die,' she said, and her voice was little more than a croak.

Theo picked her up in his arms. 'We must get her away from here and into the warm quickly,' he said.

Sam and the others were just coming over the wall, and for a few moments everyone was talking at once, jubilant that their mission had been accomplished. Beth seemed scarcely aware of anyone but Theo, and as they all worked together to lift her over the wall and away to safety, Jack felt a sharp stab of jealousy.

He had been her real rescuer. He'd planned it, got the men and organized it all. But Theo, who had done very little, had taken over once they'd found her, and to Beth it was going to seem as if he was her saviour.

Chapter Nineteen

The coffee shop where they had taken Beth was warm and steamy. She was flexing her fingers and examining her knuckles which were raw from banging on the walls.

'We should get you to a doctor,' Jack said.

'Don't fuss,' she replied, smiling weakly. 'I'm getting warmer now and I'll be fine once I've had a wash and a sleep. I just wish your friends hadn't disappeared before I could thank them.'

It had been as though her mind was as frozen as her body when Theo got her out of the cellar. She couldn't explain anything and her limbs refused to move. Theo had carried her all the way to this coffee shop, and although Jack and Sam had kept asking her questions about how and where she was snatched, she was unable to answer.

But now, after two large cups of hot, sweet coffee and some bacon and eggs, she had thawed out enough to tell them how it came about, and how her captor hadn't returned, not to bring her food or drink or even a blanket. She had told them how she kept up the shouting and banging until exhaustion overcame her, but not that she had given up hope of rescue. Now she was safe, the terror she'd felt as she sat hunched up in the dark with only the squeaking and rustlings of rats for company was fading. She could see anxiety for her etched in the men's faces and she didn't want to add to it.

Yet when she first heard Theo's and Jack's voices she had thought she was descending into madness and merely imagining what she most wanted to hear. It was only when the trapdoor began to open, light spilled into her dark prison and Theo's head was silhouetted in the opening, that she knew it was for real.

'You can come back to my place,' Theo said, taking her hand and kissing the tips of her fingers. 'Nobody knows where it is, and it's a quiet house. You can have a hot bath and a good sleep.'

That sounded like heaven to Beth, but she caught the horrified glances Sam and Jack exchanged.

Theo saw them too, and letting go of her hand, looked hard at Sam. 'You do realize that none of us will be safe? Fingers will be out for our blood, and Heaney won't offer us any protection because all he cares about is his property.'

'I can't see why Fingers would have it in for us,' Sam said belligerently. 'Even a thug like him can surely understand a man rescuing his sister.'

'It's all about keeping face,' Theo said patiently. 'He won't give a damn about the rights and wrongs of it. All he'll see is that we thwarted him.'

'He's right, Sam.' Jack sighed, running his fingers through his dark hair distractedly. 'Fingers is a madman, and the rough way he treated Beth proves that she meant nothing to him. His whole aim was to provoke Heaney. He'll have to do something else now and I wouldn't put it past him to fire-bomb the saloon tonight just to show his muscle.'

'Are you trying to say I shouldn't work there any more?' Sam said incredulously.

'Not unless you've got a death wish.' Theo smirked. 'You've got to make yourself scarce, Sam. We all have. Fingers, Heaney and their foot soldiers aren't reasonable men, they are mindless, savage brutes, determined to have a turf war, and we'll be caught in fire from both sides. The best thing you two can do is to take off to Philadelphia today. I've got some friends you can go to there, and I'll bring Beth to you as soon as she's able to travel.'

'What about my mates from the slaughterhouse?' Jack asked, his face pale and anxious.

Theo shrugged. 'I think they're safe enough. They aren't known to Fingers or Heaney.'

'We can't go just like that, it's Christmas Eve!' Sam objected.

Theo raised an eyebrow. 'You surely don't think men like them believe in the season of goodwill? They'll see tonight as the perfect time to strike when all the bars are crowded.'

Sam's belligerent expression changed to one of fear. 'But what about our belongings back at Houston Street?'

Theo looked at a clock on the wall; it was just after ten. 'I doubt word will reach Fingers or Heaney before noon. You can go and pack up now, I'll take Beth to my place first, then come round to collect her things.'

'What makes you think Beth will be safe with you?' Sam said suspiciously. 'You said you'd have to leave too!'

'So I will, for I certainly won't be able to play cards anywhere in New York for the foreseeable future,' Theo replied. 'But no one knows where I live. We'll be safe enough there until she's recovered.'

'Let me talk to Beth on her own,' Sam said curtly.

Theo nodded and said he'd give him ten minutes.

As soon as the coffee-shop door had closed behind him, Sam moved closer to his sister. 'I don't want to leave you with him,' he said. 'Especially at Christmas.'

Beth understood why he was afraid, but she was too exhausted to concern herself with that for now, and besides, she loved Theo, he'd rescued her and she'd willingly go anywhere he suggested.

'It's the only thing to do,' she said, and patted her brother's face affectionately. 'I'll be fine, I promise. I feel so weak that I'd only be a liability to you if I was to come with you now.'

'It isn't right for you to be alone with a man like him,' Sam said stubbornly. 'And I don't like him telling Jack what to do either.'

'He was talking sense,' Jack butted in. 'As soon as all this started I knew I wouldn't be able to hang around afterwards, I've heard what that crew do to anyone who gets in their way. I'd rather Beth came with us now, but she isn't up to it, Sam, so we ain't got no choice.'

Beth looked gratefully at Jack. 'I'm so sorry you had to get caught up in this and lose your job too.'

'I might get a better one in Philadelphia,' he said with a resigned grin. 'And we're not greenhorns any longer – we might even make our fortune.'

Beth could barely keep her eyes open as the cab took her and Theo to his place. He had arranged to meet Jack and Sam a little later to collect her belongings and to give them an introductory letter for his friend in Philadelphia.

'They won't know themselves there,' he said reassuringly when she'd been a little tearful as they said their goodbyes. 'Frank is a wealthy man with a finger in every pie in Philadelphia. He'll have Sam in one of his saloons and Jack in some other business before they even get a chance to unpack.'

Beth was so exhausted she didn't notice where the cab was taking them, only that it was some way uptown from Houston Street. She was vaguely aware it was a brownstone house in a quiet square, the kind of area where well-to-do families lived.

Theo took her up a flight of stairs and into a large room at the front of the house. All she really saw in her exhausted state was a big bed with ornate carved posts, and she collapsed on to it. She vaguely heard Theo telling her she needed to take her boots off and that he would tell his landlady she was there before going back to Houston Street, but she was already sinking into sleep and couldn't respond.

She woke later to the familiar sound of a fire being raked, and for a moment or two she thought she was back in Liverpool, for she had woken to that sound throughout her childhood. She was very warm; the covers over her were thick and heavy. But as she stretched a little, an ache in her back and arms brought her back to reality. To her consternation she realized that she was wearing only her camisole and petticoat; her dress, stockings and stays had all been removed.

Keeping the covers right up to her nose, she cautiously opened her eyes and saw Theo bending down to the fire. She felt rather than knew that he'd been in the room with her for quite some time for the curtains were drawn, the gas lit, and he was in his shirtsleeves.

The room looked very cosy, with two big armchairs drawn up to the fire and a thick red rug in front of it. The whole room had a rather grand air, for the gas lights on the walls had ornate glass mantles, the curtains were heavy brocade, and there was a linen press against one wall which matched the dark wood of the bed and was equally ornately carved.

'Theo,' she whispered, 'what time is it?'

He stood up straight and turned to her with a smile. 'At last! I'd begun to think you would never wake. It's seven o'clock in the evening and I saw Jack and Sam off at the station hours ago.'

'Who took my clothes off?' she asked.

'I did. I couldn't let you sleep with them on. They were wet and badly soiled and you'd have been very uncomfortable,' he replied.

Beth blushed and burrowed deeper into the covers. 'Could you get me something to put on then?' she asked nervously. 'I need to get up.'

He went over to the door and took a checked wool dressing gown from the hook. 'Put this on for now, though I have got all your own things here. If you'd like a bath it's just down the landing, and I've made sure the water is hot. But maybe you'd like to eat first? I got some fried chicken and potatoes earlier, which are being kept warm in Miss Marchment's kitchen.'

'Will she mind me staying here?' Beth asked, pulling the dressing gown under the covers with her so she could put it on without revealing any flesh.

'No, not at all. I explained what had happened to you,' he said. 'You can meet her tomorrow.'

Later that night Beth lay in the bed feeling strangely disappointed. Theo had danced attendance on her. He'd brought her a lovely big meal, run her a hot bath and given her a couple of glasses of whisky mixed with honey and lemon which he claimed would ensure she didn't come down with a bad cold. But he hadn't even kissed her.

She could smell his hair oil on the pillows, she could almost feel the imprint of his body in the mattress, but he was sleeping elsewhere in the house and he hadn't made so much as a tiny hint he'd like to share his bed with her.

Would she have let him if he had?

Beth didn't know the answer to that. Her head insisted she wouldn't have allowed it. But if that was so, why did she feel let down?

Then there was the question of where he'd been all these weeks. He'd made no explanation or apology about that. It seemed likely that he had another woman tucked away, but if that was the case, why would he say he'd take Beth to Philadelphia?

He must love her. Why else would he have planned and executed her rescue? He'd told her about how he discovered that Fingers owned property in both Blind Man's Close and Bottle Alley and that he stormed into every room of every house until he found the little girl who said she'd heard banging and shouting. Sam, Jack and Jack's friends were there too of course, but it was clear Theo was their leader.

During the evening she'd wandered around his room and taken note of many things: photographs of his family in silver frames, good-quality clothes and shoes, gold cufflinks, silver-backed hairbrushes and at least a dozen silk ties. The furnishings in the room were worn and old, but there was no mistaking that this had once been a wealthy person's residence; she wondered why he'd led her to believe that he lived much like her and Sam.

That could be because he might not know that poor people like her didn't have bathrooms or a water closet just down the hall. Maybe he actually believed he was roughing it because he had to live and sleep in one room?

But if this was roughing it, with soft sheets on the bed, a feather eiderdown and a roaring fire, then she would gladly rough it with him. This house was as quiet as a church – no babies crying, no raised voices or drunken footsteps on the stairs; the only sound she'd heard all evening was the occasional rumbling of cab wheels in the street below.

She wanted to believe that Theo had kept his distance tonight because he both loved and respected her, for that was how gentlemen behaved in romantic novels. But a small voice in her head warned her against thinking that way; he had never said he loved her, and as Ira had pointed out more than once, gamblers were a law unto themselves.

Beth woke the following morning to a knock on the door. Before she could even gather herself, the door opened and a woman came in, carrying breakfast on a large tray.

'I'm Miss Doughty, Miss Marchment's housekeeper,' she said, her face stern and cold. 'Mr Cadogan asked me to bring this up and tell you that he will see you this evening.'

'But it's Christmas Day,' Beth exclaimed. She was very pleased by the breakfast of bacon, eggs, pancakes and coffee, but she couldn't believe Theo intended to leave her alone all day.

She also sensed the housekeeper's disapproval. The woman was thin, with sharp features and iron-grey hair, and she certainly didn't look like someone Beth could win round.

'Mr Cadogan would have made his plans for today some weeks ago,' Miss Doughty retorted. 'Gentlemen do not cancel such arrangements lightly and he has asked me to make sure you rest and do not go out.'

'I'm sorry for intruding on you,' Beth said in an effort to appease the woman. 'The breakfast looks wonderful.'

'Eat it up while it's hot. I'll be back later when you are dressed to take you down to meet Miss Marchment. Make sure you put on something plain, you don't want to alarm her by looking like a saloon girl.'

She left then, sweeping out of the room and leaving Beth feeling shaken.

Meeting Miss Marchment was an even more unpleasant experience. Her room on the ground floor was gloomy and squalid. It stank of cat's urine and made the comfort and

247

cleanliness of Theo's all the more remarkable. It was difficult to judge Miss Marchment's true age, for although her wrinkled, yellow-tinged skin, her black clothes and the lacy cap over her white hair suggested she was very old, her loud, brusque voice seemed to belong to someone much younger. She was small and slender but her hands were swollen and looked painful, and Beth thought she probably suffered from rheumatics.

She didn't show the slightest sympathy or concern for Beth, instead firing questions about her family background as if she believed only someone from the gutter could have got herself into such a plight. Beth attempted to impress on her that she was in fact genteelly brought up, but the old lady retorted that any girl working in a saloon was courting trouble. She even added that she hoped Beth wasn't taking advantage of Mr Cadogan's good nature.

Beth tried not to be rude back, merely stating that it had been Theo's suggestion to bring her here because she was exhausted after her ordeal. 'I am very grateful for his kindness, and indeed to you for allowing me to stay a few days, but I shall be joining my brother as soon as possible,' she finished up.

It was clear Theo hadn't informed his landlady that he was intending to leave her shortly, and Beth didn't enlighten her.

Her spirits fell to an even lower ebb when she returned to Theo's room. She was an unwelcome guest in an area she didn't know. Nor did she know where Jack and Sam were in Philadelphia. She felt trapped and completely dependent on Theo.

Her thoughts naturally turned back to the previous Christmas at Falkner Square, and as she thought of Molly toddling around the kitchen, and all the warmth and laughter there had been, the feeling of utter safety and happiness, she ached to be back there.

Just after seven that evening Theo came back, bursting into the room and bringing with him the smell of cigars and images of a table laden with food and drink, and jovial company. 'I wish I could have taken you with me today,' he said, drawing her into his arms for a long, sensual kiss which set Beth's head reeling.

Miss Doughty came up soon afterwards, bringing them a cold supper of ham and pickles. Beth didn't have to ask why Theo got his meals cooked and his laundry and cleaning taken care of when the other four boarders, at present with their families for Christmas, had to fend for themselves. He had a way about him that would make any woman, no matter how old, want to take care of him.

After they'd eaten their supper, and Beth had moved to sit close to the fire, Theo took her fiddle out of its case and handed it to her.

'Surely you don't want me to play it now?' she said in some surprise. 'Won't I disturb Miss Marchment?'

He chuckled. 'She'd be more disturbed by silence. She'd think I was making love to you. But I thought it would keep you occupied because I have to go out again in a minute or two anyway.'

Beth felt her heart sink with disappointment. 'I thought you said it was dangerous for you to go out?' she said quietly.

'It would be if I was bound for the Bowery.' He shrugged, picking up his hairbrush and moving over to the looking-glass. 'But I have business in far more salubrious parts of the city.'

Perhaps he sensed her disappointment for he came over to her and embraced her.

'I have people to see and business arrangements to sort,' he said, kissing her forehead tenderly. 'I would of course much prefer to stay here with you, but then I would be tempted to make love to you. When we get to Philadelphia everything will be different. And you must practise your fiddle, for when we get there I'm going to present you in all the best places.'

Beth did play her fiddle after he'd gone. Her fingers were stiff and bruised, in fact her whole body ached and it took effort just to hold the instrument, but playing it was her tried and tested way of calming herself. She didn't attempt the gay-spirited jigs she'd played in Healey's, but some of the plaintive, slower melodies she had learned as a child from her grandfather. He had once said they brought back the beauty of Ireland for him: he could see Galway Bay in the mist, the purple-topped mountains and the wild flowers on the bogs in spring. For Beth they were soothing sound pictures, ones of love and security, for she could see the parlour in Church Street, her parents sitting close together on the couch, her grandfather leaning back in his chair, eyes closed and a smile on his face.

On 28 December Beth and Theo caught the train to Philadelphia. Theo had informed Miss Marchment that he was leaving just the previous night, and Beth had heard her voice raised in anger.

Theo didn't divulge to Beth what had been said. His only comment was that he'd never told Miss Marchment that he was going to stay permanently.

'I do so hate it when people try to pin me down as if I'm their property,' he added, as if by way of a warning to Beth.

*

It was dark when they arrived in Philadelphia, and a cab took them a short distance from the railway station to a street of old Federal-style houses. The door was opened by a short, squat black woman wearing a white apron and a spotted turban. 'Mr Cadogan!' she said with a smile as wide as a slice of watermelon. 'It sure is good to see you again.'

'It's good to see you again too, Pearl,' he said, patting her cheek with obvious affection. 'This is Miss Bolton, come to join her brother.'

Pearl looked appraisingly at Beth, perhaps surprised that she looked so different to Sam. 'You are very welcome, Miss Bolton, but I'm afraid Sam and Jack have gone out on some business. They'll be back later, though, so I'll get you some supper and then show you your room.'

Beth was disappointed that Sam and Jack weren't there to meet her, but it was a relief to find herself in an elegant, comfortable and warm house. The doors and banisters were shiny with varnish, there was thick carpet on the stairs, and large, gleaming mirrors framed in gold reflected the light from the gas mantles.

As Pearl led them to the kitchen at the back of the house, Beth caught a glimpse of a sumptuous parlour furnished in red and gold with a blazing fire.

'A bit different from Miss Marchment's, eh?' Theo said with a smile.

Beth had heard laughter coming from the rooms upstairs, but as neither Theo nor Pearl, who she assumed was the housekeeper, volunteered any information about the rest of the household, Beth ate the supper of soup, bread and cheese and just listened as Theo chatted to Pearl.

It was clear he'd charmed her as he had Miss Marchment, for the woman hung on his every word, fussing around him and showing her delight that he was to stay for a while.

'I've got some business to attend to,' he said to Beth as he finished his supper. 'But Pearl will take care of you until Sam and Jack return. I shall see you in the morning.'

'You look very tired,' Pearl said solicitously after Theo had gone. 'I'll take you to your room now and let you settle in.'

Pearl led the way down to the basement holding an oil lamp and Beth followed carrying her valise. It felt cold down there after the warmth of the kitchen and Pearl apologized for it, saying she'd put a hot brick in Beth's bed.

'Here we are,' she said, opening a door in a long passageway with a rough stone floor. 'That's the laundry room,' she went on, indicating a door to the left, and then, pointing to the right, explained that was Sam and Jack's room.

Beth's room was small, around nine feet by seven feet, with a barred window. 'It sure is poky but it's real quiet,' Pearl said. 'Sam and Jack won't be back till after midnight, so if you hear anything don't be alarmed – it will only be them coming back. No one else comes down here. If you need anything, just come on up to the kitchen and holler.'

The room was plain, nothing more than an iron bed, a wash stand with a tin basin and ewer, and a small clothes closet. But it looked and smelled clean and Beth was so tired she didn't even feel dismayed that Theo had left her alone again.

After Pearl had gone upstairs, she took the oil lamp and went into the next room where she was reassured to see one of Sam's shirts hanging on a peg on the wall and Jack's checked jacket on the back of a chair.

Beth had just finished unpacking her valise when a clock upstairs struck ten. Thinking she would run up and ask Pearl if she could have some hot water for a wash, she made her way back to the staircase.

The basement door opened up at the back of the hall,

and as Beth reached it she heard people coming down the stairs from the first floor. Assuming they were family members, who might not wish to run into a stranger so late in the evening, Beth shrank back into the doorway.

On the wall opposite was a large looking-glass, and suddenly reflected in it were four girls.

She gasped in shock, for they weren't the kind of sedate young ladies she had expected to see, but scantily dressed floozies, their breasts and legs partially revealed as their brightly coloured satin and lace garments fluttered around them.

It was very obvious what they were, and indeed what this house was, for Amy and Kate had shown her similar garments more than once. Even Ira had a special section in her shop where she kept such things.

All four girls, a blonde, two brunettes and one redhead, were young and pretty, and they were all giggling at a shared joke.

'If he's not done in ten minutes I'll make him give me another ten dollars,' the redhead said, spluttering with laughter.

Beth took a step backwards on to the stairs to the basement and quietly closed the door, so shocked that she no longer cared if she had a wash. She wanted to believe that there could be another explanation, but she knew there couldn't be.

Theo had brought her to a brothel.

Chapter Twenty

Beth lay rigid in the narrow bed, too upset to sleep. It was very quiet in the basement, but if she strained her ears she could just make out the sound of laughter and the tinkling sounds of a piano from above.

It was bad enough to think that women were selling their bodies to men up there, but she was even more affronted that Theo would bring her here without any warning.

Could it be that he thought she was too stupid or too innocent to realize what this house was? Or was there a more sinister reason, namely, that he was planning to recruit her to the business?

She had no idea what time it was when she finally heard Jack's and Sam's voices outside in the passage, but she guessed it to be well after one in the morning. Leaping out of bed, stopping only long enough to throw a shawl over her nightdress, she ran barefoot to the room next door.

'Beth!' Sam exclaimed. 'We weren't expecting you so soon.'

'Are you feeling better now?' Jack asked.

It was clear both of them had been drinking for they were unsteady on their feet and had glazed eyes.

She blurted out what she had seen and how upset she was that Theo hadn't warned her. 'Did he tell you what this place was before you got here?' she asked.

'Well, yes,' Jack said a little sheepishly. 'But he said we'd be down in the basement with no connection with what went on upstairs. We don't even use that door, we come in through the basement one.'

'Don't take on, sis,' Sam said, slurring his words a little. 'It's just a place to stay until we get something else, and we've already got work. Besides, it ain't as if you've never met any whores before. Kate and Amy were your friends.'

Beth had naively imagined that Sam had never known what her friends back in New York did for a living, and she felt awkward then. 'But Theo didn't tell me,' she wailed.

'Go back to bed,' Sam said impatiently. 'Yeah, Theo is a bit of a cad, why'd you think I didn't want to leave you with him? But we've got a good place to live, work and everything's just dandy. We'll talk about it tomorrow.'

Beth looked beseechingly at Jack but he just shrugged. 'There's worse places than whorehouses,' he said.

It was barely light the following morning when Beth heard Theo's voice. It sounded as if he was in the kitchen upstairs talking to someone. Full of fury that he'd not only betrayed her but corrupted her brother and friend too, she flung on her clothes and raced up there.

He was sitting calmly at the table, drinking a cup of coffee and talking to Pearl. His mussed-up hair and the dark shadow on his chin proved he'd been out all night.

'How could you do this to me?' she raged at him, before he could even say good morning. 'You led me to believe you were taking me somewhere respectable. This is a whorehouse!'

She didn't care if she offended Pearl, and when he laughed at her indignation she wanted to slap his handsome face.

'Come now, Beth,' he said, patting the chair next to him as if inviting her to sit down. 'Do you really think anyone entirely respectable would take in people on the run from New York thugs?'

That was something Beth hadn't considered and it took the wind out of her sails.

'I think you should be very grateful that a good person like Pearl was prepared to risk having trouble brought to her door,' he added reprovingly.

Beth glanced at Pearl, who was still in her night clothes with a little lacy cap over her hair. Her kindly face was full of concern and Beth felt a little ashamed of her outburst, for the woman had welcomed her so warmly last night. It also seemed that Pearl wasn't a mere housekeeper, but the owner of the house. 'You could have warned me,' she said weakly. 'It was such a shock.'

'You ought to have been smart enough to work it out for yourself.' Theo sighed, running his fingers through his hair. 'You've been in Heaney's pay for months now, you worked in a shop where most of the New York whores buy their clothes, I would've thought that would have opened your eyes to reality. Besides, you lost your respectable image the first time you played in a saloon.'

Beth stared at him for a moment, hardly able to believe what he'd just said, but then, as it dawned on her that he was probably right, she burst into tears.

It was Pearl who moved to comfort her.

'There now, don't take on,' she said, enfolding Beth against her large bosom. 'No harm's going to come to you here, you don't even have to meet my girls less you want to. But if you're set on earning a living playing your fiddle, then you've got to live with being seen as a floozy.'

'But why?' Beth sobbed. 'No one thinks anything bad about a man who plays an instrument. I'm not a bad girl, I just love music.'

'It's a man's world, honey. Dancers, singers, actresses and musicians, they all get branded the same,' Pearl said

256

soothingly. 'You can choose to be Miss Prim, go-to-church-on-Sunday, but that means you have to dress quiet, and find respectable employment and lead a dull life. But if you choose to be Miss Sassy the fiddle-player who sleeps till noon and has a heap of fun, you've got to learn not to give any mind to what people say.'

'What's it to be then, Beth?' Theo asked. 'Because I've got a debut lined up for you tonight.'

Beth disengaged herself from Pearl's arms, wiped her eyes and looked into his dark ones, hoping to see love in them. She could see amusement, but that was all.

'Then I guess I'll have to play,' she said airily. 'It wouldn't do to let you down after you've gone to so much trouble.'

Maybe if she continued to amuse him he'd come to love her.

'There you are, honey,' Pearl said as she handed over Beth's red dress which she'd just pressed for her. 'And I've got a real pretty red hair ornament you can borrow if you like.'

It was six in the evening and Beth had managed to overcome her shock about the nature of the house, for no one could have been kinder than Pearl.

After their words that morning, Theo had disappeared off to his room which was further along the passage in the basement. Pearl told her that Jack and Sam wouldn't surface until noon, and it seemed the girls upstairs were late-risers too.

After washing and dressing properly Beth went back upstairs to offer Pearl some help with the chores for she felt bad about her earlier rudeness. Pearl's wide smile showed she appreciated the offer, but she promptly brewed another pot of coffee and made it quite clear she was happier just to chat than worry too much about chores.

Beth had seen many negroes in Liverpool, and even more since she arrived in America, but Pearl was the first she'd ever had a real conversation with. She was intelligent, witty and kind. Even her voice was a delight to listen to for it was low and melodious, with just a hint of the Deep South.

But the most astonishing thing about her was her age. Her face was unlined, she moved gracefully and quickly despite her bulk, and Beth had imagined she was no more than forty. But if the stories she told were true, and Beth did believe them, then she was over sixty, and she laughingly told Beth that the reason she covered her head with a turban or a cap was because her hair was snow-white.

She said she had been born into slavery in Mississippi, but she and her mother had run away when she was thirteen and been helped by some Abolitionists in Kansas.

'Folk were making their way west then in wagon trains,' she explained. 'They were mostly good folk too and we tagged along helping them out with their children, the washing and the cooking in return for food. We meant to go all the way to Oregon, but a story got about that men had found gold in San Francisco, and a whole bunch of the folk on the train broke away to go there. Ma thought we should go too cos we could get work as cooks.'

Beth listened spellbound while Pearl described making their way over the Sierra Nevada to California as winter came upon them. 'It was so cold and the snow so deep we feared we'd die up there, like some of the others did,' she said. 'But we got through to San Francisco somehow. There weren't too many women there then, and it was a wild, rough place, but Ma was right, cooks were badly needed. We set up our tent as soon as we got there, made a big pot of stew and sold it ten cents a bowl as quick as look at you.'

Beth was expecting that Pearl would soon be telling her

that she and her mother eventually found it easier to sell their bodies than their stews, but she was wrong. They continued cooking, gradually increasing both their prices and the range of dishes. They charged miners for washing and mending their clothes, and even opened a 'hotel'.

'It sure weren't like no hotel you'd recognize.' Pearl chuckled. 'Just a big tent, and our lodgers got a straw-filled palliasse on the ground, and provided their own blankets. We made a bath-house out the back too. I could hardly lift those buckets of hot water off the fire, they were so heavy. But we made money, more than we'd ever dreamed of. We got a real hotel built in '52, a fancy place with furniture and mirrors brought all the way from France, but by then respectable women were arriving and they didn't want to stay in a place owned by darkies. They were real mean to us; if they'd had their way they'd have got us run out of town. So Ma turned the place into a brothel to teach them a lesson.'

She laughed uproariously at this, and Beth joined in, for by then she was seeing the scene through Pearl's eyes. 'But surely that would get you run out of town even quicker?' she said, spluttering with laughter.

Pearl put her hands on her wide hips and rolled her eyes. 'Ma knew a thing or two about men, especially those stuffed shirts who ran the city. She hired the kinda girls that turned those men inside out and made them come back howling for more. The polite ladies brayed for the place to be closed down, and their men nodded and agreed, but those same men slunk in the back way any chance they got.'

Beth could see why men would prefer the company of Pearl and her mother . . . She could imagine those sharp-featured, cold-hearted wives gossiping over afternoon tea, while their pompous but sex-starved husbands indulged themselves elsewhere. 'And what about you?' she asked. 'What role did you play in the business?'

'By day I cleaned rooms, cooked and did the laundry, but by night I sang in the saloon,' Pearl said. 'I was never a whore. I ain't saying there weren't men in my bed. But I never took no money for it.'

Beth could believe that. 'Were you a good singer?' she asked.

'They said so,' Pearl replied modestly. 'I loved to sing right from a small child; to me it was as natural as breathing. I had to sing, it was like my spirit being allowed to fly free. But I guess you feel the same way about playing your fiddle. I was young and pretty then too, I loved the attention, to be dressed in silk and satin, to have men looking at me as if I was their love. I'd come a long way from being a barefoot and hungry slave at the mercy of the master.'

Beth guessed that the reason Pearl's mother ran away with her daughter was probably because she wanted to protect her from that master. Although Beth hadn't suffered the kind of hardships Pearl had experienced, she understood that need to perform. 'I feel just like that when I'm playing,' she agreed. 'I know I haven't been a slave, but you can still feel bound by your background and the way you've been brought up.'

'Respectability.' Pearl nodded sagely. 'Well, I've never had that, I never will. But I get respect from my girls, and the men who come here. That's all I need.'

She went on to tell Beth that her mother was knocked down by a carriage and crippled, and it was her belief it was no accident. Her mother never walked again and Pearl had to take care of her and the business. 'But I stayed on there till she died ten years later. I wasn't going to let them win,' she said proudly. 'Then I sold the place and came here and bought this one.'

'Why here?' Beth asked.

Pearl smiled. 'A man, honey, why else would I come clear across the country?'

'Is he Frank, the friend Theo mentioned?'

Pearl nodded. 'He's good to me and a real gentleman, but a gambler and a charmer like Theo. Now, you listen closely to my advice! Don't go dreaming of happy ever after. It don't come with men like Frank or Theo. You have the good times with him, but make sure you hold on to the money you earn and anything he gives you. Give him your body freely, but don't give him your heart, for he'll break it.'

Beth was just going to try to get Pearl to enlarge on that when the girls began coming down to the kitchen. The blonde with the sulky expression was Missy, the two brunettes Lucy and Anna, and the beautiful redhead was Lola. Missy, Lucy and Anna were no more than eighteen, Lola perhaps twenty-three. All of them were wearing dressing gowns and slippers, their faces pale from lack of fresh air.

Beth sensed they weren't entirely happy at finding a strange girl in their midst and she made her excuses and went back to the basement to see if Sam and Jack were awake.

They were, but both had sore heads from the previous night's drinking. Jack went off to the kitchen to get them coffee and give Beth a chance to speak to her brother alone.

'I've kind of got over the shock of staying in a brothel,' she said cautiously. 'I've been talking to Pearl and I like her. I guess last night I panicked, but that was Theo's fault. He should've warned me.'

'I was worried about how you'd react,' Sam admitted.

'Pearl made me see things from a different viewpoint,' Beth said. 'But enough of that. Tell me what you and Jack are doing.'

'I'm managing the Bear, a big saloon just a few streets from here,' Sam said. 'Jack's learning the ropes, the bar and the cellar. But Frank Jasper, the owner, runs several gambling places and he's training me in that. He's great, sis, nothing like Heaney, a real Southern gentleman.'

Beth smiled. She wondered if he knew that Frank was, or had been, Pearl's lover. Somehow she doubted it, Sam wasn't as interested in people as she was. 'Are the wages good?' she asked.

'We haven't been here long enough to see how it will go,' he said. 'But he gave us both ten dollars last night and said he'd talk to us about it in the New Year. We don't have to pay for our keep here either, and Pearl is a great cook.'

'Theo said I would be making my debut tonight. Is it to be in your place?'

'I guess so, because as soon as we got here Frank wanted to know when you'd be coming. It seems Theo told him about you some time ago. You'll go down well, sis, it's a good place, not a rough house like Heaney's.'

'How do you get on with the girls upstairs?' Beth raised her eyebrows enquiringly.

Sam grinned mischievously. 'Pearl doesn't let them give free ones, she made that quite clear on our first night here. And anyway, we've hardly seen them. Only time we go up there is when Pearl calls us for our dinner.'

They talked for a little while, Beth telling him about how it was over Christmas.

'I hope Theo behaved himself.' Sam sniffed. 'I like him, but I don't trust him.'

'Pearl seems to think highly of him.'

'She just likes men,' Sam said wisely. 'And I guess at her age she doesn't need to worry about whether they can be trusted. But now you're here, Jack and I will look out for you.'

'I can look out for myself, thank you,' Beth said, but she softened the remark with a smile. 'I'll leave you now to get up and dressed, and perhaps you and Jack will take me out and show me around while it's still daylight. I don't want to get a pasty face like the girls upstairs.'

The hair ornament Pearl gave Beth was a pearl-studded comb with a spray of red feathers. 'Frank gave that to me when we first met back in 'Frisco,' she said as she fixed it into Beth's hair, up in the kitchen. 'It was my lucky charm, and I wore it every time I sang. You look even prettier with it than I did, and I think Frank will be pleased to see it again. He'll know I like you.'

Beth went into the hallway to look at herself in the big mirror. The brisk walk around the town with Sam and Jack had put colour back into her cheeks, and the way Pearl had caught up some of her curls at the side of her head with the comb made her look more sophisticated. She had always been a little nervous about the red dress because the neckline was low, but the feathers in her hair seemed to balance it better.

Pearl was watching Beth from the kitchen and she smiled to herself. The girl looked a picture with her black curls tumbling around her creamy shoulders. Such a pretty, expressive face, wide eyes, plump lips, the kind of girl any man would want.

She wished she could go to the Bear tonight to hear her play, but her place was here. Frank would tell her about it anyway.

As Sam and Jack had left for work some time earlier, Theo escorted Beth to the Bear. He was wearing his usual evening attire of a snowy-white shirt, bow tie, impeccably cut tail coat and top hat, with his heavy satin-lined cloak flung loosely over his shoulder.

'The Bear got its name because in an old ale house somewhere nearby, the owner kept a bear out the back,' Theo said as they walked down the street. 'If anyone made any trouble he would threaten to throw them out with the bear.'

Beth knew he was nervous because he often told her old stories when he wanted to conceal his feelings. She didn't know if he was worried that she might not live up to his expectations tonight or might be about to complain again about staying in a brothel. Or perhaps he was just a bit apprehensive because he would be playing cards later.

She didn't ask, for she was so scared herself that she thought she might be sick. Sweet reason told her that if she could play in Heaney's, she could play anywhere. But back there she'd never had anyone championing her; if she failed, it would only be she who lost face. She knew Theo, Sam and Jack must all have sung her praises, so if she was a disaster, they'd look foolish.

Her stomach churned alarmingly as they walked into the Bear. It was much bigger than Heaney's, and the high ceiling and narrow windows set in eight feet up above the ground indicated it had been built as a warehouse, but a new wood floor had been added. A long bar ran right down one side; on the other, a raised area behind a low balustrade held tables and chairs. At the far end opposite the door was a stage. The new electric lighting had been put in, twinkling in the vast mirror behind the bar.

It was already very busy, men three deep at the bar waiting to be served, and another couple of waiters taking orders from those sitting in the raised section. There was an entirely different kind of atmosphere to Heaney's too, perhaps because there were more women. Not the kind of low types that Beth was used to seeing in saloons, but ordinary, neatly and soberly dressed women, the kind who might work in offices or shops. She felt afraid of playing in front of them, sure they would not approve of her.

She could see both Sam and Jack serving, but they didn't appear to have noticed her.

'I'll take you in to meet Frank now,' Theo said, taking her arm and leading her briskly through the tables.

Beth clutched at her fiddle case with both hands as they went through a door beside the stage, down a short passage-way and then stopped outside another door while Theo knocked.

'He's a good man. Don't be scared,' he whispered.

Frank Jasper was a huge, bull-like man, with a bald head, thick neck, splayed nose and pockmarked skin. He looked like a man who had come up the hard way, but his elegant evening clothes were evidence of his success.

'So this is your little fiddle player,' he said to Theo after he'd looked Beth up and down. 'I sure hope she's as good as you claim or they'll throw her to the bear.'

Beth had no idea then that Frank was in the habit of using the bear his saloon was named after as a joke. She thought he meant his customers were very hard to please and she quaked in her boots. The size of the saloon was another worry – she wasn't sure if she would even be heard over a couple of hundred noisy drinkers.

The men left her alone in Frank's office for at least twenty nail-biting minutes. Frank hadn't told her how long she'd got to play for, or even what numbers she was going to play, and as she waited she thought she'd sooner be a laundry maid than face this kind of terror. She was just considering looking to see if there was a back door she could slip out of when Jack came in to get her.

'I'm too scared,' she admitted. 'I won't be able to play a note.'

Even he looked unfamiliar in his striped barman's apron and bow tie, and the noise from the saloon was becoming more raucous by the minute.

Jack put his arms around her. 'You'll be fine, Beth, you aren't up there on your own, Frank's got a double bass player and a pianist with you.'

'He has?' Beth instantly felt more confident. 'But why didn't he tell me?'

'Maybe he wanted to see if you'd lose your nerve,' Jack said with a grin. 'You go on in there and show him what you're made of.'

Beth slipped off her coat and lifted her fiddle and bow from the desk where she'd left it after tuning up. 'I'm ready.'

As Jack opened the door through to the bar, she heard someone ringing a bell for silence.

Then Frank spoke, welcoming his customers to the Bear, and Jack held Beth back, indicating she was to wait until she was introduced. 'Most of you already know Herb on piano, and of course Fred on double bass,' Frank said. 'But some of you have been saying you wanted someone good to look at too. So tonight, for the very first time in Philadelphia, we've got a real live English doll to play. I heard tell they called her Gypsy in New York, cos she set all their feet a-tapping with her fiddle-playing. So a big hand now for Miss Beth Bolton!'

'Go,' Jack said, and gave her a push towards the stage steps.

Hearing applause again was like taking a big swig of rum, and Beth ran up the stairs and bowed to the audience, then quickly turned to the pianist, an older man with a mournful face. '"Kitty O'Neill's Champion"?' she asked.

'Sure thing,' he said with a smile and then a nod to the double bass player.

The two musicians played an introduction and Beth smiled at the audience as she tucked her fiddle firmly under her chin and lifted her bow. Her fear was gone now, she was back on stage where she belonged, playing one of her favourite Irish-American folk songs. She was going to be Miss Sassy from now on, and touch the heart of every man in the bar.

Frank took his cigar from his lips and leaned closer to Theo across the table. 'You didn't string me a line this time – she's red-hot.'

Theo nodded and smiled. His heart was bursting with pride, for Beth wasn't just hot, she was burning the whole place up. He'd been afraid she might have lost her fire because of that ordeal in the cellar, but she was playing even better than she had at Heaney's.

He and Frank were at a table on the raised platform at the side of the saloon with an excellent view of the stage. Beth looked very small up there, like a scarlet flame in her red dress. She'd won the crowd with 'Kitty O'Neill', but then she'd gone on to play 'Tom Dooley', 'Days of '49' and 'The Irish '69', all numbers that meant a great deal to Americans. But she really came into her own with her fast Irish jigs, and down in the main part of the room they could see a hundred heads nodding and feet tapping.

Theo smirked at Frank. 'So I win the hundred bucks?'

'Sure, you son of a gun. She's good. I guess Pearl took to her too, she's wearing her feathers.'

Theo picked up his whisky and drank it down in one. He

was a happy man: he'd won his bet, Sam and Jack had proved to be assets, and he had all the gaming tables in Philadelphia awaiting him. And his little gypsy to seduce.

Chapter Twenty-one

'So what do you think of my new home?' Theo asked. 'Are you shocked into silence because of its grandeur?'

Beth giggled. She'd had a few too many drinks at the Bear tonight and Theo had sweet-talked her into coming back here with him.

He was joking about the grandeur. It was just two rooms above a coach house, not unlike the ones she and Sam had lived in at Falkner Square. The furnishings were much nicer though – thick curtains, a bright rug on the floor and an old brocade couch that wouldn't have looked out of place in a country mansion. But its real appeal was the heat coming from the enamelled pot-bellied stove in the centre of the living room. Outside in the street the snow was three feet deep, and Beth had expected that it would be equally cold inside.

'I'm impressed by the tidiness and the warmth,' she said, speaking slowly so she didn't slur her words.

'That I cannot take credit for,' Theo replied, opening the door of the stove and putting another shovel of coal into it. 'I have a maid. Actually she belongs to the people I am renting this place from, but I crossed her palm with silver and now she takes care of me too. She is old and as ugly as sin, but I appreciate how comfortable she makes me.'

Beth smiled. Theo was destined always to have some woman waiting on him hand and foot. Pearl hadn't wanted him to leave her place, for he had charmed her just as he had Miss Marchment and Miss Doughty before her.

'That will keep it going all night,' Theo said as he closed the stove door. 'Now, let me take your coat and get you a drink.'

It was the beginning of March now, but even when the church bells had rung out on New Year's Eve to welcome in 1896, and she'd only been in Philadelphia a couple of days, Beth knew she was going to be happy here.

Pearl's genteel Federal-style house in Spruce Street showed no outward signs of what went on behind its shiny, black-painted door, yet close by in Camac Street and the many narrow alleys that ran off it, brothels, gambling dens and taverns abounded. Respectable people bemoaned the crime and brawling, but to Beth and the boys the whole area was an extraordinarily colourful and joyous conclave of free spirits, who were not bound by the rigid social mores that prevailed elsewhere in the city.

The Bear was situated between Pearl's and Camac Street. Although the majority of its clientele were hard-working artisans who lived in the area, the number of artists, musicians, dancers and actors who frequented it too attracted many middle- and upper-class people who liked being seen in a place deemed risqué.

Beth had it pointed out to her that many of the men who slipped into Pearl's or other brothels on a Friday night were professional men and captains of industry. She had heard too about ladies of quality who sent their servants off to get them opium from the dives along the wharves. Even Ma Connelly, the tiny Irishwoman who assisted with unwanted pregnancies, claimed to have more genteel customers than whores or domestic servants.

Philadelphia meant 'The City of Brotherly Love', and it certainly was a more friendly place than New York, lacking the often menacing and dangerous edge she'd sensed there. There was perhaps just as much poverty, especially amongst the negro and Irish communities, but by and large immigrants appeared more settled here, and the different nationalities more integrated.

It had been terribly cold. On her nineteenth birthday in February there had been a blizzard with drifts of snow feet thick. But Pearl's kitchen was always warm, and the Bear was only a few streets away. When she got back late at night there was always a hot brick in her bed, and she'd wake in the morning to the smell of frying bacon or pancakes.

On the nights she didn't play her fiddle, she still worked at the saloon, serving drinks and collecting glasses, and she got to hear other musicians and singers. She'd made many friends too, with both the customers and the other staff.

Frank Jasper had a reputation for being hard-headed and ruthless, but Beth had found him to be jovial and fair-minded. All the money customers put into the hat for the musicians was divided between them equally, and he didn't take a percentage of it. But then, he was a real music lover, and he took pride in seeking out and nurturing new talent. Some nights he got Beth merely to accompany other musicians or singers, other nights she was the star turn, but whether she was playing, or just watching and listening from the floor, she was constantly learning, and she sensed that was Mr Jasper's intention.

He was a great enthusiast of the Italian Paganini, and the Spaniard Pablo Sarasate, both great violinists, and he'd been fortunate enough to hear Sarasate play at a concert in New York. Miss Clarkson had told Beth about these two men, and taken her to a concert where the orchestra played some of their music, so she could understand Mr Jasper's enthusiasm. Theo had said he would take her to some concerts here in Philadelphia to broaden her knowledge of other musicians.

Homesickness for England was a thing of the past. Beth wrote to the Langworthys just as regularly, and looked forward eagerly to their letters with news of Molly, but she no longer ached to go home.

It was living at Pearl's that had changed Beth's outlook the most. It was hard to disapprove of what went on in the house when she heard so much laughter and gaiety from the rooms above. She'd got to know all the girls, and none of them were hapless creatures who had been forced into the profession. They had chosen it. Some just wanted easy money, some were adventurers, and Missy had admitted to Beth she loved sex and saw no reason why she shouldn't be paid for having it too.

Pearl's entire house had a seductive atmosphere, with the girls' scent, cigar smoke and the tinkling of the piano in the parlour. Even the laundry room down by Beth's bedroom was always festooned with scanty silk and lace garments. Late at night, when she heard the sounds of bedsprings creaking, Beth found herself yearning to be in bed with Theo, to discover all that joy the girls alluded to.

She loved him, and she was reasonably secure that he cared for her too, for why else would he turn up at the end of an evening to escort her home, take her out for luncheon or bring her little presents of chocolates, flowers or a decoration for her hair? Pearl had pointed out that red-blooded men needed sex, and if they didn't get it from the one they loved, they went elsewhere. She said only a fool would believe otherwise. And Pearl should know: a constant stream of married and betrothed men came to her door every evening.

It seemed to Beth that once this hurdle was cleared, Theo would give up his disappearing acts and be more open about every aspect of his life. Marriage wasn't as important to her as it had once been. She just wanted him to say that she was his girl and make plans that included her.

Beth sat down on the couch as Theo poured her a glass of wine. 'Are you warm enough?' he asked, handing it to her.

'Yes, thank you,' she replied, suddenly nervous. She loved his kisses and being held and caressed by him, but she had no real knowledge of what came next, whether Theo would undress her, or if she had to do that. Would it hurt her? And would he know how to make sure she didn't end up with a baby?

Beth had made it her business to find out from Pearl how women could protect themselves. There were douches and tiny sponges which she'd seen, and learned the theory of how they worked. But it was all theory. Pearl had said that rubber sheaths for men were what she advocated, but she had added that most men were reluctant to use them.

Theo sat down beside her and watched as she took a gulp of her wine. 'What's going on in that pretty head?' he asked.

'Just that it is a big step coming here with you,' she replied.

He looked tenderly at her, then took her glass away and put his arms around her. 'I'm not going to hurt you,' he said softly. 'I only want to show you the delights of love-making.'

He kissed her then, the tip of his tongue flitting in and out of her lips in a way that always made her belly tighten and her nipples grow hard. In the past such kisses had either taken place late at night in the cold as they walked home, or standing in the corridor of the basement at Pearl's, with Jack or Sam expected back at any minute, so Beth was always tense.

But she was warm now, no one was going to interrupt,

and she willingly succumbed to the bliss, moulding herself into his body and letting her anxieties flow away.

'Ummm,' he sighed, running one finger down her cheek, her throat and into the valley of her cleavage. 'I've waited for this for so long.'

With just one finger he gently pulled back the bodice of her dress and the lace-trimmed camisole beneath it to reveal her right breast while looking into her eyes, his face just a couple of inches from hers. His finger met her erect nipple and he smiled before putting his head down to take it in his lips.

Beth involuntarily gasped, for she had never felt anything quite so wonderful as his sucking, licking and biting. She shamelessly held his head and arched her body towards him as a glorious tingle rushed all over her.

He had both her breasts fully exposed now and went from one to the other, kissing, caressing and sucking, and the sight of his rapturous expression in the soft light from the lamp heightened her pleasure still further.

'Too many clothes,' he murmured. 'I want to see your body and kiss it all over.'

Her dress had tiny buttons right down the back. He moved her to sit up in front of him and with his left hand still playing with her nipples he unbuttoned it, all the while kissing her neck and shoulders as he peeled it down. Laces were untied, her stays dropping to the floor, and suddenly she was sitting there, her naked upper body incongruous with her dress and petticoats ballooning around her waist.

He dropped to his knees in front of her, taking the pins and feathered ornament out of her hair and running his fingers through her curls, as he kissed her long and hard. Beth could feel her private parts growing wet and hot and she was kissing him back feverishly, wanting still more.

Theo got up from his knees, taking her with him, and as he kissed her he pushed her dress, petticoats and drawers down over her hips. Bending to take her nipple into his mouth again, his hand slipped in between her legs and slid one finger into her.

Beth was beyond caring that she was allowing a man to take such liberties with her. Her heart was racing, her breath hot and fierce, and she was shamelessly moving against his finger and moaning out how much she liked it.

Her clothes were kicked aside. She was naked apart from her stockings and boots, and he pushed her down on to the couch where he did the most appallingly rude yet thrilling things to her.

He had shed his jacket and tie at some stage – she recalled pulling his shirt out of his trousers so she could feel his back and chest – but he made no attempt to unbutton his trousers. She could feel the hardness of him against her, yet it was as if he was holding back his own desires while he fulfilled all hers.

It was much, much later before he moved her into the bedroom next door, and only then did he take off the rest of his clothes. The sheets felt very cold and stiff against her overheated skin, and he knelt up for a moment beside her and placed her hand on his rigid sex. It seemed huge, and the knowledge that soon he was going to put it inside her gave her a moment of fear.

He must have sensed it for he lay down beside her and kissed her. 'We don't have to go any further if you aren't ready for it,' he whispered.

But the heat of his body and the fingers that stroked and teased her banished the fear, and as he kissed her again she opened her legs willingly and arched her back to receive him.

*

Pearl had told Beth that if a man really cared for a woman he would withdraw before spending his seed. Theo did that. As Beth tentatively touched the sticky substance on her belly, she felt she'd been given all the reassurance she needed.

It had hurt just a little, and she was a little sore now too, but that didn't matter. Theo had transported her to heaven, and surely he couldn't do that unless he loved her as much as she loved him.

Beth turned to look at Theo asleep in bed as she buttoned up her boots and put on her coat. It was daybreak and there was just enough light to see the dark shadow coming on his chin and the softness of his mouth. She thought she ought to be ashamed of how abandoned she'd been, but she didn't, she only felt joyful. Yet she still determined to leave and get home to Pearl's before anyone knew she'd been out all night. She wasn't brave enough to be blatant about her immorality.

She went to kiss Theo's cheek, breathing in the heady, musky smell of him, but he didn't stir. Then she tiptoed out of the room, closing the door quietly behind her.

It was raw out on the street, with ice on places where the snow had been cleared or trampled. She paused in the doorway to pull her rubber galoshes over her boots and put on her gloves, then walked quickly away with a spring in her step.

'Wake up, Beth!'

Beth opened one eye to see Sam with a lighted candle in his hand. 'What time is it?' she asked.

'The middle of the night, but we've got to leave.'

It was the tone of his voice that made her sit up, not his actual words. He sounded terrified.

'Leave? Why?'

'Something happened at tonight's game,' he said. 'It will take too long to explain now, but I'm in deep trouble and we've got to get away right now.'

It was September, they had been in Philadelphia for nine months, and it had been the happiest time Beth had ever known. She had felt so secure, with Theo, her success as a musician and living here at Pearl's. She couldn't believe that Sam could have done something to destroy it.

'You'll tell me what you've done,' she demanded. 'I'm not going anywhere until I know.'

'A man is dead, that's all you need to know for now,' he said breathlessly.

Her brother's face was in shadow for he'd put the candle down, but she sensed his shame and anguish.

'At the poker game tonight?' she asked.

'Yes. One of the men accused Theo of cheating and pulled a knife on him. I tried to get him off Theo and ended up with the knife. But as God is my witness, I didn't mean to kill him.' He broke off, covering his face with his hands.

Beth understood enough and leapt out of bed. 'Where's Theo now?'

'Gone to his place to pack. He'll be round for us with a cab.'

'Turn your back while I get dressed,' Beth ordered him and flung off her nightdress. She felt sick with fear and wanted no part in this, but they were the two most important people in her life and she had to support them. 'Theo asked that I come too?' she demanded as she struggled into her petticoats.

'We can't leave you here to face the music,' he said weakly. 'Jack's coming as well.'

'Jack was involved too?' Beth's voice rose an octave.

'He only helped us get away.'

Beth's eyes were prickling with tears and she could barely fasten her stays, her fingers were trembling so much. 'What about Pearl and Frank?'

'We weren't at Frank's place, we won't be in trouble with him. I wish we could tell Pearl about it now and prepare her, but we can't, Beth. We've got to get out now.'

Jack appeared in the room just as Beth had finished dressing. He was carrying Sam's and his own bag. Without saying a word, he put them down on the floor and began laying Beth's dresses on the bed and rolling them up to put into her valise.

'So we've got to slip out of here like thieves in the night?' Beth said. 'Not a word of thanks for all Pearl's done for us?'

'We'll write and apologize,' Sam said, hastily picking up more of Beth's things and stuffing them into the valise. 'I'm so sorry, sis.'

Less than ten minutes later the three of them with their bags, and Beth carrying her fiddle case, were out in the dark street, hurrying away to meet the cab around the corner.

It was already there. The horse made a shuffling sound with its hooves as they approached and Theo leapt out.

'I'm so sorry, Beth,' he said as he helped her in. 'I'll make it up to you somehow.'

'Where are we going?' Beth asked as the cab moved away.

'Wherever the first train out takes us,' Theo replied.

Chapter Twenty-two

'I'm freezing,' Beth said, wrapping a muffler more firmly around her neck as she and the boys made their way out of Montreal station. 'If it's as cold as this when it's only September, what will it be like in the middle of winter?'

The first train out of Philadelphia station was bound for New York, but as Jack pointed out on the journey, it wouldn't be wise to stay there for they'd soon be found.

At Grand Central station they saw there was a train going to Canada just a couple of hours later. Theo thought that was the perfect destination for them to escape American justice.

'We won't be here that long. We'll just wait for the hue and cry to die down, then we can go back,' Theo said blithely.

'We can't go back to Philly or New York,' Jack said. He was shivering for he wore only a thin jacket. He'd accidentally left his overcoat hanging on the door at Pearl's. 'But maybe the West Coast of America, somewhere miles away, and warm.'

It was now thirty hours since they'd left Philadelphia. It had been a tedious, cold journey overnight, and none of them had been able to doze for more than a few minutes at a time. Beth felt as if her skin, hair and eyes were full of grit, and although Montreal looked as civilized as anywhere else she'd been, she hadn't expected it to be so cold.

'It isn't that cold, you're just feeling it because you're tired,' Theo said, taking Beth's arm. 'We'll find a hotel. A hot bath, breakfast, then a sleep will put everything right.'

'Nothing is going to make murder right,' she said tersely.

'It was self-defence,' Theo retorted. 'The man had a knife at my throat and he would have used it. To my mind Sam's a hero – he saved my life.'

Beth woke later to find Theo's arms wrapped around her. For just a few moments she thought she was in his bed in Philadelphia, and lay there listening to his soft breathing and luxuriating in the warmth. Then she remembered where she was, and why, and all the anger she'd struggled to suppress on the journey here rose up.

It was pitch dark, but she didn't know if it was early evening or the middle of the night. She was tempted to thump Theo awake rudely and ask him; in fact she had a great deal more to ask other than the time. But after a moment or two's reflection she thought it better to put her own mind in order before tackling him.

She wriggled out of his arms and the bed, took the comforter from it and wrapped it around her, then went over to the window and lifted the edge of the curtain to see out.

The street outside, which had been so busy with carts, cabs and people when they'd booked into the hotel, was silent now. All the shops and the saloon opposite were in darkness and there was not a soul in sight. But there were some lights in upstairs rooms across the street, and she reckoned it must be after eleven at night.

Jack and Sam were sharing the room next door. Theo had registered Beth as his wife, and although just a couple of days ago she would have been pleased by him passing her off that way, it grated now.

She knew Theo had been cheating at the card game even though he swore he hadn't. He was too glib, overly sympathetic to her being dragged out of bed in the middle of the night, and he had used the crowded train as an excuse not to explain how it all came about.

If it hadn't been for Jack's hasty explanation at New York's Grand Central, when Theo went off to get tickets to Montreal, Beth wouldn't have understood anything, for Sam was still in shock and had said little on the long journey.

In the past few months Jack's position at the Bear had altered from being just a barman. He muscled in when drunken brawls broke out: Beth had seen him in action many times when she was playing. He was never aggressive, but he had an instinct for sensing trouble before it turned nasty, and mostly he could defuse it just with diplomacy. But on the occasions this didn't work, he wasn't afraid to steam in, crack the two warring men's heads together and throw them out. Frank Jasper prized Jack for this, often referring to him jokingly as 'My Right Hook'.

Because of Jack's iron-fist-in-a-velvet-glove talent, Frank got him in at most private card games, ostensibly to serve drinks but with security in mind. However, the last game wasn't one run by Frank. It was organized by Rob Sheldon, a man Frank despised as he was a slum landlord and well-known racketeer. Theo and Sam had asked Jack to come along in case of trouble.

The game was in a warehouse down by the docks. The other five players were not men who ever played at the Bear; Theo had met them at other card games and knew them to be high-rollers. But Sam and Jack had never met any of them before, not even Sheldon.

Theo won the first couple of games but then began losing heavily, and when they stopped for a break around two in the morning, both Jack and Sam had advised him to cut his losses and go home, as two of the other players had done.

But Theo refused, saying he felt his luck was about to change.

The two remaining men who sat down to play with Sheldon and Theo went by their nicknames, Lively and Dixey. Theo won the first game, then lost on the second. But the third and fourth he won and the stakes had grown higher. He was up some five hundred bucks and had pocketed his winnings to leave, when Sheldon, who had been winning earlier in the evening, challenged him to one last game.

Jack said he sensed trouble then. He said there was something in the air that wasn't quite right. And he thought Theo seemed just a little too calm and confident as he sat down to play again.

Sam dealt the cards and the game commenced. The money on the table was growing. Dixey folded and left, leaving Sheldon, Lively and Theo. Then Sheldon asked to see Theo's cards.

He had four kings, which beat Sheldon's four of a kind.

'I hadn't been watching the cards played that closely,' Jack admitted. 'I was too busy keying an eye on Sheldon because I felt he might turn nasty if he lost. But I was sure that Dixey had one king when he folded. I guess Sheldon thought that too, for he leapt out of his chair, screaming that Theo had cheated and had another king up his sleeve. Before Theo could even get up, Sheldon was on him and pulled a knife out of his belt. He had it at Theo's throat.'

Jack demonstrated to Beth how Sheldon did this, with his right hand at her throat and his left arm holding her captive.

'I was afraid to go round the table and break it up in case he slit Theo's throat; he was savage enough to do it. And there was Lively too, not a big geezer, but the kind that would steam in if he believed Theo had cheated. So I tried to calm both him and Sheldon by talking, I even said if we found another card up Theo's sleeve they could have all the winnings. But Sheldon was shouting and swearing, getting madder by the minute.

'Then all at once Sam was there behind them, wresting the knife out of Sheldon's hand. I sped round the table to help, Theo suddenly got free and the knife fell on the floor, but then Lively started muscling in. He punched me in the jaw, and Sam must have snatched up the knife from the floor at the same time, because as I went to punch Lively back, Sam was just standing there with the knife in his hand, like he didn't know what to do.

'But Sheldon lunged towards him to get it back. That's when Sam stuck him.'

Beth had tried to get Sam to give his version of what happened. While he couldn't explain it as lucidly as Jack, it was basically the same, except he insisted he didn't stab Sheldon. He said the man just ran straight into the knife.

Theo's laconic view was that it hardly mattered how the knife ended up in the man's belly. After all, Sheldon was going to kill him and Sam stopped him.

But it did matter to Beth. There was a world of difference between someone running into a knife and having it shoved into them. And she blamed Theo for creating the anger in Sheldon which turned her brother from a peace-loving card dealer into a killer.

Lively ran off immediately he saw Sheldon was bleeding profusely. Jack said he believed he'd gone to get a doctor, but Theo said he was just saving his own skin.

Jack tried to staunch Sheldon's wound with his own shirt, but the man died as he was doing so. So they collected up all the money and cards from the table and left, leaving Sheldon there with the knife still embedded in his belly.

Beth wished she could feel, as Jack and Theo did, that Sheldon was a vicious brute who had preyed on the weak and defenceless all his life, and that he'd finally got his just deserts. But he must have had a wife, and maybe children who loved him.

Setting aside the crime, however, and the fact that the three people she loved most were on the run, Beth felt angry that the good life she'd had in Philadelphia was over.

She'd been so happy there. People admired her fiddle-playing and liked her as a person. She had made good money, she'd bought nice new clothes, she could buy presents to send home for Molly, she had even managed to save some money too. Life had been fun, she really felt she was going places, but now she would have to start all over again without the support and affection she'd got from Frank Jasper and Pearl.

Word would get around that Theo was cheating, and Frank might wonder how often he'd cheated at *his* games, and even whether the real reason Theo had to seek refuge in Philadelphia was for the same thing.

He'd certainly start to wonder if he should have trusted any of them, and regret getting Pearl to give them lodgings. As for Pearl, Beth knew she would be very hurt that they'd run off without even leaving a note of explanation for her.

Theo was supremely confident they wouldn't pass on any information about them to the police, and he was probably right because that was the code they lived by. But Beth had built up a close relationship with Pearl, closer even than with her own mother, and she felt she had let her down.

As Beth sat on the chair by the window in the dark, for the first time since she'd embarked on her love affair with Theo, she felt she hated him.

He'd hurt her so many times by disappearing, then

returning a week or two later without any explanation. She knew he wormed his way into the parties and soirées of the most wealthy and influential people in the city, and only a fool would believe he wouldn't abandon her if a beautiful heiress wanted him.

But he could turn her tears to laughter and her sad moods to gay ones effortlessly with his abundant charm. He was generous with both his money and affection. He made her feel she was the most beautiful, talented woman in the world, and when he made love to her he took her to heaven and back, always thinking of her pleasure before his own.

But all this had made her see another side of him, a darker one. She was absolutely certain he had cheated at that game. Why did he have to do that? Surely the whole point of gambling was taking the losing streaks with the winning ones?

Was he a cheat at everything? Was he making love to other women besides her? He had put Sam and Jack at risk. Could he be trusted never to do that again?

A rustling sound across the room alerted her that he was awake.

'Beth!' he said softly. 'Are you there?'

'Of course I am,' she snapped. 'Where else would I be in the middle of the night in a strange country?'

'Come back to bed,' he said.

'I don't think I ever want to be in a bed with you again,' she retorted.

Theo struck a match and lit the candle. 'Why are you so angry?'

He was wearing his undershirt, and with his dark hair all tousled and a dark shadow on his chin he didn't look the dapper gentleman he usually did.

'Because you are responsible for this,' she said, and moved

closer to the bed so she couldn't be overheard by any other guests. 'We all had a good life in Philly; you've ended that. Why did you have to cheat?'

He didn't answer for a moment and she waited for a further denial.

'I know you did,' she said. 'Lie to the rest of the world if you must, Theo. But not to me.'

'All right, I did cheat,' he admitted with a little tremor in his voice. 'I wasn't going to see all my money vanish into Sheldon's pocket.'

'But cheating is wrong.'

'I've been cheated too, lots of times.'

'But that doesn't make it right by you doing it as well.' She was exasperated now. 'You put my brother in danger. As it is, the police will be after him and if he's caught he might be hanged, or whatever they do with murderers here.'

'It wasn't murder, it was an accident.'

'Accident, murder, a man is still dead and my brother is on the run.'

'I doubt the police will even attempt to find out who did it; they'll just think it was gang warfare. Sheldon was a thug, not much different to Heaney in New York, no loss to the country. And even if they do find out it was Sam, they can't get him back from here. A couple of years and it will all be forgotten.'

'Not by me, and I doubt by Sam either,' Beth said.

Theo lay back against the headboard and just stared at her for some little while until Beth felt very uncomfortable.

'Are you going to stay being mad with me for much longer?' he said eventually. 'Only it's the first time we've had the chance to spend all night together without you rushing off to pretend you've been in your own bed all night. Can't we enjoy you being Mrs Cadogan instead of you sitting out there freezing to death and looking like you hate me?'

'This has all been a big shock to me,' she said, wishing she could find the right words to make him see what he'd done to her. 'I never wanted to go to Canada. As far as I know it's all wilderness and frozen up half the year – what will we do here?'

'There are bars and saloons in every corner of the world,' he said with laughter in his voice. 'And I'm sure almost every one of them would like to be entertained by you and your fiddle. Look on it as a new adventure, Beth. You've got your three musketeers with you to keep you safe. Now, come to bed and let me show you how much I love you.'

'Do you?' she asked. Her heart leapt because he'd never said that before.

'Of course I do,' he said, holding out a hand to her. 'I felt something for you right from the night we met on the *Majestic*. You looked so cold and pinched, but I liked the way you answered me back. I tried to find you on the morning we disembarked. But I didn't know your name, nothing about you. When I eventually came across you fiddling in Heaney's I was so thrilled. You were much prettier than I remembered – and your music!'

Beth had to smile then and she reached out to take his hand. 'Promise you won't ever cheat again?' she said.

'Not you anyway,' he said. 'Now, come back to bed.'

Montreal was beautiful, a city of elegant new buildings, wide roads, gracious squares and parks. Beth and the boys particularly loved going to Mount Royal, the park laid out on a mountain with a splendid view of the city and the busy port.

They marvelled at the Victoria Bridge built across the

St Lawrence river, which people called the Eighth Wonder of the World, and admired the New York Life building where an elevator whizzed you up eight floors.

There was the Golden Mile with huge and beautiful mansions where the rich lived. The Windsor Hotel was the grandest hotel Beth, Sam and Jack had ever seen, and the shops in St Catherine's Street were every bit as smart as New York's finest.

As September came to an end and the leaves on the trees turned fiery red, russet, gold and brown, everywhere became still more beautiful. But however lovely a city Montreal was, they could sense they were never going to find success here. There were plenty of saloons, there were variety shows and dance halls, but Montreal wasn't a liberal-minded city: the character of the majority of its residents was staid, sober and hard-working.

Sam and Jack both found jobs as barmen within a few days of their arrival, but although they tried to persuade their respective employers to give Beth a chance to charm their customers, they refused. Without anyone actually coming out and saying what they thought, it was clear they believed any young woman prepared to step inside a saloon was a whore.

Beth tramped round all the stores, hoping to be taken on in one of them. But it seemed they only employed men as sales clerks. If she saw a woman working in a shop, restaurant or coffee shop, she was invariably related to the owner.

Theo found it almost impossible to get anyone even to admit there was any gambling in the city, let alone get himself invited to a game. For the first time in his life, his English gentleman persona seemed to be working against him. In Montreal it appeared the French liked to be seen as the aristocrats, and he found them looking down on him. Yet the ordinary working-class men, mainly first- and second-generation English and Scots, were suspicious of him too.

He still had most of the winnings from his last poker game, but he wasn't prepared to use it just on living expenses. He said he had to keep it for a stake when he eventually found a way into a big poker game. Jack and Sam had gone along with this at first, for they both wanted to work in gambling circles and they needed Theo to get them in. But as the weeks ticked by, while they worked long hours for low wages, they had become resentful that Theo spent his days sitting around drinking in smart places like the cocktail bar in the Windsor Hotel while they were keeping him and Beth.

They moved from the hotel to a guest house, then on to a three-room flat, but even that was too expensive, bringing back to Beth memories of the difficulties she and Sam had when they first got to New York. Just as they had no choice then but to settle for one room in a tenement on the Lower East Side, now they had no alternative but to lower their sights and get a place to live in Point St Charles.

Griffintown, or the Swamp as Point St Charles was often called, was a slum area to the west of the city, between the St Lawrence river and the Canadian Pacific railway tracks. It had none of the beauty of the rest of the city which was up on a hill, its skyline dotted with church spires. Down in the Swamp, it was factories and heavy industry, tall chimneys belching black smoke day and night.

There weren't the five-storey tenements that they'd grown so used to seeing in New York, only small terraces of two or three storeys, but it was a grim place and home to the very poorest in Montreal. They found a tiny two-up, two-down clapboard house in Canning Street, one of the roughest parts, with high unemployment and large families.

Even those who did work probably brought home less than ten dollars a week.

After living in comfort at Pearl's with indoor sanitation it was miserable having to go back to an outside privy, especially as it was so cold. They managed to buy a few pieces of furniture from one of the hundreds of second-hand shops in the area, but Beth had yet to summon up enthusiasm to try to make the place a real home, for the boys just came home to sleep, and Theo only dropped in now and then.

Josie, the Irishwoman who lived next door, got Beth a job in a shirt factory with her. It was tedious, repetitive work: she machined up the side seams of the shirts, someone else put the collar on and the sleeves in.

As the autumn turned to winter and the first falls of snow, Beth was frozen all day in that factory. She saw herself becoming like the other women there, old before their time, with stooped backs and poor eyesight. They were nearly all Irish, and they had no choice but to accept the few dollars a week because they had children to feed and often feckless husbands who drank their wages away.

But at least they did have a husband. Beth was calling herself Mrs Cadogan, and she washed Theo's shirts, socks and underclothes so he could look smart, and cooked him meals when he deigned to come home – everything a wife would do. But it was Sam and Jack who appreciated her home-making skills, it was they who hauled home coal for the fire and comforted her when she felt everything was hopeless. And she couldn't bring herself to tell them that she was carrying Theo's child.

Chapter Twenty-three

Beth pulled her fur hat down more firmly over her ears and stepped out into the thick snow with some trepidation for it was five in the morning and very dark. The fur-lined boots Jack had given her at Christmas kept her feet warm and dry, but her long coat, skirt and petticoats gathered up snow as she walked and hampered her movements.

Beth had been laid off by the shirt factory in early December. She couldn't say she was sorry, for she'd grown to hate the job. She found another one as a cook soon afterwards.

Theo, Sam and Jack had been horrified, and tried very hard to talk her out of it as it was in a bunkhouse for itinerant workers in the construction business. She insisted she was going to take the job as there was nothing else on offer, but on her first day, when she was confronted by forty rough, tough, none too clean men of a dozen different nationalities, she almost turned tail and ran. But the pay was far better than at the shirt factory and it would be warm there too.

The boys were afraid the men would take liberties with her, but she'd found them to be respectful, protective and appreciative. It was a very long day, from five in the morning till seven at night, but after the breakfast was cleared away and she'd done a few other tasks like sweeping out the dormitories and cleaning the dining room, she could go home for a couple of hours. But more often she stayed in the bunkhouse, read a book or dozed by the stove until it was time to prepare the evening meal.

She could have been really happy if it hadn't been for her anxiety about telling Theo and the boys she was pregnant. From early January, when it became harder to fasten her skirt, each day she resolved to speak to them that evening. But it was the end of February now, and she still hadn't managed to do it.

It wasn't just cowardice because she feared the news would be greeted with alarm. Most days she didn't even see the boys because she went to work when they were still asleep, and they were working when she got home. But even on Sundays, when they were all home together, the time was never right. One day Sam was excited about a pay rise, and she didn't want to dampen his good mood; another time Jack had fallen in the snow and hurt his leg, and she didn't want to add to his worries. As for Theo, he couldn't be relied on to be there even on Sundays, for he had finally wormed his way into a group of wealthy men who liked to play poker.

Theo lived a double life. To his new friends he was a successful businessman with interests in America and Canada. They had no idea that his real home was in the notorious slum area. Or that he had no business other than gambling.

While Beth didn't like him disappearing for days on end, or the fact that she had no part in his other life, she was admiring of his talent for duping people into believing he was a man of means. He would book in at the Windsor Hotel, then send notes to his friends inviting them to dine with him. One night's accommodation and the price of the dinner was usually enough to get him invited back to one of their mansions in the Golden Mile, and there he would stay for a week or so, being the perfect distinguished guest, who often relieved his hosts of hundreds of dollars at poker.

Beth sometimes felt aggrieved that he lazed around in luxury while she cooked for forty men, but she understood he was working on getting backers for a gambling house which would benefit them all. Besides, he did bring money back for her and the boys, and she knew in her heart that if he didn't love her or didn't consider Sam and Jack his best friends, he would have moved on long ago.

But Theo hadn't included a baby in his long-term plans, and Beth feared it might upset the whole apple cart. It hadn't been in hers either, and at first she'd been horrified. Yet as the weeks had crept by she had found herself reliving the joy of caring for Molly, and now she wanted this baby wholeheartedly. But the fact remained that the boys were likely to view it with dismay.

She couldn't keep it secret for much longer. She reckoned she was four and a half months pregnant, the baby due in July, and the only reason no one had noticed her changing shape was because of the layers of thick winter clothes she wore. Even in bed she never removed her flannelette nightdress, and as she was mostly asleep when Theo came home, there had been no lovemaking for weeks.

'I will tell him tonight,' she resolved aloud. He didn't usually go out before she got home, and she could leave him to tell Sam and Jack the news the following morning before they went to work.

It was difficult walking in such thick snow, and treacherous too as there could be hidden obstacles beneath it, and in the darkness it wasn't easy to see a slight mound which might warn her. She took cautious little steps, her mind on her own fledgling plan for the future.

For all Theo's faults, he was loving and caring, and she was fairly certain he'd marry her to give the baby his name. But she also knew that she couldn't hope to turn him into a traditional husband who went to work each day in a bank or some other regular employment to keep his wife and child.

Beth's idea was that they should rent a whole house in a better area, then she could take in boarders to make a living. Theo could carry on with his plans, and Sam and Jack too. Even if the boys had to move away from Montreal, she'd be secure, and if she couldn't play her fiddle in public, at least she'd be mistress of her own house and wouldn't need to leave her baby with anyone while she worked.

As she turned into Fuller Street where the bunkhouse was, she was so busy thinking of how she'd present this idea to the boys that she stopped looking at the ground in front of her. Suddenly her feet slipped from under her and she fell backwards on to the snow, jarring her buttocks painfully.

As she rolled over and got cautiously up on to her knees, she saw that she'd stepped on a sheet of ice. Someone must have thrown some water out and it had frozen solid.

She expected she would have a big bruise later, but thankfully her legs and ankles felt fine.

It wasn't until she was in the bunkhouse, stirring the stove which had been banked up all night, filling the kettles and lighting the gas to start cooking, that she realized she felt a bit woozy and shaken up. But there was no time to dwell on that as the men would be up soon.

Breakfast was always more difficult than cooking the evening meal, for which she had all day to prepare. In the morning she had less than an hour to cook some eighty fried eggs, bacon and sausages in huge frying pans, slice up six large loaves of bread and make several pots of coffee and tea.

The bunkhouse had one large communal room where the men ate and relaxed. Their dormitories and washroom were out the back. The walls were rough, unpainted plaster and the floor was bare concrete. There were long, rickety deal tables, scarred wooden benches and a counter which separated it from the kitchen area. A noticeboard and pigeon holes for each of the men covered one wall; the second held pegs for outdoor clothing, for as the stove was kept alight day and night, wet coats and boots could dry out by morning.

The other wall had been decorated by artistic residents. There were sketches of bears and moose, caricatures of some of the men, and many voluptuous, semi-naked women that made Beth blush.

The first time she had gone into one of the dormitories to sweep the floor she had recoiled in horror at the stink of sweat and feet, but she supposed it couldn't be otherwise when so many men slept in such a confined, badly ventilated space. Besides, they worked long hours and could only get to the bath-house further down the street about once a month. Yet mostly they kept their few possessions and spare clothes tidy in a box or kitbag beneath the bunks. These were nomads, moving anywhere there was work. They were a tough breed, unfettered by wives or family, oblivious to cold or heat and often to injury too. All they appeared to need was a few pals, drink and food and they were content.

By the time the first group of tousled men came in yawning and coughing, Beth had got the plates, trays of food and bread on to the serving counter and was there ready to dish up. She had put the coffee and tea at the end of the counter for them to pour themselves.

Most of them only grunted a greeting, for they were only half awake, but when the big American the men called Tex got his turn to have his plate filled he looked at her sharply and frowned.

'You all right, honey?' he asked. 'You look awful pale today.'

'I slipped on some ice on the way here,' she said with a weak smile. 'No bones broken, just a bit shaken up.'

'You take it easy for the rest of the day then,' he said. 'We don't want to lose a pretty little thing like you!'

By ten in the morning Beth had finished most of her cleaning chores. She usually took a break then, had a cup of tea and a bacon sandwich and read the newspaper before starting on the preparations for the evening meal. But the meal tonight was stew, and as the meat the butcher usually sent was inclined to be tough, she liked to get it simmering early in the day.

As she hauled the big heavy stew pans from their shelf under the counter to the gas stove, she felt a sharp pain shoot through her belly. She got the pans up on to the stove, but then another pain gripped her.

She sat down on a chair, telling herself it was nothing but cramp, or that she'd just picked up the stew pans awkwardly. But then it happened again for the third time, and instinctively she clutched at her belly in exactly the same way she'd seen her mother do when she went into labour with Molly.

A feeling of dread washed over her. Could it be that she was going to lose her baby?

Maybe she hadn't been delighted about it at first, but she'd grown to welcome the idea, and in the last month she'd thought of little else but holding her baby in her arms.

What did women do to make sure they didn't lose their babies? Would lying down flat do it? Or should she ask someone to get a doctor for her?

But who? All the men were gone for the day. The bunkhouse was owned by Mr Sondheim, but aside from Friday night when he always came to collect the rent from the men, he only popped in occasionally. He had called in more often when she first started here, but it seemed he trusted her now and only came to pick up the food bills, and to check that no one had left or there weren't any men staying here without his permission. He wasn't likely to come today as he'd called the previous day.

Beth got up from her chair, hoping that the pain would just disappear, for Mr Sondheim wouldn't be pleased if she failed to have the evening meal ready for the men. She got as far as the counter where she'd put the meat ready to cut up when another pain came. This one was even more intense and lasted longer too. Somehow she knew then it wasn't going to go away and she must get help.

Gingerly, she edged her way towards the door. As she reached it another pain hit her and this time it was so bad she cried out. As it abated she could feel a sticky wetness between her legs, which she thought might be blood. In fright she opened the door and looked out on to the street.

There was no one in sight, and although the closest house was only a few yards across the street, Beth was afraid to cross it because she might fall again in the snow. Any other time she'd come out of the door there were always people about, even in the snow, for most of the residents around here lived in such cramped conditions they needed to get out.

'Someone come along, please,' she pleaded aloud as yet another pain stabbed through her. To her horror the snow between her two feet was stained red with blood, and she immediately felt nauseous with fear.

She must have stood there for ten minutes, frozen to the bone, in pain and with the pool of blood at her feet growing larger by the minute, when she finally saw a man coming along the road, pulling a sledge behind him.

'Help me, please,' she called out as loudly as she could.

By the time he reached her she was clinging to the door-post for support.

'Are you in trouble?' he asked.

She was aware he was young, no more than twenty, and Irish, with bright blue eyes. 'Yes, I think I'm losing my baby,' she blurted out, her fear cancelling out the embarrassment of saying such a thing to a stranger. 'Could you go to my home and get my husband or my brother?'

'Sure,' he said. 'But let me help you inside first. You'll catch your death of cold out here.'

He seemed to know his way around for once inside he went through the door to the dormitories and returned with a pillow and a blanket. He made her lie down on the floor and covered her up, and even took her hand as she cried out with another pain.

She rasped out where he had to go, and he promised he would run all the way.

The pain grew much worse as soon as he'd gone and it didn't abate as it had before, but kept coming like waves, each one stronger and stronger until she couldn't think beyond it or even see or hear anything else.

Dimly, through the red fog which surrounded her, she thought she heard Jack calling her name but she couldn't answer him. She felt as if she was slipping into a dark tunnel from which there was no escape.

'Mrs Cadogan! Can you hear me?'

Beth thought she was walking though a dark forest towards the man's voice. When she tried to walk faster her legs wouldn't let her.

'Open your eyes now, Mrs Cadogan, it's all over now.'

His voice so close made her realize it was a dream, and that she was in bed. She opened her eyes and saw a man with gold-rimmed spectacles looking down at her.

'You are in hospital,' he explained. 'You've given your

poor husband a terrible fright; he was afraid he was going to lose you.'

'I lost the baby?'

The doctor nodded. 'I'm very sorry, my dear, but you are young and healthy and you will soon be yourself again.'

'Can I see my husband?' she whispered.

'For just a few minutes, then you must rest. I'll send him in to you.'

She thought it must be late at night as there was only one dim light burning in the large room, and the people in the other beds appeared to be asleep. She was puzzled as to why she could remember nothing after the young Irishman came to her aid. What had they given her to make the pain go and for her to sleep for so long? Had she had an operation?

At the sound of footsteps she turned her head to see Jack coming towards her.

'Where's Theo?' she whispered when he reached her bed.

'I don't know,' he whispered back. 'It was me who came to you at the bunkhouse – Sam had already gone to work. I said I was your husband because it would look better. Did Theo know you were having a baby?'

Beth shook her head weakly. 'I was going to tell him tonight.'

'But they said you were over four months gone! I had to pretend I knew. Why didn't you tell any of us? We wouldn't have let you work at that place if we'd known.'

'There was never a right time to tell you,' she said wearily.

Jack bent down and kissed her cheek. 'How do you feel now?'

'A bit strange.' She sighed. 'But I'm not in pain any more. What did they do to me, Jack?'

'The doctor will explain to you in the morning,' he said.

'But you must go to sleep now, I'll go and find Sam and Theo and tell them. We'll come to see you tomorrow.'

It was after ten at night and as Jack walked through the deserted snowy streets, his eyes filled with tears when he thought of what the doctor had said.

'I had to perform an emergency operation to remove the parts which had not come away naturally, and sadly I have to tell you it is highly unlikely she'll ever be able to bear another child.'

Many women Jack had known wouldn't much care if they never had a child, and anyone who had ever seen Beth playing her fiddle would think that being a mother would be unimportant to her. But Jack knew different. He'd heard the sadness in her voice when she spoke of Molly, and knew that giving her sister up was something she'd never quite reconciled herself to, however much she declared she had. At Christmas, when she received a photograph of Molly, she had looked hungrily at it for hours. He had always thought that it would only be when she had a child of her own that she'd recover fully.

Now she'd lost that chance.

Theo didn't come home that night, and Jack lay awake hating the man for treating Beth so casually. Theo didn't of course know she was in hospital, but Jack was unable to understand how any man with a girl as lovely as Beth could bear to stay away from her for even one night.

Sam had looked incredulous when Jack told him the news. 'Why didn't she tell me?' he kept repeating, as if he thought that if she had done, none of this would have happened. But even Sam, close as he was to his sister, expressed the opinion that it was perhaps for the best.

'The best for who?' Jack had roared at him. 'For you and Theo maybe, so you can do what you want without any hindrance! But not for Beth. A part of her will have died with the baby, and when she finds out she can't have any more, what's that going to do to her?'

It was close to daybreak when Jack heard Theo come in. He and Beth shared what she laughingly called the parlour, which was the slightly larger of the two rooms downstairs and the one with a fire. She had to cook on that, and she'd made herself a little kitchen by putting a wooden crate with a cloth over it in the alcove beside the fire, and arranging all the crockery, pots, utensils and foodstuffs in or on it.

Her ability for home-making astounded Jack. She'd covered the bed with a bright-coloured quilt, and made cushions for the two wooden armchairs. Most people around here lived in squalor, defeated by poverty and hardship, but Beth kept the place spotlessly clean, and was always adding something to make it more homely.

Since working at the bunkhouse, she'd acquired a small table, and on Sundays when they were all home, they ate their dinner at it sitting on crates. She'd stuffed cracks around the windows with newspaper to keep out the draughts and covered the stains on the walls with theatre posters and pictures cut out of magazines. Sitting there beside a roaring fire on Sundays, a tasty dinner in front of them, they could forget the bitter cold and grimness outside for a few hours and be a real family.

Since he met Theo for the first time, Jack's feelings towards him had swung away from jealousy because he'd snatched Beth away from him and indignation that he allowed her to think he'd masterminded her rescue from the cellar. He had eventually grown to like him once they moved to Philadelphia.

For all Theo's flashiness, smart clothes, cut-glass accent and impeccable breeding, he was no snob. To him there were only two kinds of people: those he liked and those he didn't. What they had or where they came from didn't enter into it.

Once Jack had put away his old resentments, he found Theo to be generous, kind-hearted and an amusing companion – smart too, always one jump ahead of the next man.

Jack wasn't scandalized by him cheating at cards. He felt he'd have probably done the same if he'd lost a heap of money. But what he had fully expected was that Theo would run off and leave him and Sam when Sheldon died.

But he hadn't. He'd taken charge, organized their escape to Canada and paid for their tickets, and because he'd proved himself, Jack had trusted him implicitly ever since.

Yet as he heard Theo come in, and thought of where Beth was, Jack felt murderous. He leapt out of his bed and ran into the adjoining room wearing only his long underwear.

Theo had lit a candle and he was just standing there holding it, still in his top hat and fancy cloak, looking stunned because Beth wasn't in bed.

'Where is she?' he asked.

'In hospital, you bastard,' Jack snarled. 'She's lost her baby, and you want stringing up for not being with her, for letting her work in that place.'

'She was having a baby?' Theo gasped, his face suddenly pale. 'I didn't know!'

'You never gave her a chance to tell you, you're never here,' Jack roared at him. 'You swan in and out, eating meals she makes you, putting on the clean shirts she washes for you, treating her like a little skivvy!'

Theo put the candle down and dropped his hat on the

bed. 'Oh God,' he exclaimed. 'She's lost our baby? Please, Jack, sit down and tell me what happened and how she is.'

Jack could see that Theo was shocked and horrified, but that didn't appease him. He clenched his fist and took a swing at Theo, catching him squarely on the jaw, and Theo staggered back from the force of it.

'I'd beat the shit out of you without any qualms,' Jack hissed at him. 'But I don't want to smash up this room Beth has tried to make nice. Did you ever notice that? Did you see how rough her hands have become? She was someone in Philly, she wore pretty dresses and she was happy too, but you took all that away from her.'

'I suppose you had a better plan then?' Theo said with a sarcastic edge. 'One you never voiced, eh?'

'You smug bastard,' Jack yelled at him, and was just about to hit him again when Sam came running into the room and caught his arm.

'Fighting won't make anything better,' he said angrily, getting between his two friends. 'God knows I'd like to pulverize Theo too for neglecting Beth, but she'll be devastated at losing her baby, and if she comes home to find Theo gone too, she'll never recover.'

'I wouldn't leave Beth even if you two pummelled me to a pulp,' Theo said indignantly. 'You're acting like I'm responsible for this. How could I be? I didn't even know. Now, will you sit down and explain what happened and tell me how she is, for God's sake? I love her, surely you know that?'

At that unexpected declaration of love, Jack's anger faded. 'Why did you leave her here all the time then?' he asked brokenly. 'Couldn't you have introduced her to your new friends? She's a real lady, she would never have embarrassed you.'

Theo sighed and slumped down on to a chair, running his fingers through his hair. 'I was trying to get something for all of us. If I'd known I was going to be a father –' He broke off suddenly, overcome by emotion, and covered his face in his hands.

'For pity's sake, tell me how she is,' he said in a strangled voice after a few moments. 'Surely I'm entitled to that much?'

Theo stood at the ward door, looking at Beth through the small glass panel. She was lying on her side in the bed, one arm hiding her face, and he knew she was crying. He braced himself to enter the room, hoping that when he took her in his arms he'd be able to find the right words to comfort her.

His face was sore from Jack's punch a few hours earlier, but not as sore as his heart. He couldn't claim ever to have thought how it would be to become a father, yet he felt unbearably sad that he'd unwittingly created a baby with Beth and now it had gone.

Pushing the door open, he took a deep breath and walked in. Beth moved her arm from her face and he saw her eyes were red and swollen.

'You poor darling,' he said softly. 'I'm so sorry I wasn't here with you yesterday.'

Her expression was so bleak he couldn't bear to see it. 'You should have told me,' he said as he leaned over her and scooped her into his arms. 'I love you, Beth, I know I don't always show you, but you shouldn't have kept this from me.'

'They said I nearly died,' she sobbed against his chest. 'I wish I had, Theo. What is there for me in the future without ever having a child to love?'

'We don't know for certain that's true,' Theo said, and

tears ran down his cheeks too. 'We'll see another doctor, we'll make it come right.'

'There are some things that can't be made right,' she said, her voice muffled against his chest.

Instinct told Theo that she felt she had been punished for having sexual relations with a man she wasn't married to. 'I don't believe that,' he said. 'I'll take care of you, and when you're well again, everything will look different, you'll see. We'll get married one day and we'll go home to England to see Molly. Even if we can't have another baby, we'll still have each other.'

She just cried against his chest, and he felt powerless to ease her pain. What could he say? He'd never hungered to have a child, he doubted any man did. He could understand Beth's grief and disappointment, but he couldn't presume to know how it felt.

'I'm so sorry,' he whispered. 'Sorry that I haven't taken better care of you. Sorry that I didn't tell you often enough that I love you. And I'm so very sorry we lost our baby. But don't give up on me, Beth. Things may look bleak now, but they'll get better. I promise you that much.'

Chapter Twenty-four
June 1897

'Break out of it, sis, I'm sick of seeing that sad face!'

Beth blushed with embarrassment, for Sam's voice seemed to boom around the railway carriage.

'Why don't you shout a little louder?' she retorted sarcastically. 'I'm sure that the people right at the back would like to hear too.'

'Sorry,' he said, looking abashed. 'I didn't realize I was shouting. But it seems like years since I heard you laugh or even sound excited about anything. We've come clean across Canada and seen so much; we'll be in Vancouver tonight, so can't you just perk up?'

'Scrubbing floors, washing up and waiting on tables were hardly things to get excited about,' she said waspishly. 'If you can guarantee Vancouver will be better, then I might start laughing again.'

'Maybe you'll get a chance to play your fiddle there.'

Beth forced herself to smile. 'Maybe, but excuse me if I don't count on it.'

It was four months since she lost her baby, and physically she had recovered from it within a week. But hearing she would never have another child left her totally dispirited. Sometimes she stayed in bed all day, she didn't care if the room was dirty or untidy, and when she did venture out, she avoided speaking to anyone.

Theo couldn't have been kinder in those first three or four weeks. He brought her home delicacies, tonics, fresh fruit and chocolates, he took her out on a horse-drawn sleigh up on Mount Royal, and bought her a new dress from one of the best shops in Sherbrooke Street. Many evenings he stayed at home with her, and but for that she might have lapsed into permanent melancholy.

She was glad when the boys suggested moving on. She felt as soon as she was seeing new scenery and meeting new people that her old spirit would return.

They left Montreal by train in late March, when it was still very cold and the rivers still frozen, but spring was on its way. Theo's theory was that the new railway running all the way across Canada to Vancouver would have created some boom towns along the route. He was right in as much as small towns *had* sprung up wherever the train stopped, but they weren't the kind to yield the kind of opportunities Theo had hoped for.

A saloon, usually doubling as a hotel, dried goods, clothing and hardware shops, a timber yard, stabling and a blacksmith were about all most of these towns had to offer. The immigrants who had bought farmland in these remote places were sober, diligent and staid, not the kind to gamble with hard-earned money. Beth thought the only way to make a quick fortune in these towns would be to bring in bolts of dress material, hats and other luxuries to sell, for most of the women were starved of anything pretty to wear.

Yet leaving Montreal had been good for her. She had stopped dwelling on never having another child, and found the energy to work when the opportunity arose. She began to care about how she looked again, and kept up practice on her fiddle.

In most places they stopped at, the boys usually managed to find some kind of casual work, on farms, at logging camps and in sawmills. In one town Sam had helped a boot repairer out and earned nearly forty dollars. But for Beth the only work available was cleaning, laundry and occasionally some farm work, seeding and hoeing out weeds. Sometimes she had to stay alone in a rooming house while the boys stayed in the bunkhouse wherever they were working, so she was lonely too.

She had played her fiddle a few times in saloons, but although she got wild applause, her audience's appreciation didn't run to more than a few dimes in the hat. It was hard not to think back to New York and Philadelphia, and how good it had felt to be making a living doing what she loved best of all. She feared she would never get the chance to do so again.

Yet for all the disappointments, hardships and anxieties, it had been, as Sam said, an incredible journey right across this huge country, and the astounding scenery had staggered her at every turn: snow-capped mountains, vast lakes and pine forests, tumbling waterfalls, prairies that stretched almost to infinity. She could hardly believe that her world had once been confined to Church Street in Liverpool, and that a park was her idea of wide open space.

The reason for her long face today was simply weariness. She was tired of the nomadic life, tired too of approaching a new town and seeing the boys get excited, only to leave in disappointment a few days later. She felt unable to raise any enthusiasm for Vancouver as she was sure it would be no different to anywhere else.

Theo was convinced that this was where all his dreams would come true. Right now he was out on the viewing platform at the end of the carriage with Jack, and she had no doubt they were once again planning their dream gambling house.

She had known that Jack and Theo had had a fight after

she lost the baby, for she'd seen the bruise on Theo's cheek. Yet whatever animosity lay behind it had vanished, for they were the best of friends now, and Jack had more than proved his worth on this trip. When it came to hard manual work, he had no equal, for he was immensely strong and capable. He covered for Theo and Sam when they lagged behind, and his tough stance deterred any would-be troublemakers from picking on them.

All three of them were more muscular and fit now, handsome too, with sunburnt faces. Even if Beth couldn't share their boyish excitement about Vancouver, she was still very glad to be with them.

'This will do, won't it?' Jack looked nervously at Beth as he led her into the rooms he'd found for them in Gas Town.

They had arrived in Vancouver in the early hours of the morning, so they'd dozed in the station waiting room till it was daylight. Jack had gone off on his own while they were eating breakfast, and returned an hour later to tell them he'd taken this place, just a couple of streets away from the station.

'It's fine, Jack,' Beth replied, too tired to care what it was like. There were two rooms, stained mattresses on the beds, a chair with only three legs, a gas stove and a sink in the corner of the back room which overlooked the docks. But they had stayed in much worse places.

'It was the best of the ones I saw,' Jack said anxiously. 'Maybe we'd get a better place elsewhere, but I was told Gas Town is where all the saloons and gambling dives are, and it looks like our kind of place. I bet they won't be against pretty fiddlers here.'

Beth was touched he had thought of her and smiled wearily. 'You did well to find it, Jack. But then you always do well, whatever you do.'

Theo and Sam came up the stairs then. Theo wrinkled his nose, and Sam gave a strained smirk. 'Why do we always get such consistently grim rooms? You'd think once in a while we'd stumble on something decent,' he said.

Beth felt compelled to reassure them. 'At least it's quite a new building. I even saw an inside lavatory and a bathroom as we came up the stairs. I can fix it up for us, we're going to do all right here.'

'If you're happy then we all will be,' Theo said, going over to the window and looking out. 'We've got a good view of the ships, and if we find Gas Town isn't to our taste, we can sail away somewhere on one of them.'

'As long as it isn't to the north,' Beth said, as she opened up her valise to unpack. 'I've had enough of cold and snow.'

Beth woke later to hear banjo music coming from somewhere close by. It was fast and hot, reminding her of a negro banjo player who used to play in the streets back in Philadelphia. It seemed the best of omens.

All four of them had lain down fully dressed on the bare mattresses for a nap, but that must have been hours ago for she could see by the low sun that it was early evening now.

Theo was sound asleep, curled up around her back, and she wriggled away from him, suddenly energized and wanting to turn the room into a home for them.

She had unrolled their bundle of bedding, hung her dresses up in the closet, and was just dragging the table across to the window, when Theo woke.

'That's a good sign,' he said, watching her spread a checked tablecloth on it. 'Does that mean you feel at home?'

'I feel at home anywhere you are,' she said teasingly. 'But get your lazy carcase off that bed so I can make it up.'

He did as she asked but then came across the room to

her and put his arms around her. 'I've put you through such a lot,' he said regretfully.

That was something of an understatement, and if she'd been in the mood for sniping at him she could have given him a long list of hurts, starting with the inevitable feast-or-famine lifestyle of a gambler. There were the unexplained absences, flirting with other women, unreliability and selfishness too. But she wasn't in the mood for recriminations now.

'Not all of it bad,' she said, and wound her arms around his neck to kiss him. He responded eagerly, his tongue flickering into her mouth as he pressed himself up against her, and to her surprise she felt a real stirring of desire for him too.

Since she'd lost the baby she had stopped wanting him the way she used to. She had continued to go through the motions, pretending she did, out of kindness to him, but each time she faked rapture she felt unbearably sad and cheated, for their lovemaking had been such a big part of what was good between them.

He sat down on a chair and pulled her on to his knees so she sat astride him, then unfastened the bodice of her dress and released her breasts to caress and kiss them. It felt good, just the way it used to, and as his hand crept up under her skirt and petticoats to fondle her, she knew this time there would be no faking.

The indecency of knowing that Sam and Jack were just the other side of the door while Theo was arousing her to fever pitch with his fingers was so erotic that she climaxed even before he unbuttoned his trousers and slid into her. The banjo player out on the street seemed to be in time with them. She threw back her head, pressing her breasts into Theo's face with abandon, loving the sensual delight of him inside her.

He came with a roar of delight, digging his fingers into

her bottom. 'That was like winning a thousand dollars on the turn of a card,' he whispered against her shoulder. 'I love you so much, Beth.'

It was not until after ten that the four of them went out to get something to eat. They had been forced to take cold baths, for the water only got hot when the furnace in the basement was lit. But they were all reinvigorated, and Beth felt so radiant from the lovemaking earlier that she laughed at everything the boys said.

She had put on her red satin dress, even though it was creased from being packed away in her valise for so long. 'I'm taking my fiddle with me,' she announced as they left their rooms. 'I'm feeling lucky tonight.'

After a dinner of fried chicken and potatoes in a restaurant close by they walked down the main street of Gas Town.

As they understood it, Vancouver originated here. In 1867 it had been just a cluster of wooden shacks and warehouses by the wharves until John Deighton, known as Gassy Jack, arrived and opened the first saloon. The city dignitaries wanted to call the area Granville, but it had remained Gas Town to its residents.

After the sedate, quiet little towns they'd visited during the past months it was a delight to find Gas Town was buzzing with activity, noise and less pious pleasures.

People were spilling out of saloons on to the pavements with their drinks and there were stalls selling all kinds of food from baked potatoes and hot dogs to bowls of noodles. Music wafted out from a dozen different sources, and drunken sailors lurched along in groups, singing as they went.

There were touts trying to get the unwary into card games

down back alleys, and whores lounging suggestively in doorways. Beggars, buskers, street entertainers and pedlars all
added to the hurly-burly.

Jack stopped them at a very busy saloon on a street corner
in Water Street. 'Let's make a nuisance of ourselves in here,'
he said with a grin. 'There's no music, so maybe we can
persuade them they need some!'

Waiting by the door with Theo while Jack and Sam went
to the bar to get drinks, Beth reflected on how the dynamics
of their group had changed since they left Philadelphia.
Theo had been their undisputed leader then, by force of
personality and breeding and because he was the one who
had the money. Sam was his right-hand man, and Jack's role
was almost that of servant.

Once in Montreal, with Theo prone to disappearing, Jack
and Sam had begun to make decisions for themselves. Yet
even then Theo only had to click his fingers and they fell in
with his plans.

Once out of Montreal, everything changed; Theo and
Sam were both too refined and citified to be in harmony
with the tough, strong farmers, lumberjacks and construction men they met up with. But these men took to Jack,
recognizing him as one of their own.

Suddenly it was Jack making the decisions, and he carried
Sam and Theo with him. On some of the jobs they did, they
wouldn't have lasted a day without Jack helping them and
covering up their inadequacies. Sam soon began to toughen
up, and took a pride in learning new skills and keeping up
with Jack and the other men. But Theo was like a fish out
of water; he couldn't adjust. He got by solely on his charm,
and Beth often overheard men referring to him disparagingly
as 'the English gent'.

She wondered whether now they were here, in the kind

of environment Theo was at home in, he'd push his way back to being group leader again.

Jack and Sam returned with the drinks and they were grinning broadly.

'We asked the landlord if you could play,' Sam said. 'He said, "If you dare." So do you dare, sis?'

Beth took her glass of rum, glanced around at the crowded bar, and knocked her drink back in one. 'Try stopping me,' she said with a wide smile. Theo handed her the fiddle case, and she opened it and took out the instrument.

'How much of the money have we got to give the land-lord?' she asked.

'He didn't say,' Jack said. 'I guess he didn't really believe there would be any. I'll go round with the hat, we'd better offer him some of it at the end, and then maybe he'll give you a permanent spot.'

Theo watched Beth as she slithered through the crowd to the back of the saloon, her fiddle held under one arm, the bow in her other hand. She looked like a slender flame in her red dress, and he could see by her straight back and the way she held her shoulders that she was determined to succeed tonight.

She disappeared from view and Theo felt a sudden pang of anxiety, but all at once he saw her rise up behind the burly men blocking his view, and he realized she was now standing on a table.

Tucking her fiddle under her chin, she drew the bow across the strings and was off into 'Kitty O'Neill'.

For a few long moments there was no reaction from the drinkers; almost every one of them had their backs turned to her. Theo held his breath, but slowly men began to turn towards her, and smiles of appreciation began to creep on to their faces.

Theo saw how in tune Beth was with her audience. She smiled and tossed her hair, picking up the tempo as she got their complete attention, and once she'd got it she certainly knew how to hold it.

They were mainly stevedores and sailors, some already very drunk, but they began to tap their feet, their eyes never leaving her, and she took them to the far shores of their imagination with her music.

'She's better than ever,' Jack gasped. 'Look at her face!'

Theo could see nothing else. Not the men jigging on the spot in front of her, not the couple of whores eyeing him up from the corner, or even the glass of whisky in his hand. He'd seen that same blissful expression on Beth's face just hours earlier when they made love. He felt he ought to feel jealous that her music meant as much, but he didn't. He just felt bigger and more powerful than any other man in the saloon because she was his girl.

By the time she'd played for twenty minutes, people passing were elbowing their way in through the door until the saloon was packed to capacity.

'They'll never be able to serve them all,' Jack said, nudging Sam. 'We'll get up there and see if they need a hand.'

Once again Theo saw Beth's impeccable timing, for as the boys reached the bar and offered their services, she finished her number.

'I've got to take a break now,' she called out. 'Get yourselves drinks and I'll be back soon.'

That first night there was over thirty dollars in the hat, and Oris Beeking, the landlord of the Globe, was only too delighted to agree that Beth should play four nights a week. Furthermore, he took Sam and Jack on as bartenders too.

Vancouver suited them in every way. People were not as staid as they'd been everywhere else in Canada, for it was in many ways still a frontier town. It was good to be able to walk along the shore in warm sunshine, to chat to fishermen and sailors and feel they belonged here. Sam and Jack found a couple of sassy saloon girls they liked. Theo got into some poker games, and on Sunday evenings when they were all at home together, they would plan their saloon, a place with gambling, music and dancing girls.

After the uncertainty and discomfort they'd experienced on their travels, all four of them were happy to be settled again. There was no more talk of moving on, only of finding somewhere a little bigger to live.

On 16 July, Beth went to the post office to post a letter to Molly and the Langworthys. She'd been posting letters home in almost every town they'd stopped at, and she was anxious now for them to receive the address they could write back to.

Outside the post office there was a large group of men, and Beth's first thought was that they were about to start fighting, for they were pacing up and down, shouting and waving their arms. But as she got closer she saw it wasn't anger infecting them but excitement. Two of the men were stevedores she knew from the Globe, and she guessed that the others had just come in on a ship.

'What's all the excitement?' she asked, when one of the men she knew smiled and waved at her.

'Gold,' he replied, his eyes glittering. 'They've found gold up in Alaska. Tons of it. We're planning to go there on the next ship.'

Beth laughed. It sounded like a tall story to her. As far as she knew, Alaska was under thick snow all year round and the only people likely to go there were fur trappers.

She posted her letter, bought some bread, meat and vegetables, then made her way home. But as she passed a news-stand, she saw the headline 'Ton of Gold' on the front of the newspaper and a picture of a ship berthing in San Francisco on which this ton of gold was said to be.

Snatching up the paper, she read how in August of the previous year a man called George Carmack, with his two brothers-in-law, Tagish Charlie and Skookum Jim, had found gold in Rabbit Creek, one of the six tributaries of the river Klondike in the Yukon Valley. Carmack found the gold lying between flaky slabs of rock, 'like cheese in a sandwich'.

Since then, it transpired, prospectors in the area had swarmed there to stake claims, and fortunes were made overnight, but word hadn't reached the outside world about it until now, for once winter closed in up in the Yukon, no one could get out.

Beth was only mildly interested, but as she continued to read as she walked along the street, she was suddenly hearing the words 'Klondike Gold' on all sides of her.

The boys had only just got up when she returned, but as she related what she'd heard and seen on the street and gave them the newspaper to read, their eyes lit up.

'Where is the Klondike exactly?' Jack asked. 'Is it in Alaska?'

'They called it the Yukon in the paper, and I think that's part of Canada,' Theo said, and began rummaging through his valise to find his map of North America. He pushed aside the cups and plates on the table and spread it out. 'This is where it is,' he said, pointing to an area further north from Vancouver, tucked behind Alaska. 'We could go there.'

'Oh no,' Beth said flatly. 'I told you when we got here that if we had to move it would be to the south where it's warm. I am not going off on some wild goose chase to a place which is frozen solid all year.'

'But we could become millionaires,' Sam said, his voice cracking with excitement.

'We could die of cold and starvation, more likely,' she argued. 'Don't you remember learning about the Gold Rush of '49 in school? Only a few people found some. Remember what Pearl told me too? She was there, but she made her money cooking for the prospectors.'

'That's exactly why we should go,' Theo said, his eyes shining. 'The perfect place to start a gambling saloon!'

'Talk some sense into them,' Beth urged Jack. 'This is madness, we like it here, we're doing fine. It's stupid to throw it all away with all the other idiots who'll run off there half cocked.'

'I think we all ought to find out a great deal more about this first,' Jack replied, backing neither her nor Theo and Sam. 'Quietly, calmly and using our heads.'

It was impossible to be quiet and calm that day, for news of the gold was like a virulent disease sweeping through the town and infecting everyone. By the afternoon people were queuing for tickets on the next steamship to Skagway in Alaska, the town they said was the nearest point to the goldfields.

Shopkeepers were galvanized into action, putting signs outside their shops, 'Get your outfit here'. Sledges which had been stored away for the summer were suddenly out on display. Tents, fur-lined coats and boots, mackinaws and galoshes were piled up invitingly. The dried goods store had a blackboard outside listing the items the owner had in stock which could be bought in bulk.

Theo and Sam were incandescent with excitement and even Beth found her heart beating a little faster, but Jack was strangely quiet. He took himself off to see Foggy, an old man who was in the saloon most nights and who he knew had been a fur trapper in Alaska in his younger days. When he returned a couple of hours later to have a wash and a shave before going to work, Theo and Sam asked what he'd found out, and he said he would tell them in the morning.

Gold was the only subject under discussion in the saloon that night. Old-timers who had prospected in California in '49 found themselves the centre of attention. Men who knew about sledge dogs got free drinks, and any man who had ever sailed up the Inner Passage to Alaska could hold court.

'I've studied the map, and talked to old Foggy,' Jack said the following morning. 'I've made a rough list of what he thinks we would need.'

Theo took the long list and roared with laughter. 'We won't need all that! A tent, blankets, warm clothes and a bit of food will be enough. Ice picks, saws, nails! Why would we need those?'

'The Klondike is some seven or eight hundred miles from Skagway,' Jack said quietly. 'First we have to scale mountains, then we'll have to build a boat to take us the rest of the way. We'll be going through wilderness, there won't be anywhere we can buy stuff.'

'I can hunt,' Theo said, but his voice had lost its confidence.

'It's going to be tough.' Jack looked at Sam, then at Beth and back at Theo. 'Really tough. Like nothing we've ever experienced before. We're city folk, and if we aren't prepared, we could die on the way of cold or even starvation.'

'People on the way will help us, won't they?' Sam asked, a tremor in his voice.

'We can't count on anything or anyone,' Jack said sternly. 'You saw the madness last night. In a week's time when word has spread further, it will be even crazier, people flocking up there from everywhere. We need to book a passage on a ship to Skagway quickly – that is, if you want to go.'

'Do you want to go, Jack?' Beth asked. She had a queasy feeling in the pit of her stomach and whether it was fear or excitement she couldn't tell.

'Yes, I do, more than anything,' he said, grinning at her. 'It's the chance of a lifetime and I don't want it to pass me by.'

Chapter Twenty-five

Jack was right. Within a week Gas Town was caught in the grip of complete madness. The Klondike Gold Stampede was on.

Newspapers all over the world had spread the news of the gold, and every train coming into Vancouver brought hundreds more people who were desperate to get to the Yukon. They swarmed into Gas Town, bringing chaos with them as they pushed and shoved to buy equipment, provisions and tickets on any craft that would take them to Skagway. Yet Vancouver was reported to be far less frantic than Seattle, and there were also steamers setting off from Victoria, Portland and San Francisco laden with passengers.

Beth and the boys were staggered by the speed with which entrepreneurial shopkeepers in Vancouver got equipment and food supplies stacked up for all these gold stampeders. Huge banners across the shops in Cordova Street proclaimed them to be 'The Klondike Outfitter'. Sledge dogs were being advertised at exorbitant sums, booklets which listed everything needed for the trip were being printed and sold before the ink was dry. Gold fever was highly infectious, it seemed: bankers were walking out of their secure jobs; street car operators deserted their trams; policemen, salesmen and reporters abandoned their jobs; some farmers even walked away from crops before they were harvested.

There was no other subject for discussion. It was as if

people had stopped being sick, having babies, getting married or even dying. Old or young, rich or poor, whatever nationality, everyone wanted to join the stampede.

The rich could reach the Yukon in relative comfort by steamer to St Michael on the Bering Sea, then down the river Yukon to the goldfields, but it was many more miles than the overland route from Skagway. Edmonton was advertised as the All Canadian route for the patriotic, but Jack, who had pored over maps, denounced that as unfeasible as it meant crossing two mountain ranges.

It was Jack who got their steamer tickets, and almost immediately they could have resold them for four or five times the original cost. Word got out that the Canadian Mounted Police would not allow anyone across the border from Alaska to Canada without a ton of provisions. This was because they feared a famine.

Jack and Sam rushed around getting their supplies together: beef blocks, rice, sugar, coffee and evaporated eggs. A tent, mackinaw coats, wide-brimmed hats, high boots, gloves, glasses to stop snow blindness – the list was endless, and they spent all the money they had so carefully hoarded over the past months. But smooth-talking Theo found a way to keep the funds coming, moving among the new arrivals in town with his three-card monte games and relieving them of some of their savings.

As the days passed in feverish buying and packing their supplies in waterproof oilcloth sacks, Beth played her fiddle nightly to rapturous applause, ending with a hat stuffed with money. Sam and Jack poured enough drinks to float several dozen steamers, and Theo played poker and won.

Finally, on 15 August, they boarded the *Albany*, a decrepit steamer which by anyone's standards was barely seaworthy. Jack had booked them a cabin, but when they boarded they

322

were told most of the cabins had been ripped out to make room for more freight and passengers.

They could do nothing but accept this as it was clear they would be thrown off if they complained, so they found a small space on the deck and hunkered down, surrounded by their supplies.

As the steamer left Vancouver along with a huge flotilla of other vessels, all the passengers were delirious with excitement. Even if there had been room enough for people to stretch out, it was doubtful anyone could have slept.

It was only as the boat sailed into the Inside Passage of Alaska, with its breathtakingly beautiful scenery of virgin forests, snow-capped mountains and misty fiords on both sides of the narrow channel that they began to realize what lay in store for them.

They might be looking at sheer beauty beyond the ship's rail, but it was marred by the stench of coal, horse manure, vomit and sweat all around them. Pack dogs howled constantly, horses kicked and neighed, and the ship was so crowded they didn't dare vacate their tiny space on deck for fear of losing it. Huddling together under a tarpaulin against the chill wind or heavy rain, they realized the discomfort they felt now could only become greater before they reached the goldfields.

Most of their fellow passengers had not gone to the trouble Jack had, to find out exactly where the Klondike was, and they believed the goldfields were just a hike from Skagway. Few of them knew mountains had to be scaled, and a boat was needed to take them the last 500 miles.

Some people had been coerced into buying ridiculous items like bicycles on skis, or clockwork gold-panning gadgets that could never work. Others had brought enough timber to build their own cabin, a piano or a cast-iron cooking stove, but given no thought to how they would get these things up a mountain.

Yet despite the terrible conditions on the boat – waiting seven hours for a meal so dreadful it was all but inedible, the lack of washing facilities, and lavatories that made Beth retch – she and the boys remained in good spirits for there was a party-like atmosphere on the ship, everyone as excited as children going to a fair.

It was entertaining to observe the huge variety of people. Sharply dressed gentlemen were forced to share space with rough sailors and lumberjacks; there were garishly dressed women with painted faces, old-timers from previous stampedes, and clerics who appeared to be going in a missionary capacity. The vast majority were Americans and Canadians, but there were Germans, Swedes, Hungarians, Mexicans and even Japanese too. What unified them all was the dream of returning home rich. When they spoke of the gold their eyes would blaze, and they refused to allow their excitement to be diluted by mere discomfort.

'We should reach Skagway tomorrow,' Jack said as he wriggled back under the tarpaulin after a two-hour absence. It was the ninth day of the voyage and they were in the stunningly beautiful Lynn Canal which ended with the beaches of Skagway and Dyea. Sheer mountain slopes topped with a dusting of snow rose up from the clear turquoise water, dwarfing the raggle-taggle convoy of ships sailing up through the narrow corridor. 'I've been talking to one of the crew that's been there before. He said there's only a tiny wharf, so we'll have to wade ashore with our stuff. Good job we're already in our oldest clothes!'

'They could do with a wash,' Beth giggled, for they'd all had the same things on since they embarked. 'But won't the dried food get damaged in the sea water?'

'I'm more worried that our things'll be stolen.' Jack frowned. 'You can bet there'll be plenty of thieves on the lookout. I'll get you ashore first, Beth. Theo or Sam can stay here and guard our stuff, then we'll ferry it bit by bit out to you on the beach.'

'Surely we can pay a sailor to row us in with it all?' Theo asked.

Beth exchanged an amused grin with Jack. Theo thought he could pay someone to do anything he found disagreeable.

'Most of them are jumping ship too,' Jack said. 'I think we can safely say it will be every man for himself from now on.'

Once again Jack's information was correct, for when they heard the sound of anchor chains creaking, and the splash as the anchor hit the water, dry land was still a mile away.

'We surely aren't expected to swim ashore!' one alarmed, overweight matron exclaimed.

There were a few scows from other ships ferrying people and equipment to land, but it would take weeks for everyone to disembark that way. The crew were already shouting out that this was a tidal flat, and if people didn't look sharp and make their way to the beach, they'd lose their goods and maybe drown too.

Unceremoniously the terrified horses and other animals were pushed into the sea to swim ashore, and at that people began to follow, jumping into the water.

Jack put Beth's coat, boots and shawl into an oilskin bag, and led her down the ship's ladder. The water was so icy it took her breath away for a moment, but Jack put his arms around her chest, urging her to hold the bag up to keep it dry, and swam on his back with her the few yards until she could touch bottom and wade ashore.

'This is not a good start,' she said between chattering teeth.

'The sun's warm, you'll soon dry out,' Jack said cheerfully. 'You make your way to the beach and keep a place for our stuff. I'm going back to the ship.'

Once Beth reached dry land, she surveyed the scene before her with trepidation. Skagway was just a huddle of shacks and tents on marshland which was already a slick of black mud. All around were mountains, some still snow-capped, but even more daunting was the desperate scene behind her in the sea.

At least thirty boats lay at anchor, all trying to discharge their passengers and freight at once. The sea was studded with horses, goats, dogs, mules and oxen swimming to the shore, and their owners racing to keep up with them.

The noise was deafening. Men who owned the dozens of scows and primitive rafts were touting for business by shouting at the tops of their voices. People on the boats yelled back even more stridently. If goods dropped from ships missed their mark and fell into the sea, the owners cursed and swore. Animals expressed their fear by whinny-ing or barking. There were screams for help from those floundering in the icy water. Some bags of goods had split wide open, and Beth saw a sack of flour whiten the sea around it.

Someone shouted that the tide was turning and everyone should hurry. Fear for the boys made her wet clothes seem suddenly unimportant. Sam couldn't swim, maybe Theo couldn't either, and the *Albany* was too far away to spot them on the deck.

Slipping off her petticoats, she secured them with pebbles to dry in the wind, then put her boots back on. She thought she would leave her coat until her dress was dry.

Her anxiety continued to rise as the tide crept further in and she saw more people floundering in the sea and yet more sacks of goods splitting, their contents running out into the water. Her dress was nearly dry now, so she must have been waiting for nearly an hour. But she could see no sign of the boys anywhere.

Just as she was on the verge of panic she suddenly spotted Jack standing up in shallow water. He was hauling in what looked like a string of big black sausages.

Not for the first time since they left Montreal she was staggered by his ingenuity, for he'd tied all their oilskin sacks on to a rope. When she looked again she saw Sam clinging on to one of the sacks, and Theo was bringing up the rear.

'Wish we'd never come, Beth?' Jack asked later that evening.

'No,' she lied. 'But it's all a bit scary, nothing like we imagined.'

It was eight in the evening. Swarms of men who were little more than thugs out to rob the naive had descended on them, trying to get them to pay for a space to erect their tent, for wood for a fire, and countless other things.

The boys had stood their ground and refused to pay anything, and eventually they erected their tent among hundreds of others some half a mile from the shacks of Skagway. They had placed their sacks all around the tent walls, to add weight and some insulation when the autumn winds got up, and Jack had got a good fire going to dry off their clothes and cook some food.

Beth was leaning against one sack now, wrapped in a blanket, trying very hard not to give in to total despondency.

Sam had fallen asleep, and Theo had gone off to check out what the town had to offer. As they had been told Skagway was an entirely lawless place, overtaken by thugs, confidence tricksters, gamblers and prostitutes, Beth guessed he would be gone half the night.

It was bad enough to find they had landed in a place full of thugs and thieves, but it was far more disappointing to discover they'd have to stay here until February.

There were two trails over the mountains. White Pass, which started here in Skagway, was supposed to be the easier as pack animals could be taken on it, but it was longer than the Chilkoot Trail, which began at Dyea some twenty-odd miles away.

People were going off on both trails right now, but Jack had spoken to an Indian who worked as a packer taking people's goods up over the trail, and he'd advised him it would be folly to join them. The Indian explained the river Yukon would freeze over next month, long before they could reach it, and without a team of dogs to pull a sledge along it, they'd be trapped for the entire winter in the mountains and might die there.

Jack was very disappointed, but Theo had been delighted at the prospect of staying here till February. He saw Skagway as the boom town he'd been looking for, ripe for exploitation. Without a trace of shame he'd pointed out that everyone on the ship was a gambler in as much as they'd abandoned their homes and jobs to come here, and therefore he saw them as ripe for fleecing.

Sam didn't seem to mind whether they went or stayed, and it had been left to Beth to make the final decision. While she thought Skagway was hell come to earth, the prospect of freezing to death in the mountains was even more daunting, so she'd opted for staying put.

'It won't be so bad here, I'll build us a cabin,' Jack said soothingly. 'There's plenty of wood for it. Maybe when I've done one for us I can make a few dollars building them for others too.'

'Then I'll get out my fiddle tomorrow,' Beth said. It had been a huge relief to find it unharmed by the salt water. Their flour was damp, so was the sugar, but luckily there were no further casualties. 'It's going to cost us a fortune to stay here. Did you see the price of a meal?'

People had already opened up tents as saloons and restaurants. She had seen a menu stuck up on one of them offering bacon and beans at one dollar. Back in Vancouver that would have only been a few cents.

Jack nodded. 'Theo's going to get a shock at the price of whisky too. But you should make some money with that heap of ribbons you brought with you. Some of the girls in the saloons look like they need something to brighten themselves up.'

'You've been in to see them then?'

'Oh yes, and a sorry-looking sight they are too.' Jack chuckled. 'One is known as Dirty-neck Mary, another Pig-faced Sal! A man would need to be desperate to go with either of them.'

'Then maybe Theo will be safe here.' Beth smiled.

'I think it might be you who gets lured away.' Jack arched his eyebrows. 'With less than thirty women to a couple of thousand men and more arriving daily, you are a great prize.'

'Playing here tonight. The World Famous English Gypsy Queen!'

Beth giggled when she saw the board which the Clancy Brothers had erected. To her it was as huge an exaggeration as the Clancys claiming that their large tent behind the board was a saloon.

On her second day in town Beth had been told that the

brothers Frank and John Clancy were the top men in Skagway and ran everything from their saloon, so she went straight to them.

Knowing she was unique in being the only female fiddler in town and that they were charging exorbitant prices for drinks, she dared to ask for twenty-five dollars a night, plus whatever went into the hat. She expected them to agree only to what went into the hat, but to her astonishment they agreed to her nightly fee too.

Her first night was an outstanding success, with over fifty dollars going into the hat, of which she handed ten to the barman to keep him sweet. As Theo hadn't turned up to walk her back to their tent, when the Clancy brothers, two dark-haired, thick-set men with fierce-looking moustaches, asked her to stay and have a drink with them at the end of the evening, she accepted.

Frank Clancy introduced her to a tall, smartly dressed man with a thick dark beard and black stetson hat. 'This is Mr Jefferson Smith, but you'll find he's more commonly known as "Soapy",' he said.

'I'm also known as Beth Bolton,' she responded, unable to resist fluttering her eyelashes at him because he was a very handsome man with deep-set dark grey eyes. 'But why Soapy? Is that because you never wash, or do so to excess?'

'Which would you prefer, mam?' he asked, taking her hand and kissing it.

Beth giggled because he had a Deep South accent which was as attractive as he was.

'Somewhere around the middle,' she said. 'But Skagway has so few facilities I suspect I will have to get used to people who are strangers to soap.'

She was despairing of being able to tolerate Skagway until February. The sea of mud, the constant noise of barking dogs and fights, the thieves and con men out to fleece anyone they could, and the lack of even the most basic of comforts made it an inhospitable place to be.

'Ah, but I have plans,' Smith said with a little smile at her joke. 'For proper streets, a hotel, shops, lighting, a bath-house and even a church.'

'Have you now?' she said. 'So are you to be mayor of Skagway?'

'Something like that,' he said, and his self-assurance confirmed to her that he did intend to control the town.

They chatted for some time, mainly about her recent arrival. Smith himself had only been there for a week and he was in partnership with the Clancy brothers.

'Is Earl Cadogan your husband?' he asked.

The title threw Beth off balance. She had pretended to be married to Theo ever since she arrived in Montreal with him, but now she'd found he'd given himself a title, she didn't know whether that would make her Lady Cadogan, or a Countess. Unable to lie on such a grand scale, she replied that he was just a good friend and that she was with her brother and another old friend, Jack Child.

'The Londoner?' Smith asked. 'I met him this afternoon; he seems a real capable man. You will have plenty of protection then?'

'Do you think I need it, sir?' she asked teasingly.

'All ladies need protection, but someone as pretty and charming in this godforsaken town will need it by day and night.'

Sam and Jack arrived then and whisked her off back to the tent. They had been with Captain Moore who owned the sawmill here, and had arranged to get some timber from him to build a cabin.

'Did you know Theo has told people he's an earl?' Beth

asked them as they picked their way through the thick mud back to their tent.

'He called himself that back in Montreal too,' Sam admitted. 'It's nothing, sis, it just greases a few wheels. Americans are impressed by it.'

'Well, he's just lost himself a wife,' she said tartly. 'But then, I don't suppose he'll care much about that.'

There were times in the weeks that followed when Beth was tempted to catch the next boat back to Vancouver, even if she had to go alone. She woke in the mornings stiff with cold, and the prospect of yet another day tramping through mud, cooking over an open fire and never having any privacy or peace, seemed too much to bear.

Every day new ships arrived, disgorging hundreds more people, horses, dogs and other animals. The rows of tents spread further and further, more and more trees were chopped down, and still more mud and filth were created.

Ridiculously high prices for every basic commodity made Beth fear that all the money she earned at Clancy's would be wiped out before they even left on the trail to the goldfields. Rats, thieves and bears spoiled or snatched provisions; disease was rife because of the unsanitary conditions, and hardly a night passed without outbreaks of gunfire and brawling.

Beth did feel more secure once Jack and Sam had completed the cabin, for although only small, it was weatherproof and had a wood floor and a lock on the door. Jack staggered in one day with a cast-iron stove some foolish person had intended to take up over the trail, and Sam found Beth a hip bath too.

Playing nightly at Clancy's did lift her spirits, and as she saw the town improving almost overnight, with streets laid out and many new permanent buildings, she had hopes that by Christmas it would be more civilized. Clancy's was built of wood now, and there was a hotel, several more fancy saloons, most of them with brothels upstairs, real shops and a raised sidewalk so people could walk without getting stuck in mud. Even a photographer had arrived and opened up a studio.

There was much to be optimistic about in the town, but Beth was very unhappy at how Theo was behaving. He had found the boom town of his dreams, and suddenly nothing else mattered to him but making money.

Skagway had attracted hundreds of men like him. Soapy Smith and the Clancy brothers were just the same; they knew they didn't need to go to the Klondike to make their fortunes. They could do that right here. Soapy had his own saloon now, known as Jeff Smith's Parlour, complete with potted palms and a mahogany bar shipped up from Portland. Both he and the Clancy brothers had a back door from their saloons which led to a row of cribs where their girls worked. They had had a finger in every pie in town, sending in their thugs to terrorize if they weren't paid protection money.

But these men treated Beth like a lady. No one in Skagway dared steal from her or insult her for she had their protection. Theo, however, used her as if she were his housekeeper and private whore.

Beth couldn't help but like Soapy, even though she knew most of the swindlers and bully boys in town were in his employ. He flirted with her, made her laugh, and cheered her up when she was feeling glum. He had got his nickname because he'd once run a racket in which he sold tablets of soap, many of which he claimed had a ten-dollar bill tucked in the wrapper. He would get a crowd around his stall and sell a marked tablet to a stooge amongst it, who would immediately shout out that he'd found a note. Everyone clamoured to buy soap then, but there were no more ten-dollar bills.

Soapy ran a telegraph racket here. There were no telegraph lines to Alaska, but he had opened a little telegraph booth down on the shore, and had a cable running into the sea to make it look real. He would take several dollars from people sending a message home, and even fake replies from their wife or mother, begging them to send money home for a child or other family member who was sick.

Beth thought this was pretty shabby, just as the soap con was, but Soapy made up for his badness by making sure the stray dogs in the town were fed, and he gave handouts to those who were penniless, the sick and the widows.

Theo didn't seem to have a good side any more. He pretended to be an earl and charmed people into trusting him implicitly, taking from anyone who sat down at a card game with him. She knew he cheated, but he was clever enough to make sure he only did this to real greenhorns. One morning Beth had seen a man crying as he tried to sell off his kit to pay for his passage home. Theo had taken every dime he had the night before.

But it wasn't just his gambling and tricking others that upset her, it was the way he seemed to have forgotten they were supposed to be a team of four. Sam and Jack had worked hard from the day they arrived here, at the sawmill and building a cabin for them all. Now they were building cabins for other people. Beth pulled her weight too by playing at night, cooking them all meals and doing the laundry.

But Theo did nothing for the common good. He lay in bed most of the day, then demanded a clean shirt so he could swan off in style to whatever dive he hoped to find a new sucker in that evening. He rarely came into Clancy's to listen to Beth play and he left it to Sam or Jack to escort her home. The ribbons she'd brought with her had disappeared, and then she saw Dirty-neck Mary with the green ones in her hair.

But worst of all in her mind was that she was sure he was supplying girls to the brothels. The first time she saw him carrying the baggage of a couple of young women who had just got off a steamer, she thought he was just being gentlemanly. But later the same night she saw the girls in the newly built Red Onion Saloon, and it was clear from their painted faces that they had joined the prostitutes who worked upstairs there.

Every day a ship brought in a couple of dozen young women among its passengers, and it was possible some of them had been whores back in the towns they came from. But not all – some were country girls who just wanted a bit of adventure. Theo met each boat, and it was always the prettiest young women he made a beeline for to offer help and a place to live.

It seemed he didn't love Beth any more, and he'd forgotten all the plans the four of them had made back in Vancouver.

Chapter Twenty-six

'You really do have a gypsy in your soul,' Jefferson murmured as he took Beth's hand and raised it to his lips. 'I could listen to you playing for ever and never tire of it.'

'I would tire of it,' she said with a smile, and picked up the glass of French champagne he'd just poured for her.

It was the end of January and thick snow lay all around outside, but they were in Jeff Smith's Parlour, his bar and gambling den for those in his immediate circle. The stove was blazing, Beth was a little drunk, and it felt good to have a handsome man trying to seduce her.

Jefferson had been trying to woo her since December. He'd given her a rocking chair for her cabin, bought her candy and was always inviting her for a drink or a meal. But this was the first time she'd been entirely alone with him; usually, when he brought her to the saloon, most of his cronies were here too.

They had been present earlier, but they had dispersed a while ago now, and even Nate Pollack, the bartender, had left after putting more logs on the stove.

'Are you still planning to head for the goldfields next month?' Jefferson asked, taking a strand of her hair and winding it round his finger.

'Sam and Jack can't wait to go,' she replied. 'So I guess I'll go with them.'

'It's no trip for a lady,' he said, shaking his head.

'I'm as strong as most men,' she said with a smile. 'Besides,

Skagway will be a ghost town when everyone's left. What would there be for me to do?'

'As soon as the weather breaks there will be even more ships. People are making their way here from all over the world,' he said with that sparkle in his grey eyes she'd come to like so much. 'You'll make a bigger fortune here than you ever will in Dawson City. You could die on that journey; even the Indians say how difficult it is.'

'We planned to go there, so we will.' She shrugged.

'And what about the Earl?'

Beth looked down at her lap. However cross she was with Theo, she still loved him, and the prospect of parting company with him was unbearable. But he had been a louse to her for months now, and she knew that if she stayed on here when Sam and Jack had gone, she couldn't count on Theo to change his ways and she'd be very alone.

'He won't be coming with us,' she said, and tried to smile as if it didn't hurt.

'He's a fool then, for he'll get himself killed without Jack to get him out of trouble,' Jefferson said.

'Surely not!' Beth exclaimed.

'He is too cocky by half. There are many who'd like nothing better than to see him dead.'

'Not you?' she asked anxiously.

Jefferson looked at her thoughtfully for a moment. 'No, I like the man,' he said eventually. 'But then he's smart enough not to tread on my toes. I've heard the whispers, though, and I can see the signs.'

'Can't you speak to him and warn him?'

'He wouldn't listen to me. Besides, why should you care what becomes of him? You must know he's with Dolly at the Red Onion most nights?'

Beth felt as if she'd been stabbed through the heart, for until that moment it was only something she'd suspected, not known for certain.

Dolly was a voluptuous blonde who sang and danced at the Red Onion. She was a whore too, and rumour had it she charged fifty dollars a time. Every man in Skagway, it seemed, wanted to have his way with her.

'You didn't know, did you?' Jefferson said. He put his arms around her and drew her to his chest. 'I'm sorry if I've hurt you, I didn't intend to.'

Beth bit back tears. 'I'm fine. I had suspected it anyway. I guess that's all I need to confirm it's time to go.'

'You know, I'd like you to stay and be my girl. I'd get you a real nice place to live, with a maid an' all. I'd even get the Earl run out of town.'

The champagne and his honeyed Southern accent were breaking down her resistance, and when he lifted her chin to kiss her, she didn't break away. His kiss was as smooth as he was, warm and very sensual, and she was instantly aroused.

He ran his fingers down her neck lightly as he kissed her, and even though a small voice deep down inside her was telling her that to make love with him would be a mistake, she wanted him. He appreciated her, he treated her like a lady, and if Theo liked that blonde whore better than her, then it was time she showed him she didn't care.

Jefferson's hand stole into the bodice of her dress, cupping her breast, and his kisses became more passionate. 'Let me take you to my room at the back,' he murmured against her neck. 'We can be comfortable there.'

He didn't wait for her agreement, just picked her up in his arms and carried her through a door at the back of the bar. It was warm in there too, for there was another small stove, and by the light from it she saw a mahogany carved bed suitable for a grand hotel, covered with a red patterned quilt.

He didn't fumble with the small buttons on the back of her dress, or the laces of her stays, and though she knew this meant he was practised at undressing women, it didn't make her feel any less wanted.

His experience showed in his lovemaking too. He didn't rush, and his touch was firm but caressing as he whispered little endearments and told her she was beautiful.

She was whipped up into a state of near delirium even before he removed his clothes; and as she wrapped her arms around him and caressed him she found him to be all hard muscle, with none of the softness she'd expected from a Southern gentleman.

It was weeks since Theo last made love to her, and that had been a hurried, unsatisfactory snack rather than a feast. Jefferson offered her a banquet, teasing her, sucking and licking at her, and when he finally entered her she was drenched in perspiration and fevered with lust.

'You more than exceeded my expectations, mam,' he said with a mischievous smile as he propped himself up on his elbows, looking down at her, but still inside her.

'So did you, sir,' she replied, and giggled. 'I think, too, we have solved the problem of how to keep warm in Alaska.'

'Whatever happens in the future, I'll always remember this night and treasure it,' he said, bending his head to kiss her.

Beth could only smile, for she knew that his words would ease the guilt she'd feel in the morning.

'I hope I can persuade you to stay on here,' he said a little later after he'd rolled off her and was holding her in his arms. 'You and I could be a great team. And when the gold fever is gone we could go on to other towns and find new challenges.'

Beth was relieved to find the cabin empty when she got back there at noon the following day. After the comfort at Jefferson's place it looked spartan and dreary. Their beds were just sacks filled with straw, and the one she shared with Theo was as neat as she'd left it the previous evening, so she knew he had stayed out all night. Sam's and Jack's had the imprints of their bodies still and the blankets were in the usual heap.

Sam and Jack knew Beth had gone back to Jeff Smith's Parlour for a drink, and as they'd taken the trouble to bank up the stove before they left this morning, she felt they couldn't be angry she'd spent the night with him. Yet all the same she felt awkward about it. It was fine for men to bed women, but a woman who succumbed to the same temptation was considered a trollop.

She had already bathed at Jefferson's; he'd filled his bath for her and even washed her. Sitting down on the rocking chair he'd given her, she put her head back and closed her eyes, reliving the sensuality of it all, and decided she didn't care if she was a trollop. She would brazen it out when the boys came home. Jack and Sam had romantic dalliances all the time, why shouldn't she?

As for Theo, if he didn't like it he could just go off and stay with Dolly the whore. Perhaps when he discovered she was only good for one thing, that she couldn't cook, sew or wash his clothes, he'd realize how valuable his Gypsy Queen had been.

The door of the cabin crashed open late that afternoon, bringing with it an icy wind and a flurry of snow.

Beth had been dozing in the rocking chair. She woke with

a start to see Theo in the doorway, purple in the face with anger.

'How could you let that bastard fuck you?' he shouted at her. 'You've made me look like a prize idiot!'

Beth had intended to admit what she'd done, for she knew someone would eventually let it slip. But she hadn't expected that word would reach Theo so fast.

For a second she just looked at him, shocked that he was more hurt by how others would react to the news than by her faithlessness.

'You had it coming to you,' she said defiantly. 'You've been a pig to me for months, and you've been spending all your time with that whore in the Red Onion.'

'I've been involved with business,' he snarled. 'A man's business interests have to come first if he is to get anywhere.'

'There's only one kind of business going on in a brothel,' she retorted, her voice rising in anger. 'And I'm never going to play second fiddle to a whore, so get back there now and wait in line while she lets every other man in town fuck her.'

He looked at her in astonishment.

'You are a lying, cheating louse,' she continued. 'Telling people you're an earl! Robbing them blind with your marked cards! I might have been able to live with that. But I won't live with a man who doesn't value me. I've stood by you through everything, but not any more. Get out now and don't come back.'

He faltered for only a moment, then snatched up his clothes from the shelf in the corner, bundled them into a bag and left, slamming the door behind him so hard, the whole cabin shook.

Beth cried then, bitter tears which were not for sorrow that she'd been with another man, but for love turned sour. She would have gone to the ends of the earth for

Theo, and for all her harsh words she knew she loved him still.

A week later Beth and Sam were having a night in. It was so cold outside that eyelashes became covered in frost within seconds and lungs hurt just breathing in. They had banked up the stove with logs, and sat close to it, each of them wrapped in a warm quilt.

Jack had gone to see the Arnolds, a family with three children who had arrived in Skagway in early December. They had been ill equipped from the start, and what little money they'd brought with them had soon vanished. They were still living in a tent, like so many people here, and one of the children, nine-year-old Nancy, had died from pneumonia just after Christmas.

Jack had tried to get Sid Arnold, the father, some work. He had been a barber in Portland, but there was little call for barbers here where almost all the men favoured thick beards and moustaches. He lasted only one day in the saw-mill – he just didn't have the strength for heavy work – and he had proved to be something of a liability in every other job Jack had found for him. Now his wife and young son Robbie were sick, and Jack had made a collection around Skagway to send them home on the next ship. But Sid's eyes were as bright with gold fever as his wife's were with a high temperature. He kept insisting that he was setting off for the Chilkoot Pass, convinced that was the answer to everything.

'Do you think Jack will talk him round?' Sam asked Beth.

Beth shook her head. She had observed this gold madness for so long that she had come to the conclusion it was terminal. Most of the people who arrived here had no idea how far it was to Dawson City – they imagined it was a short stroll up a couple of hills. Few realized how cold and treacherous it was on the mountains, and a great many of the people who had set off last autumn on both the White Pass and the Chilkoot Pass had been forced to turn back and wait till spring.

But the Chilkoot Indians, who were accustomed to using this trail, had reported that many of those who didn't return had perished up there. The flesh had been picked clean from their bodies by birds and other scavengers.

'Maybe the only solution is to put his wife and the two remaining children on the boat alone,' Beth said sadly. 'I believe they have family in Portland who will nurse them back to health. That is, if they don't die before a ship comes in.'

'Are you afraid of going up the Pass?' Sam asked curiously.

'Yes,' she admitted. 'But we've come this far, we'd always regret it if we didn't go the rest of the way.'

'It won't be the same without Theo.'

'No, it won't,' Beth sighed. 'It will be easier.'

Sam was silent for some time, staring at the fire with blank eyes. Beth knew that both he and Jack missed Theo for his imaginative ideas and the fun he could create. They had admitted that they'd known for some time about Dolly, and had hoped Beth's night with Jefferson would bring him sharply back to heel.

But however much they liked him and thought of him almost as a brother, their primary loyalty was to Beth. So they hadn't tried to talk to him, and he in turn hadn't gone looking for them.

'What about Soapy?' Sam asked, breaking the silence. 'Do you have feelings for him?'

'Lustful ones, perhaps.' Beth giggled. 'But it's been a week now and he hasn't made any move to see me again. I guess now he's heard Theo's out of the picture, I don't look quite so attractive.'

Sam half smiled. 'Maybe that's just as well, sis, he's a dangerous man. I like him well enough, but he's more slippery than an eel. If just half the stories about him are true, there's still enough to put the wind up anyone. You'll find the right man one day, someone who is worthy of you.'

Beth reached forward and ruffled his thick blond beard. 'We've come a long way, haven't we? I doubt the Langworthys would recognize us now. Not just the way we look, but how we've changed inside. Imagine us trying to have tonight's conversation when we were back in Liverpool! Remember what Mama said about passion? I had no idea what that was then.'

'Nor did I.' Sam smirked. 'That was one of the best discoveries.'

They both laughed and went on to talk about how good it was to be away from the restrictions they'd grown up with, and that they were friends, as well as brother and sister.

'Has there ever been a woman you didn't want to say goodbye to?' Beth asked.

'It would be quicker to list those I was glad to,' Sam joked. 'I always seem to meet someone there's a real spark with just as we're moving on. Take that small redhead who helps her mother make pies down on Main Street!'

'Sarah?' Beth had spoken to the girl many times. She was very proper, never went into the saloon or encouraged any of the men's advances. But she had a feisty air about her and she was very pretty.

'Yes, Sarah from Idaho. I really like her, she's got that kind of –' He broke off suddenly at the sound of gunfire. 'That's close by,' he exclaimed, shrugging off the quilt and getting to his feet.

Gunfire was commonplace, just as brawls in the streets and saloons were. But it wasn't usual to hear it in this part of town.

'Don't go out, Sam,' Beth begged him. 'You know what it's like when a few of them are drunk and riled up. You could end up among them and get hurt.'

He hesitated. 'I'll just look out the door and see what's going on. No harm in that.'

As he pulled the door open an icy blast came in. Sam reached for his fur-lined coat and hat and quickly stepped outside, shutting the door behind him. Beth got up to look out of the tiny window, but all she could see was Sam's shoulder and the snow-covered ground. But as she heard people shouting, her curiosity was aroused, and she reached for her coat and hat too.

Sam grinned as she came out. 'Didn't think you could resist! Dare we walk down there? It sounds like it's in State Street. Let's just take a peek. We won't get involved.'

They hurried, Beth taking Sam's arm for security on the slippery ground. As they turned the corner into State Street they came upon a crowd of people huddled around a man lying on the ground. Even in the poorly lit street they could see blood staining the snow.

'Who did it?' Sam asked a man walking past.

'Dunno his name, just a guy who'd been fleeced, I guess.'

'Do you know the man that's been shot?' Beth asked.

'That guy they call the Earl.'

Chapter Twenty-seven

Sam tried to restrain her, but Beth wriggled away from him and pushed through the people crowding around Theo. Her heart was thumping with fear, but all memories of her last angry words to him were wiped from her mind.

'Theo!' she cried as she sank down on her knees beside him.

'He ain't gonna make it, mam,' a man in the crowd called out.

It didn't look good. Theo was unconscious and Beth could see a hole where the bullet had gone through his coat into his shoulder. Blood was pumping out of it. Catching hold of his wrist, she felt for a pulse. It was there, but weak. 'He certainly won't make it if we leave him here to freeze,' she said sharply. 'Someone help me get him to the doctor.'

Theo stirred and opened his eyes. 'Beth!'

His voice was so quiet, Beth leaned closer to his face. 'Yes, it's me. But don't talk or move, it will only weaken you.'

As Sam came forward to help, one of the other men suggested they got something firm to lay Theo on, and almost immediately a woman came running out of the nearest saloon with a narrow table-top in her arms. 'They busted the legs off in a brawl,' she said by way of explanation and rushed back inside out of the cold.

Sliding the table-top under Theo, Sam took his head end and two others took his feet.

Dr Chase's cabin was close by, and someone rushed ahead to knock him up. Beth had never met the doctor as she'd never needed any medical help, but she knew him to be a good man because he and Reverend Dickey were responsible for funding the building of a cabin as a hospital, due to open very soon, and the doctor was also well known for treating very poor people without charge.

Dr Chase, a small, slender man with glasses and thinning hair, was already in his apron and rolling up his sleeves as they arrived at his door.

'Put him on the table,' he said, moving the lamp closer. 'Are any of you relatives?'

Sam explained that he and Beth were Theo's friends and travelling companions and gave him their names. The doctor asked them to stay to help, and for the others who had followed on to leave.

'I hope you aren't squeamish,' he said to Beth as he began peeling Theo's clothes away at his shoulder. 'Because I'll need you as a nurse. Go and wash your hands thoroughly.'

As Beth washed her hands in the basin the doctor had pointed to, she glanced back at Theo. He had no colour in his face, his lips were blue and he was unconscious. She felt sick with fright, for as the wound was exposed it looked terrible, a mass of dark red tissue and blood.

She put on an apron and rolled up her sleeves, and the doctor asked Sam to stand firm behind Theo to restrain him if he struggled.

'It's fortunate he is unconscious,' he said quite cheerfully. 'But the chances are he'll come round when I begin probing, so be ready.'

Beth wanted to ask why the doctor couldn't give him chloroform, but she didn't quite dare, and stood by to follow his instructions.

'If one has to take a bullet, it's a pretty good place for it,' Dr Chase said, indicating Beth was to hold his tray of instruments and pass whichever one he needed. 'Why was he shot anyway?'

'We don't know because we weren't with him when it happened,' Sam said. 'We only ran to see when we heard the shot.'

'His name?'

'Theodore Cadogan,' Beth said.

'Ah, the English Earl,' the doctor said. 'From what I've heard it was only a matter of time before someone shot him. And you then,' he said, looking over his glasses at Beth, 'must be the much acclaimed Miss Bolton, the Gypsy Queen?'

Beth felt a wave of shame wash over her, for the implication in his words that she was no better than she should be for consorting with a man like Theo. But the doctor said nothing more, and cleaned the wound with swabs, then began probing into it. Theo regained consciousness once and struggled to get up, but fortunately passed out again.

'There we are!' said Dr Chase, jubilantly holding up the bullet in the jaws of his pincers. 'It hadn't gone in too far, luckily for him. But he's going to need good nursing to recover. Bullets are easy enough to extract; the real problem comes when infections move in. Are you up to that nursing, Miss Bolton?'

'Yes, of course,' she said without any hesitation.

'I shall stitch him up, and he can stay here tonight. Tomorrow I'll get someone with a cart to bring him to your cabin. I'll give you instructions then as to his diet. He has lost a lot of blood and it will take him a while to recover his strength.'

'Why did you help me?' Theo asked the following evening.

The doctor had brought him round to the cabin that morning, and the two men with him had lifted him on to the bed. Theo had been given something for the pain, and that made him sleep most of the day. Beth had made a pot of beef tea as the doctor ordered, and she was stirring it on the stove when Theo spoke.

'Because I didn't see Dolly the whore rushing to your aid,' she said waspishly. 'But if you would rather go there and lie in her flea-ridden bed, you only have to ask.'

'I would much rather be with you,' he said, his voice very weak. 'You are the only woman I've ever really loved.'

Beth felt tears welling up in her eyes, but she bit them back. 'I'll take care of you for old times' sake, but don't count on me long-term, Theo.'

Theo was in a great deal of pain for the first few days. Dr Chase came by to change the dressings daily and said he was pleased to see no sign of any infection, but showed no sympathy for Theo.

'You're lucky you aren't dead,' he said bluntly. 'I've got patients who have become sick through no fault of their own, and they are my priority.'

It appeared that the man who fired the shot had left town, perhaps because he thought he'd killed Theo, and feared he would be charged with murder. All Theo would say on the subject was that he deserved what he got. Beth took that to mean he had swindled the man.

She passed the days by reading to him and passing on any gossip, and in truth she was glad to be inside in the warm with him. Jack or Sam took over on nights when she had to play.

It was ten days after the shooting before Jefferson spoke to her about it. He hadn't come into Clancy's saloon in all that time, and she hadn't seen him around the town either. But suddenly there he was in the crowd watching her play, smiling that lazy, seductive smile that made her pulse speed up.

'Have a drink with me?' he said as she got down from the little stage.

'I've got to get back,' she said, dying to ask him where he'd been all this time, but knowing that wasn't a smart thing to do.

'Nursing duties?' he said, lifting one eyebrow. 'What does the Earl do for you that warrants such tender care? I heard you slung him out after our night together?'

'We go back a long way,' she said. 'I don't turn friends away when they need help.'

He put a glass of rum in her hand. 'And when he's recovered?'

Beth shrugged. 'I don't know. That's up to him.'

'By that I take it you will fit into his plans? If he goes back to Dolly, you'll be free; if not, you'll be tied to him?'

'Look, I don't know, Jefferson,' she said in irritation. 'When I took him in to nurse him it was because of our past, just as I would take care of Jack if something happened to him. I can't think beyond that right now and I don't understand why you are questioning me about it. You didn't even drop by to see how I was when you heard I'd chucked him out, so why should you care now?'

'Because I like you and he'll bring you down.'

'He's not that different from you,' she said indignantly.

'That's why I know how it will end.'

Beth sighed, drank down her rum and picked up her fiddle case ready to leave. 'Then I hope you'll have someone who will take care of you if you get shot,' she said crisply. 'Goodnight, Jefferson. It was nice while it lasted.'

She thought he would come after her; after all, on their night together he had said he wanted her as his girl. But perhaps that was just part of his patter and all he'd really been looking for was another conquest.

'I've been a blithering idiot,' Theo said a few days later. He was up and about now, though he couldn't do anything strenuous; even dressing himself had to be done carefully and slowly.

'What brought you round to that startling conclusion?' she asked.

'Don't be sarcastic,' he said reproachfully. 'I'm trying to make you see I do value you. I always did, but the thing that makes me saddest is the distance between us now, when we were once so close. I know it was me who caused it. But I don't know how to get you back where you used to be.'

'I don't know either,' she said sadly. 'Sometimes I think it's this town full of people with only gold on their minds. It's affected us all. Even Jack, who spends all his spare time helping people, can't wait to take off on the trail. It's like a disease.'

'Maybe the only cure for it is to take that trail then,' Theo said.

'You won't be strong enough for that for some time.'

'A month should do it. But the real question is whether you want me with you.'

'Of course I do, Theo! Maybe I don't adore you blindly the way I used to, but I still love you. If you would just be more honest!'

'Honesty didn't bother you with Soapy,' he said. 'He's far more dishonest than me, he's a liar, a thief, a swindler, and no doubt he's had people killed too, though I doubt he dirtied his own hands with that.'

'At least he was there when I needed someone,' Beth snapped. 'I didn't see Dog-faced Dolly rushing to your aid.'

*

'That's it then, sis,' Sam said as he took the last sack of their supplies out of the cabin and loaded it on to the hired cart that would take it the three miles to Dyea and on to the start of the Chilkoot Trail. 'Say goodbye to the cabin. I doubt we'll come back this way.'

Theo was sitting up on the cart. His shoulder had healed well, but the weeks of inactivity and good food had made him gain weight, giving him a flabby look. Jack, in contrast, was very lean, for he'd been working six days a week building houses, shops and cabins. This was to ensure they had enough money to pay the Indian packers to carry their goods to the top of the Pass.

Along with the compulsory ton of provisions to be allowed into Canada, carpentry tools were needed to build a boat at Lake Bennett, a shovel, sledge, stove, tent, bedding and many other essential items. As most men could only carry fifty pounds on their backs up the trail, this meant that if they didn't hire Indian packers they would have to make dozens of trips up and down, which could in effect take three months to complete.

The vast majority of their fellow gold seekers had no choice but to do that, for the packer's price per load was exorbitant. But Theo wasn't strong enough to carry more than a few pounds, and neither Sam nor Jack wanted Beth to take heavy loads. With their combined funds they had enough, and they reckoned that what they lost in money would be made up for in time, and being able to take some items that they could sell for a big profit in Dawson City.

'I have to post this letter home before we leave,' Beth said, waving an envelope. Just a couple of days earlier they had finally received a letter from England with a photograph of Molly taken on her fourth birthday just before Christmas. Beth had hastily penned a letter back enclosing a picture she and Sam had had taken here in Skagway, and telling Molly and the Langworthys that they were about to leave for the goldfields.

She had wondered as she wrote it whether people back in England had any idea of what this trip entailed. Beth had a fairly clear idea that it was going to be no picnic, as foresighted Jack had been out to the start of the trail and talked to people who had given up half-way, and what he learned was almost enough to make them abandon the idea.

'We'll go on, you catch us up when you've posted it,' Theo called out. 'But don't get waylaid!'

It was late March now, and most of the people they'd got to know during the winter had left on either the White Pass or Chilkoot Trail over a month ago. But if all went well Beth knew they'd meet up with them all on the shores of Lake Bennett. The ice on the lake wouldn't break up till the end of May, so they couldn't depart before that.

Skagway looked very different now to how it had been when they first arrived. There was a wharf, a church and a hospital, and the main streets were lined with real buildings – shops, saloons, restaurants, hotels, houses and cabins. The roads were still a slick of mud, made worse now as there had been a slight thaw in recent days. But the tent city all around the town was still there. Different tents now, for the old ones had either moved with their owner or been torn apart in gales. Ships disgorged hundreds more gold seekers daily. Some stayed only a short time before making for the trails; others would get sucked into the seedier side of the town, lose all their money and eventually catch a ship home.

Beth was glad to be leaving. She'd had some good times here, but more bad ones. She wouldn't miss the rowdiness, the filth, the exploiters or the exploited. But she was going to miss the tapping feet and handclapping as she played her fiddle. She would never forget those smiles of pure joy as she lifted her audience away from their worries and cares.

As she passed Clancy's saloon she smiled when she saw the chalk sign still up announcing 'Gypsy Queen playing tonight'. Picking up a piece of chalk lying on the ground in front of it, she added: 'Not tonight, I'm off to the Klondike. See you there.'

Turning away from the sign and still giggling to herself, she saw Jefferson leaning against a crate watching her while he smoked his pipe.

'So you're off then?' he said.

'Just posting a letter and I'll catch up with the cart.'

'Stay and have a drink with me. I'll take you to catch them up on my horse afterwards.'

She opened her mouth to refuse politely, but as she caught his twinkling eyes she couldn't resist. 'For old times' sake,' she laughed. 'But only an hour, not a moment longer, and if you don't take me then there'll be trouble.'

'You post your letter and I'll have the drinks poured when you get back,' he said.

As she walked through the door of Clancy's, he popped a bottle of champagne. 'I thought I'd give you a good send-off.' He smiled. 'It might be the last good thing in months.'

He poured her a glass and leaned on the bar looking at her. 'You'll be missed here,' he said eventually. 'There's plenty of pretty girls in town, but few with your spirit or pluck. Maybe I'll get up to Dawson one day and see how you're doing. If you haven't been snapped up by a rich gold miner, I'll whip you off to San Francisco and make an honest woman of you.'

'That would be hard for you to do, when you are so dishonest,' she retorted. 'Besides, I want to go back to England. I've got a little sister that I need to see.'

She took the picture of Molly she'd placed in the inside pocket of her coat for safekeeping, and showed him. Her hair was as long and curly as Beth's, tied up with two bows, and she was wearing a white frilled pinafore over her dark-coloured dress. She was no longer a baby but a little girl, with round dark eyes and a very serious expression.

'She looks like you,' Jefferson said. 'I guess she's the kinda kid anyone would want to go home to see. And your folks too. They must miss you.'

'They're dead,' Beth said, and suddenly found herself telling him what had happened. 'I don't know why I told you that,' she finished up, feeling embarrassed. 'I never tell anyone.'

Jefferson shrugged. 'It will be getting the picture of her, it brings things back. I've got a picture like that.'

'Of a little girl?'

'No.' He laughed. 'A picture of you, taken in here one night. I only collected it a few days ago. It made me think how things might have been, if only –' He broke off and grinned at her.

'If only what?'

'If only I'd been a different kinda man. If only I'd come round to see you after that night and told you how I felt.'

'How did you feel?' she whispered.

'Like I was all brand new again. Like there could be a life without swindling and fast talking. But I guess I wasn't brave enough to try for it.'

Beth lifted her hand and pinched his cheek tenderly. 'You were brave enough to tell me now. I'll tuck that away inside my head and think on it sometimes.'

They talked for a while about the changes in Skagway since she'd arrived, and how it might be in years to come. He asked after Sam and Jack, but didn't mention Theo.

'Don't trust anyone on the climb up the Pass,' he said suddenly. 'There's men up there who look like stampeders, a pack on their back and as dirty as anyone else. They'll offer you a little kindness, a hot drink or a warm by their fire. But they ain't real stampeders, they're con men, and they'll fleece you.'

She had a strong feeling that these men he spoke of might even be in his pay, but she thanked him for the advice and said it was time she went.

He took her hand as they left the saloon to get his horse from the stable, and the touch of his smooth hand on hers made a tremor run through her.

A man brought the chestnut mare out to him, and as he held it steady, Jefferson stretched out his hand for her foot and helped her up into the saddle. Then, leaping up behind her in one agile movement, he put his arms on either side of her to take the reins.

'Giddy-up,' he said, and they cantered down the street, out on to the track to Dyea.

In Skagway, with all its hustle and bustle, the beauty of the scenery all around the town often went unnoticed. But once away from that tumult, with the weak winter sun shining on the turquoise water of the Lynn Canal, and the snow-topped mountains all around, it suddenly came back sharply into focus.

As they jogged along, Jefferson pointed out a couple of seals in the water and a bald eagle perched on a fir tree. Beth couldn't help wishing that they'd had time before to have a little trip together like this, and really talk.

There were many groups of people trudging along the road to Dyea, some pushing handcarts, their baggage piled high, others using pack mules or horse-drawn carts. Suddenly Beth spotted the boys and their cart up ahead. 'I think you should leave me here,' she said. 'I can soon catch up with them.'

Jefferson jumped down, as lithe as a cat, then, reaching up, he caught her waist and swung her down. But he didn't let go of her. 'Farewell, my Gypsy Queen,' he said. 'Take good care on that trail, and think of me sometimes.'

He kissed her then, long and hard, holding her as though he never wanted to let her go. Then, breaking away, he leapt back on his horse, wheeled around and galloped off.

Beth stood on the path for a moment or two watching the rear of his chestnut mare, his straight back and black hat, and felt a tiny pang for what might have been.

Chapter Twenty-eight

'God save us!' Beth exclaimed as they wearily approached Sheep Camp, the last place they could get firewood or provisions before setting off up the mountain.

They had already endured three days of painfully slow progress as they and a thousand other stampeders hauled their carts and sledges up a pot-holed track from Dyea, which criss-crossed the river several times. Sleet, flurries of snow and the sheer volume of people, carts, dogs and pack animals made the path rutted and treacherous. The hastily improvised bridges were so ramshackle that on one occasion they had all ended up to their knees in icy water and had to continue with sodden boots and clothes.

But it wasn't the sight of hundreds of milling people and animals in this last real camp before climbing up to the summit that caused Beth's shocked exclamation. She wasn't even put off by the huddle of primitive shacks, abandoned heavy items like stoves, chairs and trunks, or even the torn tents and the mountains of goods piled up waiting to be moved on.

Her shock was caused by what lay beyond all that.

The Chilkoot Pass. And, more importantly, the climbing it would entail.

Every would-be gold seeker knew the Pass was tough. Back in the saloons of Skagway everyone had heard at least a dozen different horror stories from people who had either turned tail and ran when they saw it, or were driven back by bad weather. But hearing about it and seeing it for herself were entirely different.

Sheep Camp was in a hollow at the end of the timber line, encircled by mountains. Beth knew the summit they had to reach was 3,500 feet above Dyea, just four miles above her head if she could have flown straight up there like an eagle. But she wasn't a bird, and the route they would be taking sent a shudder of fear and awe down her spine.

The mountain appeared to be draped with a continuous winding black ribbon which stood out in sharp relief against the snow. It consisted of climbers, bent over like apes under their heavy backpacks and seemingly motionless. But Beth knew they were moving, for they couldn't stop; even a momentary pause would snarl up the queue coming up right behind. If anyone did choose to move out of the line to rest, they would never get back into it.

Theo had turned pale and Sam was rubbing his eyes as if unable to believe what he was seeing. Only Jack looked calm and ready to join that fearsome chain in the morning.

'There are two places to stop,' he said. He pointed out a giant boulder and said he had been told that climbers could rest a while at the base of it. He then indicated a flat ledge further up and said that was the Scales. 'That's where our packers will reweigh our load and probably charge us still more.'

Jack didn't go on to remind them that the part of the Pass which was the most difficult and hazardous was beyond the Scales, and not visible from Sheep Camp. No pack animals could climb what had been named the Golden Stairs, 1,500 steps cut out of sheer ice by some entrepreneurs who demanded a toll for using them. Once on them there was no stopping anywhere until the top was reached.

Sam, Theo and Beth looked at one another in horror. Had it not been for Jack's stalwart stance, they might have voiced their fear of making the climb. But Jack had become their commander since they left Dyea; he alone had kept his nerve when the cart nearly fell off a bridge, or got stuck in a rut; his strength, determination and calm had got them through so far and they believed he'd make sure they got all the way to Dawson City unscathed.

'If we pitch our tent here tonight, it will be hell putting it all away at first light tomorrow,' Jack went on, seemingly unaware that they didn't share his excitement. 'So I reckon Theo and Beth should go and get us a place in one of the hotels here. Sam and I will find our packers and ask where they want us to put all this.'

Beth glanced at the cart with its mountain of their equipment and the required provisions. It had seemed a formidable amount even back in Skagway, yet they'd still raged at the fee charged by the Indian packers for each sack. But now she had seen the mountain it had to be taken up, she felt faint at the thought of what it would mean if they had to carry it all themselves. She said a silent prayer of thanks that they'd managed to get the money for packers together. She doubted that she would've been able to carry even one sack on her back to the top, let alone repeat it again and again.

The so-called hotels bore no resemblance to any hotel, however humble, that Beth had ever seen, yet she was soon to discover the price was similar to that of the hotels in New York. They were just shacks, with no beds, just a tiny space on a bare floor, with dozens more people packed round them. If they bought a meal it would cost close to two days' wages.

She found you could buy almost anything at Sheep Camp, provided you had enough money. Whisky, dark glasses to prevent snow blindness, sledges, fur hats, even candy. There were whores too, who for five dollars would make sure a man enjoyed his last night of relative comfort before striking out for the summit.

Despite her exhaustion from the day's arduous trek, Beth couldn't help but smile at these whores, for they were the plainest, grubbiest women she'd seen since the shirt factory in Montreal. Some sported ragged satin dresses, a blanket tied round their shoulders like a cape, heavy men's boots on their feet and hair like rats' tails. Yet there were plenty of takers for their services.

Once into the 'hotel', hemmed in on all sides by humanity, there was no possibility of getting out again during the night. Beth was sandwiched between Theo and Sam, and the stench of feet and other body odours was so strong that she pulled her fur-lined hood right over her mouth and nose, and hoped that exhaustion would ensure she could fall asleep.

She was awake for what seemed all night, listening to an orchestra of different kinds of snores. There were loud roaring ones like steam trains, high-pitched squeaks, some regular, ordinary snores and some irregular ones, and every now and then someone would break wind, cough or groan. One man sounded as though he was praying, and another swore in his sleep. It was like a mass tuning of strange instruments.

Theo's breathing was heavy, Sam's light. Jack was lying behind Sam but she couldn't distinguish his sound from anyone else's. Beth was aware that this was probably the most comfortable and warm she could expect to be for weeks and that scared her even more. Why was she going? She didn't care about gold and she could make enough money in Skagway to ensure she could go back to England next year with a sizeable nest egg. What if there was an avalanche while they were on the mountain and she was buried alive? What if she fell and broke her leg or arm? What then?

She must have fallen asleep eventually for the next thing she knew, Jack was shaking her and saying it was time to go.

By midday Beth was already convinced she couldn't take another step. The pack on her back was small, just twenty-five pounds in weight, containing nothing more than dry clothing, while the boys had ones twice as heavy, and Sam and Jack had a sledge each too, but it felt like a ton weight. The snow was packed hard underfoot, but uneven because of the stones beneath it, so she had to watch where she was stepping, using her stout pole for support as she dragged herself, puffing and panting, ever upwards.

She was sweating from the exertion in so many clothes, but the one time she took off her fur-lined coat, the icy wind chilled her to the bone within seconds. She wanted a hot drink and a sit-down, her eyes watered in the icy wind, her lips were cracking and every bone in her body was shrieking at her to stop. She cursed her long skirt and petticoats which gathered up the loose snow with every step, and determined that when they finally got to the Scales, she would break with propriety and persuade Sam to let her wear one of his pairs of trousers.

She got the only drink of the day at the Stone House when Jack heated up water in their volcano kettle, feeding the fire he'd lit inside it with dry sticks and wood shavings he'd stored up from his carpentry work back in Skagway. As he bent over it, blowing into the fire between the double walls, Beth watched him in admiration, wondering why it was only he who had realized back in Vancouver that this curious doubled-walled invention with space to light a small fire inside it would be the single most useful piece of equipment they could own. It could be lit in a high wind or even rain and still boil the water quickly.

She recalled the skinny, pale-faced street urchin Jack had been when they first met. Even then he was resourceful and tough, but he had grown in every possible way since. His face above his thick dark beard was as brown and weather-beaten as an Indian's now, the thin scar on his cheek barely visible any longer. His broad shoulders, arms and thighs were solid muscle. He had embraced and learned something from every experience he'd had since he left the immigrant ship, whether it was butchering beef, bartending or building cabins. He was the steel in their small group, the one they all relied on, drawing on his strength when all theirs was gone.

'How are your feet?' he asked, noticing immediately that Sam was hobbling as he moved to get the coffee and sugar from his pack. 'Have you got a blister?'

'I expect so; my boots are rubbing on my ankles,' Sam groaned.

'Take them off and I'll put a bandage round them,' Jack said. 'And you, Theo! How is that wound holding up?'

'It's not too bad, a few twinges, that's all,' Theo replied, tucking his hand inside his coat as if to check the scar hadn't broken open.

'I'll check that too,' Jack said. 'But coffee first. Beth looks as if she'll collapse if she doesn't get some quickly.'

A lump came up in Beth's throat for she didn't understand how Jack had turned out to be such a caring man. From the little he'd told her about his childhood she knew it had been a harsh one, the kind you would expect to create an unfeeling brute.

*

By the time they had reached the Scales, Beth was on the point of collapse. Every part of her ached, as if she'd been stretched on a medieval torture rack.

The sky was like lead, and she'd heard someone say they thought it would snow again soon. When she looked down the way they had come, the stream of climbers was just as long as it had been that morning, and she wondered at the insanity of it all.

She dimly heard Jack say they would pitch the tent for the night and then go to check if their packers had got everything up yet.

Beth crawled into the tent even before the boys had finished hammering the pegs into the frozen ground. Every inch of ground around the Scales was covered with tents, and the sound of hundreds of voices, complaining, arguing and calling to one another, made her want to cover her ears to shut them all out.

Somehow she managed to get the blankets out of their packs, but fell on to them before she could even straighten them out or attempt to light the lantern.

It was dark when the boys had got back from checking on their kit, and although Beth had heard their voices as they came into the tent, she hadn't felt able to move or even open her eyes.

They camped at the Scales for three days because of a heavy snowfall. Others went on up the Golden Stairs regardless, but Jack thought it foolhardy, for someone had fallen and broken his leg, and had to be carried back down to Sheep Camp by Indian packers.

It was tedious huddling in the tent, but at least it gave them time to rest and gather themselves for the next gruelling part of the journey. The men Jefferson had warned her about were here at the Scales in force. They looked like bona fide stampeders, complete with backpacks and shovels, but the fires they lit, the hot drinks they offered the unwary were only to lure a few suckers into one of their pea-under-the-shell games. She recognized a few faces as being some of Soapy's foot soldiers and guessed he would get a good rake-off from them. Theo sulked for some time when she told him how she knew the games were rigged, but at least that deterred him from allowing himself to be sucked in.

On the fourth morning Jack announced it was time to pack up the tent and go, even though the sky was heavy with more snow and the temperature had dropped even lower.

'If we leave it any longer our goods will be buried under feet of snow at the top,' he said with an anxious glance at the sky. 'Besides, there's never going to be a good day for going up those steps.'

Sam took the lead with his sledge strapped on top of his pack. Beth came next, with Jack behind her, sledge and pack arranged like Sam's, and Theo bringing up the rear. It was imperative they kept in step with the person above them, and with a strong, icy wind threatening to blow them down the mountain and only a thin rope at the side of the ice steps to steady themselves, every step was tortuous.

Sweat poured off them and their muscles shrieked for mercy; the icy wind on the exposed parts of their faces felt like a thousand pinpricks. Beth didn't dare look anywhere but where she was placing her feet, for one slip could be fatal, and her back ached, bent into such an unnatural position. She counted the steps at first, but gave up after five hundred. Above the sound of the whistling wind there was a continuous, communal low groan, the sound of a couple of hundred souls all stretched to the limits of human endurance.

One man high above Beth and the boys keeled over sideways and slid back down the mountain, screaming, but no one even looked round, let alone broke their step to try to help him. It could be said they would have been risking their own lives and those of all who came behind to do so, yet all the same it seemed barbaric to ignore him. But the climb was far too hard for anyone even to waste breath on a comment. Beth felt Jack touch her back lightly as if to communicate that he felt impotent too.

On and on they went, not daring to look behind or even above them. The universal groan was growing louder, mingled with the sound of rasping breath.

It began to snow again, and suddenly Beth could see nothing more than Sam's boots just above her. Agony was mingled with terror now for she couldn't imagine how they could pitch a tent when they got to the top, and if they had no shelter they would surely die of cold.

'You *can* keep going, Beth,' Jack said from behind her, his voice eerie in the strange white world. 'We'll be fine, we're nearly there. Just think of that tea we'll make. Keep going.'

She heard a strangled cry from well below them and she guessed someone else had fallen. Then a yelp came from Theo.

Beth involuntarily turned her head, but she could see nothing but a snow-covered shape which she knew to be Jack. 'Hold on to the sledge,' she heard him say to Theo. 'I'll help pull you up.'

It was a grey-white world, in which she could see no further than two feet and sound became distorted. Surely the Scottish accent she'd heard a couple of hours earlier had come from above her? Now it seemed to be below. But

Jack's voice steadied her, reminding her they were nearly there, that Theo was holding on, and that Sam was just in front of her.

A woman screamed out that she could go no further, and a male voice urged her on, but their voices seemed to be coming from Beth's right and confused her still more.

'Just concentrate on the next step,' Jack called out as she faltered. 'It's not much further.'

Finally they reached the top to find themselves in what looked at first like a white city. The buildings were towering, snow-covered piles of goods, the streets the narrow corridors left between them.

Jack uttered an anguished oath on realizing that to find their goods would be a tall order. They had given their packers a long pole trimmed with a few bright ribbons to mark them, but they hadn't reckoned on the snow obliterating everything. Men were up on the heaps digging frantically with their shovels, and they heard one man claim he'd been digging for three days already.

There was nowhere to pitch the tent. The only shelter was within this 'city' and Jack led them through the winding streets until he found a place where they could rig up a tarpaulin for a roof over their heads.

It was warmer without the icy wind they'd struggled through all morning, and they sank down gratefully on to their sledges and once again made tea in their volcano kettle. All four were silent, and Beth had no doubt that they were all thinking the same as her, that they should have waited for spring. Darkness was already closing in, and the prospect of a night huddled here, perhaps many more too if they couldn't find their kit, was too terrible to contemplate.

Jack and Sam were revived by the hot tea, and taking the lantern went off to start a search for their goods.

'How is your wound?' Beth asked Theo as they huddled together on the sledge with a blanket around them.

'I don't think it's broken open,' he said. 'But even if it had, I deserve it for bringing you here. This is no place for a lady.'

'I'm far from the only one,' she said. 'And one day we'll look back on this and laugh about it.'

'I hope so.' He sighed. 'My wish is that I can make it all up to you by being the perfect husband and giving you the kind of home you deserve.'

'Is that a proposal?' she teased him.

He took his hand out of his glove and stroked her cheeks tenderly. 'It is if you want it to be, but I had intended to ask you somewhere a great deal more romantic than this.'

Beth glanced to her side at the narrow passage between the piled goods. It was still snowing, and other people had come along to share the passage with them; they too were fixing up tarpaulins for a roof. She laughed. 'I don't think we're going to find a romantic setting for some time yet.'

They had thought the climb up the Golden Stairs would be the absolutely worst part of the trail, but the next two days, as they tried to find their goods, were a long, drawn-out torture. It was impossible to sleep; they were filthy, cold and desperate for a hot meal, and the noise from so many people packed all around them and the ceaseless high wind and flurries of snow took them to the very edge of insanity.

They all dug snow off piles of goods, only to be disappointed, and despaired of ever finding their supplies. Digging warmed them a little, but their muscles ached unbearably, and when they stopped digging the cold seemed to freeze up every joint in their bodies.

Beth dreaded needing to relieve herself. Men went anywhere, regardless of who was nearby, but she couldn't do that, and the more she worried about it, the more often she seemed to need to go.

On the third day up there, with even heavier snow coming down, Beth really thought she couldn't survive another day. Tears froze on her cheeks and her lips were so cracked she could barely speak. Even Jack was showing signs of flagging. She watched him climbing up a snow-covered pile of goods and noticed how slow he had become. Theo looked deathly pale and staggered when he tried to walk, and although Sam was doing his best to keep up with Jack in the search, it was clear he was on the point of collapse.

Yet it was Sam who finally found their goods. He had taken himself off to try to get his circulation going again, and just happened to walk past another man who'd found his stuff. As he pulled out his last sack, Sam spotted their ribbon-trimmed pole sticking out beneath it. If he hadn't been there, within an hour the snow would have covered it again.

Packing it all on to the sledges warmed them and lifted their spirits a little, even though snow was coming down thick and fast. Finally they hauled the sledges to the snow-covered hut with a tattered Union Jack flying on it, where the North West Mounted Police, armed with their Maxim guns, stood guard over the border into Canada.

Beth was reassured to see the familiar red jackets and navy blue trousers, and heartened to know the police officers would allow no hand guns into Canada. They were determined that the violence and lawlessness of Skagway should not move across their border.

Duty had to be paid on the goods they had brought from the Alaskan side of the mountain. But Theo turned up trumps by producing a sheath of receipts for goods bought back in Vancouver, and argued that he shouldn't have to pay tax on them, only on the items bought in Skagway.

Beth wondered how the Mounties could be so pleasant and cheerful, stuck on top of a mountain for months on end in such appalling weather. They might have buffalo coats, but their shack was little warmer than a tent, and in one night the snowfall could be six feet. Yet they seemed amused at Theo's argument and nodded agreement, charging them only two dollars' tax in all, without even checking their kit.

Miraculously the snow ceased and weak sunshine appeared as they left the summit, wearing their snow shoes, for the five-mile trek to Happy Camp. Despite having to haul the heavily laden sledges and adjust to the strangeness of snow shoes, for the first time since they'd left Dyea the going was fairly easy. The number of people who had gone before had made the snow firm, and the sledges glided over it smoothly. They were astounded when someone told them they had only travelled twenty-two miles from Dyea, and eight and a half from Sheep Camp, for it seemed like a hundred.

Despite their exhaustion, the fact that they were moving at last, with the prospect of the night ahead in a tent and a fire to warm them, perked them up. At some downhill points of the trek they even rode on the sledges, shrieking with laughter like children. Some people had rigged up a sail on theirs and even overtook the few that had a dog team.

It was clear why the camp had been named Happy, for it was flat and therefore easier to pitch a tent there, and at last they were back in the timber line, so they could cut wood for fires.

Happiness was all around them that evening, despite

the thick snow and promise of more to come. The relief of being able to rest up before going on, the conviction that nothing else could be as bad as the Golden Stairs or the summit, and to be able to sit around a big fire and dry out wet clothes was enough to bring smiles and laughter back.

After they'd made a meal of bacon and rice, Beth got out her fiddle and began to play by the fire. In twos and threes people came across from their tents to listen, cheering at the end of each number. Someone brought a bottle of whisky over to share with Beth and the boys and the fiery liquid went straight to their heads, making them laugh about everything.

Later, as people left to go back to their tents, Beth stood for a moment looking around her. There was a full moon, and the sky was clear and studded with stars. The trees around the camp were poor, thin specimens, but with their snow covering they looked magical. Even the tents all around theirs, which she knew to be stained and worn, looked pretty in the golden light from the fires outside each one. In all the anxiety of the last week she hadn't noticed the scenery at all, but now, at peace again, she saw how beautiful the wilderness was, and found she was excited about the adventure before them.

'One day I'll be able to tell Molly about it all,' she thought, glancing round at the boys sitting half asleep by the fire. They were all so dirty and unkempt, with red-rimmed eyes, straggling beards, tangled hair and bundled into so many clothes, they could have been mistaken for three bears. She hoped that there might be a photographer somewhere among the people going to Dawson City. It would be good to have a permanent memento of how they all looked on this trail and something to show Molly.

A wolf howled somewhere close by, and its cry was picked up by some of the dogs in the camp. Beth shuddered and hurried back to the fire. For a moment she had forgotten that wild animals lived in this wilderness.

Chapter Twenty-nine

'We're here at last!' Jack chortled gleefully as he ran with the sledge through the narrow end of Lake Lindemann on to Lake Bennett.

Most of their fellow stampeders on the Chilkoot Trail had stayed on the shores of Lake Lindemann to build their boats to sail to Dawson City, but as Jack had heard that when the ice melted the rapids between the two lakes were very dangerous, he had decided that they should tramp through to Lake Bennett and build their boat there.

Theo had been disgruntled at what he saw as an unnecessary trek. He had liked the tented city at Lake Lindemann, where a gambling saloon, bars, shops and even restaurants had sprung up, and he'd been sure he could win enough at poker to buy one of the many collapsible boats brought over the Chilkoot Pass by a dealer. He and Jack had almost come to blows about it, for Jack had claimed these boats weren't strong enough to get them ten miles, let alone five hundred, and he accused Theo of being too lazy to work at building a safe one.

Beth had been on tenterhooks during the few days they spent at Lake Lindemann, as she could see how exasperated Jack was becoming with Theo. Jack had willingly hauled extra weight for him over the mountains. He'd let him ride on the sledge from Happy Camp to Lake Lindemann when his shoulder hurt, and excused him from helping to cut wood and other strenuous jobs. But he resented Theo swanking around treating him like his servant. Beth feared

Jack would push on to Dawson City on his own, and she wouldn't have blamed him if he had.

But as it was, Theo lost most of his remaining money in a poker game, so buying a boat was out of the question, and ultimately he had no choice but to fall in with Jack's plans.

He hadn't taken it well, though. Beth felt that underneath all Theo's superiority, he was actually jealous of Jack because so many people looked up to him, while he was seen as something of a parasite. He'd hardly said a word as they walked along the frozen lake, not even to her.

But then, Beth had her own private irritations with him too. While she wanted to put aside the hurt he'd caused her back in Skagway and have things back the way they were in Vancouver, she was finding it difficult.

As they all moved forward on to Lake Bennett, however, any ill feeling between them fell away, for the sight that met their eyes was truly astonishing.

Aside from the spellbinding beauty of the long, narrow frozen lake insinuating its way through a range of snow-covered mountains, there were tents spread along its shores for as far as the eye could see.

The thousands of tents came in all shapes and sizes, from brand-new ones to old, tattered ones, from tiny improvised ones, which would only shelter one man, to marquees big enough for a circus, and every other kind in between.

They had known that the White Pass, the alternative, longer route over the mountains from Skagway, ended up here, so they had expected a crowd of people, but they hadn't anticipated this many, or to see so many animals.

The White Pass had been dubbed 'Dead Horse Trail', because so many hundreds of horses died on it from starvation and ill treatment. One of the Mounties at the border had spoken out angrily at the cruelty and stupidity of people setting out without enough fodder for their animals. Yet there were many horses here, along with dogs, oxen, donkeys, goats, and even pens of chickens.

It was also a cacophony of sound: the thud of axes on wood, the buzz of saws, insistent hammering, dogs barking and people yelling to one another. Just a couple of years earlier this must have been a silent wilderness which only Indians and the occasional trapper passed through. Now it was a city in the making.

Theo brightened visibly as he saw a marquee advertising faro and poker games nightly, and although Beth could take no pleasure in him gambling away the last of his money, she was glad to see him smiling again. She thought too that she could make some money by playing her fiddle, as she had at Lake Lindemann.

'How much further?' Theo grumbled when an hour later Jack was still heading onwards down the lake.

'There's more trees down here. It's bad enough having to chop them down for the boat without having to haul them a distance,' Jack said tersely.

Beth exchanged glances with Sam. She knew he felt awkward being stuck in the middle, for he liked both men and had sympathies on either side. He too enjoyed a game of cards and a drink, and he still believed that Theo was the one who would eventually make them all rich. Yet at the same time he knew the three of them depended on Jack, for he had all the skills required to get them to Dawson safely.

Sam pulled a face at Beth. He didn't need to say a word – she knew he was thinking that Jack was a little too forceful and bossy, and that they could all do with a couple of days of complete rest before starting to build a boat.

She decided that she should intervene, so, picking up her skirt, she ran after Jack. 'Can't we have a couple of days off before we start on the boat?' she asked him. 'I mean, it's only March, and the ice won't melt until the end of May, so we've got lots of time.'

Jack stopped short, letting go of the rope on the sledge he was dragging, and looked at her with some amusement. 'Do you see how many people are here already?'

'Well, yes.' She shrugged.

'Every single day that number will grow larger,' he said patiently. 'They are pouring over the two trails in their thousands, and before long all the trees we see now will be chopped down. We have to start getting our wood right now as soon as we've made camp, or risk someone else getting it.'

Beth looked at him appraisingly. He was as dirty and bedraggled as every other man, with his bushy beard, matted long hair and his exposed skin raw from the bitter weather. But he didn't have that intense gold lust that was in every other man's eyes. She doubted he even dreamed of great riches the way Theo and Sam did.

'Fair enough.' She nodded. 'That makes sense, but tell me, Jack Child, what drives you? I don't think it's the gold.'

He chuckled softly, looking back at Sam and Theo who were resting on their sledge. 'Someone has to make sure you three get there safely.'

'That doesn't really answer my question,' she retorted.

He smiled and reached out and patted her cheek. 'I thought it did.'

By the middle of May their craft was completed, a sturdily built raft with a mast, a rudder to guide it, and slats around the sides to keep them and their kit safe in turbulent water. The boys had named it *Gypsy*, painting the name and the craft number, 682, on the rail across the prow. Samuel Steel, the superintendent of the Mounted Police, had decreed that all craft must be registered, and he had gone around the stampeders giving them each a number and logging down the names of everyone on each craft and their next of kin, in case of accidents on the long sail to Dawson City.

The raft sat on the ice on the edge of the shore, along with thousands of other craft, waiting for the day when the ice would break up. Many bore little resemblance to any boats Beth and the boys had ever seen; triangular shapes, round and oval ones, huge rafts big enough to take horses, scows, skiffs, catamarans, canoes, and some were little more than crude boxes.

Many were still being built, and despite the sunshine and clear blue sky, the air rang with squabbles, sawing, hammering and often curses, for those who hadn't finished their boats were stressed and panicked, and everyone else was in a state of high expectancy.

It was estimated that there were now 20,000 people here on the shores of Lake Bennett, their tents and equipment covering the entire length of it. Every possible amenity was here, including bath tents, barber-shop tents, a church, casino and post office, along with shops selling everything from bread to gum boots. Yet because of the Mounties' vigilance, there was none of the crime and skulduggery seen in Skagway. It was said that some of Soapy's henchmen had come over the Pass, but had been sent back with dire warnings not to return.

The only serious trouble was between men in their saw-pits, cutting green timber into planks for their boats. They had to work in pairs either end of a six-foot-long blade. The one above on the scaffolding guided the saw along the chalk line on the lumber, while the man below had to pull it down, but as the big saw teeth bit into the wood, the one below

377

was showered by falling sawdust. He was often convinced that his mate was not guiding the saw correctly, just as the man above claimed the lower one was holding the saw handle too tightly. Bitter arguments often exploded into bloody fights, and life-long friendships that had endured through all the trail had thrown at them were destroyed permanently.

Jack, Sam and Theo had avoided much of that because they had decided to build a raft made from whole slender trees rather than a boat of planks, but even so there had been a great deal of cursing and squabbling. Theo felt he was above manual work, and often disappeared. Sam was willing, but he would cut corners if Jack wasn't standing over him. Beth had often heard Jack berating both of them and threatening that he would leave without them if they didn't pull their weight.

But the work was all done now. All that was left to do was fix up the sail and stow their kit on board, and as the spring sunshine became a little warmer each day, and the days grew longer, they could hear the distant rumble of avalanches in the mountains and the gurgle of melting snow.

Mostly everyone who had finished their boat tended to spend their days now sitting on the shore, idly watching the dark green lake water visible through the ice as they whittled another paddle or oar. Someone had joked a few days earlier about the rush to the goldfields being called a 'stampede'. To all of them such a name was a joke, for it had been quite the opposite so far. It had been a slow, painful trudge, a three-month trial of endurance. There were no pot-bellies on any of the men now, their bodies were lean and muscular, and their gaunt faces, thick beards and long hair were all proof that they were no longer greenhorns. They smirked with pride as they spoke of those who had given up and gone home. There was a bond between them because of all the hardships and obstacles they'd overcome.

The women still had no time to sit on the shore. For them there were clothes to wash and mend, food to be prepared, letters to be written and dozens of other small jobs to be done which would make their men's lives more comfortable. But Beth took time off to watch the geese flying overhead, to study the carpets of flowers that appeared as the snow melted – mountain forget-me-nots, Dutchman's breeches and wild bleeding hearts.

After living in an all-white, snow-filled world for so long, the colours that appeared as the snow melted seemed fantastically bright. Red mountains, dark green fir trees and the acid green of lichen and mosses vied with the pink, blue and yellow alpine flowers that carpeted the ground away from the squalor of the camp. The sparrows and robins were coming back, and often the sound of birdsong almost drowned out the sawing and hammering.

Sometimes Beth would go off with her fiddle, away from the constant noise of the camp, and play for herself, glad to be alone. One day she saw two baby bears frolicking in the sunshine beneath a big rock and she hid herself away to watch from a safe distance, feeling privileged that she'd seen them. Their mother soon returned to them, cuffing them playfully with her big paws, and the sight evoked memories of Molly back home and brought tears to Beth's eyes.

It often struck her when she was entirely alone that she had no plans or even dreams for the future any more. Everyone else on the trail had the dream of gold; at night around the campfires they discussed what they'd spend it on, where they'd go next. But Beth seemed unable to think beyond the next day. There were many things she wanted – a real weatherproof house, a hot bath, a soft bed, fresh fruit, and to be able to put on a pretty dress and know it wouldn't be soiled with mud in five minutes. She would like Theo to make love to her, for that had been impossible since they left Dyea, what with the cold, how dirty they were, and always having Sam and Jack so close. She also longed to see Molly and England again, but even that seemed so far away she couldn't call it a plan.

She wondered what had happened to all the dreams she used to have. Of the house with a lovely garden. Of her wedding day, or a holiday by the seaside. She thought of them only occasionally now. Was that just because she'd already seen so much more than she could ever dream about? Or that she'd become disillusioned?

Theo often wove dreams about them living in a fancy apartment in New York, or in a grand mansion back in England. She would have liked to believe they might come true, but she couldn't. Theo had won back the money he lost by Lake Lindemann, but then he'd lost it again. The reality was that this was how it would always be with him, never secure, never settled, always looking out for the big chance.

Beth was aware of all his faults, and knew too that they were major ones that would never change. Sometimes she wished she'd taken note of what Ira had said about gambling men and had never given him her heart. But when things were good between them it was wonderful, for he was funny, clever and so loving, and she tended to overlook the bad parts – the disappearing acts, the lies or half truths, the laziness and conceit.

Her real security came from within her. She knew she could earn a living anywhere with her fiddle, and she loved that as much as she loved Theo. Maybe she didn't need a dream because she was already living it?

*

They heard the first crack in the early hours of 29 May. Beth thought it was a gunshot and sat upright in alarm. But then another came and she realized it was the ice breaking up.

It never really got dark at night now. The sky turned pink and purple around midnight, as if the sun was finally setting, but it didn't go completely dark at all. So she leapt up, pulled on her boots and, shouting to the others, ran down the few yards to the shore.

By the time the boys had joined her, there were hundreds of people gathered to watch. The ice was creaking and rumbling, dark green water spurting out through the cracks and washing away the building detritus, wood shavings, nails and patches of tar where they'd caulked their boats. Someone cheered and everyone joined in, holding hands and spinning one another round like children in a playground

That last day on Lake Bennett was one of pure joy for everyone, for the following morning they would be able to sail away. Beth dug her red satin dress out to wear in the evening. It had some black mould on it from being packed away so long, but she sluiced it off and hung it up to dry, excited by the prospect of looking like a real woman again, even if it was only for one night. She washed her hair too, leaving it to dry in the warm sunshine.

Everyone else was busying themselves with similar tasks. The queue for the bath tent was the longest she'd ever seen it, and someone told her that they were resorting to using the same water for twelve men, and offering them a rinse-off with cold water.

Some of the men, Jack included, pitched in to help the folk who hadn't yet finished their boats. Even the dogs picked up on the excitement and ran around the camp barking wildly.

At eight that evening, Beth played her fiddle to a packed house in the Golden Goose, the big gambling saloon marquee. People who had never been seen in there before turned up, and everyone danced.

Much later, as Beth was leaving to go back to the tent with Theo, the sound of the thunderous applause still ringing in her head, and over thirty-five dollars in Theo's hat, she heard a young man singing 'Sweet Molly'. Until that moment she'd forgotten her mother used to sing it to Sam and her when they were small, and hearing it again now, so far from home, on the eve of the last stage of their journey, seemed portentous.

Sam and Jack had stayed behind in the saloon, and for the first time in months, Theo made love to her. Later, as Beth lay sleepily snuggled into his shoulder, listening to all the merrymaking throughout the camp, she felt she must be the happiest woman there.

The late-night revels didn't prevent anyone getting up early the following morning and running down to check on the state of the ice.

There were still some large chunks floating by but it was clear enough to set sail and go. Suddenly everyone was striking their tents, packing up their pots and bedding, and hauling their provisions and equipment down to their boats.

Beth smiled to herself as she folded up her red satin dress and put out her best boots for Theo to seal up in one of the big waterproof sacks which they wouldn't open again until they got to Dawson City. She was wearing her old dark blue cotton dress again, her mackinaw coat, wide-brimmed hat and rubber boots. A change of clothing and her fiddle were packed in a small waterproof bag for the journey.

She watched Sam as he packed away his things. He was bare-chested, the first time she'd seen him without a shirt since the previous summer, and it was a surprise to see that the boyish, slender chest and back that she remembered from their days in Liverpool were now rippling with hard-packed muscle. But then, she'd got muscles in her legs and arms too. All that pack-carrying, sledge-pulling and carrying buckets of water had made her almost as strong as the men.

'Are you excited, Sam?' she asked.

'You bet!' he said, his handsome face breaking into a wide smile. 'I know we've got a long way to go yet, but it'll be an easy ride, and the weather's so good now.'

'I wonder if we'll still stick together when we get there,' she said thoughtfully. 'Do you still think you and Theo can make a go of a gambling saloon?'

''Course we can, sis.' He laughed. 'With you pulling them in with your fiddle, we can't fail.'

'Do you ever think of England?' she asked. This was a question she'd never thought to ask him before.

He smiled. 'To be honest, not much. What is there to go back for? We'd never have the thrills we get here.'

'But there's Molly,' she said.

He scratched his blond head and looked a little perplexed. 'We'd be nothing to her now. She won't even remember us. Besides, I know I wouldn't fit into that narrow way of life again. Not after this.'

Beth felt a lump come up in her throat and her eyes prickled with tears. 'Then I guess I'll have to go back alone.'

Sam caught hold of both her arms and squeezed them. 'What's up with you, sis? You shouldn't be thinking about stuff like that today. We're off on an adventure.'

'How many times do you think you've said that to me

383

since we left Liverpool?' she asked. 'It's always what's going to happen next, never a pause to think on the past.'

'Was the past that good it needs digging up?' he asked with a trace of scorn in his voice. 'As I recall, it was all about being told what I had to do – no one ever asked what I wanted. Well, I wanted to be rich even as a boy, and I want it more than ever now. It's up there in Dawson City, Beth, just lying around waiting for us, whether we dig it out the ground, or take it from others at gambling. Being rich will wipe out Papa killing himself because Mama was unfaithful to him.'

Beth was shocked to hear him say such a thing. She'd thought he'd put that aside a long time ago.

'I can't forget,' he said, as if he'd read her thoughts. 'It stops me trusting women too – except you of course.'

'Well, I'm glad of that much,' she said sarcastically. 'But what happens if you don't get rich in Dawson?'

'I will,' he said blithely. 'I know it.'

Over 7,000 boats sailed that afternoon in the warm sunshine, a vast armada of the strangest craft ever to be seen anywhere. Some had only an old coat or shirt as a sail; most sported a kind of home-made flag with the boat's name painted or sewn on to it. Some of the craft were already listing danger-ously; others looked jaunty and sporty. Old folk, young folk, bankers, shop clerks, farmers, soldiers, sailors and dance-hall girls – every walk of life was represented here. Some had left wives and families behind, some escaping the law; there were those from privileged backgrounds and those from big city slums. Yet the vast majority had never done anything exciting in their lives before and had invested their life savings in this mad adventure.

Beth felt all their hopes as she sat in the stern of *Gypsy*, with Jack and Sam paddling like fury, and Theo at the rudder. The cries of 'See you in Dawson' rang out over the lake and echoed in the mountains. She glanced towards the shore to see what looked like a vast waste tip: abandoned sawmills, ragged remains of tents, clothes and packing cases. Empty bottles and cans glinting in the sunshine, thousands of tree stumps, a whole forest cut down to build boats.

Everyone paddled and rowed frantically at first, all wanting to be up with the front runners, but as they reached deeper water, a breeze got up and caught the sails, and the paddles and oars were put down.

Later, the wind dropped and they were all becalmed, but as if by some silent message sent from boat to boat, no one reached for their oars, but just settled down, lit their pipes and let the current take them. Singing broke out all over the lake, the joyful sound of people who believed the worst was all behind them and that tomorrow was soon enough to rush for the gold.

The race resumed early the following morning, and Jack was delighted to find their big sail came into its own and took them along at a good speed. There were perhaps forty or fifty boats ahead, but behind them the rest of the vast armada was bunched up in clusters.

What with the warm sun, shining water and because their raft appeared to be far more stable and manageable than any other they'd seen, their spirits rose even higher. Jack had built low stools for them to sit on, so any water splashing up through the cracks of the raft wouldn't soak their clothes, and they lounged on them, complimenting themselves on their good workmanship and foresight.

It was during the afternoon that Beth noticed some of the people in the boats ahead were pointing to what looked like a red flag hanging from a tree, and a scrawled one-word message on a piece of wood, saying, 'Cannon'.

'Seems like a warning,' Jack said, and the words had barely left his lips when they heard the roar of tumbling water beyond.

As the lake made a slight turn to the left, they suddenly saw a narrow gorge before them, with steep black stone sides.

Beth gasped, Theo turned pale, and Sam waved his hat in excitement. 'Hold tight,' Jack shouted. 'This must be Miles Canyon.'

One of the Mounties had told them about the canyon. He said it was a terrifyingly dangerous place with two lots of rapids beyond it, but none of them had expected it to come so soon. It was too late for them to paddle over to the shore and check it out, for the raft was being sucked straight into the gorge.

'Take the paddles and use them to stop us being smashed against the sides,' Jack yelled, thrusting a paddle into both Sam's and Theo's hands. 'I'll try and steer us. Beth, you just hold on for dear life.'

They all looked on in sheer horror as the raft hurtled into the canyon. It was a third of the width of the river they'd been in previously, and because the water was being forced into a much narrower space, it created a crest some four feet high in the middle. They were virtually teetering on this crest, going at breakneck speed, and the roar of the water was so loud they couldn't hear one another speak.

The water was full of drifting timber, brought along here on the current from the mountain lakes, and large boulders and sharp rocks. Beth clung to the rail, watching in terror as Jack tried to steer them round the obstacles, and each time she heard a scrape on the bottom of the raft she braced herself for it being overturned.

Ahead of them they saw a large scow capsize, and five or six men desperately trying to cling on to it as it swirled around, smashing into rocks and boulders.

Beth glanced behind her and saw a canoe upturned, with no sign of the owner. But it was too frightening even to think about others, for their own raft was spinning round and round, up at the prow one minute, and then the stern would rear up like a bucking horse. Huge, icy waves washed over the raft, and they had to cling on to the sides in fear of being thrown overboard.

Beth closed her eyes involuntarily, and when she opened them she saw two more boats crash into boulders. One broke up instantly as if it were built from matchsticks.

Only Jack was standing. He'd lashed himself to the raft rail with rope, and with every muscle in his body straining, he held his paddle in his hands, using it to steer them past rocks and avoid crashing into the canyon walls.

One minute Sam had been kneeling at the prow, also wielding his paddle to push them away from rocks, but when Beth looked again he was gone.

'Sam!' she shrieked at the top of her lungs. 'Sam's gone over!'

She clung to the rail as she frantically looked for him but she could see nothing in the dark, boiling water but chunks of timber.

Theo and Jack were searching too, but like her they couldn't see him.

'He'll have been swept ahead of us!' Jack yelled out. 'He'll have the sense to grab some timber to hold him up.'

She had to hope Jack was right, for it was clear there was nothing they could do to rescue Sam even if they should see him in the canyon.

The raft went into a spin then as it was caught in a

whirlpool and all they could do was cling on tightly, praying that the nightmare would soon be over.

Out of the whirlpool they came and were shot into an even narrower canyon, then spat out with force at the end into rapids. They felt the sharp rocks scraping the bottom timbers of the raft and heard screams coming from other boats, but they were being swept along so fast they could barely see who or what they were passing.

Then, just as suddenly as it had started, it stopped. They were in calm water again.

Jack paddled to the shore, leapt out and secured the raft. All along the bank there were boats doing the same thing, some smashed up, some holed underneath. Most of them had lost goods or people overboard.

The roar of the rapids was behind them, but the sound of people wailing in distress was all around. Huge sacks of goods floated by, flour, sugar and rice spilling out. A cage of squawking chickens crashed into the bank, dogs swam for shore and shook themselves. There were many people in the water, most clinging to a big log or a packing case. Theo and Jack jumped in and swam to their aid, while Beth ran back along the bank, looking for Sam.

She saw two people pulled out lifeless, their friends and relatives desperately trying to revive them, and finally she caught sight of Sam. Even from a distance of some hundred yards she knew it was him by his butter-coloured hair and the red neckerchief around his neck. She knew too that he was dead, for he was floating on the current, his limbs not moving.

'He's there!' she shouted to Theo and Jack, pointing to where he was. 'Get him quickly.'

The swift current flashed Sam along to them, and together they hauled him over towards the shore. Beth plunged into the shallows to help them and, taking her brother's head in her hands, she saw it had been cracked wide open on a rock.

All three were silent as they lifted Sam on to the shore, each of them knowing that the frantic life-saving efforts others were making with their loved ones were of no use to their friend and brother.

Beth dropped to her knees beside Sam, sobbing as she dried his handsome face with her skirt. He had been far more than a brother; he was her childhood playmate, her ally, friend and confidant and they'd shared everything for their whole lives. She couldn't believe that fate could have been cruel enough to snatch him from her.

She could hear a terrible wailing sound, and as Jack and Theo tried to take her arms to lift her away from Sam's body, she realized that the sound was coming from herself.

'I can't go on without him,' she cried angrily. 'He's all I had left of my family.'

'You've still got us,' Theo said, pulling her into his arms. 'We know how you feel. Jack and I loved him too.'

It was only then that she saw they were both crying as well. There was no attempt to hide their grief in a manly way; tears streamed down their faces unchecked and their eyes mirrored the pain she felt.

How long they stood huddled together by Sam's body weeping, Beth didn't know. They were all soaking wet and shivering with the cold, but it was as if shock and grief had paralysed them. More craft must have been overturned coming through the rapids, for she dimly heard others screaming and shrieking. But it was only when a man spoke their names and offered to help dig a grave that they came out of their frozen state sufficiently to recognize him and his companions as men they knew from Lake Bennett, and to acknowledge that they did have to bury Sam.

'He was a good man,' their leader said, his eyes full of real sympathy and understanding. 'We are so very sorry for your loss. Let us help you.'

'It isn't right,' Beth sobbed as she watched the men start digging into some softer ground a few yards from the water's edge. 'We've come so far and been through so much. Why did we have to lose him now?'

'I didn't see him go,' Jack said wildly, as if he believed he might have been able to change the outcome if he had.

Theo knelt down beside Sam and smoothed his blood-streaked hair back from his forehead. 'Oh, Sam, Sam, what will we do without you?' he asked, his voice cracking with sorrow.

It didn't seem real to Beth as she watched Jack and Theo lower Sam into the hastily dug grave. Her mother and father had both been buried on cold, grey days; she'd said goodbye to Molly in similar weather; even the day she'd lost her baby had been cold and bleak. Funerals were meant to be on grey days, in sober places, not here in bright sunshine by a sparkling river with clumps of vivid spring flowers growing along its banks. Sam was young and strong – he had his whole life ahead of him and so many plans and dreams; it couldn't be right that he wasn't going to achieve any of them. Beth almost felt as if any moment she would wake and find it had been a terrible nightmare, and Sam would laugh with her about it.

But it was real, for Theo was reciting a passage from the Bible, his voice trembling as he struggled not to break down. The wooden cross Jack had nailed together and roughly chiselled Sam's name on to was lying on the mound of soil waiting to be speared into the grave.

Their voices were thin and reedy as they sang 'Rock of

Ages', and Beth thought bitterly that God had deserted her once again.

All along the river bank others were dealing with the aftermath of the canyon, some digging a grave, some tending those who'd been injured. She could hear weeping and the distressed cries of those who'd lost their boats and goods. And she could hear the sound of her own heart breaking.

Chapter Thirty

'How muchee? How muchee?' Another group of Stick Indians called out from their camp on the river bank. Beth averted her eyes for they were dirty, ragged and sick-looking, and she felt guilty at not giving them anything. But they'd already given food to other groups further back along the river, and they could spare no more. Besides, she'd been told that the Indians sold whatever they were given back to other stampeders, and with thousands of boats passing every day, they were probably making a good living.

The early spring flowers had given way to bluebells and lupins, a sea of blue along the river banks. Every now and then Beth would spot a moose, sometimes with a calf, drinking from the river, or a black bear peeping from behind a tree as if astounded at so many humans going through its domain. Wild fruits – cranberries, blackcurrants and rasp-berries – were ripening amongst the rocks and mosses and the scent of wild roses wafted to her on the breeze.

It was spectacular scenery, and she wished she could delight in it all. But since Sam died back at the Squaw Rapids, it was as though the sun had gone in for good and she'd never rejoice in anything again.

Five men lost their lives that day, and countless more would have done if Steele of the Mounties hadn't arrived to avert further disaster. Aside from the deaths, there were dozens of boats smashed up; all those sacks of provisions carried over the Pass were split open and ruined in the water, and many treasured possessions were lost. Some people were so distraught they were tearing at their hair, sobbing and screaming.

Steele made rules on the spot that no more boats should sail through the rapids without a competent person in charge, and that all women should bypass the rapids by walking the five-mile overland route.

Jack had hardly said a word since they buried Sam. Beth knew he was torturing himself with the thought that he could have prevented the accident. But both she and Theo knew he could not have done. He had done well to get the raft through in one piece with all their goods intact. Sam must have been careless and let go of the rail.

But rationalizing how it came about didn't help their grief. No one would ever be able to take Sam's place in their lives, and right now Beth couldn't see how she could go on without him.

When she tried to stop thinking about her brother she found herself dwelling on the baby she lost and feeling desperate to see Molly again. She supposed this was natural; Molly was after all her only living relative now. She couldn't count the times she had got out her photograph, drinking in her sweet face and curly hair, and thinking back to those early days when she'd fed and changed her.

Beth couldn't expect Jack and Theo to understand her feelings about Molly, but it did give her some comfort that they felt just as keenly as she did about Sam. Maybe she had the lion's share of memories and the blood tie, yet they had loved him too. The pain was still too raw for any of them to speak freely about their feelings, or to share their best memories of him. But maybe that would come in time.

They were close to Dawson City now, and the river Yukon was a seething mass of boats. Joining all those who like them had come down from the mountain lakes were many Sourdoughs. Beth understood the name came from the habit of old-timers up here keeping a small piece of bread dough in a bag inside their shirt so that it stayed warm and could be used like yeast to make the next batch of bread they cooked. These men were grizzled old prospectors who'd been holed up all winter at their claims on small creeks. Some of them had been in the region for years searching for gold.

The excitement that they were nearing their destination was palpable. People shouted out greetings; they wanted to share their stories about their journey and hopes for what lay ahead. But Beth and the boys couldn't bring themselves to enter into conversation, for one mention of Sam might make them break down.

Beth hoped that everyone assumed their silence and grim faces were symptomatic of the fearsome heat and the tormenting mosquitoes, for that appeared to be making some people act irrationally. She and the boys had witnessed many vicious fights and slanging matches, usually between men who had soldiered amicably through so much already. Whatever it was that was causing it, it was terrible to see, for they seemed to hate one another like poison now, wanting to separate to go it alone. They watched two men on the bank, actually sawing their boat and provisions in half as they screamed abuse at each. Another couple were fighting for ownership of a frying pan, until someone else came along and solved the problem by throwing it into the river, so neither could have it.

It was a madness that Beth and the boys found impossible to understand. Sam's death had made them realize how much they valued one another, and how little mere goods and chattels meant.

*

Darkness never came now, just a slight dimming of the light around midnight, but by two in the morning daylight had returned. They would make camp on the shore just long enough to light a fire and cook a hurried meal, then set sail on the raft again, Theo and Jack taking it in turns to sleep. It wasn't that they wanted to beat others to Dawson, for their hearts had gone out of that, but because they needed to be occupied. They realized now, too late, that it was Sam's enthusiasm, cheeriness and constant optimism that had kept conversations flowing in the past, and without him there seemed nothing to say.

On the morning of 12 June, Beth was half dozing at the stern when she heard Jack shout, 'It's Dawson City! At last we're there.'

They hadn't known exactly where it was, and they'd been hugging the river bank for the last two days for fear of coming upon it suddenly and being swept past by the strong current. But as they rounded a rocky bluff, there it was in front of them. The fabled city of gold.

Beth didn't know what she had expected it to look like, but the reality, a sprawl of tents, log cabins, false-fronted emporiums and teetering piles of lumber, wasn't that different to Skagway. There was even the same black oozing mud.

Yet this mud stretched from the shoreline right into the little town, and she could see no planks put down to walk on, no boardwalks or even stones as there had been in Skagway. Horses and carts were floundering in it, and people were trying in vain to pull heavily laden sledges through it.

Later, they were to discover that the town had been flooded when the ice melted a couple of weeks earlier, and the people who had built cabins right down on the shoreline saw them swept away. But it seemed such things were just a minor setback in Dawson City, for as soon as boats began arriving with provisions, especially longed-for luxuries like eggs, whisky and newspapers, the muddy streets were a mere inconvenience.

They managed to find a spot along the boat-crowded shoreline to moor the raft, and hauled their kit right up to the back of the town, the only place they could find free to pitch their tent. They heard that to rent one room cost a hundred dollars a month, and every commodity changed hands for extortionate prices.

'Good job I brought those nails,' Jack said, spotting a sign advertising them for eight dollars a pound. 'Not that I want to sell them – we'll need them to build a place of our own.'

'Maybe I'll get a good price for that silk and satin I brought along,' Beth said thoughtfully. The boys had argued with her back in Skagway and said she should take something more useful, but she had stuck to her guns, insisting that she knew there would be women desperate for dress material once they got to Dawson. Judging by the stained and dreary clothes most of the women here were wearing, she was right.

After they'd pitched their tent, they went back down to Front Street to take a look around. This street overlooking the river was clearly where everything happened and where everyone gathered. It was lined with saloons, hotels, restaurants and dance halls, though all of them had clearly been thrown up in a hurry. Every minute or so another boat moored and the owners hauled their belongings on to the shore, adding to the utter chaos. Thousands of new arrivals were wandering around aimlessly, while the veterans, who had by all accounts suffered all winter from a scarcity of almost everything, harassed the newcomers for everything from brooms to books.

As at Lake Bennett, there were huge piles of lumber everywhere, and the buzz of saws and the hammering of nails made it difficult to hear what anyone was saying. Building work was going on everywhere – shops, saloons, banks and even a church – yet disconcertingly there appeared to be no overall plan.

Down by the shoreline people had set up stalls selling everything from boots to boxes of tomatoes, all at sky-high prices. Many of these goods had been brought in by a steamer just a few days earlier, but they saw an elderly woman they'd met in Lake Bennett, who'd managed to get her chickens up the Chilkoot Trail, selling them for twenty-five dollars each.

There were countless signs proclaiming 'Gold Dust Bought and Sold'. Outside some of these cabins, grizzled-looking men with shaggy beards, and small leather bags hanging from their belts, stood in line smoking their pipes. A man in a loud checked suit and a black stetson hat informed Beth and the boys that these were Sourdoughs, who'd struck it rich on their claims at Forty Mile and Eldorado Creek. He said he thought the gold they were selling today was worth a king's ransom, yet they looked like tramps, without a cent to their names.

However strange everything was, it was colourful and vibrant. Men in smart suits and homburg hats mingled with others in ragged, mud-splattered trail clothes. They saw a pretty blonde in a pink satin dress being carried over the mud by a bare-chested man who looked like a prize fighter. There were dogs everywhere, mostly malamutes and other sledge dogs, but there were also women carrying toy dogs under their arms, and greyhounds and spaniels picked their way daintily through the mud.

'It don't feel right seeing this without Sam,' Jack sighed.

It was a pivotal moment, for Beth had thought the same and she guessed Theo had too. She felt grateful to Jack for being brave enough to come out with it.

'If he was here we'd all be arguing what to do next,' she said, half smiling as she imagined how excited he would have been.

'Then we must do what we aimed for, for him,' Theo said unexpectedly. 'He wanted to get here more than all of us. So we can't let him down now.'

Tears prickled in Beth's eyes and she buried her face against Theo's chest to hold them back. He was right – the best kind of memorial they could give to Sam would be to succeed here. That way, maybe they'd be able to cope with their loss.

Beth lifted her head away from Theo and wiped her moist eyes. 'Then I must find somewhere to play tonight,' she said. 'And you two must start looking for opportunities.'

Beth went into the Monte Carlo Saloon on Front Street while Theo and Jack went to check out a few other places.

From the outside the Monte Carlo looked the smartest and busiest of all the saloons, with fresh paint and a large picture of Queen Victoria over the door, and it had signs claiming to have gaming rooms and a theatre. But the timber facade which promised sophistication was false. Inside it was unprepossessing, only one step up from a rough and ready shed, the gaming rooms dark and dreary, the theatre small and spartan with hard benches.

Undeterred, Beth approached a man with a swirling moustache and a fancy waistcoat behind the bar and asked him if she could play her fiddle there.

He looked her up and down and shrugged. 'You wanna take the risk, then that's your funeral,' he said. It was clear he didn't believe the young woman before him, in her shabby dress and gumboots, could possibly entertain his customers.

'So if I just come in and start playing, and pass a hat round at the end, it will be all right with you?'

'Sure, honey,' he said, already turning away to reach for a glass and bottle. 'But don't expect too much, or fer me to look out fer you. It gets rough in here at nights.'

The man's obvious conviction she would only make a fool of herself made Beth anxious to prove him wrong. She went back to the tent, washed her hair in a bucket, dug out her scarlet dress and polished up her best boots. It was only a couple of hours later that she learned from the people in the next tent that the man behind the bar was Jack Smith, one of the men who'd struck it rich out on Bonanza Creek and built the Monte Carlo.

But it transpired he wasn't such a good judge of character, for he'd sent his partner, Swiftwater Bill Gates, off to Seattle with ten thousand dollars in gold to buy mirrors, velvet carpets and chandeliers for the saloon. News had already filtered back here that Gates had actually gone to San Francisco and was being called the King of the Klondike because he was distributing the gold to one and all while he lived the high life in the city's best hotel.

Beth was amused by the story and it made her even more purposeful. At seven that evening she was back outside the Monte Carlo, which was almost shaking with the thunderous noise coming from within. But with shining hair trimmed with a feathered comb, her red dress and determination in her heart, she was ready for anything. She slipped off her muddy gumboots, leaving them by the door with her fiddle case, put on her clean, shiny boots and, with Theo and Jack looking anxiously on, tucked her fiddle under her chin, striking up a spirited jig, she walked in.

It took a few minutes for the music to percolate around the saloon. Beth was nervous, her fingers sticky with sweat from the heat, and she was intimidated by quite so many rough-looking men in one small space, but she let her mind conjure up Sam, imagined him standing before her as he'd so often done in the past when she played. And she played only for him.

She could see his smile, the way his wide mouth turned up at the corners and a dimple appeared in his right cheek. She could see his blue eyes sparkle and the way he pushed his blond hair impatiently out of his eyes.

Mentally, she left the sweaty saloon and went back to the immigrant ship, watching him charm the girls and laughing with him on deck. She saw him lounging on the bed in their room in New York, or pouring drinks in Heaney's, with a host of Bowery whores batting their eyelashes at him.

It was some time before she realized that the noise in the saloon had stopped, and she opened her eyes to see a hundred or more men looking at her. Most were probably about Sam's age, but they had that weatherbeaten look that made them look far older. Some were in fancy suits, boiled shirts, ties and homburgs, others in grubby shirtsleeves, with braces holding up trousers that had seen better days and broad-brimmed hats that could tell a few stories. There were pale-faced Europeans, brown faces from South America, black faces and Indians too. Some had untrimmed beards and moustaches, others were clean-shaven. In amongst them were a few women as well: a prettily plump one with a straw hat trimmed with feathers, another with roses on hers; women in silk and lace, others in plain cotton from the trail. But regardless of who they were, whether they'd already found gold or were helping someone who had, to spend it, they were all listening to her play.

'Bravo!' a big man in a checked jacket called out as she finished the first number. 'Don't stop now, give us more!'

It was after one when Beth picked her way through the mud to get back to the tent. She was exhausted but satisfied that she'd made her mark on Dawson, for Jack Smith had claimed she was the finest fiddle player he'd ever heard.

She had no idea where Theo and Jack were. They'd been in the Monte Carlo for the first hour she was playing, but then left and hadn't returned. She hadn't minded, for while she wasn't playing, there were plenty of people only too happy to buy her a drink and keep her company.

The sky was as bright as day, and no one else appeared even to be thinking of sleeping, for the muddy tracks between tents and cabins were full of jostling people. Above the sounds of thousands enjoying themselves down on Front Street, laughter, chatter and clinking glasses, she could hear thumping feet on a dance floor, the wheeze of a mechanical organ, and a saxophone playing a plaintive ballad.

She'd been told Dawson City buzzed until eight in the morning, and she supposed that was understandable in a place where they were cut off from the Outside by snow and ice from September till the end of May.

Tied around her waist was a leather bag which someone had thrown at her, with a quantity of gold dust in it. She'd added to it the small fortune in notes and coins that had been collected for her. As she walked, it clonked against her hip bone, making her smile with satisfaction. Money and success would never compensate for her brother's death, or make her miss him any less, but tonight those black clouds of grief had rolled back sufficiently to make her want to live again.

*

A week later, at four in the morning, Beth was being walked back to her tent along Front Street by Wilbur, one of the bartenders at the Monte Carlo.

'Looks like there's a big game on at the Golden Horse Shoe,' he said, indicating a crowd of people outside a saloon up ahead. 'You can bet it's Mack Dundridge playing poker in there. Folks always want to watch him play; when he's winning everyone gets free drinks.'

Beth smiled up at Wilbur, for this tall, lanky young bartender from Seattle was not only her regular escort home, he always had tales to tell her about the larger than life characters of Dawson City.

He'd told her about Mack Dundridge just the day before, for Mack was one of the celebrated Eldorado Kings. He had been drifting around Alaska and the Yukon for years searching for gold, and he was close by when George Carmack and Skookum Jim discovered it in Rabbit Creek. Mack rushed there when he heard the news and staked a claim that was soon to bring him a fortune. And Rabbit Creek became known as Eldorado.

But like many of the old-timers who'd struck it rich, Mack was feckless with his fortune. He would come into town and sling his poke, a leather bag of gold nuggets, down on the bar and treat everyone. It was said that one evening he gave a dance-hall girl a gold nugget worth over five hundred dollars so she'd only dance with him.

'Can we go in and watch?' Beth asked. While barely an hour passed without her thinking about Sam, her popularity at the Monte Carlo and the constant excitement and gaiety in the town had lifted her spirits. She liked Wilbur and felt safe in his company, and as Theo and Jack never got back to the tent until at least seven in the morning, she saw no reason why she shouldn't have a bit of fun too.

402

'As it's a big game they'll have someone on the door stopping common folks getting in. But you ain't common folks, so I guess I can use my powers of persuasion.' Wilbur grinned.

He took her arm firmly and pushed his way through the people around the door of the saloon who were trying to peer through the door and windows to see the action inside.

'You'll let the Klondike Gypsy in, won't you?' he said to the burly man barring the way. 'She's got a mind to see the high-rollers, and maybe she'll return the favour by playing for you one night.'

The way the big man beamed down at her made Beth realize that she'd already established a name for herself in town and it made her feel good.

'You're welcome in the Golden Horse Shoe, Miss Gypsy,' he said. 'But don't you go distracting the game with your pretty face, or your fiddle.'

Despite the bright light on the street, inside the saloon it was gloomy and impossible to see anything, for men stood packed shoulder to shoulder, intently watching something at the back of the place. But Wilbur took Beth's arm and led her over to the side of the room where the crowd was thinner.

He left her there to go and buy them both a drink. Beth couldn't see the players beyond the thick wall of male shoulders, but she could sense by the tension in the room that something out of the ordinary was going on.

'Is Mack winning?' she whispered to a tall man she'd found herself beside.

'He was, but he's lost the last couple of games,' he whispered back. 'I reckon it might be one of the nights he throws his claim in fer a stake.'

Wilbur had told her that Mack had built his reputation as a high-roller by going right to the edge, prepared to gamble everything he had. It was said he lost half a million dollars one night, but turned up again the following evening and won it all back.

'Who's he playing with?' she whispered.

'The Swede, Dangle and a guy I ain't seen before,' the whisper came back.

People gave everyone nicknames in Dawson; it appeared to be a way of showing their acceptance of them. But as Beth hadn't met either the Swede or Dangle, she felt she must take a look at them, so she moved along to where there was a pillar holding up the roof, wriggled round it and elbowed the men there out of the way.

She gasped when she finally saw the players, for one of them was Theo.

Above the table was an ornate oil lamp which created a circle of golden light in the otherwise dark room. Just beyond this circle and behind Theo she could make out Jack standing against the wall watching the game, and she could see from his stance that he was very nervous.

The three men Theo was playing with were typical Sourdoughs, bearded, with untidy hair, rough clothes and weatherbeaten faces. Clean-shaven Theo in his smart clothes and polished boots looked incongruous, even though he wasn't much younger than the others. He'd had some good wins since they got to Dawson, but she was fairly certain he hadn't won anything like enough to be playing for such high stakes as this.

'Which one is Mack Dundridge?' she whispered to the man next to her.

'The gingery-haired fella,' he replied. 'No one can beat him at poker, and he'll stay until he's wiped out the others.'

Beth slunk further back so Theo wouldn't spot her, and watched him for just a moment or two longer. He looked so casual and relaxed, almost lounging in his chair, the light above accentuating his high cheekbones. But she had enough knowledge of poker to know it was based on bluff, so he could well be as nervous as Jack.

The tension in the room was growing tighter by the second, and Beth knew she couldn't bear to witness Theo being beaten.

'I've changed my mind. I don't want to stay,' she said, meeting Wilbur as he came back across the saloon. She took the drink from his hand and downed it in one. 'Will you take me home now, please?'

The bright daylight always made it hard to sleep, but Beth was so nervous she could barely manage to shut her eyes. She had grown accustomed to Theo's losses over the last year, but to her knowledge he'd never before gambled more than he could afford to lose. It was different here: prospectors, saloon owners, shop keepers and dancing girls – they were all basically gamblers. With fortunes casually changing hands nightly, even the most level-headed person could easily lose their grip on reality.

She must have been lying awake for a couple of hours when she finally heard Theo and Jack approaching the tent. They were stumbling as if they were very drunk and that made her feel even angrier at them.

Theo stuck his face through the tent-door flap. 'Are you awake, my sweetheart? he asked, grinning inanely.

'I am now,' she said sarcastically.

Theo withdrew his head and spoke to Jack. 'She's cross with me,' he said. 'D'you think she'll be even crosser when I tell her our news?'

'You'll have our neighbours cross with you if you wake them up,' Beth said tersely. 'So come in here and be quiet.'

They came stumbling in and Jack flopped down beside her. 'Sorry we're drunk. But we had to celebrate cos Theo's won a building lot on Front Street.'

Beth sat bolt upright. 'He has?' She was astounded: a building lot on Front Street cost around forty thousand dollars.

'Sure thing, my darling,' Theo said, dropping down on the other side of her. 'A knuckle-biting game with Mack Dundridge. They said he couldn't be beat, but they were wrong.'

Beth frowned. She didn't like it when Theo became boastful, and it crossed her mind he might have cheated.

'Don't worry, Beth.' Jack grinned at her as if reading her mind. 'He won it fair and square. And he had the sense to stop once he'd twisted the bloke's arm to throw the building lot in. Might have been a different story if it had been his goldmine.'

'We're made now,' Theo chortled. 'We can build our own gambling saloon and we'll have rooms upstairs to live in. We'll even give you the bathroom you've always wanted.'

They were too drunk to explain properly how it had come about, but Beth understood enough to realize Theo had set out with the intention of getting Mack to use the Front Street lot as a stake.

'I reckoned he wouldn't care so much about that,' Theo said smugly. 'If his goldmine was on the table, he'd have kept me there playing till he won it back.'

'Theo played a blinder,' Jack said, his face alight with awe. 'I thought he had a bad hand at the end; he was sweating like a pig and looked shit scared. You could have heard a pin drop when Mack asked to see him. I couldn't even look. But he had four nines, Mack had four eights. The whole place went wild. Even Mack said he'd met his match.'

Beth lay down again and tried to go back to sleep when the boys went outside to smoke their pipes, but the rise and fall of their drunken, excited voices as they planned their gambling saloon prevented her from sleeping.

She was thrilled, and had no doubt they would get it built. Jack would see to that. She even felt it would lessen the sorrow of losing Sam for all of them, for they would be making his dream come true.

But getting what they had planned for so long, so easily, just by the turn of a card, felt strange and unreal.

In the days that followed, as the boys started organizing the building of their gambling saloon, Beth often reflected that everything in the town was strange: sunshine that lasted twenty-two hours a day, the mud that didn't dry up, the false fronts of the saloons, and steamers arriving from Seattle and San Francisco almost daily bringing champagne, oysters and every other kind of luxury.

It seemed bizarre that they'd each been forced to haul a ton of provisions over those mountains only to find no one wanted or needed flour, sugar and rice. Even more bizarre was that all these thousands of people who had hocked everything they had to make the trip, risked their health and sanity for the dream of riches, were doing nothing now to find gold.

She and the boys had never intended to be prospectors. But almost everyone else had. Yet as soon as they tied up their boats, and they were six deep along the shore now, these people just hung around in town, not even taking a trip out to the creeks where gold had been found. It was as if getting here was enough.

Beth could understand weariness, for the majority of these people had spent a whole year getting here and they'd been challenged in every conceivable way. Most had burned all their bridges, walked out on jobs, homes, sometimes wives and children, and blown all their money. They'd risked their health, sanity and in some cases their lives. But surely a couple of days' rest would revive them? Why were they now trying to sell their kit to buy a ticket home on a steamer? How could that lust for gold suddenly vanish? Or was it that the gold had never been the real aim, only to have the biggest adventure of all time?

It was said that there were approximately 18,000 people now in Dawson, and another 5,000 out prospecting on the surrounding creeks, making it almost as big a population as Seattle. With no more room for tents or cabins, people were now going across the river to a place generally known as Louse Town.

Down on the shore a huge market place had sprung up. Dogs, horses, sledges, and bags of flour, patched shirts, worn-out axes, long winter underwear, mackinaws and high-sided boots were all for sale. People picked over them endlessly, and to the disappointment of the sellers who wanted to go home, their stuff was mostly rejected.

But each steamer spilled out many more hundreds of people: dancing girls, actresses and whores, bank clerks, doctors, even ministers. There were whole families, elegant ladies with feathered hats, their husbands with wing collars and tail coats, and small children. They too had mostly only come to take a look, for they surely weren't intending to pan for gold.

It was a mad, wild place, a city of runaways, some from

the law, or from nagging wives or brutal husbands, debt, dull jobs or city slums. The morality and social status of the Outside meant nothing here. Men took up with dance-hall girls, a woman could drink in the saloons without a man beside her, even the whores were treated with respect. You could be anything you wanted here; where you came from didn't matter. Those who'd struck lucky helped those who had nothing. It was almost as if people shed their old skin the moment they stepped off the boat, and grew another more comfortable one.

Yet for now it suited Beth. For as long as she could play her fiddle, she could forget all she had lost and that she had no real place to call home.

The deep sadness at the core of her seemed to give her music a new dimension and she'd found she was using it to twist her audience's emotions. If one of her tunes reminded them of an old lover, their mother, their children, they put more money in the hat. She didn't feel this was exploiting anyone; after all, the money she earned was passed on to the woman who baked bread, the boy who sold eggs, and the couple from Idaho who ran a diner. It would also take her home one day to see Molly.

Late in the afternoon of 3 July, Beth was down on Front Street watching as Jack and a couple of his hired men built the facade of their saloon. The speed with which Jack had gone to work on it was astounding. Within a week he had the skeleton of the saloon up; by the end of the second the roof was on and he was laying the floorboards on the first floor. The long hours of daylight and the number of men needing paid work helped. Now the building was close to completion, with three rooms upstairs, a large room for the saloon downstairs and a kitchen and storerooms out the back.

'It's looking good, Jack,' Beth called to him. 'But you aren't going to work tomorrow, I hope? It's Independence Day.'

Despite the fact that Dawson City was in Canada, because such a big majority of its residents were American there was to be a big celebration with dancing, hog roasts and fireworks. Beth had found a good seamstress and had a new dress made with the pink silk she'd brought over the pass with her.

Jack paused in his work and grinned at her. 'I guess one day off won't kill me! Have you seen Theo today? I could do with a hand.'

'He went to the post office,' Beth called back. 'You know what that's like!'

Getting mail was a big problem in Dawson. It was brought in and out on many boats, but was often dropped off by mistake in Juneau, Haines or any of the little towns along the Inner Passage. With so many thousands of people here, the queues at the post office were so long it could take all day to reach the front, and most came away disappointed that there were no letters for them. Beth hadn't bothered to queue, for the only people who wrote to her were the Langworthys, and even if they'd got the letter she'd written in Lake Lindemann with the approximate date they'd reach Dawson City, a reply could take a month or more to reach her.

She had written again when she got here to tell them of Sam's death, but that would still be on the steamer to Seattle.

Theo, however, had gone to join the long queue to send his folks a telegram to let them know where he was. He laughingly said that even if his father and older brother didn't care, his mother and younger sisters would. Beth privately thought his real motive was to boast he was doing well, knowing word would reach all his old friends.

'If you see him, tell him I need him,' Jack said. 'He's a lazy devil, never around except when it suits him.'

Beth made no comment. Theo wasn't pulling his weight, but then he never had. He seemed to think that winning the building lot and handing over the money for the lumber and other materials was enough. Jack had to handle everything, from building the saloon to buying the timber and hauling it here. At night Theo rarely came into the Monte Carlo to hear Beth play, she often had to eat alone, and he seldom came back to the tent before seven or eight in the morning, then slept all day. Sometimes she wondered if he valued her at all.

She decided to walk down to the post office and check how far up the queue he'd got. But as she took the turn off Front Street, she saw him coming towards her through the crowd. She waved, and as he saw her his face broke into a wide smile.

Despite having become a little disenchanted with his character, hardly a day went past without Beth thinking how handsome he was. Even back in the winter, bundled up in a heavy coat, with a hat and a muffler and a thick beard covering half his face, his dark, expressive eyes could still make her heart flutter.

He had somehow achieved the image of the perfect English gentleman even here in this rough-and-ready town. He had shaved off his beard back on the river, and one of his first priorities when they arrived here was to get his hair cut. Wearing a fawn linen jacket, a red cravat at the neck of his shirt and a Panama hat, he could have been on his way to Ascot. Only the mud on his brown leather riding boots spoiled the image, something he groused about almost daily as he cleaned them.

'You've got a letter,' he called out as they drew closer,

and he took the envelope from his pocket and waved it at her. 'They weren't going to let me have it as it's addressed to Miss and Mr Bolton, but when I told them that was Gypsy of the Monte Carlo's maiden name, they gave in.'

Beth laughed. 'It's from the Langworthys,' she said, recognizing the handwriting even from a distance, and she rushed forward the last few feet to grab it from him. 'They surely hadn't got my letter from Lake Lindemann already?'

'Dawson City's in the news everywhere in the world,' Theo said. 'I guess they decided to write here knowing you'd get here eventually.'

'It looks as if it's been in the wet,' Beth said, for the envelope was stained and the ink smeared.

'Some of the mail was so badly soaked the envelopes are unreadable or missing,' Theo said. 'There were lots of disappointed people today, but you're a lucky one.'

Beth tore it open, unable to wait till later. *'My dear Beth and Sam,'* she read. *'There isn't any way to give you this terrible news, except straight out.'*

A cold shudder ran down Beth's spine, but she had to read on.

So please forgive my bluntness when I tell you our precious little Molly died of pneumonia, ten days ago on 7 March. She had a bad chesty cold in February and despite everything we and the doctor did, all the medicine and care, it turned to pneumonia. She died in her sleep while I was sitting with her.

Edward and I are bereft. We loved her so much, and everything is so bleak and cold without her. But my heart goes out to you and Sam so far away too, for we know this will be a tremendous shock to you as it has been for everyone who loved her. Please believe we did everything we could for her. Her funeral was a week after her death on the 14th, a beautiful moving service at St Brides . . . Edward,

Mrs Bruce, Cook and Kathleen all send their condolences, and we sincerely hope this letter will find its way to you. We always read everything in the papers about the Klondike, wondering if you got there safely. You are in our thoughts and prayers, please come to see us when you return to England. And Edward and I wish to thank you for all the past joy you gave us by leaving Molly in our care. She may have only had just four short years with us, but they have been the happiest times we've known.

Thinking of you at this saddest of times
Ruth Langworthy

'What is it, Beth?' Theo asked, shocked by her stricken face.

'Molly's dead,' she replied in hushed, anguished tones, looking at him beseechingly. 'She died of pneumonia.'

Chapter Thirty-one

'I know it's terribly sad to hear of a child dying, Beth, but you've got to pull yourself together,' Theo said, a sharp undercurrent to his voice.

'She wasn't just any child, she was my sister,' Beth retorted, breaking into fresh tears. 'First Sam, now Molly. I've got no one left.'

A week had passed since she received the shattering letter. Theo had been kind and comforting then, yet the day after, Independence Day, he left her crying in the tent and joined everyone else in Dawson for the celebrations.

Jack came back to the tent in the early evening, having run into Theo in a saloon and realized he'd left her all alone.

'I expect he just doesn't know what more he can say to comfort you,' he said in Theo's defence. 'I don't either, Beth, I just knew you shouldn't be alone.'

'Why is it that you know that and he doesn't?' she asked Jack bitterly. 'It wasn't your baby I lost, it was his. He promised me up on the Chilkoot Pass that he loved me and wanted to get married; he knows how hard Sam's death hit me, so surely if he really loved me he could put himself in my shoes now and understand?'

'Oh, Beth, you've had so much sadness.' Jack sighed and sat down beside her, holding her. 'Right from when you first told me about Molly on the ship, I could see how low you felt about leaving her behind. But you did do the right thing for her. Look at all the hardships we all had in New York. You wouldn't have wanted to put her through that?'

'But I keep thinking if she'd been with me she wouldn't have died.'

Jack stroked her hair back from her face and mopped her eyes. 'She would've been even more likely to have caught something nasty. At least she had four happy years, in a loving, caring home. It's tragic that she died, a terrible thing, and all I can offer you is a shoulder to cry on.'

He listened patiently as she sobbed out all her sadness, for Molly, Sam's death and losing her baby and being told she'd never have another. 'It's like I'm jinxed,' she said. 'What have I ever done that was so bad I had to have all this thrown at me?'

Jack couldn't find an answer to that, but he stayed all evening and held her, letting her spill out all her grief. When it grew darker, thousands of fireworks were let off and they stood outside the tent watching them together. But the fierce noise from the fireworks wasn't enough for the revellers in the town; they fired rifles and made huge explosions with dynamite, too. The town dogs were so frightened they swam across the Yukon to Louse Town in one long streak to escape.

Beth hated everyone for celebrating while she was so desperately unhappy, and she wouldn't even allow Jack to persuade her to put on a pretty dress and go and play at the Monte Carlo. 'I'll never play again,' she vowed.

Since Independence Day, Beth had hardly set foot outside the tent, preferring to lie there feeling bitter and hurt. Jack and Theo had been working long hours on the saloon, and although Jack had tried many times to persuade her to come down and see how the work was progressing, or to go back to the Monte Carlo to play, Theo had said little on the subject until today.

'You *have* got someone left, there's Jack and me,' Theo said wearily. 'The saloon is finished, so we can move in tomorrow. But you haven't even been to see it.'

'I don't care about it. I don't care about anything,' Beth sobbed. 'I left Molly with the Langworthys because I thought she'd have a good life with them, but she still got sick and died. Maybe if I'd stayed with her she'd be alive now.'

'It's foolish to say such things,' Theo replied, his voice softening. He sat down beside her on the floor of the tent and wiped her tears from her face with his handkerchief. 'It was fate, just as Sam's death was too. I don't believe we can change our destiny, whatever we do. But you can't stay here moping for ever, that won't make it better. If you put your energy into turning our new place into a home, it will take your mind off Molly. So come with me now and look around. Jack was going to put the name up today. We've decided to call it the Golden Nugget.'

Beth was tempted to refuse, but in her heart she knew everything he'd said was right, and staying in the tent wallowing in grief wasn't going to make anything better. So reluctantly she got up, found a comb and ran it through her hair.

Theo patted her on the shoulder in approval. 'You can have a bath tonight if you want. Jack managed to get the boiler going. Imagine that, sweetheart, a real bath, we'll be the envy of everyone else in town. That is, if you don't run out on us and take the steamer back to Vancouver at the end of August.'

'Why would I do that?' she said. 'There's nothing for me there.'

Realizing that sounded self-pitying, she blushed. 'We've got the gambling saloon we wanted, and I'm glad about that,' she continued. 'Just be patient with me a little longer. Two deaths in such a short time are more than anyone could bear.'

'I know, darling,' he said, enfolding her in his arms. 'But you must play on opening night, everyone's expecting it.'

Beth washed her face and walked with Theo to the new place. It seemed many people had heard about her loss, for they stopped her and said how sorry they were. She hadn't expected that, and it helped to know people cared about her.

Jack had just finished putting up the sign as they approached the new place. He shinned down the ladder and hugged her.

'What d'you think?' he asked.

Beth stepped back into the street to look properly. When she'd last seen it the facade was only half done, and raw timber at that. The wood was painted red and shiny now, with a black sign bearing the words 'The Golden Nugget' painted in gold.

'It looks marvellous,' she said, and smiled for the first time since she'd received the news of Molly's death. 'You are a miracle worker, Jack.'

He glowed at the praise. 'I had a lot of help,' he said quickly. 'Now, come and look inside.'

Beth had grown accustomed to the tricks used to create a sense of permanence and luxury in saloons since her time in Skagway. False facades led into the most flimsy of buildings, often tents, and even those that were built of wood had only canvas tacked on to the timber posts to make interior walls.

But Jack had lined the wood walls with another layer of timber, making it warm and windproof, and he'd painted them the same red as outside.

But even more astounding was the picture painted on the side wall opposite the bar. It was of the Chilkoot Pass, complete with the endless winding ribbon of climbers against the snow.

'Who did that?' she asked.

'Enrico, that little bloke from San Francisco I helped with his boat at Lake Bennett.'

Beth nodded. She remembered the small, dark-haired man who she had thought was a Mexican. 'It's fantastic,' she said. 'It really sets the whole place off. But the bar is marvellous too, Jack, you are so clever.'

It was first-class timber, planed and varnished to a gleaming finish. She ran her hand along it admiringly.

'I've got to put another coat of varnish on the floor tonight, then we can get the furniture in tomorrow morning,' Jack said. 'It's all piled up out the back.'

Beth looked at the big mirror behind the bar and noticed it was covered in fingerprints and smears. 'I'd better polish that,' she said.

Jack and Theo grinned at each other. 'What's so funny?' she asked.

'We left it like that purposely. We thought it would stir you into action,' Jack said.

Beth smiled. 'You'd better show me upstairs, I expect some action will be required there too.'

Jack hadn't had time to do anything much upstairs. Just three rooms with bare, rough timber walls and floors, but after living in a tent it would be luxury to all of them. As for the bathroom, she could hardly believe that Jack had been clever enough to run pipes from the boiler downstairs to fill the tub with hot water.

'I had a lot of help from an engineer,' he said modestly. 'But there was no possibility of putting in a lavatory as there are no sewers in the town yet. So we're stuck with an outside privy until there are.'

Front Street was the main artery of Dawson City. It pulsated with people all round the clock. By day it was like a gigantic market where you could buy anything from medicine to a horse or dog and every kind of foodstuff and luxury item brought in by traders. By night it was a rip-roaring hedonistic paradise, where you could drink, gamble, see a show or just parade up and down watching others if you were broke.

Even on Sundays when the law stated that nothing should open, and this was rigorously enforced by the Mounted Police, people still thronged up and down. All the most popular saloons, dance halls and theatres were in Front Street and they vied with one another to be the best. They wanted the prettiest dance-hall girls, the highest stakes in a poker game or the best singers and entertainers.

Although Beth, Theo and Jack had only been in Dawson a short while, they had an advantage over other new arrivals setting up in business because they had already attracted enough attention in town to be given nicknames. People liked nicknames here; Lime-juice Lil, Two-step Louie, Billy the Horse and Deep-hole Johnson were just some they'd heard. Theo's English gentleman image and his reputation as a good poker player landed him with 'The Gent'. Jack was affectionately called 'Cockney Jack' and widely regarded as the man to talk to if you wanted to build anything. Beth was still called 'Gypsy', for the name had come with her on the trail, and at the Monte Carlo she'd been billed as 'The Klondike Gypsy Queen'.

Yet when they opened the saloon doors for the first time at six in the evening, they were still very anxious. Most of the other places on Front Street were owned by Eldorado

Kings, men with claims that had netted them fortunes, and they could afford to splash out on chandeliers, velvet carpets, a five-piece band and a host of girls to lure big spenders in. But Theo's money had run out, and he owed a couple of thousand dollars for drink, timber and the tables and chairs.

He had hung a sign outside proclaiming half-price drinks, and they had to hope that that, and Beth playing, would be enough. Theo was wearing a white tuxedo he'd accepted in settlement of a gambling debt back at Lake Bennett. With a frilled shirt and bow tie and his dark hair shiny with oil, he looked the image of a successful saloon owner. Jack sported a red waistcoat, a red and white spotted bow tie and a straw boater.

Beth had put on the new pink dress she'd planned to wear on Independence Day. She'd lost weight because she'd barely eaten anything since she got the letter about Molly, and she looked so peaky she'd even resorted to rouge on her cheeks.

She began to play a jig as soon as six men walked up to the bar.

They'd hired Will and Herbert, two men from Portland they'd got to know at Lake Bennett. They were desperate to raise the cash to get a boat home, and Theo had promised if they worked for two weeks for him, he'd buy their tickets and give them fifty dollars each too.

By the time Beth was on the third number, a goodly crowd had come in, and all at once she felt exhilarated because she was pulling people in to spend money in *their* place. She hoped Sam was looking down on them, thrilled that they'd finally reached their goal.

As the evening progressed, more and more people came in, until they were jammed up like tinned sardines. Theo was running a game of faro, a favourite in Dawson because it was fast, and gave the players a fighting chance.

Theo had bought the faro table from a steamship owner who was short of cash. Every card from ace to king was painted on it, and the players laid their chips on the card they wanted to bet on. The dealer lifted the top card off the deck; if the one beneath was one someone was betting on, he lost, but if it came up second, he won. If neither, he bet again.

On the wall behind Theo there was a rack which held the players' pokes. Into the rack went a slip of paper charging the owner for the chips he bought. At the end of play, chips were balanced against slips, and the player's poke was increased or decreased, according to whether he'd won or lost.

Gold, dust or nuggets, was the main currency in Dawson, and every shop, saloon or other business had scales to weigh it out. When Beth and the boys first got to Dawson they were all astounded by the casual way men tossed pokes containing hundreds of dollars worth of gold around, but they were used to it now.

While Theo was dealing at the faro table, Jack greeted customers, keeping an eye on the bar and on Will and Herbert. Later, Jack would take over at faro, leaving Theo to begin a poker game, and in between her fiddle sessions, Beth would keep her eye on things.

It was soon clear that they would require several more staff, just as they would need more supplies of drink and another entertainer to keep things going all night. But that first night they muddled through, all working flat out. The whisky ran out at four in the morning, but most of the customers stayed and drank anything available. Theo had a huge smile on his face because Sam Bonnifield, known as 'Silent Sam', the owner of the Bank Saloon and Gambling

House on the corner of Front and King Streets, had come in to play faro. He got his nickname because he never said a word or smiled as he played. His luck was not in tonight and he was five hundred dollars down, yet he kept on playing.

At six in the morning, Theo finally closed the doors. He was too tired to count what they'd taken that night, but he reckoned it was close on 15,000 dollars. Enough to pay off the debts, restock with drink and get some furniture upstairs.

'Later today I'll buy you a big brass bed with a feather mattress,' he said as he embraced Beth. 'I promise you that you'll never sleep on the ground ever again.'

The Golden Nugget soon became established as one of the most popular gambling saloons in Dawson. Theo used his charms to lure four girls to work there, paying them a small commission for every glass of champagne they managed to persuade men to buy for them. It wasn't real champagne, but then very few people in Dawson knew what the real stuff tasted like. The girls added colour to the place as they teased and flirted with the men, and if they sold their bodies later to the highest bidder, no one was concerned.

Paradise Alley, behind Front Street, was where the real whores did their business, in a row of tents called cribs, each with her name above the door. They were mostly plain, sturdy women, for the difficult journey across the mountains to get here ruled out the delicate. They serviced around fifty men a day and their pimps took most of their earnings, and to Beth they had the worst life she could imagine.

But then, women generally had a poor deal in Dawson. They baked bread, did laundry and cooked in restaurants, and though some of them made an excellent living, they had to work incredibly hard, and often had men who spent it as fast as they earned it. Those who were married to miners spent their days panning for gold in remote creeks, living in terrible conditions with no other female company.

Only a small percentage of women lived the high life, and they were the actresses, singers and dance-hall girls. Most of the dance-hall girls took far more from men than they gave. For a dollar, a man got less than a minute with them in his arms before they moved on to their next partner. One girl had a belt made with seventeen twenty-dollar gold pieces, a present from a miner. Almost all the girls made no secret of the fact that they were there to separate the men from their pokes.

Beth worked too hard and for too long hours to live the high life, but she didn't mind, for it stopped her dwelling on Sam and Molly. True to his word, Theo had bought furniture for their rooms upstairs, including the promised brass bed and carpets too. Every night in the saloon was fun, and to see it becoming such a big success gave her great satisfaction.

When sad thoughts came into her mind, she reminded herself she was living her dream. It wasn't hard to be happy in Dawson; people were warm and friendly, and never a day passed without someone doing something outrageous that made them all laugh. She might feel a little disappointed that she and Theo had so little time together alone, but as August arrived and the cold weather and dark days grew imminent, many people began departing on the boats for the Outside, and she knew their time alone would come.

She knew, too, that she had forged herself a place in Dawson's folklore. There were many fiddle players in town, but no one as good as she, and they were all men. She was also considered the prettiest girl in Dawson, something Theo and Jack took great pride in.

People in Dawson liked stories, and there were enough

bandied around about the Eldorado Kings, the fortunes they'd won and lost at gambling tables, and all the lesser characters, to fill several books. It didn't surprise her one bit when she found people were embellishing tales of her, Theo and Jack. One night in the saloon, she overheard one man telling another that Theo had carried her on his shoulders up the Chilkoot Pass. Then he went on to describe how Sam died in Squaw Rapids, as if he'd been standing there while it happened.

Yet what intrigued people most, it seemed, was her relationship with Theo and Jack, for word had got around that she wasn't married to Theo.

She was well aware that many of the dance-hall girls had their eyes on him. She couldn't blame them – he was handsome, charismatic and rich now too, for they were making money hand over fist. It made Beth smile when they came slinking into the Golden Nugget in their best finery, flirted with him and tried to lure him away to whatever dance hall they worked in. She knew Theo well enough to be fairly certain that if he was to be lured away by another woman, it wouldn't be a mere dance-hall girl.

One rainy evening in early August a man came into the Golden Nugget who not only had a story to tell but was to start a chain of events that would alter everything for Beth.

She was playing her fiddle as he walked in, a tall man in a mackinaw and a broad-brimmed hat who looked slightly familiar, but the saloon was too dark and smoky to see him clearly.

As always, she played for around half an hour before having a short break, and as she went up to the bar to get a drink, the man caught hold of her arm.

'Howdy, Miss Gypsy,' he said. 'I was hoping I'd run into you.'

Looking up into his face, Beth recognized him as Moss Atkins, one of Soapy's henchmen from Skagway. He had often come into Clancy's when she was there, and though she hadn't ever spoken to him, he had a reputation for being vicious. He also had the kind of face she couldn't fail to notice, for his eyes were a brilliant blue and he had pock-marks on his cheeks.

'Hello, Moss,' she said. 'Good to see you again. Have you just arrived?'

'It's been a few days now, just asking myself whether it would be smarter to push off before the river freezes, or to stay for the winter and do some business here.'

'I think you'd do better in Skagway,' she said with a smile. 'The Mounties are very vigilant here. No guns, no skulduggery. If they catch you putting a foot out of line they'll give you up to ninety days on the woodpile.'

It was said that few people caught out in a crime cared much about the fine given to them – they could usually afford it. But the punishment of being forced to chop wood for the town council did act as a deterrent. It was boring, back-breaking work, and most high-tailed out of town rather than do it.

'Well, maybe I'd best skidaddle,' he said, giving a humourless chuckle. 'But to where I don't know. Skagway's lost its way since Soapy was gunned down.'

'Soapy's dead!' Beth exclaimed.

Maybe if she hadn't been so surprised, she might have realized people were listening to their conversation. But she was so keen to hear how it came about that it never occurred to her it would be wise to be more discreet.

'You ain't heard? It was back on 8 July. Shot down by Frank Reid on the dock.'

'But why?' she asked, as she recalled Frank Reid was an

innocuous sort of man who was more interested in town planning than fighting.

Moss launched into the story of how a prospector called J. D. Stewart had come back to Skagway from the Yukon with 2,800 dollars in gold dust. It was stolen, and the general view was that it was by one of Soapy's men. The Skagway traders were afraid that if word got around that it wasn't safe for anyone with gold to leave from their town, all prospectors would take the sea route and bypass it, robbing them of lucrative business. Demands were made that Soapy was to give Stewart back his gold immediately, and the townsfolk began to turn against him.

'The upshot of it was that Soapy started drinking, got his dander up and went off down to the docks with a derringer in his sleeve, a .45 Colt in his pocket and a Winchester rifle slung over his shoulder,' Moss told her. 'Frank Reid was down there, and told Soapy not to go any further. Soapy put his rifle to Reid's head. Reid seized the muzzle with his left hand and reached for his own six-gun in his belt with the other. He fired, but the cartridge was faulty, and instantaneously Soapy fired his rifle, shooting Reid in the groin. But Reid fired his six-gun again; this time he shot Soapy right through the heart. He died instantly.'

Beth gasped, as did others within earshot, for everyone in Dawson had heard about 'Soapy' Jefferson Smith, even if they hadn't actually gone through Skagway on the way here.

People around them started asking Moss questions, and he was clearly delighted to be the one to bring the news of this to Dawson and find himself the centre of attention. 'Yeah, Reid died too, but a slow, lingering death. At least Soapy's was quick.'

Both Theo and Jack came closer, as interested as anyone else in such a big story. Moss continued to hold forth, saying that many of Soapy's men had taken to the trails and the mountains to avoid being captured by the gang of vigilantes who had lynching on their mind.

'Maybe it's a good thing you left Soapy when you did,' he suddenly said to Beth. 'He told me you was his girl, but I guess it must've been hard for you to swallow all his badness. Especially when he had that other fella of yourn shot.'

Beth's stomach lurched, and she saw Theo's face had stiffened. 'There was nothing between Soapy and me,' she said. 'And I'm sure it wasn't him who had Theo shot, you've got that all wrong.'

Moss laughed scornfully. 'I ain't got nothing wrong, babe, I was with Soapy when he ordered the shooting. "Take out the English guy," was what he said, "I've got plans for his lady." I saw you dozens of times with him, too, so if that don't mean there was something between you, then I'm a Dutchman.'

Jack intervened at that point, suggesting it was time Beth played again. Moss left the saloon soon after.

The following day was Saturday, and as they'd slept late, they had to rush to open the saloon at midday. Beth was aware Theo was being a bit cool with her, but they were so busy there was no time to bring it out into the open.

On Sunday they didn't wake until mid-afternoon, but when Beth snuggled up close to Theo, expecting that they would make love as they usually did, he got up and began dressing.

'Where are you going?' she asked.

'I've got stuff to do,' he said curtly.

After he'd gone out, Beth stood at the window, looking out across Front Street on to the river, and she could feel winter drawing close. The trees on the mountains were all evergreen so there was no autumnal colour like back in

England, America and Montreal. She'd been told that the temperature could reach 50 degrees below freezing here in the winter months, and she shivered at the thought of it

Four hours later, Theo still hadn't come back. Beth had spent the time catching up on little jobs, stitching up the hem of one of her dresses, doing some washing and writing a letter to the Langworthys. Outside it was still raining heavily, and she couldn't imagine where Theo could have gone as nothing was open.

She and Jack made a meal down in the kitchen later, and stayed down there afterwards as it was warm by the stove.

'He's angry about what Moss said,' Beth blurted out later. 'But I don't understand why he'd take it out on me. After all, he was the one that went off with that whore in the Red Onion, and I took care of him after he was shot.'

'I wouldn't take the word of anyone who worked for Soapy Smith,' Jack said. 'And I'd be surprised if Theo did. But the word was all over town by last night, and several people made jokes about it to him. I suppose he's smarting a bit.'

Theo didn't come home that night. He turned up at midday on Monday to open the saloon but offered no explanation as to where he'd been. As he didn't seem to be brooding on anything and was just a little quiet, Beth let it go and went out to do some shopping.

She was gone a couple of hours and as she was walking back to the Golden Nugget, she heard the now very familiar sound of a steam horn on a departing boat. As she turned into Front Street, a large crowd were gathered to wave goodbye, and she waved too, as was the custom if you were nearby.

*

428

When Beth got back, Jack said Theo had gone to the bank with the takings. An hour passed, then another, and still he hadn't returned.

'He'll be having a game of poker somewhere. Let's just hope he took the takings to the bank first,' Jack said laughingly.

It was just after seven when Wilf Donahue, better known as 'One Eye' on account of having a glass eye, came in. He was a regular at the Golden Nugget, even though he owned a similar establishment on King Street. Beth thought the rotund, red-faced man from Kansas coarse and over-familiar, but Jack and Theo found him amusing and claimed he was a man's man.

'I want you up there playing, my girl,' Wilf said to Beth, pointing to the little stand she usually played from. 'We won't get any punters in without some music.'

'Since when did you give the orders around here?' she asked lightly, assuming it was his idea of a little joke.

'Since two o'clock this afternoon when I bought the place,' he said.

Chapter Thirty-two

'Where are Jack and I going to sleep?' Beth asked One Eye indignantly the following day. She was livid as she'd just overheard him telling Dolores and Mary, two of the saloon girls, that they could move in upstairs.

'I won't be taking your room unless you keep giving me lip,' he said. He was half turned away from her, his one good eye looking in her direction but the glass one staring sightlessly ahead. 'Jack will have to move down to the kitchen, though, as I've promised his room to another couple of girls.'

Beth felt she might explode, but she didn't dare for fear he'd boot her and Jack out. 'This isn't right, Mr Donahue,' she pleaded. 'Jack built this place and it's our home. Don't do this to us! It's been enough of a shock that Theo sold the place to you without a word to us.'

The previous day, she and Jack had thought at first that One Eye was pulling their leg by saying he'd bought the saloon. He was known as something of a joker, and every time he'd come into the Golden Nugget in the past wearing a loud checked suit and stetson hat decorated with feathers, he'd said something outrageous. He was prone to splashing his money around too, and though they'd thought him a fool, they'd seen him as a harmless one.

But to their shock and dismay, he pulled out a legal document drawn up by a lawyer here in Dawson, and signed by Theo, proving he had bought the place, lock, stock and barrel, for 80,000 dollars.

They had found it astounding that Theo had been ruthless enough to clinch this deal on Sunday, but so cowardly that he stayed out all night so he didn't have to face them. Yet he'd had the nerve to return on Monday after he'd signed the document and cashed the banker's draft, and coolly pick up the takings and secretly pack a few of his things. He'd even spoken jovially to Jack, reminding him they needed more supplies of whisky, then calmly left to catch the steamer – ironically, the very one Beth had waved at.

Jack was incandescent with rage; Theo wouldn't have got the saloon built but for him. But the glint of tears in his eyes suggested that the thing which hurt most was that he'd thought he and Theo were like brothers, and he couldn't believe he'd betray him.

Beth saw the utter treachery of it. She would have stood by Theo whatever life threw at him, even if he'd lost the saloon in a poker game. Maybe their affair had grown cooler of late, but she still loved him and thought that love was returned. But to find he could just walk away from her, after all they'd been through and been to each other, that he cared more for money than her, was simply devastating.

There was no legal recourse, however. Theo had owned the land, and no agreement had ever been drawn up to give his partners a share in the business, even though he'd always said this was what he intended. If One Eye chose to throw her and Jack out on the streets he could legally do so.

To add insult to injury, they now had to be grateful he was prepared to keep them on in his employ and give them a roof over their heads.

Since the Golden Nugget opened, they hadn't even had proper wages, and Jack had never been paid for the building work. All they'd had was a few dollars here and there when they needed something, foolishly trusting that the money going into the saloon account belonged to all of them, just as they'd shared everything in the past.

One Eye looked at Beth with cold calculation. He didn't like the hurt and anger in her eyes; wronged women were invariably trouble. But he had to find some way of appeasing her, for he knew only too well that she was the Golden Nugget's real attraction. In truth, he wouldn't have wanted the place if not for her. Smart dealers, dancing girls, skilled barmen were all as common as drunks. But pretty fiddle players were as rare as a domesticated grizzly bear.

He knew he must string her along for another week or so till the river froze, then she'd have no choice but to stay all winter. And if he could get rid of Cockney Jack without putting her back up, maybe she'd even end up in his bed.

'Look, my little Gypsy Queen,' he said in honeyed tones. 'I feel bad your man ran out on you; he was a louse to do that to you. But I've paid top dollar for this place and now I've got to make it work for me. So I've gotta let those two rooms. But I tell you what, I'll pass the hat round when you play, and you can keep whatever they put in it. How's that?'

Beth felt too numb to protest any further. It wouldn't feel like her home without Theo anyway, so she supposed it didn't matter if there were going to be four girls living in it.

As always, playing her fiddle that evening soothed her. Maybe she didn't make anyone want to get up and dance – in fact her mournful tunes brought tears to the eyes of some of her audience. But when the hat had been passed round and come back to her, she counted up over thirty-five dollars, confirmation that she had a unique talent which would ensure she'd never starve.

It was a quiet night, and One Eye let them close up at one o'clock for there were few people around. The girls weren't moving in until tomorrow, so Jack grabbed a bottle of whisky and said they should drown their sorrows.

'I bet Theo cooked up this deal with One Eye some time ago, but didn't have the brass neck to go through with it then,' Jack said a little later as they sat up at either end of Beth's bed, drinking, the comforter over their legs. 'Then when he heard that geezer talking about Soapy Smith and you, he saw it as the perfect way out, without him looking like a complete cad.'

'But that means he must have stopped caring about me ages ago,' Beth said brokenly, yet more tears threatening to flow. 'Why couldn't he have admitted it?'

'I doubt it was that. He was a gambler through and through,' Jack reminded her. 'I'd bet all he thought about was the money he'd have in his hand. All in all it must have been over eighty thousand with the takings and whatever was in the bank. That would set him up for a lot of big poker games. Or maybe he just saw that money as one huge win, and felt he had to quit while he was ahead.'

'But I've been with him through thick and thin. He said he loved me and he knew I would have gone anywhere with him. So why didn't he want to take me with him?'

'I don't know, Beth.' Jack shook his head in bewilderment. 'But look back at how things have been since we left Philadelphia. Sam and I always carried him. Granted, he did share when he had a win, but without us he would never have got across Canada, let alone reached here. Maybe he realized that, and it made him uncomfortable. Taking off with the loot might have made him feel free.'

'To find some society woman who won't embarrass him,' she said bitterly. 'Look what he was like in Montreal, always looking out for nobs to socialize with. He didn't care that

I had to work in a factory and live in a hovel. I bet he was delighted when I lost our baby and the doctor said I couldn't have any more. That way he had no responsibilities. What a fool I've been!'

Jack reached out and took her hand, squeezing it in sympathy. But he didn't protest and say she was wrong.

'Well, I really hope he loses all that money in his next game,' she said viciously. 'When he's down in the gutter with nothing I hope he'll come crawling back to me. Then I'll kick him in the face.'

They drank silently for some little while, both deep in bitter thoughts.

'Was there something between you and Soapy?' Jack asked later. 'I know you did spend a night with him, but was there more to it than that?'

'No, but there could have been.' She sighed, then told Jack about how she'd met Soapy and had a drink with him on the last day in Skagway, and that it was he who took her down to Dyea later on his horse. 'I liked him a lot, but as it turned out it was a very good job I didn't pick him. There wasn't that much difference between him and Theo, was there? Do you think it was true Soapy ordered someone to kill him?'

'I think it might have been, but I doubt it was over you. I expect Theo stepped out of line. They were two of a kind, both cheats. I don't mean just at cards or with women, but in everything. They used their charm to get people in their thrall, just so they could take advantage of them. Theo suckered me, that's for sure, and what sticks in my craw is that I would have died for him.'

By mid-October, Dawson was a great deal quieter. Snow had fallen and the Yukon was frozen solid, used only by dog teams hauling supplies out to the goldmines or bringing in wood for fires.

The stampeders who'd arrived in June and wandered through the mud like lost souls had mostly gone home while it was still possible to get to the Outside. With no more boats bringing people in or taking them away, the shore was deserted. Smoke from a thousand chimneys rose up to create a grey fog before an even greyer sky.

The lower slopes of the mountains that surrounded Dawson were denuded of trees, the black stumps left behind like so many rotten teeth, and sickness lurked among the many people still living in tattered tents. The town was built on swampland, and all through the hot summer, with no proper drainage or sanitation, diseases like typhoid, dysentery and malaria took their toll. Scurvy was on the increase too, as were pneumonia and chest complaints.

The Front Street residents were mostly unaware of or uninterested in the plight of the poorer citizens for they could afford to keep their boilers, fires and stoves blazing away, their privies emptied and their larders full. Electricity had arrived, so had the telephone, and for those with adequate means, Dawson was as gay and colourful as Paris, even if it was bitterly cold.

Beth found she couldn't ignore the plight of the poor and sick. Every day she made a large pot of soup and took it on a sledge up to Father William Judge, the frail and bony priest who ran a little hospital under the hill at the north end of Dawson.

To her mind, Father Judge was a saint. He worked tirelessly from early morning till late at night, wearing nothing but a ragged cassock despite the extreme cold. Beth suspected his nurses were not so pure, and stole from the patients while they lay dying, so she'd stay until she saw the sick drink the soup, to be certain it wasn't being spirited away and sold somewhere else at a profit.

Jack was also becoming increasingly disillusioned about the way things worked in Dawson. Most people toadied to the rich and admired their flamboyant displays of their wealth, while doing their best to make sure some of it came their way. He found it offensive that many of the very richest people in town cheated the poor, paying them a pittance to do their laundry, chop their wood and other menial tasks. When One Eye ordered him to throw people out of the saloon who sat in the warm nursing one drink for long periods, Jack refused. He knew some of these men would die of cold in their tents and unheated cabins, and it was his view that One Eye should show some Christian charity.

There had been many spats between the two men, for One Eye showed no respect for Jack's honesty or his humanity.

'I've got to leave,' Jack finally announced to Beth one night in November after the bar was closed. 'If I don't, one of these days I'll lose my temper and attack One Eye. He's watering down the spirits, he's turned the girls into whores and takes most of the money they make, and I think he's got the games rigged. I can't stand by and be part of it any more.'

Beth had been horrified too when the four saloon girls began slipping off upstairs during the evening with men, for though none of them had been innocents when Theo took them on, they hadn't been whores. Dolores had confided in her and said One Eye told them he would fire them if they refused to go with any man he ordered them to.

He had the girls over a barrel, and Beth had the utmost sympathy for them. None of them were outstandingly pretty or even very bright, and all the other saloons had their quota of girls, so they wouldn't find work anywhere else. The best they could hope for was that one of the miners would take them for a 'winter wife', to warm his bed and cook his meals. But a cold, primitive cabin on the edge of town, with no money of their own and a man they didn't love, was probably as bad as being a whore.

'Where will you go?' Beth asked Jack. The prospect of him leaving made her feel as though a cold steel clamp was being squeezed around her heart. She thought she'd come to terms with losing Sam and Molly, but when Theo left her it was as if every one of her past sorrows had come back at once. Without Jack, her one entirely true friend, she would have caved in, perhaps even been tempted to end it all, as other jilted women had done in Dawson.

But for weeks she'd been aware that Jack hated and despised One Eye, and it would be wrong to try to make him stay purely for her sake.

'Out to Bonanza.' He shrugged. 'There's plenty of work there.'

'But it's such a very hard life,' she protested.

'Not as hard as bowing and scraping to old One Eye,' he said with a grin. 'I'll come back when the ice breaks up in spring, and if some rich and handsome man hasn't claimed you by then, maybe we'll both be ready to go back to the Outside.'

Beth smiled weakly. She could tell by the glint in Jack's eye that he was actually savouring the idea of working out at Bonanza. He had never been afraid of hard work or rough conditions, and he had more in common with many of the miners than he did with the gamblers, parasites and toffs here in Dawson. It was only Theo's influence that had got him into being a bartender, and in reality he was worth far more than that.

437

'I've no interest in any more love affairs, but I know I'm going to miss you terribly.' She reached out to hug him. 'Take care of yourself, and send notes with someone so I know how you are.'

Jack left two days later with a miner called Cal Burgess on his dog sledge. Beth went down to the frozen shore to wave him off, smiling brightly even though she wanted to cry. The malamutes were barking furiously and straining at their harnesses to go. When Cal jumped on the back of the sledge and gave the dogs their signal, they leapt forward eagerly.

Jack turned, his face half hidden in his wolf fur-lined hood, his mittened hand raised, but she guessed by the straight line of his lips that he was worried about leaving her.

It *had* been terrible when Theo walked out on her. She felt exposed, humiliated and that her hopes and dreams were shattered. But she had been able to pick over the bones of their relationship, list his many faults and past failings, and see for herself that he'd always been out for the main chance. She really ought to have known better than trust him implicitly.

But there were no such feelings to counterbalance the sadness she felt at Jack moving on. Hardly an hour went by when she didn't miss him. When she made the first cup of coffee of the day, she'd imagine his sleepy morning face with a dark rash of stubble, breaking into a smile as she woke him. Later, when the saloon was open, she'd remember how in quiet times she used to sit up on a stool by the bar and chat to him as he cleaned the shelves and polished glasses.

There were the jokes they shared about customers. Jack could convey a message to her about a very large nose, a speech impediment, a compulsive liar or any other defect, with no more than a smirk or a raised eyebrow. Sometimes they couldn't contain their laughter and had to duck down under the bar or rush out to the back, for fear of being asked for an explanation.

But it was in the evenings that she missed him most, for they had always gone to get supper together around six. She would change and do her hair when they got back, and later, when she walked back into the saloon to play, he'd give her a wolf whistle. He was always there, always admiring and supportive, always the friend who never let her down. He had been ready to talk at any time, night or day, and happy to sit in companionable silence too when that was what she wanted.

When she looked back, that was the way it had always been. If he hadn't fired her up to go to Heaney's, maybe she would never have played in public, but found a job in a store. He didn't falter when she jilted him for Theo, and despite all the girls he'd had, and there had been many, he'd never let them come between them.

He gave her strength and consolation when she lost her baby and took control of everything in Skagway. He had got them up the Chilkoot Pass. He'd shared her grief at losing Sam, and understood how she felt about Molly's death. He'd even shared her hurt when Theo ran off.

But now he was off to have a life of his own, and however much she missed him, she was glad for him. He'd spent too long supporting her, Sam and Theo; it was time he used all that energy and ability he had for himself.

She realized too that she must do the same.

From the moment she met and fell for Theo, she'd virtually given her life into his keeping. She'd never stopped to ask herself if she really wanted to be part of his grandiose plans; in fact she lost the ability to make any of her own. Looking back, it seemed incredible that she'd travelled so many thousands of miles, put up with so many hardships, just to be at his side.

She was brushing her hair in her room one morning a few weeks after Jack had gone, when all at once it occurred to her that One Eye was using her in just the same way as Heaney had back in New York. Accepting the money put into the hat each night and being grateful he let her keep her room was playing into his hands. She was being exploited, and if she wasn't careful she'd become trapped like Dolores and the other saloon girls.

She was making some 200 dollars or more a week, but the high cost of everything in Dawson soon whittled that down, for she'd bought new dresses, a fur to keep warm outside, and thick, fur-lined boots.

In all the giddiness of getting here and being part of the madness that was Dawson, she'd lost sight of the reason why they made the hazardous journey in the first place. The plan had been to make their fortunes.

Theo had done that, but all she'd got to show for her hard work was savings of 160 dollars. That wasn't going to get her very far.

'Come on now, honey, give me a kiss!'

Beth recoiled in horror as One Eye drunkenly tried to lunge at her. He was wearing his yellow and black checked suit, the waistcoat so tight around his middle that part of his belly protruded beneath it. His face was red and shiny with sweat and his breath was rank.

It was four in the morning and it had been a very busy night, with a poker game running for huge stakes. As usual, One Eye had sat at a table drinking with his cronies all evening, only shifting himself to call for more drinks, to order one of the barmen to eject a drunk, or to fondle one of the Paradise Alley whores who had taken to frequenting the place lately.

The poker game had finished an hour ago. All the gamblers had gone home, and the only customers left were six or seven men so drunk they were either asleep with their heads on the table, or wavering precariously on their seats.

The current bartender, known as Sly, an appropriate name for a man Beth was fairly certain pocketed the price of many drinks, had been trying to close up so he could go home. He'd asked Beth to help, and it was when she suggested to One Eye that the drunks should be ejected that he got up.

But he hadn't ejected anyone; instead, he'd made a play for her.

Suddenly Beth knew she had to make a stand and prove herself.

'Back off, you loathsome creep,' she snapped at him. 'I am not your woman. Lay one hand on me and you'll regret it.'

'You speak to me like that and I'll throw you out on the street,' he slurred.

She looked scornfully at him swaying on his feet, and this time remembered that she was popular in the town, while he was laughed at. 'Just throw this lot out,' she said, indicating the drunks. 'Then go home. I'll deal with you in the morning.'

She flounced off upstairs, locking her door behind her. She doubted One Eye would go home or throw the drunks out, for despite all his talk, he was in fact a weak man. The chances were they'd all still be there in the morning, out cold on the saloon floor.

It was early December now, so cold that the snow on the streets was as hard as brick and it hurt to breathe. The reason she'd stalled on implementing the plan she'd made two weeks earlier was purely because her room above the Golden Nugget was warm and comfortable. She felt secure here, even though she loathed One Eye. But that security was gone now he'd got the idea she was his property. He'd been very drunk tonight, but he was much more dangerous sober. She wouldn't put it past him to force himself on her, or even to hatch up some plot to implicate her in some kind of criminal act as his revenge for rebuffing him.

She barely slept for the remainder of the night, for each and every creak in the building made her think the man was coming up the stairs. She gave up trying to sleep at nine, and got up.

Going first into the saloon, she found all the men sprawled out cold on the floor. One Eye was still clutching a whisky bottle, his mouth wide open and snoring loudly. The stink in there made her gag; it wasn't just the vomit on the floor, but something even more disgusting.

Closing the door on them, she put on her coat and fur hat, then left through the back door.

She had made a point of trying never to think about Theo, yet she couldn't help but imagine his horror at what she'd just seen. He'd been scrupulous about refusing to serve any more drink to men once they didn't know what they were doing. If a man looked about to collapse, he ordered the man's friends to take him home to sleep it off. No one would have got away with lying drunk on his floor.

It was too early for the saloons to be open, so she went into a café in King Street and ordered breakfast.

At eleven, she walked through the door of the Monte Carlo. 'I'd like to see Mr Fallon,' she said to a young man who was sweeping the floor. 'Tell him it's Gypsy.'

The Monte Carlo had changed hands several times since the previous June when she played there, and with every new owner it had been made grander with mirrors, chandeliers, oil paintings and carpets. The current owner, John Fallon, was said to be a Southern gentleman, with even bigger plans for the place. She hadn't ever met him but she was banking on his having heard of her.

'He's still in bed,' the young man said.

'Well, get him up then,' she said crisply. 'I have other people to see this morning.'

He disappeared out the back and she heard his feet clonking up the stairs. A few minutes later she heard them coming down, and her heart sank because she assumed Fallon had told him to say he wasn't getting up for anyone.

But to her surprise it wasn't the young man, but a man in his late thirties. His fair hair was tousled, and he was wearing a satin smoking jacket over a rather grubby collarless shirt.

'John Fallon at your service, mam,' he said, taking her hand and kissing it. 'Please excuse my appearance. Had I known the Klondike Gypsy Queen would come a-calling, I would have been spruced up, ready to meet you.'

Beth was delighted that the gossip she'd heard was true, and he really was a Southern gentleman.

'It is I who should apologize for calling so early,' she said.

'It is an honour to make your acquaintance, mam.' He smiled. 'I am a great admirer of your music. I've often lingered outside the Golden Nugget to listen to you play. Back in Virginia we have many great fiddle players, but I don't think I ever heard any better than you.'

Beth's heart began to beat a little faster. 'Why, thank you, sir,' she said breathlessly. 'Then perhaps I've come to the right place.'

His wide smile and interested pale blue eyes were

443

reassurance enough for her to keep her nerve. 'You see, I'm looking for a new establishment to play in. And the Monte Carlo would suit me just fine, providing you would be happy with my terms.'

'Suppose you tell me what they are?' he said, his smile fading into a foxy smirk.

'Fifty dollars a night, plus whatever your customers put in the hat. And a room too.'

He sucked in his breath. 'Fifty dollars a night is too much. I could only run to twenty-five.'

The figure in Beth's head to settle on had been just fifteen, but to be offered more made her confidence rise.

'Then I'm sorry, Mr Fallon, I can't play for you,' she said, and turned to walk out the door.

She was just about to push it open when he coughed. 'Maybe I could run to thirty-five,' he said.

Beth turned. 'Come now, Mr Fallon. You don't want me playing at the Criterion, do you? Agree on forty-five and I won't call on them. Providing the room you give me is a good one.'

He wavered for just a second. 'It's a deal,' he said, coming forward to take her hand and shake it. 'When can you start?'

'When will my room be ready?' she said.

'An hour?' he suggested.

She nodded. 'Do you have anyone who could escort me back to the Golden Nugget to collect my things? I fear One Eye may be a little unpleasant about me leaving.'

'I'll come myself, mam,' he said with a wide grin. 'Just give me five minutes to get dressed properly.'

It was the most deliciously satisfying moment to see One Eye's look of sheer outrage when he encountered John Fallon on the stairs with his arms full of Beth's dresses.

'Wh-wh-where you going with that?' he stuttered.

'To my place,' Fallon said breezily. He turned to Beth on the stairs behind him. 'Have you got everything now?'

'All that's important to me,' she said, smirking at One Eye. She had her fiddle in one hand and her valise packed with everything else in the other. 'You can let my room to a couple more whores now. You'll need some new attraction without me to pull folk in.'

'You can't leave me in the lurch like this,' One Eye protested.

'Come, come, Mr Donahue,' Beth said silkily. 'Customers who shit their pants and vomit on the floor don't much care for fiddle playing, and you can turn the whole place into a brothel now. You'll do just fine.'

She had the delight of knowing that Dolores, one of the biggest gossips in Dawson, was at the top of the stairs listening. By tonight the story would be right round town.

One Eye made an attempt at blocking Fallon from reaching the back door, but Fallon pushed past him.

'Do make sure the saloon is cleaned up before opening up today,' Beth said crisply as she breezed past One Eye. 'Otherwise people might just think you've got the skids under you!'

'The Gent must have been feeble-minded to walk out on you,' Fallon said as he carried Beth's clothes into one of the front bedrooms at the Monte Carlo. 'It was admirably dignified, the way you put One Eye in his place.'

'My time at the Golden Nugget is over now,' she said sternly. 'I'd rather you didn't speak of it again.'

He laid her dresses down on the bed and smiled. 'That's fine by me, and I think we should have some champagne to celebrate a new beginning.'

445

'That would be very nice.' She smiled. She liked the look and sound of this man. From now on she intended to stop looking back over her shoulder and make the most of any opportunities that came her way.

The Monte Carlo was packed to capacity that evening, and when Beth peeped down over the banisters before she was due to start playing, she guessed that the latest story about her was circulating, gathering even more drama with each telling.

Fallon had put signs outside proclaiming she was playing there tonight, and young Tom had just informed her that he'd been past the Golden Nugget and there were only three or four customers in there.

She was going to earn a great deal of money here. She had the best room in the house, complete with a feather mattress on the bed, and a dressing table grand enough for the Queen of Sheba. Even electricity had been installed, and the place was as warm as toast.

Theo was just a slight ache now. She could live very well without him.

As she turned back to her room to collect her fiddle, she looked at herself in a long mirror on the landing. Her hair shone like wet tar, her eyes were bright with excitement, and her cheeks flushed a becoming pink. In the purple satin gown with black lace flounces she'd recently had made by a dressmaker, with elbow-length black lace fingerless gloves and a purple flower in her hair, she knew she looked sensational.

'Use it to your advantage,' she whispered to herself. 'Be the Gypsy Queen!'

All through the remainder of December, into the New Year of '99, Beth triumphed at the Monte Carlo. She did two hour-long sets each night, but often sat in with other musicians too. John Fallon liked her to mix with his customers, and it was like a party almost every night.

New Year's Eve and her twenty-second birthday later in January were special highlights, for Fallon threw a private party to celebrate the New Year for all the wealthiest and most influential people in town, and on her birthday he organized one especially for her, and presented her with a gold bracelet.

Beth sensed by the way Fallon slipped the bracelet on to her wrist and kissed her hand that he wanted her, and it delighted her to find she wanted him too, for that meant she was free of Theo at last.

She wasn't looking for another serious love affair, but she was ready to have a little fling. Not immediately – she wanted to get Fallon's full measure first – but in the meantime she could flirt with him.

Sometimes in the dark and icy January and February days, Beth actually felt glad Theo had left her, for if he'd still been around she would never have discovered how strong and independent she really was. She had taken control of her own life, she was a living legend in Dawson, and she knew that wherever she decided to go after here, she had enough confidence and belief in herself to succeed.

In early March she decided the time was ripe for a night of love. She had found it hard to think of anything else for a few weeks, often waking in the night from erotic dreams.

It was the law in Dawson that on Saturday nights everything should be closed by midnight, and ever since Beth came to the Monte Carlo, Fallon had always opened a bottle of champagne once the doors were shut, and asked her to join him.

She had been saving all her money since she began at the Monte Carlo, but because she wanted to look extra special for Fallon, she got a seamstress to run her up a new scarlet gown. It was modelled on the style of a flamenco dancer's dress, with a low-cut neckline, frilled sleeves, and a close-fitting boned bodice taken right down over her hips, then flaring out in layers of frills to her feet.

It was a sensational gown, one that she would never have dared wear anywhere but Dawson, and part of its delight was knowing that it was risqué and would raise eyebrows. She knew people still gossiped about Theo leaving her, and perhaps this gown would prove she was over him. She knew she was, for as she slipped it on over new silk, lace-trimmed underwear, all she could think of was Fallon undoing her laces and buttons, and it brought a flush to her cheeks.

She played for him alone all evening. The saloon was crammed with people, all looking up at her on the little stage, tapping their feet, clapping their hands and smiling. But her dark eyes were on his face as he stood at the corner of the bar. He wasn't dashingly handsome like Theo; his skin was pale and he had unremarkable features and pale blue eyes. But he had style – tonight he wore a sea-green silk waistcoat beneath his dark suit, his hands were soft and manicured, and the smile on his lips was just for her.

'You look very beautiful tonight,' Fallon said as he handed her a glass of champagne in his parlour after the saloon had closed. 'And your new gown is very becoming.'

The parlour was small, with no room for anything more than a couch in front of the fire, a large polished wood desk and chair, and a safe stacked high with papers. He ran the saloon from here, and the adjoining room was his bedroom.

'Well, thank you, Mr Fallon,' she said with a smile.

'It's John,' he said, standing with his back to the fire. 'I can hardly seduce a lady who calls me Mister.'

'So you intend to seduce me, do you?' she said impishly.

'I have been intending to do that from the first day you walked into my saloon.' He grinned. 'But I sense that you are giving me the signal to go ahead tonight. Am I right?'

'Would a lady admit to that?'

'One as honest as you would.'

She got up, putting her glass down on his desk. 'Then maybe you'd better kiss me,' she said.

Beth had studied his mouth a great deal recently. It was in fact his most attractive feature. His lips were well shaped and plump, turning up at the corners, almost as though he was constantly smiling. She hoped that meant he was good at kissing.

He put his hands on her waist and drew her close, looking down at her in amusement. 'I hope you aren't being a tease!'

She didn't answer, for his lips came down on hers and his arms went round her.

He was good at kissing, not too forceful nor yet too hesitant, and as the tip of his tongue insinuated itself between her lips, she felt dizzy with desire.

The walls in the Monte Carlo were nothing more than thin wood partitions, and the sound of the various residents talking, laughing and going up and down the stairs was a little disconcerting. Beth was afraid they could hear her heavy breathing as John moved her back to recline on the couch and kissed her again and again. When he put his hand down the bodice of her gown and released her breasts, she had to stifle a gasp of delight as he kissed them.

'Beautiful breasts,' he murmured, licking at her nipples

449

with the tip of his tongue. 'I have dreamed of doing this for so long.'

His hand stole up under her skirt, caressing the soft skin above her stockings, slowly working his way up under her drawers until his fingers found her sex. 'So wet,' he whispered. 'I think you must really want me.'

Beth forgot about the people who might overhear, for John was doing things to her with his fingers that made her want to scream out how good it was. But he was rude with her too, pushing her skirt up so he could look at her body, which made her feel so wicked and wanton.

He took her there on the couch while they were both still dressed, thrusting into her with such force it both shocked and thrilled her.

'I'm so sorry, that wasn't very gallant of me,' he said when he was spent. 'Please forgive me.'

'There's no need to apologize,' she said, for even if it hadn't been entirely satisfying, it had been very good.

'I've crumpled your gown too,' he said, looking concerned.

'It will recover.' She laughed. 'Now, are we going to get into your bed, or am I to go back to my own?'

'Please stay with me,' he said, kissing her again. 'I want to prove I can be a sensitive lover.'

Chapter Thirty-three

'Wake up, John, something's going on outside,' Beth said, shaking his arm roughly.

It was some six or seven weeks since she first went to bed with John, and she'd never had cause to regret it. John had proved he was capable of being not only a sensitive lover, but also an extremely demanding one. He would often search her out during the day while the bar downstairs was full of people, between her two sets in the evenings, and still be ready for more when he finally shut the saloon in the early hours of the morning.

For Beth it was just what she needed. She hardly ever thought of Theo now, and when she did it was with faint amusement rather than hurt. She had made many new friends, she had money saved for the future, and because she only worked in the evenings, she had time to help out at the hospital during the day.

She still missed Jack, but every couple of weeks someone coming in from Bonanza would bring a letter from him. He was working for Ed Osborne, an old Sourdough known affectionately as Ostrich or Oz because he so rarely left his claim. Beth could tell Jack was happy out there for his letters were full of funny little stories about miners he'd met.

Beth was entirely content. Her relationship with John was built on mutual passion, but she didn't feel the need to dress it up as love, or hope it had a future. John had a wife and three children back in Virginia, and he'd been honest enough to admit from the outset that it was his intention to sell the Monte Carlo by midsummer and return home.

'There's always something going on out there,' John said sleepily, trying to draw her into his arms. 'Go back to sleep.'

Beth was just about to snuggle down again when she heard the cry of 'Fire' and she was instantly out of the bed and at the window.

All she could see was a golden glow further along Front Street, but that was more than enough. This time she pounded John with her fists to wake him, for she'd seen how quickly fire could spread back at the end of '98. That night the Greentree and Worden hotels and the post office had all burned down, and men had to chop down other structures to stop the fire spreading right through the town.

John rushed off to wake everyone in the Monte Carlo while Beth pulled on her warmest clothes, for it was some 40 degrees below freezing outside.

With a hammering heart, Beth ran beside John towards the fire. By now most of the residents and owners of property in Front Street were outside, men hastily organizing themselves to break the ice on the river to get water. Everyone was asking where the fire engine, bought only the previous year, was. But it seemed that the newly trained fire fighters had been in dispute about their wages and the boilers in the engines had not been kept alight.

Beth looked on in horror as men built fires on the river ice to melt it and reach the water, but that was taking far too long, and the fire was jumping from building to building, devouring everything in its path.

At last the fire fighters arrived with hoses and the pumps were started. Beth saw the hoses slowly begin to swell as they sucked up water, and like everyone else, thought the fire would soon be under control. But then a ripping sound burst out, and to the assembled crowd's horror, the hoses split open, for the water within had frozen and expanded.

Beth saw Tim Chisholm, owner of the Aurora, covering his face with his hands as the flames began to spread to his saloon. 'What's to be done?' he cried.

'Blow up the buildings in front of the fire,' Captain Starnes of the Mounted Police commanded, and quickly ordered a dog team to race to get some explosive.

Thousands of people turned out to try to help. Every cart or sledge was commandeered to carry away articles from the condemned buildings in the path of the fire. Men even rushed into places already ablaze to try to rescue as much as they could.

'I'll give a thousand dollars to save my bank,' Beth heard David Doig, the manager of the Bank of British North America, pledge. But his plea was in vain, for it was soon gobbled up, along with scores of saloons and dance halls.

The whole town shuddered under the force of the dynamite explosions, and Beth saw men she knew to be as hard as nails weep openly as their buildings crackled and burned.

John was helping soak blankets in river water to try to save the Fairview, Dawson's best hotel at the north end of the town, and she turned her attentions to the whores of Paradise Alley, as the flames approached their rickety shacks. Many of the girls came running out almost naked, screaming with fear, but then stupidly trying to rush back in to rescue their clothes and possessions.

With some help from a few men, many of whom took off their coats to cover the girls, Beth managed to lead them all well away to safety.

The night was so cold that many people watching the fire couldn't feel the heat from the flames until their coats became singed. Hogsheads of whisky exploded in the flames and the contents ran out on to the snow, freezing instantly. And the gold in the bank safe, along with all the jewellery and other treasures put there for safe keeping, melted in the fierce heat.

Finally, there was nothing more anyone could do but stand and watch the inferno, hoping that the fire breaks made by blowing up buildings would be enough to contain it.

John came back to find Beth and they stood as close as they dared to the Monte Carlo, which so far had only been scorched. With their faces red-hot from the blaze, backs freezing and lungs full of smoke, they couldn't even speak of the disaster. Most of Front Street, including the Golden Nugget, with all its memories, was gone. Beth had fleetingly seen One Eye lurching around holding his head and sobbing out that he was ruined, and she even found it in her heart to feel sorry for him.

When daylight eventually filtered through the fog of smoke they saw that the entire heart of the business part of Dawson had been destroyed. The Fairview Hotel was saved at the north end of town, and the scorched Monte Carlo at the north end. Between them, where once there had been gaiety, light and warmth, was a huge black gap. The odd burnt timber still stood erect in a thick bed of grey ash, and it was the most desolate sight Beth had ever seen.

There was no joy that the Monte Carlo had been saved, for the scale of the disaster was too devastating, with thousands now homeless and ruined. John and Beth took in hundreds of people, letting them bed down wherever they could find room and providing coffee and whatever food they could rustle up.

Down at the Fairview, hundreds more were camping out in the lobby. Later in the day it was said that one hundred and seventeen buildings were lost in the fire, their loss totalling more than a million dollars.

But Dawson people were robust in spirit as well as body. Less than twelve hours later Tom Chisholm had erected a large tent where his old saloon had been and was back in business as the Aurora Saloon again, even before the ash had completely settled. That was the signal for everyone else to buckle to. Within a day or two the all too familiar sound of sawing wood and nails being hammered began again, and dray horses were out hauling lumber from the sawmills.

Beth spent her time cooking up huge pans of soup and stew to feed the homeless and destitute. She dragged a sledge around the town begging for bread, meat and vegetables from those who had supplies, and organized a collection of donated clothes, boots and blankets too.

John had been very active in the first day or two after the fire, and she thought nothing of it when he didn't come to her bed at night, because with the saloon packed with distressed people sleeping on the floor, it clearly wasn't an appropriate thing to do.

But suddenly she became aware that he was acting strangely. She kept seeing him standing out on the singed boardwalk looking at the blackened gap in the town, and he wasn't talking to anyone, least of all her.

She was too busy with the food and clothes collections to concern herself with him at first. But as the days ticked past, and everyone else was pulling together to plan and

455

rebuild the town, and still he stood for hours out there alone, she became puzzled and irritated.

He hadn't lost anything. Business was even brisker than before the fire, and now most of the refugees were gradually finding other places to stay and leaving the Monte Carlo, his staff needed direction.

She was coming back from the hospital one afternoon eight days after the fire when once again she saw him outside on the boardwalk. She noticed how dishevelled he was, unshaven, still wearing the same trousers, shirt and jacket he'd changed into after the fire.

As she got to the boardwalk he looked round at her but didn't speak or even smile.

'What's the matter?' she asked. 'Are you sick?'

'No, I'm not sick,' he replied, but his eyes had no light in them.

'Then come on inside with me, it's very cold out here,' she said, putting her hand on his arm.

He shrugged off her hand as if it had burned him.

'Tell me what I've done to offend you,' she said in bewilderment. 'Is it because I've been out in the town helping people? Do you think I'm neglecting you and the saloon?'

'Not that,' he said, giving her a look cold enough to freeze. 'The fire. It was the Lord's way of showing me how I've sinned.'

'But you were spared,' she said in puzzlement.

'Precisely. That's the Lord's way of saying, "Sin no more." Don't you see that?'

Beth suddenly saw what he was getting at. 'You mean with me?' she asked incredulously.

He nodded. 'I knew it was adultery, but I could not resist the temptation.'

She wanted to laugh as all this Holy Joe stuff sounded

like a joke; he had never told her he had any deep religious convictions. But she checked herself just in time as she remembered he'd begun praying out loud when the men were trying to light fires to melt the river ice. She had thought that odd then, but later almost everyone she'd spoken to said they'd been offering up frantic prayers, and she supposed she had done so silently too.

'This town is just like Sodom and Gomorrah,' he went on, his voice flat and dispirited. 'Now the Lord has destroyed it to show us what wickedness dwelt here.'

Beth had heard enough. She had always found him rather formal and pompous, not a man to make a woman laugh, or even a great conversationalist. What she'd liked about him was his lovemaking and his good manners, and now the lovemaking had clearly gone for good, and he was implying she was the serpent in the Garden of Eden, they'd obviously reached the end of the road.

'So, like Lot and his wife, you are going to flee,' she said sarcastically. 'Mind you don't look back while you're fleeing or you might turn to a pillar of salt.'

'You would do well to consider your sins too,' he said reproachfully. 'You seduce men with your Devil's music.'

Beth did laugh then. She wouldn't have been surprised to hear a statement like that back in England, but it was ludicrous here in a Frontier town coming from the lips of a man who just a week ago couldn't have his way with her often enough.

'So why, if you were a religious man, did you come here and buy a saloon?'

'I guess the Devil tempted me away from the Lord.'

'Then you'd better get back in his good books by selling this place and giving the money to the deserving poor or the Church,' Beth snapped. 'But pardon me if I don't do the same.

457

Your precious Lord took my parents, my brother and my little sister from me. I've learned to trust in no one but myself.'

That night Beth sat up in her room. Downstairs the saloon was packed because there were so few places left for people to drink in, and their booming voices and laughter wafted up to her. John had said he didn't want her to play tonight, and it was clear, even though he hadn't actually said so, that he wanted her out of his saloon.

She could see the funny side of it, for none of the dancers in his theatre or his saloon girls were pure as the driven snow. Gambling, drinking – it was all ungodly, so why single her out as the source of evil? She wished Jack was here, for he had always enjoyed a good joke.

She could of course go to any one of the remaining saloons in Dawson and they'd welcome her playing for them with open arms. But the fire, and now John's strange reaction, had put her off Dawson City.

But it would be another month before the ice broke and she could get a steamer.

She groped under her bed for her valise so she could count her savings. As she opened it, the first thing she saw was the photograph the four of them had had taken in Skagway, soon after they arrived. It was less than two years ago, but it seemed far longer. They all looked so young and fresh-faced, and the backdrop of mountains behind, painted on canvas, which at the time they'd thought marvellous, now looked so unrealistic. The boys had borrowed the rifles they carried on their shoulders – for Sam and Jack, the first guns they'd ever held. Beth was wearing a straw boater and a high-necked blue dress with a little bustle. At the time she'd been foolish enough to think that attire, with just a coat over it, would be suitable for the trail.

She smiled and ran one finger over Sam's stern, unsmiling face in the picture. He'd grown a beard soon after it was taken to make him look tougher, but it didn't work; he'd still looked young and starry-eyed. Theo, in an embroidered waistcoat and well-tailored jacket, looked what he was: an aristocratic gambling man.

Jack was the only one smiling, almost as if he knew even then what the mountains had in store for them. He had learned to shoot, just as he'd gone out of his way to learn everything about the trail, and to build cabins and a raft. How odd it was that he'd never had the lust for gold, yet he was the only one who finally got to the goldfields.

Just looking at the picture made a thousand little memories pop up in her head. The terrible night squashed up in the hotel in Sheep Camp, and the ones where they nearly froze to death at the top of the Chilkoot Pass. So many people in Dawson had shared that hideous ordeal, yet they all took pride in having suffered it, like a badge of honour.

Beth preferred to savour the good memories – speeding downhill on the sledge to Happy Camp, and the great evenings they'd had at Lake Lindemann and Lake Bennett. Sam was dead now, and Theo gone. Only she and Jack were left.

She thought back to the second day on the immigrant ship to New York, and smiled at the memory of their first conversation. Who would have thought that skinny street urchin would become her dearest friend?

All at once she knew what she wanted to do. Tomorrow she would ask someone to take her out to Bonanza Creek to see the goldfields and Jack.

Chapter Thirty-four

The five-dog team were raring to go, barking and pawing impatiently at the snow-covered ice of the river.

'Sitting comfortably?' Cal Burgess asked Beth as he tucked the bearskin tighter around her.

Beth nodded. With a wolf-fur hood, a coon-skin coat and several other layers of clothes beneath, she felt very cosy.

At Cal's signal the dogs leapt forward, and Beth's head whipped to and fro alarmingly. But as the dogs got into their stride it was smoother, the fine snow on the ice rising up and sprinkling on her like icing sugar.

She had packed her belongings the previous night. All the gowns she wore in the saloon and her daintier clothes, shoes and boots were packed into a box which this morning she'd left in safe keeping with friends who owned a restaurant. Her valise was packed with everything else, and before leaving she'd bought some luxuries for Jack – fruit cake, jam, chocolate, fruit, a quantity of lamb and bacon, cheese and several bottles of whisky. Her fiddle was wedged in the seat next to her and if it hadn't been for her run-in with John that morning she would have been bubbling over with excitement at this trip to see Jack.

She had been making some coffee about seven that morning when John came into the kitchen. She could smell whisky on his breath and judging by his heavy eyes and crumpled, grubby shirt, he'd drunk himself insensible and slept in his clothes.

She offered him some coffee, but his only reply was a

baleful stare which implied she shouldn't even be in his kitchen.

'There's no need to be so hostile,' she said gently. 'I'm leaving for good in a short while.'

'Where?' he asked.

She knew this wasn't concern for her, only fear she was going to another saloon and might talk about him.

'I don't think you have the right to ask me that when you've been so unpleasant,' she said airily.

He gave her another baleful look. 'Whores like you should be run out of town,' he retorted.

Until that moment she'd had every intention of leaving quietly without any recriminations, but calling her a whore changed everything.

'Why, you hypocritical arsewipe!' she exclaimed. 'You were lusting after me from the first day I moved in here. I held you at arm's length for three months, and when I did succumb, you couldn't get enough of me.'

'You tempted me,' he whined. 'You are a Jezebel preying on men's weakness.'

Beth put her hands on her hips defiantly. 'You pathetic snake in the grass,' she hissed. 'How dare you try and ease your own conscience by putting all the blame on to me? You are the guilty one because you have a wife and children. I think your poor wife would see it as *you* taking advantage of *me*!'

'My wife is a gentlewoman,' he snapped back. 'She would understand that I was no match for a whore like you.'

Beth was outraged. 'Gentlewoman! What the hell does that mean? That she only lets you fuck her in the dark with her nightdress buttoned up to her neck? No wonder you wanted me – I bet you fulfilled every last little dirty fantasy you've ever had. But then there's every chance someone else has been fucking your wife while you've been up here. She might even have found out what it's like to be loved by a real man, not some sanctimonious weakling.'

He lifted his hand to strike her, but Beth slapped it away. 'Lay one finger on me and you'll regret it,' she snarled. 'I could go out on to Front Street right now and raise a posse who would skin you alive. I have friends in this town. Now, get out of my way!'

He slunk away then like the snake he was, leaving her shaking with anger and a little ashamed that she hadn't seen what he was right from the start.

Tearing along at what seemed a great speed, the cold wind prickling her face like tiny pins, Beth did her best to wipe the memory of John from her mind. She did feel a little pride that she'd stood up for herself and had put him in his place – a year or two ago she'd never have been able to do that. But it shouldn't have come to that, and now she felt bruised and ashamed.

The snow lay in a thick and pristine white blanket on the river banks, the stumps of all the felled trees making a curious lumpy pattern. But further back, where the hills were too steep for logging, the snow-covered firs looked beautiful. There was no sound but the dogs panting, their paws thudding rhythmically and the swish of metal skids on the snow. She knew Cal was standing on the back of the sledge, but he was so silent, it was as if she was entirely alone with the racing dogs.

Weak rays of sun were slanting through the clouds, and it was good to leave the noise, ugliness and gossip of Dawson behind.

It occurred to Beth that she'd never experienced such utter peace before. As far back as she could remember there had always been people and noise all around her. Even up in the mountains on the trail, there had always been people close by. Back in Dawson, she often asked old Sourdoughs who lived miles from their nearest neighbour how they stood such isolation. Almost all of them said they loved it. She had an inkling now why that was. Silence was a great healer.

'Almost there now.' Cal bent down by her ear to speak to her. 'In a couple of minutes we'll be in Bonanza. It was called Rabbit Creek until they found the gold and I bet it was a pretty place then.'

The dogs veered off from the Yukon into the creek. Within minutes they passed the first of many small snow-covered cabins, smoke rising from the chimneys. Dogs barked as they went by, and from then on others joined in, almost as if each dog was passing the message along that a stranger was coming their way.

All Beth's imaginings about the fabled goldfields were set in summer, an idyllic scene with flower-strewn meadows, men in shirtsleeves panning in the water and shady trees overhead. Perhaps it had been that way before the stampede, but the trees were cut down now, and each tiny cabin or shack they passed was surrounded by snow-covered machin-ery; sluice boxes, picks, shovels and wheelbarrows were strewn around on the dirty, trampled snow. Men who looked more like apes in their heavy coats and hats were bent over fires or shovelling out dirt from holes in the ground.

'This is Ostrich's claim up ahead,' Cal shouted to her. 'See his flag flying? He hoists it up every morning. He sewed it himself.'

Beth could see a blue flag fluttering, with something brown on it, but it wasn't until the dogs began to slow down that she smiled as she saw that the brown shape was an ostrich cut out of leather.

Two big malamutes, one black and white, the other grey and white, came charging down from the cabin, tails wagging and making that woo-woo sound Beth had come to know was typical of their breed.

'They know I always bring them something,' Cal said, pulling up his dogs and jumping off the back of the sledge. 'But you give it to them.'

Beth got off the sledge and took the bag Cal was holding out. It contained two large bones and she gave them to the dogs a little nervously. She must have met thousands of sledge dogs, this breed and huskies too, since she'd started out in Skagway. She admired their strength and courage enormously, but she had never been at such close quarters with them before.

'Don't be scared of them,' Cal said. 'Malamutes like people, and they'll like you.'

'Howdy, Cal,' a voice called from the cabin, and an older man with a bushy beard, in a thick coat and matted fur hat, came shuffling down the path towards them. 'You stoppin', or are you taking that purty young lady on a jaunt?'

Beth smiled.

'Her jaunt ends here, Oz,' Cal said. 'This is Miss Bolton, the famed Klondike Gypsy Queen. She's come to see Jack.'

Before Beth could even shake Oz's hand, he turned and yelled to Jack to come, his voice so loud it made the sledge dogs howl.

'Well, missy,' Oz said, turning back to her. 'I sure do hope you've brought your fiddle with you, for I've heard a great deal about how sweet you play it.'

Suddenly Jack was up on a hill above them, running down

464

as though the hounds of hell were after him, whooping as he came.

'I'd say the lad is pleased to see you, missy,' Oz said with a toothless grin.

Jack had grown a thick beard, his hair was touching his shoulders, and in mud-daubed clothes and boots he looked just the way all the miners did. But his face glowed with health and he'd lost that strained look he'd had in the last weeks at the Golden Nugget.

He hugged Beth and spun her round, laughing with delight.

But her heart sank when Oz asked them into his cabin for a cup of coffee, for she couldn't see how Jack could fit in there, let alone her too. It was tiny, with a hard-packed dirt floor, a bed made out of old packing cases, a table, stool and another chair, all made out of rough wood. But it was very warm, for there was a tin stove, and Oz laced the coffee liberally with whisky.

Both Jack and Oz were anxious to hear every detail about the fire. They'd got news of it a couple of days after the event, and Jack said he'd been set to come to Dawson to see if Beth was all right. But then he was told that the Monte Carlo was still standing and she'd been looking after the homeless.

It was only when Cal got up to go, saying that he'd get her bag from the sledge, and then he must be on his way to pick up a load of timber, that Beth realized both Jack and Oz thought she'd just come for the day and would be returning with Cal.

'I had hoped I could stay with you for a while,' she explained. 'But I can see there's no room. So perhaps I'd better go back with Cal.'

'You certainly won't,' Jack exclaimed. 'I don't live here

465

with Oz. I've got my own cabin up on the hill. If you can stand the roughness of it, I'd be more than glad for you to stay.'

They waved Cal off and, picking up Beth's valise, Jack led the way round Oz's cabin and on up the steep hill, past a great deal of snow-covered equipment.

'It's real good to see you,' Jack said, his dark eyes shining the warmest of welcomes. 'I guess something went wrong with you and Fallon? But you don't have to tell me if you don't want to.'

Beth was too out of breath to speak, and she was a little horrified that Jack had heard that there had been something between her and John. She ought to have expected it, though, for no one could do anything in Dawson without everyone hearing about it.

Jack's cabin was a log one, much like Oz's, but larger and newer and the furniture was less crude.

'You can have the bed,' he said as he stirred up his stove and put some more wood on it. 'I've got a camp bed, that'll do me.'

'What did you hear about Fallon and me?' she asked, sitting down on a miner's string chair.

Jack shrugged. 'Just that you'd taken up with him, but I was a bit sad you didn't feel able to tell me in any of your letters.'

'Do you tell me every time you have a new woman in your life?' she retorted.

'I would if she meant anything special.'

'Well, Fallon wasn't special. It was just a bit of –' She paused, not knowing how to explain without admitting it was just sex.

'A fling?' he prompted.

'Yes, that's all it was.'

466

Jack nodded in understanding. 'So who ended it?'

There was nothing for it but to tell him how it was. But as she began to tell him what John had said after the fire, she saw the funny side of it and began to laugh.

'Oh, Jack, it was so weird. I'd never have put him down as a Holy Joe, and when he came out with all that turning away from wickedness, and saying Dawson was like Sodom and Gomorrah, I couldn't keep a straight face.'

Jack laughed too. 'I sometimes think that all the strangest people in the world end up in Dawson. I always found Fallon a bit of an oddball. He used to come into the Nugget and have just one drink while you were playing. He didn't seem to have any pals, he never gambled, I couldn't see what attracted him to the Klondike, or why he bought the Monte Carlo.'

'He never told me why.' Beth shrugged. 'But then we didn't talk much about anything now I come to think of it. He said I was a whore this morning. Isn't that awful, Jack? But I guess I brought it on myself.'

Jack came over to her chair and knelt in front of her, his eyes full of understanding. 'I'd like to go into Dawson tomorrow and beat him to a pulp, but that would only create more gossip. He's to be pitied if he doesn't see the difference between a woman who gives herself willingly and one who demands payment.

'Don't torture yourself, Beth, just put it down to experience. You are still the prettiest girl I know, my best pal and the greatest fiddle player. So the way I see it, you haven't lost anything but a bit of pride.'

'I shouldn't have taken up with a married man,' she said sadly. 'It *was* wrong.'

'Now, don't you come all holy on me.' Jack laughed and got to his feet, pulling her out of her chair. 'Let me show you what I've been doing before it gets dark, and tonight we'll get blinding drunk to celebrate you finally making it to Bonanza.'

Jack led her up some fifty yards behind his cabin. He warned her to take care to walk carefully around any indentations in the snow as they were holes he'd dug. He explained what he was doing.

'The ground is frozen two feet or so down, even in summer,' he said. 'So I dig down as far as I can, then light a fire in the hole. That melts the ice, and the next day I shovel out all the slushy dirt, which is what those piles are.' He indicated huge snow-covered mounds and a fresh one that he'd been digging out when she arrived. 'They are called dumps.'

He swept the snow off a long trough with crossbars running all along the bottom. 'This is a sluice, and when the thaw comes, I'll shovel the dump into the sluice, then wash it with water. All the gravel and dirt gets washed away, and if I'm lucky I'll find some gold stuck at the bottom of the sluice.'

'And you give it to Oz?' she asked.

'Not if I find it here. I've taken a "lay" on this bit of his claim. I didn't pay him any money for it. Our arrangement is that I work for him down there for part of the day, and anything we find there belongs to him. In return I get this.'

Beth nodded. 'So have you found any gold?'

'Not yet, that will only be revealed when I start sluicing. Maybe I won't ever find any. But Oz has found a lot in the last two years. He could, if he wanted, sell this claim for a fortune.'

Beth smiled. Ever since she arrived in Dawson she'd heard so many fantastic stories about claims along Bonanza and Eldorado changing hands for staggering amounts. Many

468

of the men who originally staked the claim now owned the hotels and saloons in Dawson, or had gone back to the Outside very rich men.

Yet there were still many old Sourdoughs like Oz who would never sell up. They continued to live in their primitive cabins, going into town once in a while to blow a great chunk of their gold, then back they'd go to the cabin and start again.

'Oz can't dig much now,' Jack explained. 'He's getting old, tired and achy. He don't really need any more gold, but he don't want to give up either. So with me here he's got what he wants – help, company and the excitement that comes with finding more gold.'

They walked on then right up the hill to where it turned to woodland.

'I come up here and shoot,' Jack said. 'I got a moose a couple of weeks ago and we've got enough meat to last till the thaw. It was so pretty last autumn, so many different berries growing and the leaves changing colour, not like down there,' he said, thumbing in the direction of the view down towards the creek.

Beth turned to look at the snow-covered scene. 'It's pretty now,' she replied. 'But I suppose that's because all the scars of holes, dumps and mining equipment are disguised by the snow. I bet it will look like a junkyard set in a slick of mud come the thaw.'

'Worse. There's huge ditches cut from the streams to wash out the sluices. It looks hideous.'

Jack had to light more fires in his holes, so Beth went back into the cabin as it was so cold.

She didn't need to ask if he'd built it. His stamp was all over it, from the way he'd fitted the bed into an alcove to the carefully crafted shutters at the windows. She guessed he'd made most of the furniture during the worst weather when he couldn't go outside. She ran her hand over the table legs, marvelling that he'd whittled the curves and rubbed them down till they were smooth.

Everything was so tidy too. Plates and dishes were stacked away on the shelves, a shirt hung drying on a rack by the stove, and he'd even made his bed.

It was while looking at the bed that she saw the pictures. They were pinned to the wall in the alcove and wouldn't be seen by anyone just coming into the cabin for tea and a chat.

One was of Jack and herself when they first got to New York, which they'd had taken in a booth down by South Seaport. Beth's copy was lost when they had to move so hastily out of the flat on Houston Street, and it was good to see it again. Another picture was of her playing her fiddle at the Bear in Philadelphia. She had no idea who had taken it or when, as she'd never seen it before.

There was one of Jack and her taken at Skagway. That one, she remembered, was taken by a man who was compiling a photographic journal of the Chilkoot Trail. She didn't know how Jack had got a copy of it, for they never saw the man again. Finally, there was one of her playing on the opening night at the Golden Nugget. It was taken by the editor of Dawson's newspaper, *The Nugget*, and it appeared in the paper along with an article about her, Jack and Theo, and how they'd lost Sam on the trail. Jack must have begged him for a copy of the picture.

She felt warm inside at him displaying pictures of her. She thought most miners would have pictures of pretty, scantily dressed ladies, not just an old friend.

*

470

'Those pictures of yours brought back a few memories,' she said later when he got back.

He looked a little sheepish. 'It's good to look at them when I go to bed,' he said. 'I had the one with the four of us taken in Skagway up there for a while too, but I took it down because Sam's face made me sad, and Theo's made me angry.'

Beth pointed to the one of them together in New York. 'You look so young and skinny,' she said. 'And I look very prim. How we've changed!'

'You wouldn't even invite me up to your room in those days.' He grinned. 'And here we are all this time later, alone together miles from anywhere. That's progress!'

In the days following her arrival at Jack's, Beth felt like a tightly coiled spring gradually unwinding. The fire in Dawson, helping the homeless and the unpleasantness with John afterwards must have taken a lot out of her.

It was good to wake in the morning to absolute silence and to know the day ahead would make no demands on her. Sometimes Jack took her out for an exhilarating ride on the sledge, with Oz's dogs, Flash and Silver, pulling them. But mostly she read a little, mended Jack's torn clothes and took walks along the frozen creek or up through the woods, with the dogs happily accompanying her.

The temperature had risen, and when the sun came out it felt almost like spring. Jack was the easiest of people to live with, always calm, never complaining. His face broke into a wide smile when she took him coffee and cake while he was digging, and appreciated it when she'd heated hot water for him to wash when he came in. But he didn't expect anything.

Yet the thing she liked best of all was that he made her

laugh. She would be sitting reading and she'd suddenly look up to see his face pressed grotesquely at the window. Once she heard a growling and scraping at the door and took fright, thinking it was a bear, but it was only him playing the fool. Most of the laughter, however, came from light-hearted banter between them, shared memories or observations about people. She realized that she hadn't really had that with Theo, nor long conversations either. She suspected that if they hadn't always had Sam and Jack around them, they might have been very bored.

The days were growing longer now and sometimes they would go down to Oz's cabin after supper, and Beth would play her fiddle for him. Some evenings men from nearby claims would hear her and come along too. They were the best of times, for some of the men would sing with her, they had good stories to tell and appreciated some feminine company.

There were a few women along Bonanza. In the main they were a tough, hard-bitten breed who dug holes in the frozen ground as efficiently as their men, and often did other jobs as well, like washing for other miners or baking bread and pies to earn badly needed extra money. They rebuffed Beth's tentative overtures of friendship, and while Jack said this was because they didn't want a pretty woman near their men, Beth felt it was more likely that they had heard the gossip about her.

While that didn't matter here, Beth realized with a little alarm that once back on the Outside she was going to face more serious social disapproval.

A dance-hall girl, or even a whore, might get married, or become a nurse or a secretary, with little fear of anyone discovering what she had done here. But Beth knew she was up there with Klondike Kate, Diamond Tooth Gertie and other women who'd made a big splash in Dawson City,

472

and the stories about them all had spread all over the world through newspaper articles about the Klondike.

So unless she gave up playing her fiddle in public, and never told a soul on the Outside that she'd been to Dawson City during the Gold Rush, the more scandalous parts of her time here in Dawson were going to get out.

Beth had been thinking about this problem one morning as she got washed and dressed. She had no solution as her fiddle-playing was the only way she had of making a living. But as the sun was shining, she thought she would stop worrying about her future and see if she could tempt Jack into leaving his digging to go for a walk with her.

She knew the temperature had risen the second she walked out of the cabin for her face didn't tingle as it usually did. Then she heard dripping. It was all around her, coming from the snow-covered machinery, the roof of the cabin, the path down to Oz's, everywhere.

The snow was melting!

Excitedly, she ran up behind the cabin and up the hill, calling to Jack. He paused in his digging as she approached him and leaned on his shovel with a wide grin on his face.

Beth stopped short, whatever she was going to say forgotten at the sight of him without his beard.

'When did you do that?' she asked.

'Do what?'

'You know! Your beard's gone.'

'Oh, that.' He rubbed his chin as if he was surprised to find no hairy mass there. 'I saw the thaw had come this morning, and I thought it was time the beard went too.'

'You look much nicer,' she said. In fact he looked very handsome, for his square jaw and wide mouth were two good features he never should have covered. 'And much younger.'

'I'm glad it meets with your approval,' he said. 'But what were you rushing up here to tell me? Is Queen Victoria dead?'

'Not as far as I know.' Beth laughed. 'I was just excited because the snow is melting.'

'Remember how it was last year?' Jack mused. 'Up to our knees in mud at Lake Bennett and you skipping off to look for spring flowers!'

'Let's go and do that again,' she suggested.

'There won't be any flowers for a while,' he reminded her.

'But there might be in sheltered places. Let's go and look?'

Jack stuck his shovel hard into the ground. 'All right, just to please you.'

As they reached the woods at the top of the hill, the thaw was even more apparent, for the sound of snow plopping from the branches of trees was almost a symphony. Beth made a snowball and threw it at Jack, and he quickly retaliated. She ran for it, but each time she took shelter behind a tree, she made another snowball to hurl at him.

The game went on and on, both of them shrieking with laughter each time they were hit and jeering at each other when they missed.

They had gone further and further into the wood, and Beth found a very big tree to hide behind. Jack was suddenly silent, so she peeped round the tree trunk to see where he was.

Suddenly she felt his hand clamp on to her shoulder. 'Boo!' he shouted, making her nearly jump out of her skin as she hadn't heard him creep up behind her.

She had a snowball ready in her hand, and she brought it

up and pushed it into his face. 'Boo to you too,' she giggled.

He laughed and brushed the snow off his face, but there was still some on his nose. They were only a foot apart, and Beth took off her mitten and reached out to brush the snow away. But as her hand touched his cheek, she suddenly saw something in his eyes. It was the same look she'd seen the last night on the ship before they got to New York. She was so innocent then that she hadn't known what it meant, except that it was special. But she knew what it was now.

Raw longing.

She couldn't take her hand away from his cheek. She had a feeling welling up inside her that was so strong and sweet she felt she might cry. He took her hand and moved it to his mouth, kissing her palm. The warmth and softness of his lips sent an exquisite tingle down her spine.

It was she who moved closer, moving her hand to his cheeks to kiss him on the lips. For a moment or two he didn't move, her lips on his, their bodies not quite touching, but then his hand came up to cup her face and he was kissing her back with such tenderness it made her feel she was an innocent seventeen-year-old again.

How long they stood there kissing she didn't know, but she knew she didn't want it to stop. Every part of her body was tingling with desire, wanting more than kissing but afraid to break away even for a second in case the spell broke.

Snow continued to plop from the trees all around them and the sun felt warm as it slanted across her cheek. In the distance she could hear the clank of a windlass as a miner hauled his bucket of mud out of a hole in the ground, and a bird chirruped on a nearby tree.

It was Jack who drew away first. His bare hands went

back to cup her face and he looked deep into her eyes. 'My beautiful Beth,' he sighed. 'I hope this isn't just a dream and I wake up to find it didn't really happen.'

Chapter Thirty-five

As they stopped outside the cabin to remove their boots, Beth felt awkward. The kissing had happened spontaneously up on the hill and it felt pure and right. But now they were going inside she was very aware that she had to decide whether or not they would move on to the next stage. She wanted to, but she wasn't sure if it was wise.

Jack was her best and closest friend, the one person in the whole world who really knew her inside out. She was afraid of jeopardizing that friendship.

'Scared?' Jack asked as they stepped into the cabin.

'No,' she lied.

'Well, I am,' he admitted, kissing her nose as he took off her hat and ran his fingers through her hair. 'But then I've been dreaming of making love to you ever since I first met you.'

'Really?'

'Yes, really. If you could have read my thoughts sometimes, you would've blushed.'

'You're teasing me?'

'I'm not,' he said, unbuttoning her coat. 'Thoughts of you have kept me warm on many a cold night.'

He dropped her coat on the floor, drew her into his arms and kissed her again. As his tongue flickered against hers, Beth felt the tugging of desire inside her and she knew she was lost and couldn't back away.

Still kissing her, he managed to remove all her clothes down to her chemise, then took her over to the bed and knelt beside it to peel off her stockings. 'I always used to wonder what your legs were like,' he said, running his hand up them while looking into her eyes. 'I saw them as far as your knees once when we were on the raft, and I nearly fell in I was so excited.'

'Oh, Jack,' she said reprovingly.

'You don't like to think I was lusting after you all that time?' he asked, his eyes glinting with mischief as his hands slid further up her thighs, stopping just an inch away from her sex.

Delicious waves of desire had rendered her speechless. All she could do was reach out for him.

He was out of his clothes in a couple of seconds, just long enough for her to pull the blankets back and get under them as the cabin was growing cold. But the moment he was in beside her, his arms around her, she forgot her anxiety, modesty and cold, for his warm, silky skin against hers felt so right.

She had thought Theo, Jefferson and John Fallon all to be good lovers, but they were only mediocre compared with Jack. He used his fingers with such sensitivity, stroking, probing and kissing in such an unhurried way that every nerve in her body came alive. Again and again she reached out to fondle his penis but he always stopped her. It was only when she felt something erupting inside her, and all sense of where she was and even who she was had left her, that he finally entered her, driving forcefully into her as tremendous shock waves engulfed her.

She heard herself cry out, felt tears course down her face, and she knew then that he had taken her to a place that none of her previous lovers had.

Jack propped himself up on one elbow and watched Beth as she lay sleeping next to him, his heart swelling with love for her. It was close to midnight, but there was enough light from the stove and the lantern hanging above it to see her clearly. It was midday when they came into the cabin, and since then he'd made love to her three times, along with making food, washing each other, drinking half a bottle of whisky between them and talking about anything and everything. He thought he ought to be exhausted, but he was too excited to sleep. She had been his first love, his only true love, and now she was finally his.

There had been many other girls during the six years since they first met on the ship. Straitlaced ones, wanton ones, kind girls, cruel girls, happy and sad ones. Some he'd tried to tell himself he loved, others he just made love to and hoped the pleasure he gave them made up for his lack of commitment. But inevitably he was always left with a sense of disappointment.

Beth had always been his lode star, even when he knew she had eyes for no one but Theo. But for her he would still be in New York; he'd never have gone to Montreal, travelled across Canada or come here. He had become her self-appointed guardian just to be near her. He would have done anything for her, even if she never saw him as anything more than a friend.

Now she was here, her slender body curled into his, deep in sleep, her face as soft as a child's. He remembered how she'd looked when they rescued her from the cellar, frozen to the bone and her face haunted by the horror of her imprisonment. Her indignation when she discovered Pearl's place in Philadelphia was a brothel. The night at the hospital in Montreal was etched on his mind too, when she'd cried out for Theo but had to settle for comfort from him.

Her courage on the Chilkoot Pass and her powers of endurance throughout that trail had astounded him. Then,

479

in Dawson, having so recently lost Sam, she lost Molly too. Yet she gritted her teeth and played her heart out night after night in the Nugget. Many stampeders who had no money for drinks had told him they stood outside the saloon to listen to her play. They said she made them feel less hungry and thirsty, and that her music gave them hope they'd find a way to make their fortune.

Jack could understand how they felt, for he had fallen under the spell of her music the very first time he heard it on the ship.

Slipping out of bed, he put a little more wood on the stove to keep it going till morning, and blew out the lantern. In another couple of weeks the river ice would break up, and once again thousands of people would arrive in search of gold.

He smiled, for here in his little cabin he knew he had something far more precious than gold.

A loud whoop of excitement from Oz wafted up the hill to Jack and Beth who were busy at the sluice washing through stones and gravel.

'What's got into him?' Jack said, standing up and moving to a place where he could see what was going on below.

'Most likely he's found a full bottle of whisky he'd forgotten about,' Beth joked.

It was the middle of June. Two weeks earlier the ice had broken up on the creek and Oz's claim had become a slick of glutinous mud. But constant warm sunshine since then had dried the worst of it, grass and wild flowers had sprung up around the cabin and birdsong filled the air.

Beth had never known such happiness. From the moment she opened her eyes in the morning to see Jack beside her, till they fell back into bed late at night, she was filled with the joy of knowing she'd made the right decision to come out here.

They hadn't spoken of love or even of the future, for it seemed unnecessary when it was so clear that they were meant to be together for all time. Beth worked alongside Jack and Oz, shovelling and sluicing the dump piles cheerfully. She didn't mind that it was hard, dirty work, or that at times it seemed pointless. It was enough to be beside Jack, to laugh and chat and feel utterly secure.

Sometimes in the afternoons he would take her fishing on the creek in Oz's little rowing boat, and she would lie back, basking in the sunshine, and greedily contemplate making love when they got back to the cabin. Other times they would tramp up to the woods at the top of the claim and she'd pick flowers while he chopped wood for the stove. Lust often overtook them up there, for there was something deliciously wicked and dangerous about making love in the open air, especially when a bear or even a human could come along and surprise them.

'Let's go down and see what he's up to,' Jack said. 'It's time for something to eat anyway. Maybe a bit of canoodling later would be in order?'

Hand in hand, they ran down the hill to find Oz in a tattered checked shirt with his trousers held up with string, bent over his sluice.

As they approached he looked up, his wide smile revealing his blackened teeth. 'Lookee here at what I've found!' He picked up an old baking soda tin and handed it to them.

It contained four small gold nuggets. Jack shook them out into his palm. 'Jesus Christ!' he exclaimed. 'You found them all together?'

'Yup,' Oz said. 'I've sluiced through five dumps this

morning and nothing, then on the sixth I was left with those.'

'I'm so glad for you, Oz.' Beth went over to him and gave him a hug. 'How marvellous!'

'Which hole did they come out of?' Jack asked, looking around. All the ground to the side of his cabin was full of holes and dumps beside them.

'That one there.' Oz pointed to the one nearest his cabin. 'That one was the last we did. Remember you was afeared I'd fall into it when I came out the cabin?'

Jack smiled and turned to Beth. 'It was just before you came. When he asked me to dig it, I tried to put him off.'

'I suppose you'll be wanting to move the cabin now to dig underneath it?' Beth asked.

Oz grinned. 'Maybe. But first I had it in mind to get myself spruced up and go into town and spread the word around that old Ostrich has struck it rich again. There's been folks laughing at me for a long time. This'll stop 'em.'

'You'll get some eager to buy the claim off you,' Jack reminded him.

'If they offers me enough I just might take it,' he retorted.

Beth looked at Jack in alarm, wondering where that would leave him, but to her surprise he was smiling at Oz. 'You go on into town,' he said. 'We'll do some sluicing down here while you're gone, see if we can find more for you. But look after what you've got there, won't you? That might be all there is!'

An hour later, Jack and Beth waved goodbye to Oz as he went off in the boat to Dawson. His sprucing up consisted only of trimming his beard and changing his clothes into slightly less tattered ones. Beth had made him put the nuggets into a poke around his neck and tucked inside his shirt.

Jack had advised him to deposit them at the bank before he began drinking or playing cards.

'What if he does sell the claim?' Beth asked when they'd waved the older man out of sight. He had left Flash and Silver with them and they remained sitting on the creek bank looking towards where their master had gone.

'I hope he does,' Jack replied. 'He won't last another winter here.'

'But what about you? The new owner won't want you here.'

Jack shrugged. 'I don't mind. If you hadn't turned up I'd have been on my way somewhere else by now.'

'You would?'

He laughed at her surprised look and stroked her cheek. 'I didn't come here for gold, only to get away from Dawson. Now you're with me I could be happy anywhere.'

That was exactly how she felt too, but hearing Jack voice her feelings was wonderful.

'What will *we* do then?' she asked. 'If we're chucked off.'

'Whatever you want,' he said, taking her in his arms. 'My dream has already come true.'

She cupped his face in her hands. 'I love you, Jack Child,' she said.

'You do?' He looked astonished.

'Of course. A hundred per cent. But I expect you to make plans. If you don't I'll start pushing you around.'

'There is no one I would rather be pushed by.' He laughed.

'Aren't you forgetting something?' She playfully bit the end of his nose.

'What?'

'Well, I said I loved you. Aren't you supposed to respond to that?'

'How?' he said.

She knew he was teasing and boxed his ear. 'Say it,' she ordered him.

He caught hold of her round the waist and spun her around. 'I love you, Miss Bossy Bolton. I have for five long years,' he said, still spinning her.

He let go and she wobbled with dizziness. 'That's hardly a romantic way to tell a girl,' she said indignantly.

'I'm more of a practical sort of bloke.' He grinned at her. 'So I'm going to be really romantic now and suggest we get on with sluicing down here for Oz, and see what else we can find for him.'

They found five more small nuggets that afternoon. Jack put them into Oz's tin. 'They must be worth a few hundred dollars,' he said thoughtfully. 'There was a time when I might have pocketed them, but meeting you changed that in me.'

'It did?'

'Yup.' He nodded. 'You were so sparkly clean and honest, I didn't think I'd have any chance with you unless I became that way too. I've got a lot to thank you for.'

Beth was very touched. 'I was a fool not to have realized straight off how right you were for me.'

'Hell, Beth, if we'd settled down and become ordinary folks back in New York it probably would have fallen apart in no time. Look at the adventures we've had together!'

She knew that was his way of saying that he didn't feel bitter about her choosing Theo back then, and that made her love him even more.

Oz didn't come back within a few days as he'd promised. Jack and Beth carried on sluicing, finding no gold amongst Jack's dumps but more small nuggets in Oz's, and they scooped a quantity of gold dust from the bottom of his sluice.

It was glorious weather in the main, though the mosquitoes were irritating, but as the days grew into one week and then two and still Oz didn't return, Jack became worried about him. He had never known him leave his dogs with anyone for that long and they spent all day waiting on the river bank looking out for their master. But Jack didn't dare leave the claim to go and look for him.

News from Dawson City travelled quickly, even out to the farthest creeks, for everyone passing by had something to tell. They had heard that the town was almost completely rebuilt since the fire, with sewerage, electricity, steam heat and telephones being put in. Since the ice broke up, thousands more people had arrived, the rich by sea, and the poor over the trails, and it was said that vast numbers of them were flat broke, tramping around looking for work. Men like Jack who were mining for the claim owners were becoming jittery that their wages would drop with the surplus of workers, and even those who owned the claims were worried that desperate men might try claim-jumping, or come out here to rob.

On 4 July, they heard the bangs and fizz of fireworks from Dawson, a reminder to Beth that it was a year since she'd got the news of Molly's death. But still Oz didn't return.

One afternoon in mid-July, Flash and Silver began howling, and finally Jack spotted Oz rowing his boat back up the creek.

They were overjoyed to see him, but as Oz clambered unsteadily ashore, stinking to high heaven, it was clear he had been drinking solidly for the past few days and they thought the worst.

'Have you lost it all?' Jack asked as he helped the old man to his cabin.

'Yeah, I reckon so,' Oz said before collapsing on to his bed and immediately falling into a dead sleep.

Jack went down to Oz's cabin twice during the evening to check he was all right, but he didn't wake.

'He'll have gambled the claim away,' Jack said sadly as he returned to Beth. 'He's brought nothing back with him but a couple of bottles of whisky. No provisions or anything. I guess we'll have to brace ourselves for moving on quicker than we expected.'

'That's fine,' Beth said. 'Let's get a boat back to Vancouver. I can play in the Globe again, you'll get work easily enough. I've got the money I saved, that will see us through.'

'Would you like to go home?' Jack asked.

'To England?' she asked.

Jack nodded.

'I don't think of it as home any more,' she said thoughtfully. 'There wouldn't be anything there for me.'

'That's how I see it too,' Jack agreed. 'Home is wherever you are. I guess we've got to find the place where we feel we both belong.'

That night their lovemaking had a tinge of sadness because it was the end of an era for them. For weeks they'd enjoyed the kind of total privacy that they knew they'd never get anywhere else, and freedom to do exactly as they pleased. They'd even put the tin bath outside and bathed in the sunshine in the happy knowledge no one could hear or see them. Back in any city they could only expect to find a couple of rooms, with all the noise, smells and disagreements that accompanied crowded conditions.

The following morning Beth made a pile of pancakes and

took them down to Oz; Jack followed on with a pot of coffee. But to their surprise he was sitting on the bench outside his cabin in clean clothes, his beard shaved off and his hair soaking wet.

Beth had always imagined he was at least sixty, but with the beard gone she could see he was twenty years younger.

'Well,' she said, placing the plate of pancakes down on the bench beside him and putting her hands on her hips. 'We expected to find you still sleeping it off. Or are you the younger brother of the Ostrich?'

His smile was a faintly embarrassed one. 'I had a dip in the creek,' he said. 'I guess it was the shock of the cold water that made me shave off the beard. I sure am sorry I left you to look after Silver and Flash so long, but things got sort of complicated.'

'Eat your pancakes while they're hot,' Jack said, and poured coffee for them all. 'So when have we all got to leave here?'

'Olsen will be out later today,' Oz said.

Jack nodded. Olsen the Swede had already made a fortune from his mine on the Eldorado and owned a lot of property in Dawson. A formidable giant of a man and a first-class poker player, he'd probably targeted Oz the moment he heard he was in town with gold.

'It ain't the same in Dawson any more,' Oz said sadly. 'Sure, they've spruced it up, but there's a kinda gloom about the place, like the bubble's burst. And there's ladies arriving now!'

'Well, that's good, isn't it?' Beth said, sitting down on a tree stump. 'There never were enough to go round.'

'They ain't good-time girls.' Oz shook his head as if that grieved him. 'They's real ladies, bankers' wives, society dames, school marms and such with their parasols and fancy hats. Come to settle with their husbands and children too. There's a fancy dress shop now, some Frenchy dame owns it, they reckons you can get the latest Paris fashions there.'

Beth and Jack looked at each other, wondering if this was true or just Oz imagining it. 'How's the Monte Carlo?' Beth asked.

'All painted up again like there never was a fire. Fallon's long gone. They said he high-tailed out of town soon after you left there.'

'What about One Eye?' Jack asked.

'He's still there. They reckon he's got a saloon over in Louse Town and runs a few whores there.'

'So where are you going today then?' Jack asked.

'That depends.'

'On how much you can scrape together here?' Jack asked. 'It's lucky I kept on panning for you while you were gone.' He reached into his pocket and pulled out a small leather bag which contained the nuggets he'd found, and tossed it into the older man's lap. 'Just do me a favour, Oz, and don't gamble that away too. We don't want to think of you broke and cold next winter.'

Oz opened the bag and tipped the nuggets on to his palm, looking up at Jack in shocked surprise.

'There's some gold dust too. I didn't bring that down with me, but I'll get it for you,' Jack added.

'You kept this for me even though you knew you'd have to go?' Oz asked, squinting up at Jack.

'Sure I did, it's not mine to keep.'

'There's not many that honest,' Oz said thoughtfully. 'Reckon I did the right thing after all.'

'You did, Oz,' Jack said, assuming he meant letting him stay and build a cabin on his claim. 'I've been happy here, and since Beth came out, even happier.'

'So are you gonna get hitched?'

Beth giggled. 'He hasn't asked me, Oz. Don't embarrass him.'

'A girl who can make pancakes like these and play the fiddle as sweet as you is worth her weight in gold,' Oz said, stuffing in another mouthful. 'I'll ask her meself, Jack, if you don't look sharp and do it.'

'I ain't gonna ask her in front of you,' Jack said, and grinned. 'But we've got plans to go to Vancouver. I'd better go down the creek and see if someone can row us to Dawson later. We can't all get in your boat, not with the dogs too.'

'You can take my boat. I've got it in mind to walk with the dogs, maybe drop in here and there on some old pals on the way. But first we got some business to do.'

'I'll get the gold dust,' Jack said.

'I didn't mean that, son,' Oz said, getting to his feet and walking into his cabin.

'He'll want me to sign something about giving up the lay,' Jack whispered to Beth.

Oz came back holding a piece of paper in his hand. 'There you are, son,' he said. 'Your ten per cent.'

Jack looked puzzled as he looked at the piece of paper. Beth came closer and saw it was a banker's draft for 20,000 dollars, made payable to Jack Child.

She gasped. 'You sold the claim for two hundred thousand?' she exclaimed.

'You didn't lose it in a poker game to Olsen?' Jack asked.

''Course I didn't. I seen too many men go down that way.' Oz chuckled. 'I won some money and lost it too, got myself drunker than I thought possible. But I weren't gonna gamble that away. I sold it to Olsen.'

'But why give me ten per cent?' Jack asked, his voice shaking with emotion.

489

'Cos you've looked after me good all winter. Been like a son to me. Besides, if you hadn't dug them holes, I'd never have found more gold. Word in Dawson was that I was all washed up. Olsen wouldn't have given me ten cents for the claim without seeing some gold.'

'I can't take it,' Jack said, tears glinting in his eyes. 'It's too much!'

'You took a lay here, you might a struck gold yerself any time. Only fair I give you a share. We've been pardners, ain't we?'

Jack looked stunned. He kept glancing at the banker's draft and then back to Oz.

'You clinched it when you gave me those nuggets,' Oz said. 'I'm gonna spread it around Honest Jack is gonna marry Gypsy Queen. Think of it as a wedding present.'

Chapter Thirty-six

'We'll stay at the Fairview Hotel tonight,' Jack said as he tied the boat up at the shore in Dawson. 'You put on your prettiest dress and later we'll parade up and down Front Street.'

'I'll have to get my good clothes from the restaurant,' she said absentmindedly, distracted by all the new buildings erected since the fire. It was as though the disaster had never happened except that the replacement shops, saloons and dance halls were more substantial and grander than before.

There were also thousands of people milling around. Many of them were just as shabbily dressed and weary-looking as the newcomers had been the previous year, but it was staggering how many were fashionably dressed, city-type folk. As Oz had said, there were also a great many very respectable-looking women and children.

Beth had heard that a railway had been built to take passengers from Skagway over the White Pass, but she doubted any of these smart people had come that way, for not one of them looked capable of building a boat and sailing on down the Yukon.

A man in a tailed coat, striped trousers and top hat was walking arm in arm with a woman wearing white muslin and a large pin hat trimmed with roses, seemingly unaware that her dress was trailing in the dust. Another woman in a very elegant brocade jacket and toning skirt was perched on a leather trunk, the kind Beth had only ever seen being carried from first class on the ship coming to America.

There were similarly well-dressed men and women everywhere, and she couldn't imagine why they had come. What did they hope to find in this little pioneer town which was cut off from the Outside for eight months of the year?

As they began to walk down Front Street, Beth carrying her fiddle and one small bag, and Jack carrying the rest of their belongings, she felt as if she was having one of those strange dreams where she was in a familiar place, but nothing was as it should be.

It had been like that since they woke preparing themselves for buying the very cheapest tickets out of here, and a struggle ahead of them in Vancouver.

Then, without any warning, they were rich.

While that was the best of surprises, there was sadness too at saying goodbye to a place where they'd found so much happiness. Then, after the emotional farewell to Oz, they rowed here, an eerie reminder of how they had arrived a year earlier, still wrapped in grief at losing Sam.

Last year, as they'd walked down this very street in thick mud, they'd been cheechakos, the local word for greenhorns, excited, frightened, weary, expectant and totally confused. Dawson City had changed them. It couldn't have been otherwise for it was like being thrown into a huge mixer where the outrageous characters, the dawn-to-dusk frivolity, hardships, overcrowding, lax morality and visions of fortunes being made tossed everyone out slightly changed.

Beth wondered now if she would ever be able to fit into conventional society again. She had been mulling this thought over on the boat ride, hardly speaking at all, and as Jack had been silent too she guessed he was as apprehensive about coming back here as she was.

'We'll be fine, we've got each other,' Jack said suddenly,

as if he'd read her thoughts. 'If we want, we can leave on the very next boat.'

Beth flashed a grateful smile at him. She found it remarkable that he always seemed to know what she was thinking.

At eight that evening, they were almost ready to go out and look around the town. They had been given one of the best rooms at the Fairview. It was sumptuous, with a thick carpet, fancy French furniture, a feather mattress and velvet drapes at the window. Beth thought cynically that it was a shame the owners hadn't made any effort to make the interior walls more robust. She and Jack could hear every word the people in the next room were saying.

They'd collected Beth's clothes from the restaurant, cashed the banker's draft, and Jack had bought a smart new suit, had his hair cut and his best shoes polished.

Beth was tying his bow tie for him when a knock came on the door. Jack opened it to find the young uniformed bellboy holding out a letter. 'This came for Miss Bolton,' he said. 'They said I was to wait for your reply.'

Surprised and puzzled, Beth opened it to see it was from Percy Turnball, the current owner of the Monte Carlo.

Dear Miss Bolton, she read.
I was delighted to hear the news that you and Mr Child are back in town. I would consider it a very great honour if you would both come to the Monte Carlo tonight as my guests, and hope you might consider playing a couple of numbers for all those who have missed you so sorely. Your humble servant. P. Turnball.

She handed it to Jack to read. 'What d'you think?'

'Is he the Scotsman they used to call "Big Balls"?' Jack asked. 'The big bloke with a diamond tie pin who used to come in the Nugget?'

Beth giggled. Dolores had called him Percy the Pig, because he had very small dark eyes and a high colour. Like One Eye, he went in for loud checked suits, but he was a decent, generous man, and she had liked him.

'Yes, fancy him ending up owning the Monte! Shall we go?'

'If you want to. Maybe it would be good for you to play here one last time.'

Beth turned to the bellboy. 'Tell him we'll be delighted to come.'

It was nine o'clock before they got to the Monte Carlo. A pianist was playing but they could barely hear him for the noise in the crowded saloon. As Beth and Jack walked in, people turned their heads to look at them and a kind of buzz went around the room.

'That's her,' Beth heard one man say. 'She's even prettier than they said.'

Percy Turnball must have noticed the stir because he came pushing his way through the crowd to meet them.

'Welcome to you both,' he said, his big florid face breaking into a wide smile. 'There was a good deal of jubilation when you were seen coming into town earlier today. You're one of the legends of Dawson, Miss Bolton, even the cheechakos have heard of you and were disappointed they couldn't get to hear you play. As for you, Jack, I've heard tales that you were attacked by a bear, struck it rich and married our Gypsy Queen in secret. Are any of them true?'

Jack laughed. 'Just tall tales. If I marry the Gypsy Queen it won't be in secret.'

Turnball slapped him on the back. 'Good for you. I always did think you two were good together. Let's have some champagne to celebrate you being back here.'

*

Turnball led them to a table he had reserved and the bartender brought over champagne in a silver bucket. It was far better quality than the stuff Fallon used to give Beth, and the glasses were real crystal.

Dozens of people she'd never seen before came up to the table to say how thrilled they were to meet her. It was a good feeling, and with Jack holding her hand under the table, the anxiety she'd felt earlier in the day disappeared.

There were many familiar faces in the crowd, all qualifying for the title of Sourdough now they'd spent a winter here. Some had been fresh-faced boys back in Skagway, innocents who had left their small towns in search of a dream. Now they were rugged men who could turn their hand to anything. As they were still here, that meant they'd found some sort of niche, even if they hadn't struck gold.

Here and there were the dance-hall and saloon girls with their gaudy dresses and elaborate hair styles. They might look plump, pretty and welcoming, but most were calculating, tough and mercenary. Yet they had injected Dawson with glamour and no doubt given comfort to many a miner, even if he was down on his luck.

Other faces, equally familiar to Beth, were of those who had set up businesses here. Some she'd met on the trail, some came by other routes, but they were entrepreneurs all. A lot of them had lost everything in fires, for even before the big one in April there had been many others. Defeat was not in their nature; as one venture crashed, they began another. Doggedly determined, with steel in their spines, they would probably survive anything life threw at them.

Yet the majority of the customers were strangers to Beth. Among them were the latest cheechakos, gaunt-looking men in shabby mackinaws and high trail boots, yet most of the strangers were sleek, well dressed and prosperous looking.

'They are just tourists,' Turnball said disparagingly when he caught her curious stare. 'No trails and hardships for them; they've come with their leather trunks, even their maids in some cases, just to say they've seen Dawson City. None of us knew last year that newspapers all over the world were following everything that went on here. Some of these newcomers know more about us than we do ourselves! Of course, there's still plenty coming here thinking they'll find gold, but more just want to see what it is all about.'

At ten Turnball got up on the small stage and banged on a cymbal to get everyone's attention.

'Ladies and gentlemen,' he said when the place was hushed. 'All of you here will have heard some of the legends of the Klondike. Even if you came here the easy way by boat, you know about those courageous ones who defied death on the infamous Chilkoot and White Passes, carrying their kit on their backs.

'The little lady I've got here tonight climbed the Chilkoot in February last year. She lost her brother to drowning in the Squaw Rapids too. But she battled on here, carrying her famous fiddle, and enchanted us all with her music.

'I remember the first time I heard her play, and it was in this very saloon, just a couple of days after she'd arrived. Her reputation had gone before her, but I hadn't expected that the English fiddle player that captured hearts in Skagway would be a mere slip of a girl.

'That night she brought tears to my eyes, she made my feet tap and my heart sing, and like every other man in town I was dazzled by her guts, talent and beauty.'

Turnball turned towards Beth, indicating she was to come up on stage.

With a flamboyant, open-armed gesture, he raised his voice to a boom. 'I give you now, our very own darling. The world-famous Beth Bolton, the Klondike Gypsy Queen!'

To a round of applause Beth jumped up on to the stage with her fiddle in her hand and dropped a curtsey to the huge crowd beneath her. For old times' sake she began with 'Kitty O'Neill's Champion,' and within seconds the crowd were tapping their feet and smiling up at her. Next was 'The Days of '49', the old 'California Gold Rush Jig', then 'The Lass of Glenshee'.

She paused to tumultuous applause. Waving her bow for silence, she addressed her audience.

'I composed this next number myself,' she said. 'I hope you'll hear in it the blizzard blowing in my face on the Chilkoot Pass, the saws of the boat builders on Lake Bennett, and our joy at setting sail when the ice broke. A middle section is the heartbreak of my brother's drowning, and the beauty of the Yukon in spring. Finally, there is the gaiety of Dawson City at the end of the trail.'

Jack had heard her playing something beautiful many times while he was working at Oz's claim, a number he hadn't heard before. He had thought it was a classical piece, and had always meant to ask her to play it one evening, for him.

Now, as she began to play, he realized this was what he'd heard before. From the achingly beautiful, chill-to-the-bone opening bars, he found himself reliving the Chilkoot Pass. He could feel himself bent almost double with the load on his back and dragging the sledge behind him as he struggled onwards and upwards through the snow. Somehow she'd managed to portray in her music the desperation, exhaustion and fear all the stampeders went through. Yet at the time he only remembered her smiling brightly whenever he looked at her.

497

There was gay humour in the saws of Lake Bennett, and he noticed many of the Sourdoughs looking at one another and smiling as they recalled their bitter arguments.

Everyone in the audience, whether they'd been on the trail or not, could feel the joy of setting sail, for Beth had managed to inject the flavour of a sailor's hornpipe, the fluttering of wind in the sails and even the warmth of the spring sunshine on their backs.

A fast, spine-tingling passage mirrored the thrill and terror of the rapids in Miles Canyon, but it flowed into a plaintive memorial to Sam. Jack could see him as they pulled him from the water, dark red blood from the wound on his head staining his blond hair. He could picture Beth kneeling beside his body, her sobs cutting through him like a knife. And then laying him to rest in his riverside grave, and singing 'Rock of Ages' after they'd prayed over him.

A lump came up in Jack's throat because all this was in the music. When he looked around him he could see that even those in the audience who knew nothing of Sam or the Miles Canyon understood Beth's anguish.

In her portrayal of the voyage on down the Yukon, all her heartbreak and feeling of hopelessness were there, but she'd also managed to paint in the beauty of the winding river, the surrounding mountains, spring flowers, and moose drinking at the water's edge.

On that journey, they had come upon Dawson suddenly. Beth illustrated this by an abrupt change of tempo. All at once her composition was frantic, loud and gay, prompting Jack to remember the market by the shore, the thick mud, the thousands of people. She had the Spielers there, shouting out that their saloon, restaurant or dance hall was the best. She portrayed the romantic 'Long Juicy Waltz', so heavily promoted by the kings of the dance halls. Men soon discovered their dollar bought only one minute to hold the girl in his arms, yet some spent a hundred dollars a night for that privilege.

A touch of burlesque in the theatre at the Monte, saucy, vulgar, but never indecent or the Mounties would close it down. The faro tables, the girls in Paradise Alley, the howling of dogs, the drunks, the losers and the winners, they were all there in Beth's music, and Jack had never been more proud of her.

He looked at her up on the stage, head bent over her fiddle, dark curls tumbling down her back, her slender body moving sensuously with the music. He realized she'd grown from a pretty girl into a beautiful woman in the years he'd known her, without him noticing the changes.

As the piece ended and Beth lowered her bow, the audience went wild. Those sitting leapt up, stamping their feet, clapping their hands and cheering. On and on it went, everyone calling for an encore. But Beth smiled and shook her head, mouthed her thanks to the audience for she couldn't be heard above the applause, and turned to leave the stage.

Jack understood why. That composition of her own had drained her. All the pain, hardships, joys and delights were in it. She couldn't surpass it, and didn't even want to try.

They couldn't leave Dawson the following day as they'd hoped, for all the boats were fully booked, but Jack managed to get them a first-class cabin on the *Maybelline* on 3 August, in five days' time.

The following afternoon, while out on her own buying a few things she needed, Beth spotted Dolores, who used to work in the Golden Nugget, coming out of a grocery shop. She was heavily pregnant.

When she saw Beth she came running over, almost breathless with excitement at seeing her. 'I was so worried about you when you disappeared. No one seemed to know where you'd gone!' she exclaimed.

'I went off to Bonanza to stay with Jack,' Beth explained. 'I'd had enough of Dawson. But what about you? Where did you go after the Nugget burned down?'

Dolores laughed. 'That fire was a lucky break for me. I met Sol that night, he was one of the firemen. He took me back to his place and we've been together ever since.'

They chatted for some time, Beth telling her that she and Jack were going off to Vancouver. Dolores said she helped out in the laundry, and Sol was building an extra room on to their cabin for the baby.

'So when is it due?' Beth asked, pleased to hear it had all worked out for the girl.

'Well, the doctor thinks it's going to be in November,' Dolores said. 'But we can't be sure of the date cos I can't remember when I had my last do-da.'

Beth smiled at Dolores' name for menstruation. Having ascertained that Sol appeared to be delighted he was going to be a father and that Dolores was well and happy, she said goodbye and went back to the Fairview.

Thinking over their conversation as she walked, it suddenly occurred to Beth that she hadn't had a do-da either for some time. She could remember having one soon after she got to Jack's, and a second one which must have been a month later in early June, but nothing since then.

Because she'd been told back in Montreal that she'd never get pregnant again, she'd had no reason to expect or want any man to be careful, and it certainly never occurred to her that the doctor could have been wrong.

Back in the room at the Fairview, she looked carefully at

herself in the mirror. She could see nothing different about herself, she certainly didn't feel any different either, yet she was over a month late. What if she was pregnant?

She closed her eyes and held her stomach, wishing with all her heart that she was. To have Jack's baby would be the very best thing in the whole world.

But she said nothing to him when he returned. She needed to be sure first, and as he'd run into some old friends that afternoon and was full of their news, it was easy for her to hide her excitement.

The following day, Jack went off to help someone build a new cabin, and Beth tried to put the thought of a baby right out of her mind by going to visit some old friends. But it didn't work; whether it was just the power of suggestion, or for real, her breasts felt tender, and she'd even had a touch of nausea in the morning. She chatted and laughed as she visited people, but foremost in her mind was how happy Jack was going to be when it was confirmed.

On the evening of the 31st, a rumour ran round Dawson that gold had been found in Nome on the Bering Sea in Alaska.

Beth and Jack first heard about it from a fellow guest who'd just received a telegraph from a friend somewhere nearby. They thought nothing of it, for there had been a rumour about another new gold strike back in January, and many men had rushed off to it, some of them so ill prepared they got frostbite, only to find it was a hoax.

But when they walked down Front Street later, everyone was talking about it. In the saloon they went into, men were saying that the gold was just lying on the beach waiting to be picked up, and all of them were intending to leave for Nome as soon as they could get a passage.

The rumour spread like wildfire, and suddenly all the men

with vacant expressions who had been spending their days lounging around on the boardwalk had that old familiar fire in their eyes.

Jack found it very funny. He roared with laughter when an old Sourdough stopped him in Front Street to ask if he'd be going. 'Not me,' he said. 'I've had enough of gold fever to last me a lifetime. I just want to go home with my girl.'

The following day, the whole town was buzzing with excitement. People were fighting to get on to boats, and when they couldn't get tickets were commandeering pole and row boats to sail themselves.

Jack seemed to find the whole thing very disturbing, and said he was going off for a tramp up the hills. Before he left, he peeled off five hundred dollars from their stash of money and suggested Beth went to Madame Aubert to buy something smart and fashionable to wear in Vancouver.

The Frenchwoman was a marvellous dressmaker, but she also had ready-made clothes in her shop that were the latest fashions from Paris.

'I can't buy something there,' Beth said in horror. 'She's too expensive.'

Jack laughed. 'We're rich now, and all your clothes will look very shabby in Vancouver. Besides, with so many people leaving for Nome, I bet you can beat her down in price.'

Beth wanted a new dress, but she told Jack five hundred dollars was far too much to give her.

'You hang on to it,' he said. 'You'll need shoes and other things too.'

Jack was a little distant over dinner that evening. Beth had found a lovely costume at Madame Aubert's, a dark green and cream striped peplum-style jacket with a matching plain green skirt, and a little green hat with a veil. She was excited about it, and all the gossip she'd got from the Frenchwoman, and she felt rather disappointed that Jack wasn't more receptive.

She had a couple of glasses of whisky after the meal and it went straight to her head. She could barely stand, and Jack helped her up to the room and into bed.

'I think I'll go out for a bit of a wander and see what's going on,' he said. 'It's too early for me to go to sleep. Sweet dreams.'

Beth was woken abruptly in the morning by noise in the street below. But to her surprise she was alone in the bed. She got up and looked out of the window to see what the noise was about, only to see hundreds and hundreds of men with packs on their backs heading down to the landing stage.

It was just like it had been two years ago in Vancouver, and she assumed Jack had slipped out quietly to watch. But when she looked back at the bed, it didn't look as if he'd slept there. No indentation on the pillow, and the sheets and blankets were still tucked in on his side.

Yet even more curious was that his new suit was hanging on the back of the chair, his best boots beside it. He must've come back here last night when she was asleep and changed into his old clothes.

She looked in the closet and saw his bag of tools was gone too. Jack had always been a sucker for a hard luck story, and if someone had asked for his help last night, he would've found it hard to refuse. But what she didn't understand was why, if he came back here for old clothes and his tools, he hadn't either woken her to tell her where he was going or left her a note.

She felt nauseous again, but decided that was due to

hunger, and went downstairs to have some breakfast, hoping there might be a note from Jack at the reception desk.

But there was no note, and she had to rush out of the dining room to be sick after just smelling the coffee.

Back in the room, she sat by the open window looking down at the men trooping past the hotel, and suddenly her heart contracted with fear. Could Jack have left for Nome?

That seemed an absurd thought, for he'd shown nothing more than amusement and curiosity about the gold strike. He'd even said that if prospecting for gold here was hard, it would be even worse there, for Nome was almost in the Arctic Circle.

Yet a cold chill ran down her spine, for this whole town wouldn't exist but for the irrationality and greed which gold brought out in men. She couldn't even say that there was only one kind who would succumb to the lure of it, for she knew they came from every walk of life, and honest, decent men were far more common than crooks and swindlers.

She also knew that how much money a man already had made no difference, for she'd seen men with fortunes lose it all at the turn of a card. Theo had his dream come true when he got the Golden Nugget, yet he'd sold it behind her back and disappeared with the money. Why should she think Jack was any different?

She turned from the window and looked at the bed. They'd put the money in a cloth bag under the mattress after they got it from the bank. Jack had only kept back about a thousand dollars, and five hundred of that he'd given to her. If the bag was gone, so was he, just like Theo.

Shaking with nerves, she gingerly approached the bed and lifted the mattress. She slid her hand under it, but could feel nothing. An involuntary cry of despair came from deep within her. She ran her hands right round the bed, and on finding nothing, grabbed the mattress and tossed it on to the floor. But there was nothing beneath it, just the thin horsehair padding above the springs.

The shock made her reel, for however much she had rationalized that Jack was no different to other men, in her heart she'd felt he could never do anything so low.

He'd claimed he didn't come here for the gold, only to be near her, and she'd believed that.

The betrayal was too much to bear, far worse than what Theo had done, for she'd always known he was a wild card. But Honest Jack, the man she had trusted implicitly for so many years, her comforter, her friend, how could he do this to her?

Sobbing hysterically, she flung herself down on to the bedding. She remembered how he'd pressed those five hundred dollars into her hands and said she couldn't arrive in Vancouver looking like a pauper.

The rat must have been planning his escape then, and only gave her that money to salve his conscience so she wouldn't be utterly destitute.

How could he do that to her?

Chapter Thirty-seven

Beth lay crying on the heap of bedding for hours. As the tickets were still there on the dressing table it seemed obvious to her that Jack wanted her to leave on the boat in the morning. That way he'd be free to go with that deranged brotherhood of men who would rather spend their lives in stinking shacks in remote places, dreaming of finding gold, than have a wife and family who loved them.

She relived the past few weeks, trying to see if she'd ignored something which might have been a hint that Jack wasn't as deeply committed to her as she'd believed him to be.

There was the moment when she said she loved him and he had stalled on saying he loved her too. Yet at the time she'd thought that was just teasing.

She knew he had been happy out in Bonanza, but perhaps she'd been presumptuous to think he could be happier still living with her in the Outside. Now she came to think of it, he hadn't ever talked about how he intended to make a living when they left Dawson.

His silence on the boat trip to Dawson looked suspicious now too. She'd thought he was merely stunned by Oz giving him the money, but what if it was because he felt he was being drawn into a trap?

That seemed laughable, but maybe to a man who liked a simple life well away from others, the prospect of living in a real house, surrounded by staid, respectable people, was a living death.

Yet surely he knew he could voice such fears to her? So

perhaps it was in the Monte Carlo that he began drawing back? When Percy Turnball spoke of her being a legend, perhaps Jack was afraid he would always be in her shadow? That he would be expected to mould himself around her playing, and never again be able to choose how he wanted to live?

But why would he think that? She thought she'd made it plain enough that she didn't care about anything other than him. Even playing her fiddle was secondary; she was just as happy playing for him alone and no longer craved an audience.

Would he have gone if she'd told him she thought she was carrying his child?

In the early evening Beth's pride roused her from the floor.

'If he'd rather be scrabbling around in the Arctic with a bunch of half-wits than going off on the boat to Vancouver with me, then that's his funeral,' she said to herself.

She slung the mattress back on to the bed and threw the covers over it, washed her face in the basin and scowled at her swollen eyes.

'You will not cry any more,' she told her image in the mirror. 'You'll go down to the dining room, eat a good meal, then pack your things ready for tomorrow. You won't let anyone see you care that he's gone.'

'I'd like someone to help me to the boat with my luggage, please,' Beth asked the hotel manager as she paid the bill the following morning.

The lobby was full of people departing for Nome, and though hardly any of them looked capable of braving an Arctic winter, they appeared to be following like sheep because so many others were leaving.

'Of course, Miss Bolton,' the manager said, smiling slimily at her. 'Mr Child will be meeting you there?'

'Yes, he will. He's been called away on business,' she said, smarting because the weasel had made a point of calling her Miss Bolton to show he knew she wasn't married to Jack.

She had packed Jack's new clothes, for if she'd left them in the room that would make it obvious she'd been abandoned, but she thought the manager knew that already, and was relishing her distress.

The bellboy walked behind her along Front Street with the luggage on a small handcart. The street was packed with people departing Dawson, and she guessed the boat would be grossly overcrowded as captains were like everyone else, only too happy to make a fast buck. But at least all the extra people would only be going as far as St Michael before jumping off to find some other way of reaching their destination.

Beth kept her head up high as she walked along. She might have a broken heart, but she knew she looked good in her new costume, with her hair pinned up under her hat. Yet all the same she dreaded seeing anyone she knew, for they were bound to ask where Jack was.

The *Maybelline* was a small but sturdy-looking steamer and relatively new, unlike most of the boats that had been pressed into service during the previous year. One of the crew took Beth's luggage and showed her to her cabin which was up on the top deck. It was tiny, with only a foot of floor space next to the bunks, but as she'd seen how crowded it was down on the lower two decks, she didn't care. Putting her luggage on the bottom bunk, she climbed on to the upper one and lay there watching the scene on the wharf through the tiny porthole.

If she hadn't felt so miserable, she might have laughed to

see people fighting to reach the front of the queue for tickets, then trying to bribe the crew to get them aboard. She didn't understand their desperation. Only people you loved were worth fighting for. She'd certainly have fought tooth and nail to save Sam, and turned her back on a fortune if it had meant Molly could stay alive and well back in England.

The boat was juddering with the sound of hobnailed boots stomping across its deck. Outside her cabin she could hear a man with a booming voice complaining that his cabin was too small, and the crew member responding by telling him in no uncertain terms that if he didn't like it he could get off the boat and he'd sell his tickets to someone else for double.

A woman's voice piped up then, saying it was a disgrace that the boat was so overcrowded. She got a similar reply to the one given to the male complainant.

Beth got down off the bunk when she heard the steam horn blast out to hurry the last stragglers on board. She felt she had to take one last look at the place which two years earlier she'd set off for with such excitement.

The window was only a square foot of glass and it didn't open, so her view was limited only to what was directly in front of it: just a group of young men with kitbags, heavy coats and shovels, still hoping they might be allowed on at the last minute. Behind them was a saloon, the fancy carved decoration on its facade suggesting the interior would be equally lavish. But it was a false image; inside it was little better than a shed, and tears welled up in Beth's eyes for it seemed to symbolize how she'd been suckered into believing Jack was the real thing. She had believed he had no false facade, no tricks or cons. Honest Jack, a man she could depend on, who could be her friend, her love, her everything.

She was certain now that his baby was growing inside her, for she'd felt that nausea again as soon as she smelled coffee this morning. She knew she would love the baby despite Jack's betrayal. Perhaps in time she would even forgive him. But she also knew she would never trust another man, not for as long as she lived.

Her view was out of focus because her eyes were swimming. She saw a man running behind the men in the queue, and although she only saw him for a brief second, she had the fleeting impression that he was tall, with dark hair. Her heart leapt involuntarily, yet she turned away from the window, irritated that she could imagine it was Jack.

But then she heard shouting and she pricked up her ears, for the man yelling that his wife had his ticket sounded just like Jack.

She was out through the cabin door and running down the steps to the crowded lower deck like the wind. There were passengers and luggage taking up every inch of space, but beyond them she could see the crew had already pulled in the gangplank and cast off, and on the wharf, with the boat moving slowly away from it, was Jack, red-faced and furious.

'That's my husband,' she shouted, jumping over cases and kitbags and pushing people aside. 'Let him on, please!'

The crew looked round at her in surprise. Jack took a few steps back, then ran forward and leapt out to the boat.

There was a united gasp from all the passengers on the lower deck, for the gap between boat and wharf was widening fast.

Beth clamped her hand over her mouth, for it seemed that Jack was suspended in space and would surely land in the water. But he landed on the boat with less than an inch to spare, falling forward on to his knees.

He was filthy and unshaven, but to Beth he looked wonderful. She ran forward, arms outstretched to hug him.

'Thank God I made it,' he panted as she ran to him. 'You would've thought I'd run out on you!'

Ten minutes later in their cabin, Jack was still breathless. 'I had to go to see to Oz,' he wheezed out. 'He'd been attacked. Willy the Whistle couldn't get him in his boat.'

It was some little time before he got his breath back to explain fully. He was on his way back to the hotel the night he'd left her to go for a wander, when Willy the Whistle (so named because he played a penny whistle), an old-timer who'd been panning for gold around Dawson for years before the stampede began, shouted for him to stop.

Earlier in the evening, Willy had been in his cabin in the woods, some four or five miles from Oz's claim, when he heard dogs barking and scraping at the door. He recognized them immediately as Flash and Silver, and knowing that they'd come for help, he followed them through the woods. About a mile away he found Oz lying in the undergrowth, badly beaten up, barely conscious and bleeding from a knife wound in his chest.

Willy was only a small man, and though he managed to rig up a rough stretcher and, with the dogs pulling it, succeeded in getting Oz to his cabin, he knew he didn't have the strength to get Oz down to his boat and into it. So he shoved an old towel into Oz's wound, gave him some whisky, and leaving him with his dogs to guard him, rowed into Dawson to get help.

Jack explained that he came back to the hotel to change into his old clothes, but as he was in such a hurry and expected to be back by morning anyway, he didn't think to leave a note or even wake Beth.

When he and Willy got back to the cabin it was still dark,

but on examining Oz Jack felt that moving him into the boat to take him to hospital might kill him. So he patched him up as best he could, and sent Willy off again to get a doctor while he stayed there.

'I told him to go and tell you where I was,' Jack said. 'But the idiot drank the best part of a bottle of whisky on the way, fell asleep and drifted past Dawson. I was stuck out at Willy's cabin, with no boat to go for help, and I couldn't leave Oz anyway. By the time Willy had woken up, nearly killed himself rowing back to Dawson against the current and got a doctor, it was late last night. The doctor came out in his own boat with another man at first light. I came back here with them. Once Oz was in the hospital, I ran round to the Fairview, but you'd already left.'

'I thought you'd left me and gone to Nome,' she blurted out. She was ashamed now that she'd doubted him, for the blood and dirt on his clothes and his exhaustion were ample evidence that he was telling her the truth.

'How could you think that?' he exclaimed, his eyes full of hurt. 'Surely you know you are the most important thing in the world to me? I wouldn't trade you for a ton of gold. I love you, Beth.'

'But you'd taken your tool bag and the money,' she said weakly. 'What else was there to think?'

'I took my tools in case I needed them,' he said. 'But I didn't take the money. That was in the safe at the Fairview.'

He put his hand into his shirt and pulled out the money bag. 'I put it in the safe after I gave you the money for your dress. Word had got around about Oz giving it to me. I was afraid we'd be robbed.'

'The manager didn't tell me,' she said.

Jack shook his head in disbelief. 'That arsewipe,' he hissed. 'Bet he hoped I wouldn't come back and he could keep it. He looked surprised to see me. I ran like the wind from there, no time to even wash myself. And I can't even hug you now to make up for it all, I'll mess up your nice outfit.'

'I can get water for you to wash, and I brought your clothes with me because I didn't want everyone to find out you'd run out on me.'

Jack smiled. 'Run out on you! If I'd had to swim to catch up with the boat I would have.'

Beth felt all the tension and hurt inside her fading away. 'How is Oz now?'

'He'll pull through. The chest wound needed stitching, and the Mounties will be rounding up the blokes who did it. Luckily he'd left all his money in the bank here at Dawson, and he'd even put the nuggets I found in a bag and tied them to Flash's collar.'

'But why didn't the dogs defend Oz?' she asked.

'Willy and I were mystified by that too. But Oz came round enough on the way to hospital to tell us he'd been drinking with two blokes he thought were pals, in their cabin, which was about a mile from Willy's. He tied the dogs up outside. I guess the men thought Oz had the money on him, and greed made them set about him. But they scarpered when they didn't find anything on him, and Oz crawled out and let the dogs loose.'

'Some pals!' she exclaimed. 'If the dogs hadn't been so clever he might have died out there.'

Beth got a bucket of water for Jack to wash, and once he was clean he hugged and kissed her. 'I'd like to show you just how much I love you,' he said softly. 'But after two nights without any sleep I don't think I could prove my point.'

Leaving him to sleep, Beth went out on the top deck to watch the river. She had been told that Yukon was the Indian name for 'Greatest' and she thought it was well named, for it was over 2,000 miles long, ranging from deep and narrow stretches through canyons and sharp bends, to miles wide where it slopped over flat land. The glacial water was so cold in the rapids that if a man fell in he would die from that alone, or be sucked to the bottom in minutes by its strong and deadly current.

But it was so beautiful too, sometimes emerald green, sometimes turquoise. Caribou and moose waded in its shallows, ducks and geese idled in its more placid water, and swallows nested in its banks. Yet she had loved it in winter too, when the ice was four feet thick and she and Jack had sped along its bumpy surface on a sledge, with Flash and Silver pulling them.

She looked around at the other passengers sitting on the decks, squashed up with their luggage, and felt sad for them that they weren't seeing the beauty of this country, only craving the riches they could take from it.

Coming here had been a complete education. A lifetime in England or even New York would never have tested her, pummelled or taught her as much as the two years spent here. She could live without comfort now, make a meal out of anything, knew that the human body could endure far more than anyone would suppose.

But the greatest, most important thing of all, and she'd only realized she'd learned it today, was the knowledge of who she was and that she was capable of being independent. She had been horrified and terribly saddened by the thought that Jack had run off and left her, yet she hadn't been frightened of the prospect of coping alone.

Last night as she packed her bags she felt that was it, the

sad end of a chapter, and there was nothing for it but to go on to a new one. She knew that when she arrived in Vancouver, she was capable of getting herself a place to live, and work. She wouldn't have crumbled because she was alone.

Even the prospect of bringing their child up alone hadn't frightened her. She might have chosen to call herself Mrs for convention's sake, but not because she was ashamed. She was a musician, and a good one, and she would always get work somewhere.

She was of course overjoyed and relieved that Jack had turned up. But in a way she was glad she'd had this chance to discover she had grown into a strong, dignified and capable woman.

'When should I tell him about the baby?' she murmured to herself, putting her hand under her jacket on to her stomach. She was certain there was one, but perhaps it would be better to wait until a doctor had confirmed it.

Jack didn't wake until the daylight was fading. He opened his eyes as Beth came into the cabin and smiled.

'Feeling better?' she asked, bending over to stroke his face.

'I am now I'm with you,' he said, taking her hand in his and kissing it. 'I got a fright thinking you were going without me. I wouldn't have got another boat for days and I would have had no way of contacting you.'

'And I wouldn't have been meeting every boat in the hope you were on it,' she said teasingly.

He smiled, studying her face. 'I would have tracked you down eventually. I'd have run round Vancouver putting up posters saying, "Missing! Fiddle-playing Gypsy Queen. Reward given for information".'

'What are we going to do when we get there?' she asked, gently pushing him over so she could sit on the bunk with him.

'Whatever you want to do,' he replied. 'We could get another boat down to California to be warm all winter. New York, Philadelphia, Constantinople, Paris or Rome, we can go anywhere we fancy. What do you want to do?'

'Just to be with you,' she said. 'In a warm, quiet house with a proper kitchen and a bathroom. I want you at home with me every evening.'

He looked at her quizzically. 'No grandiose plans for another saloon? A shop, a boarding house?'

She shook her head.

'But you've got something up your sleeve? I can sense it!'

'Maybe,' she said, lying down beside him and wrapping her arms around him. 'But for now there's just the two of us, scrunched up in this tiny bunk, so we should make the most of it.'

Acknowledgements

I would like to thank all those who helped me in my research into the Klondike Gold Rush.

Malcolm Latchem was a great help with background information about violin playing and the folk music of this period. Thank you, Malcolm, you made me wish I'd persisted with learning the violin beyond 'Twinkle, Twinkle, Little Star'.

A big thank you to Patrick Griffin of Wexus Travellers' Club, who made all my travel arrangements for the complicated journey following in the footsteps of my heroine to Alaska and on to Dawson City in Canada. His knowledge, enthusiasm and sense of humour made it seem a much less daunting trip.

I read every book I could get my hands on about the Gold Rush and its characters, but the two which stood out over all the others were by Pierre Berton, Canada's leading historian. *Klondike, the Last Great Gold Rush, 1868–1899*, was simply marvellous. Exciting, fantastically descriptive, a book everyone should read to get the full picture of the madness of gold fever. *The Klondike Quest*, also by Berton, is a photographic essay of the same story. With fabulous photographs along with the narrative, you can almost feel you were there.

Special thanks to Bombay Peggy's, the one-time brothel I stayed at in Dawson City, which managed to re-create the decadence and naughty aspects of how it was once, with twenty-first century comfort and a warm welcome.

I never managed to get the names of that wonderful

bunch of Aussies I fell in with on my first night in Dawson. I have photos of you all and lovely memories, so I just hope one of you remembered my name and bought the book. You'll know who you are, so get in touch!

Last but not least, my thanks to Mari Evans, my editor, for her boundless enthusiasm and editing skills. Love you, Mari!

Lesley Pearse

ABOUT LESLEY

Lesley Pearse is one of the UK's best-loved novelists, with fans across the globe and book sales of over two million copies to date.

A true storyteller and a master of gripping storylines that keep the reader hooked from beginning to end, Lesley introduces readers to unforgettable characters who it is impossible not to care about. There is no easily defined genre or formula; her books, whether crime, as in *Till We Meet Again*, historical adventure like *Never Look Back*, or the passionately emotive *Trust Me*, based on the true-life scandal of British child migrants sent to Australia in the post-war period, engage the reader completely.

'Lesley's life has been as packed with drama as her books'

Truth is often stranger than fiction and Lesley's life has been as packed with drama as her books. She was three when her mother died under tragic circumstances. Her father was away at sea and it was only when a neighbour saw Lesley and her brother playing outside without coats that suspicion was aroused – their mother had been dead for some time. With her father in the Royal Marines, they spent three years in grim orphanages before her father remarried (his new wife was a veritable dragon of an ex-army nurse) and Lesley and her older brother were brought home again, to be joined by two other children who were later adopted by her father and stepmother, and a continuing stream of foster children. The impact of constant change and uncertainty in Lesley's early years is reflected in one of the recurring themes in her books: what happens to those emotionally damaged as children. Hers was an extraordinary childhood and, in all her books, Lesley has skilfully married the pain and unhappiness of her early experiences with a unique gift for story telling.

'She was three when her mother died under tragic circumstances'

Lesley's desperate need for love and affection as a young girl was almost certainly the reason she kept making bad choices in men in her youth. A party girl during the swinging sixties, Lesley did it all – from nanny to bunny girl to designing clothes. She lived in damp bedsits while burning the candle at both ends as a 'Dolly Bird' with twelve-inch mini-skirts. She was married, fleetingly, to her first husband at twenty and met her second, John Pritchard, a trumpet player in a rock band, soon after. Her debut novel, *Georgia*, was inspired by her life with John, the London clubs, crooked managers and the many musicians she met during that time, including David Bowie and Steve Marriot of the Small Faces. Lesley's first child, Lucy, was born in this period, but with John's erratic lifestyle and a small child in the house, the marriage was doomed to failure. They parted when Lucy was four.

This was a real turning point in Lesley's life – she was young and alone with a small child – but in another twist of fate, Lesley met her third husband, Nigel, while on her way to Bristol for an interview. They married a few years later and had two more daughters, Sammy and Jo. The following years were the happiest of her life – she ran a playgroup, started writing short stories and then opened a card and gift shop in Bristol's Clifton area. Writing by night, running the shop by day and fitting in all the other household chores, along with the needs of her husband and children, was tough.

'Some strange compulsion kept me writing, even when it seemed hopeless,' she says. 'I wrote three books before *Georgia*, then along came Darley Anderson, who offered to be my agent. Even so, a further six years of disappointment and massive re-writes followed before we finally found a publisher'.

There was more turmoil to follow, however, when Lesley's shop failed in the 90s recession, leaving her with a mountain of debts and bruised pride. Her eighteen-year marriage broke down, and at fifty years old she hit rock bottom. It seemed she was back where she had started in a grim flat with barely enough money for her youngest daughter's bus fares to school.

'Lesley did it all – from nanny to bunny girl to designing clothes'

'I wrote my way out of it,' she says. 'My second book, *Tara*, was shortlisted for the Romantic Novel of the Year, and I knew I was on my way.'

Lesley's own life is a rich source of material for her books; whether she is writing about the pain of first love, the experience of being an unwanted abused child, adoption, rejection, fear, poverty or revenge, she knows about it first hand. She is a fighter, and with her long fight for success has come security. She now owns a cottage in a pretty village between Bristol and Bath, which she is renovating, and a creek-side retreat in Cornwall. Her three daughters, grandson, friends, dogs and gardening have brought her great happiness. She is president of the Bath and West Wiltshire branch of the NSPCC – the charity closest to her heart.

ABOUT *GYPSY*

Why did you choose to set this novel during the Klondike Gold Rush?

I liked the whole concept of people being swept up in Gold Fever. The drama of them leaving their homes and families, travelling hundreds of miles across snow-covered mountains, living under terrible conditions and risking their lives for something that there was no certainty they'd ever find. It was a kind of madness, yet a brave and dramatic one, which offered such tremendous scope for an exciting story.

How did you research the period and the arduous journey made by so many in search of gold?

I first read dozens of books on the subject, and then went to Alaska and Canada, following the main route the gold stampeders took. I didn't of course have to climb up the Chilcoot Pass with a fifty pound pack on my back, yet even today it is still a difficult, complicated journey to get to Dawson City. I was aware that should I miss one connection, be that plane, boat or train, I would be in trouble. I went through every kind of weather – rain, snow, sleet and sunshine. Even at the end of May there was still thick ice on the sides of the river Yukon. Most of the area is still wilderness, the terrain and the distances formidable, so it was fairly easy to imagine the problems and hardships greenhorn city folk would have faced there.

Beth and Sam fall on hard times when they first reach America. What made them stay and pursue their dreams?

I don't think many of us like to admit failure, and Beth and Sam would have had little to go back to England for anyway. America was a young and promising country which wasn't hidebound with class distinction, so it would have been better to stay there and work at becoming a success.

Beth is a strong, independent woman, who's determined to earn her own living. What was it like to be an unmarried, working woman at that time? Where did Beth find the courage to defy convention?

In this period, only women from poor backgrounds worked. If Beth's parents hadn't died, she would have stayed at home, helping her mother until she married. Beth actually wanted to work even before her parents died, but that was just a girlish dream of getting out of the house and meeting people. She was in fact ignorant of what long hours women workers had to put in, or what low wages they received.

Her courage was initially forged by being left to care for her baby sister when her mother died. She suddenly found out what being poor really meant and she had no choice but to become a laundress just to put food on the table. Hardships have a habit of making us braver and stronger, and Beth would have observed the unfairness of a male-dominated society, noted how few opportunities there were for women, and decided she must make her own.

Even in America it would have been unacceptable for a carefully brought-up young lady to play a musical instrument in a public house. But Beth had nothing to lose, no family there to shame, and everything to gain if she became popular. She was brave taking that path, but she loved her music, she needed to play and she soon found she cared nothing for convention.

In the two years since the launch of the Women of Courage Award, you must have met many extraordinary and courageous women ...

I certainly have. Wonderful women who think far more of others than they do themselves, make light of the huge burdens put upon them and never complain. Some have children with serious and permanent health problems that require care twenty-four/seven. Others have lost a child through sickness or injury, yet offer support and help to other mothers with sick children. We had a wonderful woman who, while sick herself with a rare blood disease, at her own expense brought children from Chernobyl over to Scotland for respite care. There were severely disabled young women who have studied hard against all the odds to gain qualifications so they can get a good job to support themselves. So many inspirational carers, others who have pulled their relatives through drink and drug abuse, and some who were abused by their partners who now help other women going through the same thing.

This year our winner was Karen Baker, a woman who not only gives full-time support to her disabled daughter Nicky so she can work, but cares for her father who has Alzheimer's disease, and yet somehow manages to find time to keep up with her own career of tutoring hairdressers as well as learning British sign language and visiting the elderly. I felt honoured to have met this remarkable, wonderful lady.

'Amongst Friends'

The Lesley Pearse Newsletter

A fantastic new way to keep up-to-date with your favourite author. *Amongst Friends* is a regular email with all the latest news and views from Lesley, plus information on her forthcoming titles and the chance to win exclusive prizes.

Just go to **www.penguin.co.uk** and type your email address in the 'Join our newsletter' panel and tick the box marked 'Lesley Pearse'. Then fill in your details and you will be added to Lesley's list.

THE BOOKS

GEORGIA
Raped by her foster-father, fifteen-year-old
Georgia runs away from home to the seedy
back streets of Soho ...

TARA
Anne changes her name to Tara to forget her
shocking past – but can she really become
someone else?

CHARITY
Charity Stratton's bleak life is changed forever
when her parents die in a fire. Alone and pregnant,
she runs away to London ...

ELLIE
Eastender Ellie and spoilt Bonny set off to make
a living on the stage. Can their friendship survive
sacrifice and ambition?

CAMELLIA
Orphaned Camellia discovers that the past she has
always been so sure of has been built on lies. Can
she bear to uncover the truth about herself?

ROSIE
Rosie is a girl without a mother, with a past full of
trouble. But could the man who ruined her family
also save Rosie?

CHARLIE
Charlie helplessly watches her mother being
senselessly attacked. What secrets have her parents
kept from her?

NEVER LOOK BACK
An act of charity sends flower girl Matilda on a trip
to the New World and a new life ...

TRUST ME
Dulcie Taylor and her sister are sent to an
orphanage and then to Australia. Is their love strong
enough to keep them together?

FATHER UNKNOWN
Daisy Buchan is left a scrapbook with details about
her real mother. But should she go and find her?

TILL WE MEET AGAIN
Susan and Beth were childhood friends. Now
Susan is accused of murder, and Beth finds she
must defend her.

REMEMBER ME
Mary Broad is transported to Australia as a convict
and encounters both cruelty and passion. Can she
make a life for herself so far from home?

The Books

SECRETS
Adele Talbot escapes a children's home to find her grandmother – but soon her unhappy mother is on her trail . . .

A LESSER EVIL
Bristol, the 1960s, and young Fif Brown defies her parents to marry a man they think is beneath her.

HOPE
Somerset, 1836, and baby Hope is cast out from a world of privilege as proof of her other's adultery . . .

FAITH
Scotland, 1995, and Laura Brannigan is in prison for a murder she claims she didn't commit.

The
Lesley
PEARSE
Women of Courage Award

The Lesley Pearse Women of Courage Award was launched in 2006 to celebrate the extraordinary achievements of ordinary women; women who have done something special for themselves or someone else; women of courage.

THE 2006 WINNER NICOLE GALLAGHER

'Winning the inaugural woman of courage award was a unique experience which I shall always remember'

NICOLE GALLAGHER from Kent was nominated by her best friend because of her care and devotion to her children who both suffer from rare medical conditions. Aishling was born with internal malformations and Nicole spent the first four months of her new daughter's life at her hospital bedside. It was during this time that her first daughter, Niamh, was diagnosed with Arnold Chiari malformation – where parts of the brain protrude into the spinal column. Niamh and Aishling have between them endured more than twenty operations.

THE 2007 WINNER KAREN BAKER

'I still have to pinch myself to remind me that I did actually win the award. I would like to thank Lesley and Penguin for even considering me for such a wonderful honour'

KAREN BAKER from Harrow was nominated by colleague Angela Dias. She provides full time support for her disabled daughter, Nicky, gives support to her colleagues in a busy role, looks after her father who has Alzheimer's disease and is the key support for her husband who has epilepsy. On the side, Karen is pursuing a career in hairdressing and visits the elderly. She has also been learning sign language in her spare time. As if that wasn't enough, Karen has been living with cancer for years.

PLEASE TURN OVER TO FIND OUT HOW YOU CAN NOMINATE SOMEONE FOR THE AWARD

'I know there are real heroines out there who would put my fictional ones to shame, and I really want to hear about them'
LESLEY PEARSE

Is there an amazing woman out there who deserves recognition?

Whether it is someone who has had to cope with problems and come out the other side; someone who has spent her whole life looking out for other people; or someone who has shown strength and determination in doing something great for herself, show her how much she is appreciated by nominating her for an award.

The Lesley Pearse Women of Courage Award gives recognition to all those ordinary women who show extraordinary strength and dedication in their everyday lives. It is an annual event that was launched by Lesley and Penguin in 2006.

Five finalists and their families are invited to London for a sumptuous awards lunch, where the winner is announced and presented with a cheque for £1000 by Lesley, as well as a host of other prizes.

Let us know about an amazing lady you know and make a difference to her life by nominating her for this prestigious award.

To nominate someone you know:

Complete the form opposite, or send us the details required on a separate piece of paper, and post it to:

The Lesley Pearse Women of Courage Award, Penguin General, 80 Strand, London, WC2R 0RL

or visit:

www.womenofcourageaward.co.uk

where you can print out a nomination form, enter your nomination details onto our online form and read all about the award and its previous nominees and winners.

The Lesley PEARSE

Women of Courage Award

OFFICIAL ENTRY FORM

NAME OF YOUR WOMAN OF COURAGE:

HER ADDRESS:

POSTCODE:

HER CONTACT NUMBER:

YOUR RELATIONSHIP TO HER:

YOUR NAME:

YOUR ADDRESS:

POSTCODE:

YOUR DAYTIME TELEPHONE NUMBER:

YOUR EMAIL :

**ON A SEPARATE SHEET, TELL US IN NO MORE THAN
250 WORDS WHY YOU THINK YOUR NOMINEE DESERVES TO WIN
THE LESLEY PEARSE WOMEN OF COURAGE AWARD**

For Terms and Conditions please visit **www.womenofcourageaward.co.uk**